The Launching of
Barbara Fabrikant

The Launching of Barbara Fabrikant

Louise Blecher Rose

David McKay Company, Inc.

NEW YORK

The Launching of Barbara Fabrikant

Second Printing, April 1974

Acknowledgment is made for use of lyrics, as follows:

From "Somethin's Comin' " from *West Side Story*. © 1957 by Leonard
Bernstein and Stephen Sondheim. *Used by permission of G. Schirmer, Inc.*

From "Love Is a Many Splendored Thing." Lyrics by Paul Francis
Webster. Music by Sammy Fain. © 1955 Twentieth Century Music
Corporation. Rights controlled by Miller Music Corporation. *Used by
permission.*

From "Put Your Finger in the Air." Words and music by Woodie
Guthrie. TRO— © 1954 Folkways Music Publishers, Inc., New York,
N.Y. *Used by permission..*

From "You Can Fly! You Can Fly! You Can Fly!" from *Peter Pan*. Words
by Sammy Cahn. Music by Sammy Fain. © 1951 Walt Disney Music
Company. *Used by permission.*

From "I Cain't Say No" from *Oklahoma!* Words by Oscar Hammerstein
II. Music by Richard Rodgers. © 1943 by Williamson Music, Inc.
Copyright renewed. All rights reserved. *Used by permission.*

Library of Congress Catalog Card Number: 73-91119
ISBN: 0-679-50453-2
MANUFACTURED IN THE UNITED STATES OF AMERICA

For Michael Porder and Margaret Sommers

The Launching of
Barbara Fabrikant

Chapter One

🌷

How do most people go to college? I'd like to do a study of that
someday. A year-by-year study, to see if they go differently
now, kicking and screaming maybe, the way they should if
they have any sense, or hopefully, like idiots, the way I did.
With teased bouffant hair, plaid knee socks, plaid skirt, green
Shetland sweater, guitar to hold in bed instead of men, who are
forbidden in the dorms, three huge valises full of clothes, and a
list of synagogues in The Boston Area.

1961. September. The day is warm; hot sun glares off the
pavement and road, causing those heat shimmers that are like
mirages—asphalt pools; no breeze. The only way you can tell
it is fall is by the traffic on the Connecticut Turnpike;
everybody is going to college in Massachusetts. No weather,
believe me, for a Shetland sweater and knee socks, but since
these are my College Clothes (just like for marriage, an
entirely new wardrobe to mark the beginning of a New Life),

and my parents are certain that Boston, five hours north of Morrisville, New Jersey, is a lot colder than the Connecticut Turnpike, I swelter in the back seat.

My brother, only a junior in high school and therefore dressed in khaki Bermudas and a Dacron short-sleeved white shirt, says, "Even your hair looks hot. It's starting to droop."

Now I know perfectly well, from years of watching *Father Knows Best*, that I am supposed to grimace and be annoyed and yell, "Oh, Bud," and then wait for my younger sister (I have one of them too; we are the ideal television family) to say something cute or stupid or both and to wrinkle her little nose. Unfortunately my sister and I, with Jewish genes and chromosomes, have between us three or four little noses. Plus, all I am able to say is, "I think it's the hair spray starting to sizzle," and Danny and Lisa both laugh. We like each other, and that's because we have a common enemy: the people sitting in the front seat. So my advice to all you moms and dads out there who want your children to be friends and not fight is: be lousy parents; who else will your kids have to turn to but each other?

"Are you scared?" Lisa asks.

My father, who has never yet heard of a question that is not directed at him, says, "Why should she be afraid? Here is a golden opportunity to improve herself, to meet new people, become finished. . . . I'm only afraid that a co-ed school is not quite the right place. They don't finish you the way one of the sister schools would."

All of us in the back seat raise our eyebrows and sigh quietly. Luckily I was not accepted by any of the sister schools. I say luckily because if I had been I would've had to go. And frankly, finishing sounds too much like varnishing to make me happy. I keep thinking, if what they wanted was attractive pieces of furniture, why did they have children? But to that, for sure, there is no answer.

My mother says, "All she needs to do is lose a few pounds

and she'll be perfect." This has been her contribution to my education for the last ten years.

"Please, let's not start this again," Lisa says, and right away my father yells, "That little one has no manners at all. What do you mean speaking to your parents that way? We'll say anything we want, when we want, and how we want."

"You're absolutely right, Dad," I say. He scares me to death. "Lisa is a little tired." She mouths, "I am not." At least she's beginning to learn stealth; in our family that's one of the keys to survival.

"If she would go to bed at a normal hour instead of watching so much television . . ." He leaves the sentence unfinished, a very rare occurrence. I look up to see why, just as the car screeches to a stop.

We're near Hartford; there are traffic lights every minute, all of them red, traffic in every direction, orange-roofed Howard Johnson's, gas stations, restaurants, pavements, flat, ugly, and hot.

The sun is attacking the makeup on the right side of my face, actually not makeup, Clearasil, which turns the pimples from angry red to big brown blobs. Once my mother read about something called Covermark—it's used to cover birth defects, huge blotches, real problems, I mean, not a few adolescent pimples. But in my family everything is enormous —there is no such thing as a small problem—so Mom goes to a drugstore and asks about this product that she has read about, this latex paint for the face, and the lady behind the counter gasps when she hears the use it's going to be put to. She gives my mother the Clearasil, and that's how it gets brought into our house. Normally my parents don't try any remedies except yelling, punishing, smacking, and Friday night services; these are their cure-alls. Thanks to some counter lady, we've branched out. Unfortunately, sun and Clearasil are an unhappy combination. I feel like half my face is melting away, turning to plastic goo first and then dripping down. I have a fantasy that by the time we get to The Boston Area I will be part Silly Putty, part skin, only half human whichever way you look at it.

"First impressions are very important," my father points out as I put a hand to my face to see if it's still there. The red light is endless; it feels something like eternity—will it ever cease? "I'm not sure how you should introduce me. Should you say, 'The Rabbi, my father, Dr. Moses Fabrikant,' or 'my father, the Rabbi Dr. Moses Fabrikant'?"

Danny, sandwiched between sisters, whispers, "Why doesn't he wear a sign?" Mom shushes him immediately; the Rabbi, my father, can't tolerate interruptions. Even when people sneeze or cough in temple, he pointedly waits for them to stop before continuing with his prayers or sermon. The congregation is very respectful of this idiosyncrasy—they think it proves he's doing something important up there in the pulpit. For all I know, maybe he is. We his children keep quiet and respectful for another reason, because he has a bad heart, and we were brought up on the dictum: "Do you want to kill your father?" Rather than have to search our hearts for the answer to that question, we stand still to be slapped (didn't God smite his erring people? If God, why not the Rabbi?), yelled at, ordered about; if the meek ever inherit the earth we three are in for a big chunk. On the strength of a coronary ten years ago, he has become an absolute monarch; my father, the Rabbi, can make strength out of the most incredible weaknesses.

It takes an effort, sitting there in the back seat, sweating, trying to figure out what some poor unwary freshman is going to say when I introduce the Rabbi My Father Dr. Moses Fabrikant, not to say to him right then and there, "Hey, it's ME going to college, nobody is interested in you." However, the thought of him slumped over in the front seat, my mother crying, "See what you've done, father-murderer?" is a tremendous aid to self-control.

The light finally changes, traffic creeps slowly ahead. I feel like the whole car is melting, the entire road, the world, everything is turning into glue, gummy glue, and we are sticking here, sticking there, crawling forward like a bug trapped in a jar of paste, smothering. My mother says, "Soon it'll clear up."

"Is it moving up ahead?" Lisa asks, thinking that Mom must have some good reason for her statement.

"Not that I can see," Mom answers.

"So why do you think it'll clear up soon?" Lisa wants to know.

"It can't go on like this forever," she answers.

Who is going to deny that?

All four windows of the big white Chrysler with the huge fins (gift of the congregation, whose idea of spiritual life is: the bigger the car, the better the rabbi) are rolled down, but we're moving so slowly that the air is hardly circulating. My sweater is sticking to me, as are my socks and slip; my pores feel like they've closed up shop entirely. I breathe deeply and often to try to compensate for their lack. I think maybe if I keep breathing I will ventilate my body from the inside. Because if I don't, who knows. I might suffocate.

"Can you die from heat?" I ask. There is nothing that, in my imagination, one cannot die from. Cars, bridges, tunnels, planes, smog, aspirins, and wine in the same evening: the entire world looks to me to be filled with lethal possibilities.

"Don't be silly," Dad says. Why should he worry? Even heart attacks don't kill him; he is invincible. The way he drives proves it too; on the road he's always in a race with someone, with that truck up ahead he doesn't like the looks of, with that little bug on the road his big American car ought to pass, with the blue convertible that is weaving in and out of traffic (he must get away from it—the driver is too crazy). A thousand good reasons to go seventy miles an hour and win moral victories over all his enemies: every other car on his road, in his way. I feel that I take my life in my hands every time he's at the wheel. All the way to Massachusetts I keep thinking, so what if we DO make it up there? On the way back he could crash and my entire family might be wiped out. Then where would I be?

Right now at least I'm safe in the back seat of a car so hemmed in that even the Rabbi cannot get out. It may take us ten hours to get to college, but at least we'll be alive for a while longer.

Danny says, "I don't worry about the heat so much as the exhaust fumes. Carbon monoxide all around, maybe we're dying right now and don't know it. I feel kind of drowsy myself, do you?"

In answer, I point to the front seat, where Dad is gripping the wheel, leaning forward; he looks like a greyhound being restrained by a powerful owner. No drowsiness up there, that's for sure. Danny looks, gets the point, and laughs. It's lucky his fears aren't mine; I can reassure him so easily.

Once we make it past Hartford the road widens, and the traffic unsnarls. Perfect for the big-finned, three-hundred-horsepower wonder. Air starts rushing in through the windows, soon it's whipping my hair around, beating against the prescription sunglasses. I roll the windows halfway up and try to prepare myself for an eternity with Our Heavenly Father and my earthly one,· both haranguing me about getting polished and finished forever and ever and ever. Amen. Who says that Jews have no hell?

Mom says, "Moses, what's the rush? We'll get there a few minutes later. You're going over seventy."

"Nonsense," Moses tells her. "It just looks that way from your side of the car. You have to be directly in front of the speedometer to read it correctly."

Lisa surreptitiously leans forward and mouths to us, "Seventy-three miles an hour." She sits directly behind him and the speedometer, and although only thirteen years old, is perfectly reliable in this matter. Dad would probably insist that it takes years of experience, practice, knowledge, and old age to read a speedometer correctly, so we don't say anything, just sit back and watch the cars we're leaving behind, blurring trees, dotted white lines running together so fast that they seem solid, unbroken. Lisa pulls up her window, and we ask Mom to raise hers. We've gone from torpor to hurricane velocity in such a short time; see how powerful the Rabbi is? Even the weather is under his control.

Soon he's up to eighty miles an hour; at this rate we'll be at school in ten minutes; he's whistling cheerfully to himself. We've outdistanced the whole state of Connecticut, when, as if in chorus with his tenor whistle, comes the soprano squeal of a siren and the flashing red light of a black-and-white less-impressive car, practically no fins to speak of, which zooms next to us. The blue-suited driver waves us over to the far side of the road. My mother takes out a Kleenex and says, "Moses, don't get excited. Remember your heart."

The cop walks over, pencil and ticket book in hand, and says, "Okay, Mac, let's see your license."

My father has the clergy sign in the front window, but the cop doesn't notice it, so he says, "Officer, I am the Rabbi Dr. Moses Fabrikant," and the cop says in a very pleasant way, "I don't care if you're Almighty God, hand over your license. You were going eighty miles per hour; what do you think this is, a skyway to paradise?"

The Rabbi is turning red, it clashes with his silver-gray hair, and Mom says, "Dear, don't argue with him."

"Don't tell ME who to argue with!" he answers, and having yelled at her, has relieved himself enough to hand his license over to the waiting policeman.

"One speeding ticket already, I see, Rabbi," he says. "Have you had any accidents yet?"

"Absolutely not," my father says, and of course it's true. He was born under a fleet of lucky stars. Once my mother whispered to me that she wished he WOULD have an accident, a small one, just enough to scare him. As if anything actually *could*.

"Believe me when I tell you this," the cop goes on, "you're

pushing your luck. With you in this car it's a weapon, not a vehicle." He hands him the ticket.

Dad says nothing until the policeman drives away and then he says, "Gentiles. Always looking for Jews to give tickets to."

"From so far away he could see your nose?" Lisa whispers, only not softly enough. I have a sudden eerie feeling, prophetic, about who is going to take over my role as chief victim when I'm gone. Poor Lisa, if only Dad could have seen how frightened she was with the cop standing there; who knows what was running through her mind? A fight, jail, heart attacks—she's related to me, so I imagine that the hands clasped tightly together and the wide eyes meant something, sitting there waiting; because, listen, even if we hate him, still we also love him. However, he is not interested in our love. He has told us from childhood on that he doesn't want us to love him, he wants us to respect him.

He abruptly turns the motor off and leans back and smacks Lisa; she starts crying, I start crying, Danny puts an arm around her, Mom watches her husband, distressed: has he gotten too excited? Dad puts the key back in the ignition, starts the motor, and drives onto the highway saying, "When are you going to learn to behave yourself?" For an answer Lisa just cries.

I whisper to her, "Remember, they also had lousy parents." (How can one live if one can't forgive?)

That's not all, either. Do you know what kind of a lousy job a rabbi's is? Because, and this is a known fact, no one hates rabbis like Jews. The only other Being (or non-Being as the case may be) that Jews hate as much as the rabbi is God. For hating God they have the best reasons: gold-plated, fourteen-carat reasons; and when the rabbi tells the whole congregation on Passover what a big, happy celebration it is because He spared their first-born sons and smote the Egyptians, do you think they don't puzzle it out what God was doing during Auschwitz? In Miami to get a tan, maybe, and didn't have his portable radio with him for the duration? Missed that entire time because his heavenly newspapers weren't being delivered. And do you think none of this (very justifiable, in my opinion) bitterness doesn't spill over onto the rabbi?

They came to him for comfort, and they go away angry. Because if you're the parents of a little boy, say, who died in a car accident, and the rabbi says to you, "Trust in God. His goodness and mercy surpass our understanding," you tell me how you'd feel. You'd like to get your hands on this God of such tremendous Understanding and wring his neck. Instead, his flock complain about the rabbi—God not having the courage to show Himself to them recently—his sermons aren't long enough, they're too long, he only likes his rich members, not his poor, his children are snobs, his older daughter had a nose job, his son doesn't do so well even in private school.

The rabbi is at a terrific disadvantage, having to be the spiritual emissary of so bad a Supreme Being, and his flock lose faith easily, which is completely understandable. The mystery is that they have any faith at all. But what they do have they hold tenuously, perilously, and if the rabbi, his wife, his children, or his wirehaired fox terrier should bother anybody, they could easily lose it. His life, and ours to a lesser extent, is one long receiving line: smiling, shaking hands, dressed well, friendly, kind, and perfect. Because, believe me, even when he plays golf, once a week, they criticize. They want him never to be off that receiving line. Plus, and need I even say this, somewhere, well hidden, the rabbi must have his own doubts about all the reassuring stories he tells. Could he have produced a skeptical child from out of nowhere?

By the way, I did have a nose job; even with it my nose isn't small, only manageable. At least now you notice there is something on my face besides it. I got permission for it two years ago when my mother was nagging me about my weight, trying to involve my father so he shouldn't notice how fat *she's* gotten recently, and I said, "Let me have a nose job, it'll probably take ten pounds off me." And at this the Rabbi, from whom I inherited in a direct line that massive growth between my eyes and mouth, laughs, and to my surprise, says, "Okay." So you see, he's not all bad.

Now he's driving a leisurely sixty-five miles an hour, telling stories about how the entire state of Georgia consists of troopers who hide behind magnolia trees and Spanish moss and watch for Miami-bound Jews going a mile or two above the speed limit and giving them fifty-dollar fines they have to pay on the spot or be hauled away to prison.

Danny whispers, this time low enough, "I wonder what's gonna happen the first time he gets stopped by a Jewish cop?"

Lisa wipes her eyes, puts her prescription sunglasses back on her yet unfixed nose, and smiles at him. "What am I going to do when you go away to school?" she asks. "I'll be at home alone with them for two years." She looks as though she's about to start crying again. "Two whole years."

"Don't worry, you'll visit us a lot, it'll be all right." Suddenly I feel like a rabbi myself—what nonsense I'm telling her.

"Welcome to Massachusetts" the sign says at the end of the short stretch beyond the toll booths. My heart goes faster: I'm leaving home, going to the land of pilgrims, Thoreau, Harvard, M.I.T., Boston, John Quincy Adams, the Founding Fathers, Cambridge—an older, more cultured civilization. This is the place where I'm finally going to learn something. New Jersey hasn't taught me much besides getting decent Board scores and faking my way through *Moby Dick* with the aid of little summary booklets and cheating on exams. Don't ask how the Rabbi's daughter can cheat, either, because I'll tell you how: Very Quietly. Can you imagine the furor if I were ever caught? A wave of atheism might hit the entire Jewish community. It's like necking, I mean, really, I'm eighteen years old, and Jews think God will smite them down for kissing the Rabbi's daughter. Who knows? Maybe they're right. What has God done recently to prove differently?

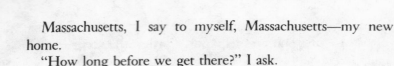

Massachusetts, I say to myself, Massachusetts—my new home.

"How long before we get there?" I ask.

"Two and a half, three hours at least," Dad says.

I can't believe it; living in New Jersey for so long, you forget how much bigger other states are. "Can I see the map?"

"*May* I," my mother says, and hands me the map. She feels terrible because she has a Brooklyn accent and we don't. They spirited us out of Brooklyn just to avoid the possibility that we also would spend the rest of our lives reversing our *t*'s and *d*'s, as both of them do. They want us to sound like the British Royal Family AND still be proud that we're Jewish. They don't realize that being Jewish means being it all the way through, not keeping it hidden in your heart, a Jewish heart and a Queen Elizabeth exterior. (By the way, another study: how many Jewesses are named Elizabeth?) After I get my nose job my father says proudly, "She looks like a shiksa." And I do, reddish-brown hair, blue eyes, and new Irish nose. From Countee Killjew, overweight, glasses, ah well, why shouldn't even the Rabbi have mixed feelings about this stiff-necked, irritating ethnic group? As a matter of fact, who has a better right than he, who is forced to deal with Jews all the time? It takes dealing with Gentiles to make you appreciate Jews, as I soon find out; the college that I go to has a ten percent quota, like most schools. I have a B'nai B'rith handbook, courtesy of my father, that explains the quota system. These are the facts of life Jews accept easily; we may be irritating, but without a quota we'd take over the world. And who wants it? Without a quota Harvard would be ninety-three percent Jewish; every state would have two Jewish senators, one a lawyer and the other a doctor; every president would be a Jewish accountant. Then the Jews and Chinese would run the world and have nothing but aggravation on their hands for thousands of years. So take it, goyim, Harvard and then the world! It's all yours.

My father thinks my opinions are crazy. All he likes is

Judaism; Jews he can't stand. That's why he wants me to be "finished"—then no one will know I'm Jewish except when I light the Sabbath candles. Perfect.

I look at the map and then out the window, trying to fit the two together, the turnpike and rolling hills, autumn trees and hot sun, so far not very different from New Jersey; even the air is as warm, sky the color of some real shiksa's eyes, and so even though my own blue eyes aren't able to tell the difference, I still think—a new place, a ʼ me. It will be perfect, I will be perfect.

We're coming to some big signs hanging over the turnpike. Dad says, "Give your mother the map so I can find out where to go."

"I'll read it," I offer. "We should be heading toward Boston."

"Give your mother the map," he says.

I hand it over to her. Life will be perfect—very different from what it is right now.

"What would you take if you were going to college?" Lisa asks Danny, but it naturally is taken for a general question.

"Do you mean if I were myself or if I were Barbara?" Dad wants to know.

"Oh, either way," Lisa says, rolling her eyes upward.

"Well, if I were myself I'd take World History, mainly Ancient History, and I'd take Greek to read parts of the New Testament in the original. I believe the translations have been wrong for centuries."

"You mean," I ask, "you think Christ never said he was the messiah?" Maybe he was just delivering the milk one morning, and these Gentiles, who can't do *anything* right, mistook him for the son of God.

"Who knows?" he says. "And Physics to understand Einstein, because even Einstein said how his theorems postulate a God because only God could have created such an orderly universe."

I look out the window at the green flying by and wonder

how it is that the universe has always struck me as entirely chaotic. Maybe it takes genius to see it differently. A genius or a rabbi.

"However," Dad continues, "if I were Barbara, I would take French and literature and art history. . . ."

"Not tatting and embroidery?" WHY can I never keep my mouth shut?

"And manners, if they teach it," he goes on, voice raised. "And being a LADY, if it's still possible to get that across to you."

"Moses, Moses," Mom says, "don't get excited."

"What would you take, Mom?" Danny asks. It's amazing how he manages to stay out of trouble; from the looks of things you'd guess he's the smartest of the three of us. Then why does he do so lousily in school whereas Lisa and I do well? The mysteries of an orderly universe.

"I'd take piano lessons and music theory," she says.

"Why don't you take them at home?" I ask.

For answer she waves her hand. We have a Steinway baby grand in our home that no one touches except her, once or twice a month. What does she do with her time? Sisterhood and Hadassah don't meet all that often.

Danny says, "I'm glad I'm not going to college yet; I have no idea what I'd take."

"I don't either," I tell him.

"It seems to me it would behoove you to listen to your parents in that case," my father opines. "You need to be toned down, your mouth is going to scare men away. Take something that is refining."

To melt me down and start all over again? Oh Daddy, I'd do it if I could; you think I'm so pleased with myself either?

"I think you ought to major in English," he continues, and I know he thinks this will make me into the Queen. "If only you had gotten into a sister school."

"Dad," I say irritatedly, "Harter is harder to get into than Mount Holyoke." Which it is: outside the state it has a fabulous reputation: co-ed, close to Cambridge, Harvard, Boston, Brandeis, still out in the country, a beautiful campus, a Hillel Club—what more could anyone want? And who knows why I didn't get into a sister school with my Board scores so high? Maybe they could tell from the interview, where I sat stiff and nervous, saying what I thought were all the right things, that their brand of varnish wouldn't stick to my stubborn wood.

I sit back against the red vinyl seat (the inside of this car looks like a fire engine) and stare sullenly at the ash tray on my side filled with half-eaten pumpkin seeds, the lowest-calorie thing you can take into your mouth besides water and air. One thing my parents can't nag me about is my academic achievement. Especially since no one *ever* caught me cheating.

"No one is blaming you," my father says. "They obviously didn't want a rabbi's daughter this year."

At this, looking at the pumpkin seed shells, my teeth marks all over them, nervous, with the traffic starting to build up again, I become nauseated. Is this all any school notices when they look at me: that behind me, the man who sired me, whose little sperm cell was wearing a yarmulke as it traversed the length of my mother's vagina, is a Man of God?

"I don't feel so good, Dad," I say. "Would you mind pulling over for a minute?" This hasn't happened to me since my childhood, when during every drive that lasted over an hour I would get out and puke. When we went in to Brooklyn to visit the family I would make it past Newark, then start gagging, Dad would pull over, Mom would rush out with a bunch of Kleenexes, I'd vomit, she'd wipe my mouth, they'd give me a drink of tea from the Thermos they'd bring along for every trip, and we'd continue on. Today is like a replay of an old movie, something I haven't seen for years. I walk out of the car over to the side of the road that is grassy, bend over, and puke. Luckily some of the iced tea brought along for the trip is left. I drink it and get back in the car.

"I worry about you," Dad says.

I lean my head out the window, figuring the hell with my hair, and then take off my knee socks and shoes and sit barefoot. If I could, I'd peel everything off; I'm so damn hot. Short of that I'm following my uncle the doctor's advice. He says that if your feet are cold then your body is cold; sometimes he modifies this to include the wrists—if you pour cold water on your wrists you cool all the blood that's passing through your body and you'll feel like you're being air-conditioned. So I stick my hands out the window too; no harm in trying even though I know my uncle is as crazy as my father, maybe worse. In a while I feel a little better.

The Mass. Turnpike seems to attract cars the way half-rotten fruit does flies. Once again the big white Chrysler finds itself surrounded, not being stopped this time, only slowed down. Dad weaves in and out, trying to get away from all the crazy drivers out on the road today.

"Why don't we sing?" Lisa suggests. "You think you could play the guitar if we both scrunch over?"

The guitar in its hard plastic case is lying at our feet. "I can try." I bend over and click it open. There it is, covered by my *Sing Outs*, handwritten music, a notebook of chords I always forget, and songs I haven't been able to memorize. Danny moves over, and I pick it up and strum it. "Well, it's love, O love, O careless love," I begin. Lisa and Danny immediately join in, and I can switch from melody to harmony, "love, O love, O careless, careless love, love, O love, O careless love, can't you see what love has done to me." Mom and Dad hum along; we all enjoy singing. My nicest memories are of my father singing Yiddish songs or my mother at the piano playing selections from Gilbert and Sullivan, with the three of us behind her taking all the different parts. Even Danny has no shame about singing. We could all carry a tune at an early age, and when I was seven, Danny five, and Lisa three, Mom and Dad took us to a little recording studio and had us sing our favorite songs. They still have them, our little voices doing "Yankee Doodle," "Happy Birthday" (with me singing,

"Happy Birthday, dear Barbara and Danny and Lisa" (learning to share was the hardest thing in the world for me) and Danny bellowing out his favorites and then arguing with Mom for the last third of the record, insisting he was absolutely finished, wasn't going to sing any more. So there is this argument preserved for life, Mom saying, "But Danny, dear, you know how you LOVE 'Put your finger in the air, in the air,'" and she begins singing it, and he says, "I sang THREE songs already." She suggests another one, he rejects it, and so on to the end of the record, which, when the needle catches in the groove, catches her saying, "But Danny but Danny but Danny" on to eternity, or however long a seventy-eight is likely to last.

The very best of the performances is the one by Lisa, who at three years of age believes nothing that is told her. Mom has explained how she will sing into a little microphone and then will be able to hear herself, her very own voice. So she goes in and sings "Happy Birthday, dear Lisa" (she has no trouble learning to share, simply refuses to do it), and when my mother says, "Fine, now let's do 'Yankee Doodle,'" Lisa bawls out, "But wait till it, wait till it PLAYS!" And Mom says, "First you have to sing and THEN it plays!" "NO!" Lisa shouts. "Now come on, darling," Mom says, "sing 'Yankee Doodle went to town riding on a pony,'" and Lisa, being only three years old and hearing Mom start the song, goes along and finishes it. "How about 'Mary Had a Little Lamb'?" Mom asks, and Lisa, distressed, you can hear it clearly ten years later on the record, asks, "But where IS IT?" Mom says, "Later you'll hear it. Now you have to sing." And she starts, "Mary had a little lamb," and Lisa exasperatedly joins in, "Mary had a little lamb, a little lamb, a little . . ." Then she pauses and shouts out with real conviction, having finally mastered the whole business, "and then MY voice will come out," pauses; you can hear Mom laugh, "Mary had a little lamb, her fleece was white as snow."

My record is the least interesting of the three because I don't misbehave; all you hear is a little kid's voice woodenly singing song after song. I get half a dozen in on one record, twice as much as either sibling; but forever after when company or family listen to the records and enjoy Danny's and Lisa's much more, I have this dull, shamed feeling about my own performance, so perfect and so nothing, just a bore.

"Let's sing 'Five Hundred Miles,' " Lisa says. The harmony is easy, I've memorized the *Sing Out* version, so the chords are good (when I make up my own chords they very often aren't so terrific). We sing, Mom and Dad hum, air pours in through the half-opened windows. In the distance are whole forests of green, brown, and gold, the sun is high in the sky, no longer beating in through any windows. If only life could be enjoyable this way more often.

We continue for more than an hour. I'd be happy to keep it up forever, because as soon as the music stops my mother turns around and says, "Barbara, your hair! your face!"

"I'll fix it when we get closer to school," I say.

She stares at the pimples on my face. No one can stare like my mother. It looks like she's weighing and measuring each one; then she sweeps her eye down the rest of me, rumpled skirt and sweater, belly, heavy thighs (can she see them now too?) and shakes her head. "When I was sixteen I went on a diet even though my parents thought it was dangerous to eat small amounts of food. Do you realize that? They were pushing potatoes at me and yet I managed to lose weight, and here you are eighteen years old with parents that are willing to *help* you"; she shakes her head. There just are no words to describe what a wretch I am. Why am I killing my parents with my extra twenty-five pounds? Why am I wrecking my entire life, sacrificing a future husband and their grandchildren while they are so helpful? Once when the Rabbi catches me downstairs at midnight stuffing into my mouth a piece of pound cake I wasn't allowed to have at dinner, he grabs it and smacks me, and I cry and say, honestly for a change, "I don't know why I'm doing this. I'm not even hungry." For that he smacks me again. "Don't make excuses to *me!*" he yells.

"You're ruining your first impression at college," my mother goes on.

I take out a comb and try to get my hair into place. It's snarled and tangled by the wind; I really need a brush for the job, but mine is packed, so I draw the comb through, pull my scalp, pull out some strands of hair, and roll up the window so it won't blow around so badly. I take out my compact with the hypoallergenic powder and look into the little mirror; there I see the glasses, thick, shoulder-length dark hair, the full face, big mouth, excellent nose.

All I need is to lose twenty-five pounds and take off the glasses for good and I'd be beautiful. Oh yes, I know it too; in this I don't argue with my parents. You think they even want me to wear glasses? My uncle says glasses are bad for eyes anyway, you get too dependent on them, and he gives me eye exercises to do. I take my finger and hold it in front of my face and move it from side to side, following it with my little myopic eyeballs, back and forth, up and down. While doing this exercise I look like someone recently escaped from a mental institution; but I do it, and at the end of the exercise do you know what I have? I have the tiredest eyeballs in the world—maybe they even lose weight from all the moving— and I still can't see a damned thing. Plus I hate to be blind; this seems to be another one of my idiosyncrasies—every other girl in the world is vain enough to tolerate nearsightedness but me. When I can't see I can't hear; I feel like I'm all alone in a world that's probably laughing at me, and who knows what *they're* up to?

Danny wears glasses, but he's a boy so it doesn't matter; Lisa doesn't wear hers. When I pass her in the school halls I have to reach out and grab her to say hello; she doesn't recognize me she's so blind. Frankly I don't know how she manages to cross the street without getting killed. Does she put her ear to the ground like Indians in Tom Mix Westerns, or what?

Mom says, still staring at me, "Your father and I met just after I had lost all my weight. He was the new rabbi, and all the girls were interested in him. Now where would I have been if I had still been fat?"

God only knows, Mother, I should say but can't. When I was eight and she was giving me the same folk tale and putting me on a diet (Oh yes, ladies and gentlemen, I have been dieting for the past ten years, with what fantastic success you already know), I had the brains to say, "But you're fat now. Why can't YOU lose weight? Why do I have to and you don't?"

"Because I'm already married," she says.

"Which way now?" my father asks as we come to the toll booths.

"Let me see," Mom says. "Why don't you pull over to the side for a minute while I look?"

"Why didn't you do this before?" he snaps. He pulls over to the side and takes the map from her. This doesn't strike her as bad behavior; she doesn't need to worry about his heart to be a good slave; it comes naturally to her. "Here we are, Wetton; we have to head west, so let's watch for signs." He drives off the turnpike, and we all stare dutifully at the road.

"Hannah," my father turns to my mother as we drive along this beautiful tree-lined road, "did you remember the mezuzah?"

I lean so far forward at this that my nose nearly touches the back of my mother's head.

"Yes, dear, I have it right in my pocketbook." She reaches in and pulls out a little silver ornament, a rail spike with curlicues.

"What's that for?" I ask.

"Your room," Dad says.

"My room?" I begin to bite my thumbnail, something I

haven't done since they put bitter goop on each finger years ago to train me out of the habit.

"For a blessing," he says, "on your college career."

"Will it help me with grades or men?" I ask.

"Bar-ba-ra," my mother says. Who knew my name had so many syllables?

"What if my roommate isn't Jewish? Maybe she'd be offended, maybe in retaliation she'll put up a cross."

"Are you ashamed of your religion?" he asks.

What can I say? My own personal philosophy is, God or not, I'm on my own here on this planet. I don't want God's help, even if He would give it. I can just see it now, God flitting through the dorms of Harter College, whizzing up and down, arms crossed over His heavenly chest, till He spots my mezuzah, then He stops and raises His arms, like my father giving the benediction at the end of services, and says, "Let this girl have A's and a doctor for a husband." And me, jackass that I am, I'll be sitting there studying, memorizing this and that, anxious and upset, drinking Metrecal, not even realizing that it has all been fixed up in advance. I could relax and eat chocolate chip cookies and see a movie. Why, I wouldn't even need to cheat! And to all the angels on high I'll be like their favorite TV show, *The Barbara Fabrikant Comedy Hour*, me sweating and aggravated, all the while not knowing that God has fixed it up for me, my grades are in, my spouse picked out while I'm crying myself to sleep worrying about everything.

"Couldn't you just leave the mezuzah with me?" I ask. "Does it have to be on the door?"

"You know the answer to that," Dad says.

But he's wrong; there isn't a ritual in the world I understand, and it's not for lack of trying. How can the God Who created Heaven and earth and the moon and sun and stars worry about little silver plaques on doors? Who is this Nut On High that after doing such a bang-up job with the universe He should suddenly be concentrating on bacon? Once I tasted ham and hated it, and it's fattening besides; I'm willing to stay off pig for life. But to think that beyond these clouds is some Large Person who actually is happy about my decision? This is all He has to worry about? Nuclear weapons and Auschwitz He sits through, but a mezuzah hidden safely in my underwear drawer is going to get Him up in arms? I sit back and think, don't worry, first impressions don't count, it's only Orientation Week, not everyone will be there, maybe my roommate is home sick.

I look out the window. The little winding road we're on goes through small towns, which I examine for signs of New Englandness, something to differentiate them from towns I've already known. So far all I have seen are Houses of Donuts, Dunkin' Donuts, Donutland, Seventy-one Varieties of Donuts. For this we've traveled three hundred miles? There are more hills anyway, more round, rolling hills, and lots of old churches with the really tall spires, trying to give God a little jab no doubt on His Heavenly Ass.

"Would you mind putting on the news?" Danny asks. It's nearly one o'clock, he'd like to hear some baseball scores, but he has to pretend to be interested in politics, Israel, the United Nations, and Khrushchev, just for the sake of the Yankees. They should only appreciate it. My father turns on WQXR but gets static.

"We can't get WQXR up here," he says after fiddling with the dial, and that's how, folks, for the first time I know we are someplace new.

"I wonder if you can get WNEW or WABC," Lisa says.

Dad tries these, also with no success. Lisa looks at me pityingly. We're both hooked on those two stations, secretly of course; we each have clock radios in our rooms that are permanently set there; we've never found out if the radios can get anything else. Being addicted to rock and roll scares me; it's like being addicted to food—once I start I can't stop. Why is it that my likes turn so quickly to pathology? That's one of the reasons I try to transfer my affection to folk music. Only half succeed too, although I run to New York for Pete Seeger concerts; all the most authentic performers, the old ladies with zithers and their mountain melodies, the old blacks with a two-string bass I can't stand. Joan Baez I like best when she sings (she thinks she's parodying them, but I know better) rock and roll hits. I feel like the only fraud in Carnegie Hall: I play the guitar and for the rest of my life can sing all the words to "Born Too Late," and every other rock and roll song I hear.

Dreck, I know, but I love it.

Dad flips the dial around; it's Sunday, so we're getting church services from all over Massachusetts, and finally we hook on to a voice that's forecasting the weather; we listen carefully and, my God, it sounds like John F. Kennedy. Can this be what he's doing in his spare time? Besides reading two thousand words per second and rocking in his chair? But no, wait, it can't be—this is how everybody speaks around here; they all have an accent! The announcer is talking about the traffic on the Mass. Turnpike, he says the caaaahs are backed up to, where? We can't catch the name of the town. A new world, a strange tongue. We listen to the news: Russia is exploding an A-bomb, the whole world is protesting; will our milk turn sour? Will Strontium-90 clouds descend and beat us to death? The movie *Exodus* is being advertised, thank you Ferrante and Teicher, and the Yankees are doing fine. The weather is warm.

Soon I fade out, thinking, we're almost there, and guess what scares me? I'm afraid I won't be able to find music I like or stations I like up here, and I'm going to miss *Piano Personalities*, a program my mother has on every single day.

When I remember *Piano Personalities* I nearly cry. I'm leaving home. It doesn't seem to my rational mind to be much to cry over, but tears well up in my eyes anyway. My heart pounds and I look around at the town we're passing through, trolley tracks and doughnut places, and wonder am I old enough to be on my own?

"Wetton six miles," Dad reads from a road sign.

Lisa and Danny turn to look at me. I see that they, too,

don't know whether to envy me or be grateful that they're not the ones going off to college.

"How do you feel?" Lisa asks. She takes a Kleenex from her pocketbook and blows her nose.

"Who knows?" I lean over and pat her shoulder. "Anyway, don't worry, if I don't like it I'll just pack my bags and come home."

"What did you say?" Dad roars.

"Just joking," I hasten to explain. Because, believe me, coming home is not one of the options I have. I'm like a slave. I've been sold to Harter College for four years; love it or hate it I've been sentenced to a B.A. (don't ask what my crime was either, because it's for sure I don't know). I'll be paroled in four years.

"Maybe it'll be lots of fun," Danny says hopefully.

"It'll be quiet around the house without you," Lisa says.

"You must be kidding." I try to make her smile. "Subtract one voice from the din and what've you got? Still a din."

"Ah," Danny says, "she's just sorry there'll be no one around to help her with algebra."

At this we laugh. I still don't know my multiplication tables.

"I feel bad," he goes on, "for every fight we've ever had."

"Of course. You've lost so many of them." Sentiment is the last thing I need right now.

"Lost?" Mom echoes. "Did someone lose something?"

"Just like those kids," Dad reflects, "losing all the time, no sense of the value of things. They're spoiled is the problem. Why, when I was a child I was glad to have a nickel, it seemed like a million dollars to me. But what do they know? If you haven't lived through the Depression, you can't appreciate value." How this man can talk talk talk talk.

"Nobody lost anything, Dad," I say wearily, but this offends him; you cannot contradict him on *anything*, even if you're stating a fact.

"And who lost their prescription sunglasses at the beach just one month ago, answer me that?"

"I did." Naturally.

"Thirty dollars you bury in Asbury Park."

"Maybe some poor nearsighted person will find them," I say, "and it'll be a *mitzvah* for him. He'll be walking along the beach, picking his way carefully across the sand and he'll trip on driftwood and land right next to my sunglasses, pick them up, and get down on his hands and knees and thank God for a miracle."

"Probably it'll be the middle of the night and he'll see worse with them on than off," Lisa says.

"Who knows?" I might as well continue; as long as he isn't speaking or yelling yet, what do I have to lose? "It might even be some Jewish person who has lost faith in God and by finding my glasses his faith AND eyesight will be restored unto him. Maybe I didn't even lose the sunglasses," I finish in a burst of inspiration, "maybe God took them from me for a purpose."

At this my father actually laughs, and there is a slight smile on Mom's face. A miracle.

"You'll write, won't you?" Lisa asks.

"Sure. And I'll send you mail care of the post office like we planned." I'm whispering; these arrangements we worked out before—the surface news I'll send to the entire family, the real poop I'll write to the siblings. If I haven't confided in my parents all the way through high school, am I going to begin now?

"What are you whispering about?" Dad asks.

"Nothing," I answer.

"They're always whispering," he says to Mom.

I have an urge to lean forward and shout in his ear, "HEY, IS IT LOUD ENOUGH FOR YOU NOW? MAYBE YOU'D LIKE TO HAVE A DIRECT LINE TO OUR THOUGHTS ALSO?" Because we even think quietly, secretly; unlike him we don't think out loud. Which he disapproves of, I'm certain. Look, we're not allowed to lock

· 24 ·

our bedroom doors, I don't want to know why, because between him and his wife must be a collection of fantasies so dirty they'd make the Marquis de Sade blush. They don't like it if we lock the bathroom, and do you know the reason for this? Because they don't want us to hide diarrhea from them; many is the child who has died from unnoticed diarrhea, this information courtesy of my uncle. They don't want us to sneak any loose shits past them. Frankly, they're welcome to them all.

"I packed your Confirmation Bible for you," Mom says.

"Terrific." I roll my eyes heavenward.

"Those that don't respect their religion have no respect for themselves," my father thunders. I remember the line—it's from one of last month's sermons. Usually it leads up to a plea for more contributions to the everlasting building fund, the Reform Jewish God is clearly of an architectural bent; nothing pleases Him more than new wings added on to old temples.

"I've always told you this: people who talk badly about their parents, family, or religion are never thought well of. The world recognizes them for what they are: TRAITORS!"

"I'm not talking badly," I say.

"I hear the tone of your voice!" he shouts. "You're sneering."

At this I sneeze. I must be allergic to sneering on top of everything else.

"Why are you sneezing?" he asks. "You been running around barefoot again?"

Now I don't know whether this is a Jewish belief in general or a specific Fabrikant one, but my parents seriously believe that going barefoot is like having a surgeon perform an operation without washing his hands: death immediately attends. With them a cold isn't something you get from germs, but is from a lack of oranges, going barefoot, or not wearing a hat in winter. In vain I point out to them the Russian men who swim in the Volga in midwinter. I remind them that they themselves catch colds and never go barefoot, also in vain; once you believe something, nothing, not even hard facts, will change your mind.

My mother turns around and peers down the back seat. "Moses, you're right," she tells him, as though he's just come down from the mountain with the stone tablets. "She's barefoot."

At this I pull on my wool knee socks, slip back into the loafers. Then I'm struck by a comforting thought: when I'm in the dorm away from them I'll walk around barefoot, yes, and no one will stop me. I'll take off the knee socks, oh joy, and even the shoes. I'll eat without being nagged, sleep, shit, study, go to movies, date, talk, say anything I want, my God I'm FREE. I won't even have to go to Friday night services!

"Wetton, home of Harter University," Lisa reads from a big sign at the crossroad. "Harter College is to the right, where that arrow is pointing."

We have to drive through the town of Wetton, which I was expecting to be a model of New Englandness, quaint and historical. The first sight that greets you in Wetton is Spina's Funeral Service; it juts out on a peninsula surrounded by three roads that converge in the middle of town. Next to Spina's is Marino of Italy Coiffure; when you go you should go looking good. Down the block is Donut King—hand-cut donuts. Farther on down the same block is a barbershop, then a supermarket, and on the opposite side of the funeral parlor is a huge drugstore, bigger even than the supermarket, a super-drugstore. I see how cleverly the town is laid out; either you go to the drugstore and are saved, ushered back to the realm of the living, or it's across the street, to wherever that place ushers you.

Right smack in the middle of town is a park on a hill; on top of the hill is a powder house, and by this I don't mean a ladies' room. All over Massachusetts these constant reminders of the Revolutionary War, everybody's favorite war. In Boston there's Paul Revere's house and the Freedom Trail, little red footprints on sidewalks and streets leading you to freedom, or is it to the Italian store that hand cuts noodles and ravioli?—anyway much preferable to freedom, which is inedible. In Cambridge there is Henry Wadsworth Longfellow's house, which is described by the copper plaque on the front gate (copper plaque-making must be the biggest industry in this area) as General Washington's headquarters. All right, *Hiawatha* and *Evangeline* are no great shakes, but surely they represent something at least as important as where Washington placed his ass. I learn not to expect too much from Cambridge; on one of the bridges leading to it is this little saying: "The multitude of the wise is the welfare of the world." Isn't that nice? In this state wisdom is scattered all over the place.

Meanwhile in the Wetton park is an identifying plaque so bizarre I soon visit it regularly just to read and marvel at the style, the grammar, the content. This is how it goes: "This stone windmill was built by John Mallet about 1703 and was sold to the province for a gun powder magazine in 1747. Rifled by General Gage of the Colony's Powder on 1 September 1774, it became a magazine of the American Army in 1775–1776." I read it fifty times and can never understand: does it commemorate A Good Thing or A Bad Thing?

Down the street from the park are Dandy Donuts, a florist, a driving school, and one huge liquor store. Surrounding the business district, creeping practically all the way up to Harter University itself, are ten thousand houses, all close together, made of wood and painted white or green. The land is covered, completely covered by houses. This is the countryside Harter describes itself as being in the middle of.

I have no time to puzzle this out or worry about it, for we are suddenly at the foot of a big fenced-in hill, which the sign identifies as Harter. Another sign lists all the schools and divisions and indicates how to find the one you're interested in. We turn right and follow the wire fence up and up, past a football field and a domed building, several parking lots, and then finally we see the buildings, rows and rows and acres and acres of buildings, red brick mostly, some wood, a few new glassy structures that remind me of the plans for the temple wing.

Then we see an entrance, the one break so far in the wire fence. It's manned by two uniformed men, and a line of cars is waiting to get in. We take our place on line, my heart is pounding—there's something ominous about fences and guards. We creep slowly up to the gate. I think even Dad is nervous; he's quiet.

"We're supposed to go straight to my dorm, Bailey Hall," I say.

But it is perfectly impossible for my father to repeat such a brief sentence. When we get to the guard he introduces himself, The Rabbi Dr. Moses Fabrikant, and says that he is taking his daughter, a freshman at Harter College, to school. Her first time away from home.

The guard looks as though my father has just recently escaped from somewhere and he'd rather not know all the details, so he smiles politely and asks, "What dawm ah ye headed faw?"

"Bailey Hall," I say.

"Foller this road all the way around till ye come to the first left. Don't turn left, keep going for two houses, the second house, it's red brick with a white picket fence in front, is Bailey."

We foller his directions around this little road that is sort of midway up the big hill. To the right of the road is another seven-foot-high wire fence enclosing lots of red-brick buildings and the famous Harter Museum, way on top of the hill; it has two spires, and inside it is Jumbo, the famous first elephant of the Barnum and Bailey circus, now stuffed and glassy-eyed.

No one is inside this second wire fence; all the bustle is down here, around the dorms, where cars are parked on the sidewalk, on grass, lined up in chaotic rows. Girls are dragging huge valises, boys are helping; the contents of a thousand homes seem to be emptying into Harter College dormitories. We drive slowly around cars and people; it's an obstacle course, and the Rabbi isn't used to it. The only time he drives this slowly is when he's backing out of the garage, to avoid hitting his power mower.

We come to the left, don't take it, and shortly see what must be Bailey—white picket fence, a flood of College Clothes pouring into it. Danny starts singing, "O Miss Bailey, unfortunate Miss Bailey": I glare at him and he stops. But you know how it is with some songs, you think of them and the tune or words keep running through your brain over and over. All the while we're getting out of the car and Dad and I start walking down the path, followed by Mom and Lisa and Danny at a respectful distance, this ballad is in my mind accompanying us.

Bailey Hall is near the corner of Professors' Row and Greek Way; how intellectual of it. I notice a sign posted over the entrance that says Fallout Shelter In Basement Capacity Two Hundred. The little lawn in front is guarded by a neatly trimmed bush, and the door is surrounded by two huge granite columns and covered by a granite arch and led to by granite steps and a granite stoop. The little path leading to the entrance is a nice curving one made up of big flat stones; it looks like it ought to be going across a stream rather than a strip of lawn.

I sneak a look at my father as we near the door to make sure he doesn't slip on a yarmulke and do a benediction right here. But he seems content to gaze around in a calm manner befitting the spiritual leader of Temple B'nai Jeshuran. He's wearing a nice dark summer suit, dark shoes; I've never seen him in anything light-colored except for the constant white shirt he always wears with the thin, sober tie. He's never dressed casually; even his pajamas are serious-looking, dark stripes, jacket and trousers too. God never catches him off the job—even in his sleep. He's a handsome man, six feet tall, a mass of kinky salt and pepper Philip Roth Jewish hair that's a trial for him to keep cut short enough—for that kind of hair to be neat you practically need to be bald.

However, the Rabbi comes from a long line of unbalding men—his father had a perfect head of hair when he was seventy; what was inside that head only God knew, but the outside was magnificent. Besides it's good for a rabbi to have hair, because if there's one thing a yarmulke sticks to it's that nice kinky Jewish stuff.

In temple, to relieve my constant boredom, I watch the baldies try to keep their yarmulkes on: trouble, believe me—they need Elmer's glue for the job. Once in a while, when Dad is all charged up, highly moved in the pulpit, he throws his head back and even *his* yarmulke starts slipping. I always like to see him then right in the middle of his emotional fit reach calmly back and push his yarmulke forward; I always feel that's the Real Rabbi Fabrikant.

He has the regulation eagle nose, brown eyes with unusually long eyelashes that he flutters during the high spots of services, and, ever since the coronary ten years ago, keeps himself only moderately overweight. When I first knew him he had a huge belly, but somehow it got transferred to my mother, a tall lady who hasn't had a heart attack yet and so can afford to be fat. After all, she's MARRIED. She has matching salt and pepper hair that she wears tied back, because the rabbi's wife isn't supposed to dye and set her hair like the other yentas.

I look back at her, flanked by Danny and Lisa. She also is in a dark summer suit; she and the Rabbi wear interchangeable clothes, except for the trousers, but she's the only one in the family with a short nose. Her side of the family specializes in short noses, but so strong were Dad's genes and chromosomes, so overpowering were his sperm cells that each one of us got his nose. On Danny it looks fine, he's tall and skinny, the girls are already crazy about him, Jewish boys on the whole running mainly to short; he has dark curly hair, darker than mine, and a sweet smile, with slightly crooked teeth, the result of a botched job of orthodontia one of the temple members gave him free. •

Lisa has the only straight hair in the family, reddish-brown, big eyes and eyelashes like my father, a pretty mouth, and is thin thin thin. Next year when she has her nose job she'll be magnificent.

What an attractive family marching up to the door, except for the overweight older daughter! Dad holds the door open and we walk in. I take a few steps in the foyer and nearly run headlong into a row of smiling female faces, a receiving line, how could I have missed it? The first girl on line has short blond hair, a cap cut with little circlets all around her face, upturned tiny nose, incredibly neat white blouse and gray skirt, WASP unlimited. She steps forward and says, "You must be a new freshman. I'm Betty Ann Fraser, chairman of the orientation committee, and here are your house president, vice president, secretary, and your house mother, Mrs. Hibbard."

"Hi. I'm Barbara Fabrikant." I feel bad I have no title but am saved from total ignominy by the appearance at my side of the Rabbi Dr. Moses Fabrikant, my father. Betty Ann goes to the long table right behind her and brings forth a name tag that she then pins to my sweater. I notice that everyone is wearing one of these, we look like human packages, signed and sealed; all we need is a stamp and we'll be ready to send.

"Mrs. Hibbard will show you your room and you can start making yourself at home. There'll be a compulsory house meeting tonight after dinner in the living room." She points to the room opposite her and flashes a smile containing at least fifty gleaming white teeth.

"Glad to have you aboard," a dark-haired girl whispers as we march by.

"Thank you."

I follow Mrs. Hibbard through a closed door down a long corridor with numbered doors on each side, practically every other foot. This is what "close quarters" must mean. The corridor is gray, and Mrs. Hibbard from the back reminds me of my old third-grade teacher, Miss Wicker, known to us as

Miss Wicked. Mrs. Hibbard has tight, brown-dyed finger curls that shake as she walks, just like Miss Wicker had. When I was in the sixth grade and read Greek mythology for the first time and came across Medusa with the hair-snakes and a face that turned people to stone, I immediately thought of Miss Wicker.

Mrs. Hibbard is wearing a midcalf-length brown print dress that looks as though it was always old-fashioned, even when it first saw action fifty years ago. Her face, when she turns to stop, look at us, and open a door with one of the keys on a chain fastened to a dress pocket, is composed of a pursed prune-smile, little pince-nez glasses perched on a thin nose, and the tiniest eyes you can imagine.

"Here is your room, Number Ten," she booms out.

"Thank you." I peek in.

"Now your father and brother should take a good look—this is the very last time they'll be allowed down this corridor until school is over." She *beams*.

"Why?" Danny asks.

"No men are allowed in any part of the dorm but the living room." Her voice sags a little as she mentions the living room; poor lady, she'd like to bar men completely, keep them outside the white picket fence. "Even a father or brother," she continues with a satisfied leer; she probably doesn't believe in fathers or brothers, only in dangerous mad rapist males. "You know college must function *in loco parentis*."

At this I gasp, for I think the expression means "your crazy parents," and she uses it, that Harter is to function like my loco folks. It makes plenty of sense that way, and I take no offense, just wonder how she had already heard.

Down the corridor I notice other families, other freshmen unpacking and moving in. We smile feebly at each other, all of us with the same look on our faces: what are we in for?

My father, who has his pleasantly serene look on says, "Let's see your room."

Unfortunately the entire family cannot fit inside my room,

so Dad and Mom go first. Mrs. Hibbard departs, saying that if we need anything we should call her. I follow my parents inside, and Danny and Lisa peer in through the door.

"It is small, isn't it?" I look around at the identical unmade beds, identical dressers, and desks carved out of the same used maple wood, the flat-backed wood chairs, and the wrought-iron bookcase. The one window has a sad gray shade on it.

"Nonsense. It's big enough!" Dad assures me. "Why are you always looking for trouble? You're never satisfied. Spoiled, you've been spoiled."

"It's a nice big walk-in closet, dear," Mom says. I think she's referring to the entire room until I turn around and see that she's rustling the hangers inside the closet to the right of the door. "As long as you're here first, why don't you take this side; it's nearer the window."

Less chance of suffocating, I know; listen, my mother won't let us keep plants in our bedrooms on the grounds that they use up too much air, and no amount of showing her biology books illustrating how plants give off oxygen, breathe in the bad and give out the good, can persuade her out of this notion.

"Fine." I walk over to the window; we're on the ground floor with an excellent view of the white picket fence, the road, the wire fence, and the bottom of the hill, but at least I'll never have to worry about fires, it's only a two-foot drop to a pair of piney hedges underneath the window. "Let's start unpacking."

We lug in suitcases, typewriter, clock radio, shoes, boots, coats, a copy of *Jane Eyre*, the guitar, my hair dryer and rollers, throw them onto the bed and floor, except for the coats, which Mom hangs up; then Dad offers to stay and help me unpack.

"That's not necessary," I say. "You have a long drive back."

"All right," he agrees. "Then let me take out my hammer and I'll put up the mezuzah, and we'll get going."

He goes out to the car to the glove compartment, where he keeps his silver mezuzah-hammer, tiny religious nails, and one white yarmulke (he's always prepared), and walks back down the corridor wearing that yarmulke, holding the hammer, looking like an overgrown elf. We gather around him at the door, I try to shield him from the curious looks of parents and kids marching back and forth with suitcases, and he begins hammering. Suddenly from out of nowhere comes Mrs. Hibbard and her curls, flying down the hall, shrieking, "What's going on here? Who's putting something in with nails? Nails aren't allowed in dorm rooms!"

She stops in front of my room, and Dad says, "I'm putting up a mezuzah."

"Oh no, I'm sorry," she says; clearly she has no idea what a mezuzah is. "You'll have to put it up with masking tape or hang it from the cornices. The college fines you at the end of the year if it finds any nail holes in your room."

Needless to say, I could die. I want to explain to her, look Mrs. Hibbard, pardon him, he doesn't know any better, he's just a crazy rabbi trying to do his job, but how far would that get me with either of them?

"All right," Dad says. Then he stretches out his arms in a gesture that seems to include even Mrs. Hibbard, and says the room-blessing in Hebrew. Mrs. Hibbard darts out of reach of the benediction; she looks as though she's just come across a coven of witches, and she flies back down the corridor. I wish I could join her, fly down the hall and out the door, find some happy place free of rabbis. Oh Lord, I pray, GET ME OUT OF HERE. Please God if you're there, *get me away*.

God answers by allowing my father to finish his prayer, then I kiss them good-bye, walk down the corridor with them, past the still-smiling receiving line, and hold the door open as they file out. They get away, and I stay. Thank you, God.

Chapter Two

❦

Sitting on an unmade bed in the middle of a strange room is not a joyful experience, especially if there are bare white walls, no curtains on the window, and one's possessions scattered on the floor. Of course who am I to talk of joyful experiences? Maybe this is one and I don't know it; maybe other girls are whistling as they unpack, free of fears and trepidations, not terribly lonely. Maybe life just unrolls for them day by day, unravels; not like my life that starts and stops and jerks and bounces like a standard shift car being driven by a beginner. I never have any idea what will come next, and believe me, if a prehistoric monster, Tyrannosaurus Rex, suddenly crashed down the hill and through the dorm, laying waste to Bailey Hall, it would no more surprise me than tomorrow. Or next week.

I unpack my guitar and strum a few chords, then stop and feel the calluses on my fingers. I take my left-hand thumb and pat gently the tips of all the fingers on that same hand. I love those hard, grooved calluses, proof that I can accomplish *something*. I rub them on my right arm, which feels as though it's being stroked by tough nails. It's nice to know that skin doesn't always need to be pinprick soft; and when I touch these calluses with my other hand or a pencil or even the stiff nylon strings of the guitar, *they don't feel a thing*.

I pull the biggest suitcase, red plaid material folded over, onto the bed and open it. There on top of a pile of skirts, blouses, dresses, with underwear smashed into a corner, girdles and bras still stiff from being unworn, is my white Confirmation Bible. For a laugh I pick it up, close my eyes, and open to a random page, then put my finger on it. If my father saw me do this he'd kill me because, you must know, Jews are not superstitious. No indeed, they don't eat pork because of *trichinosis,* not from fear.

When I open my eyes I see that I'm pointing to Psalms 4:4, "Be angry, but sin not;/commune with your own hearts/on your beds, and be silent." There's nothing like the Bible for sound, sensible advice, and I'm sure I'd take it if I could ever understand what it means. I shut it and put it on the top shelf of the bookcase along with *Jane Eyre* and my clock radio. I figure as long as I'm at it why not try Charlotte Brontë, see if she has any words for me in my hour of need. I close my eyes and point to the second paragraph of Chapter Fifteen: "I had not, it seems, the originality to chalk out a new road to shame and destruction, but trode the old track with stupid exactness not to deviate an inch from the beaten centre." I throw her back on the bookshelf.

I'm not cheered up, but then with me superstitions never help. Other people find them comforting: do this and you'll be safe. I KNOW I'm not safe, and little things like stepping out the door on my right foot (which I do) only remind me that I'm doomed.

I unpack underwear first and put in a top drawer a bunch of bras so wired and rubbery they stand up by themselves, something my heavy breasts are unable to do, and rubber girdles of all kinds—with pants to squeeze my thighs, without squeezing everything else; a "merry widow" to whip my waist and middle into shape. I get depressed just looking at all of them. At this very moment I'm wearing a bra that cuts deep into the skin underneath my breasts whenever I sit down and a "long-line" girdle that pushes the flab up; it feels as though there's a war going on between my bra and girdle: which is pushing hardest? . . . Without the iron and rubber undergarments I have a small, not flabby (after all I'm still young) roll around my middle, but when I'm all cinched up and in, the hill becomes an uncomfortable mountain. Listen, when you push fat around it has to go somewhere, it doesn't just disappear. This is a law of nature I've apparently discovered; everyone else thinks you "lose three inches off waist and thighs," but I know better; what you lose one place you gain in another, and all the bra salesladies and mothers in the world cannot prove differently.

My mother insists that girdles keep your muscles toned up and firm, just like bras keep your breasts from drooping. It drives her crazy that I hate girdles and only wear them because otherwise none of my clothes will fit, but when I'm reading in my room or lounging around with a bathrobe on I do not wear a bra. Mom has been in tears over this perverse part of my nature; she feels it is immoral and unnatural and unfeminine and against all the rules and scientific laws. The Wisdom of Hannah Fabrikant: People need to be boxed in else they go to hell. Meanwhile she has a figure that could make you vomit, breasts that droop far below their bra-level and a belly you have to see to believe, and very few people have that privilege, for my mother's first act upon arising is to put on an all-in-one, a girdle that stretches from breasts to thighs, and if they came up with one that went from neck to ankles, she would have it too, and if you saw her without the armored supports you'd know why.

Underneath the fat-pushers in the suitcase are muu-muus,

my favorites; under them I wear nothing and, if you follow the gospel according to Hannah F., am ruining my figure for life. On this planet, says my mother, you pay a heavy price for comfort.

Further down in the valise are boxes of stockings that I'll never rinse before wearing, another crime to be committed; socks, sweaters, dresses, one long red and gold scarf (rah rah Harter), gloves and mittens, my hairbrush wrapped in silver-foil, my manicure set (ever since I've been six years old I've been pushing my cuticles back, how lovely the half-moons on my fingernails are you can't believe), toothbrush and tooth-paste, jewelry box with the two Jewish star necklaces (I must have a hundred of them, all gifts of members of the congregation).

From another valise I take out shampoo, Neutrogena soap (my uncle gets it free), Fostex cream (he also gets this free, it's made of ground stone and bits of glass and is excellent for acne because it tears the living shit out of pimples, skin, eyes, if you're not careful; I use it only in extreme emergencies). There are more Shetland sweaters, here nicely folded (that won't last forever); blouses, dungarees, slacks, and a Yankees T-shirt that Danny sneaked in, I laugh when I unfold it, and wait, what's this? A note from my father, I can recognize his lousy handwriting eight miles away—is it a prayer? Or a command? It says, "Thou shalt love the Lord thy God with all thy heart, with all thy soul and with all thy might."

I tear it up and then notice there's no wastebasket in the room, so I head for the door with God's holy word in shreds in my hand; I aim to flush it down the toilet immediately. I'm at the door, when it opens, hits my hand, and scatters the bits all over the room, at the very moment that a nice-looking girl appears with a gray-haired lady right behind her.

The girl looks at the room, already littered (I don't know whether to talk first or pick up the papers) and says, "Room and board is how much a year? The food had better be fantastic."

"Sorry for the mess," I reply. "I just got here a while ago," and I bend to scoop up the shredded prayer.

"Baabra?" she asks as I straighten up. "I'm Maasha Green, and this is my mathah. Listen, I wasn't looking at the floor, just at the size of this place. Maaa, you think all the stuff we brought will fit in?"

Her mother walks in and I back up, transfer the shreds to my left hand, and shake hands with her. Marsha and I have been corresponding all summer; this is one of the rules of Harter College, along with the required reading of Joseph Wood Krutch (whom I pronounce to rhyme with much). I thought writing letters to someone you didn't know was pretty boring until I came to Krutch; he made the letters seem perfectly fascinating.

From Marsha's letters I've learned that she likes to swim, dance, play tennis, and read J. D. Salinger. In sum I know nothing at all about her. Now I see that she's pretty, with short blond hair, a small nose that looks like mine, blue eyes, no glasses, and a nice, moderate mouth except when it's opened. Her opened mouth is the only Jewish thing about her, except for her mother, who has my father's nose, a Sisterhood hairdo, bubbled and sprayed into place, and a nicely girdled, overweight body, but I'm still not sure they're Jewish; maybe other ethnic groups breed mothers like this. Marsha has a great body, long legs, nice waist. I look longingly at it, maybe it's contagious, a thin waist and narrow hips, maybe I can catch them from her. I notice she isn't wearing socks or a sweater, just loafers and a gray cotton skirt and red blouse, Peter Pan collar naturally; I don't know if there is a blouse available in America at this time that doesn't have either a button-down or a Peter Pan collar.

"I brought curtains and bedspreads and two little rugs," Mrs. Green says. "We live so close by I'll return them if you don't like them."

"How nice of you."

"Watch your step," Marsha says to me. "You treat her too

well she'll move right in, huh, Ma?" She pats her mother's shoulder.

"I can't believe my baby is in college," Mrs. Green says, eyes moistening.

And I, I can't believe that Marsha isn't being yelled at, smacked, murdered even, for being so flippant. Perhaps when her father steps in, but no, imagine this. He didn't come. He's very busy. He'll take her out for dinner soon, or she can go home and see him. This is the strangest family I've ever seen. Marsha's older brother, a junior at the University of Pennsylvania, apparently *drove himself* to college last week. I can never tell the Rabbi all these details, for I know what he'd say: "There are parents who don't really care about their children and let them do as they please. But I'm not a Block of Wood. I can't help worrying about what will happen!"

Generally this block of wood metaphor is pulled out when we ask to: 1. drive the car down to the shore (an hour away); 2. come in late from a date; 3. go away to camp—any activities that require our being out of His reach. Because if we're not THERE, God only knows what might happen. And me, fool that I am, I've always believed him (if you can't trust your father and you can't trust your rabbi, who pray tell is left?). I've always thought that parents who permit their children to fly on a plane, for instance, are *murderers*.

"I'm nearly unpacked," I say. "Let me throw these papers out and I'll help you unload your car."

"That's very sweet of you, dear," Mrs. Green tells me, "but Jeff will be along any minute now with . . . ah . . ."

The door opens slowly and outside it is a middle-aged black man covered with suitcases and boxes and plastic-wrapped bright red plaid material that could match my suitcase perfectly. Marsha says, "Thanks Jeff, you're a doll," and goes over and kisses him good-bye on the cheek. He wishes her good luck and exits.

"Do you want to see the spreads and curtains?" Marsha asks.

"I already see them. They're nice. I like red; it's my favorite color." There's now so much stuff in the room, the only place I can go is back to my bed.

"I'll put up the curtains if you start unpacking," Mrs. Green says.

I wad the papers, which I see I'm never going to throw away, God's punishment for ignoring His Holy Word, and put them underneath my pillow. I help Mrs. Green hang the curtain and feel guilty for having appropriated this side of the room. "If you want to switch sides halfway through the year, we could," I suggest.

Marsha shrugs her shoulders. "If we could crash down the wall and extend the room, say, twenty feet, that might help, but otherwise . . ."

"Was Harter your first choice?" Mrs. Green asks.

"Yes. Was it yours?" I ask Marsha.

"Yes," she says. "No," Mrs. Green says.

"I wanted her to go to Vassar—" Mrs. Green begins.

"To get me away from Bob," Marsha finishes. "And here he is." She pulls out a large framed photograph of a gorgeous young man; from the picture he looks like Tab Hunter, everybody's idol.

"He's cute!" I give the ultimate compliment.

"He's a doll," Marsha adds, "and Ma is mad at me because I brought him along, right?"

"You're too young to get married. You should be dating a lot, not settling down." If this sounds angry to Marsha, she should hear my family.

"I will date, I promised to and I will, but he's so sweet and nice and fun and I'm crazy about him." Marsha kisses the picture. Mrs. Green takes out a handkerchief (monogrammed, I notice) and blows her nose. Marsha looks like she enjoys teasing her mother, prodding her, hugging the picture and all. I've never seen anything like this in my entire life: Is Marsha sick, crazy, perverse? Or is this normal behavior? I have very little foundation on which to judge.

· *41* ·

"Do you have a steady boyfriend?" Mrs. Green wants to know.

"Neither steady nor unsteady."

"Where else did you get into school?" she asks.

"Oh, Smith, Vassar, Pembroke," I lie.

She's impressed. She believes me, she actually assumes, on the basis of a five-minute acquaintance, that I'm telling the truth. That's because I wear glasses; anyone who wears them automatically looks honest, and people tend to believe anything they say. Besides, I'm a good liar. I've had a lot of practice.

"What were your Board scores?" Mrs. Green wants to know. Now this makes me almost certain that she's Jewish; only Jewish mothers sound like college admittance officers.

"Seven hundred eighty in English and six hundred thirty in math." I crib the seven-eighty from my afternoon English Board, which I cheated on; it takes something to figure out how to cheat on a College Board, but I do. I go back and take extra time on English, rush through the chemistry, where I know there's a low ceiling on my possible score since I haven't learned *anything* by the time I take the test (and in chemistry, by the way, I fill in the blanks at random, blacken here, there, everywhere, with wild abandon. I got a five hundred and fifty on that too. Pure brute luck). My math score is from my junior year College Board, another fluke I don't equal, not even senior year.

"Wow," Marsha says. I smile modestly; it was nothing, really.

"What did you get?"

"Both in the high five hundreds," she says.

Now I'm not so sure she's Jewish; first of all, Jews don't get scores that low, and secondly, they don't admit them.

"What does your father do?" Mrs. Green asks.

Now this is the one question Marsha and I have managed to avoid so far; on my side you already know why, and on hers? Who knows, maybe her father is a convict, an embezzler, a forger, rapist, looter, pillager.

"My father's a rabbi," I finally blurt out.

"A rabbi?" Marsha cries. "Then you're Jewish. How terrific! So am I!" And she rushes off her bed and hugs me. Mrs. Green looks delighted. I say, "What does your father do?"

"Businessman," Marsha says.

So what did she have to be ashamed of?

"You'll have to come to our house for High Holy Days," Mrs. Green says. "We belong to a lovely temple."

"Wonderful." My God, am I doomed by a rabbinical father to a lifetime of temples?

"Any Friday night you feel like going, my goodness, won't Rabbi Elman be pleased?"

"Jesus, Ma," Marsha groans, "does that mean I'll have to go too? On Friday nights?"

Mrs. Green looks at me as though I'm going to take terrific offense at this, perhaps call in the Chief Rabbi of Israel. "Don't worry about me," I reassure her. "I've had enough Friday night services to last me a lifetime." Mrs. Green looks relieved, and who blames her? How much do you think *she'd* like to see Reb Elman? Weekly?

I've never known a rabbi's daughter before," Marsha says. "Are you holier than most people? Do you keep kosher?"

I pause for a moment thinking of myself: liar, cheater; no, I'm sure I'm not holier than anybody. "I don't know what I am."

"Well, isn't this a nice surprise," Mrs. Green says. "You know you don't look Jewish."

"I had a nose job."

At this Marsha laughs so hard that tears run down her cheeks. "So did I," she finally gasps. "So did I." When she catches her breath she says, "You have a beautiful nose. It's just like mine."

"I know." We laugh again, the Nose Sisters.

Mrs. Green walks over to her daughter's bed, sits down at

the foot of it near the cartons, and starts unpacking. "I see if I don't begin this, it'll never get done."

Marsha pulls herself up next to her, and I roll to the foot of my bed. The first thing Mrs. Green takes out is a huge AM/FM radio, a silver Zenith with lots of dials and numbers. Then a stereo with speakers. I'm impressed. Then Marsha unwraps an electric coffeemaker. "It's illegal," she tells me, "but breakfast is from seven to seven forty-five—can you believe that? I'm never going to make it." So we hide the coffeepot in her closet.

"Here, put the coil there too," Mrs. Green suggests.

"For soup," Marsha explains. "I'll show you how to use it later."

I'm thanking my lucky stars I got such a roommate; she seems to have an idea of what's coming and how to prepare for it. I watch her unpack a huge Webster's College Edition Dictionary and a *Roget's Thesaurus,* brand new, a typewriter, and lots of paper and ribbon, a pencil sharpener that is weighted to stand on the desk without screws, she even seems to know the no-nails rule in advance! Then she takes out records; the top one is a Berlitz *Learning French.* "I'm lousy in French and we need to take at least one year of it, did you know?" She looks at the ugly jacket. *"Je déteste cette langue."*

I see immediately what her problem is. She hasn't learned never to use a word that sounds like its English counterpart, even if it's the right one; that makes all French teachers think you're cheating. They think using the wrong word, a REAL French word, is better than using a familiar half-English right one.

Marsha pulls out a box of fruit, oranges, apples, and pears, and says to her mother, "You know all I'm going to eat are the pears."

"Maybe your roommate would enjoy some different kinds."

I smile and nod; fruit, I'd like to tell her, I've eaten so much fruit in my life, all the while my parents assuring me how

SWEET it is and how GOOD it is and how much like a chocolate bar it is. I HATE fruit.

Next comes out a box of cookies.

"How did they get in there?" Mrs. Green asks.

"I put them," Marsha answers.

"You KNOW how bad they are for you."

"Yeah. I love them too. They help me study." Marsha opens the box and takes out a cookie and bites into it and offers the box to me. Pepperidge Farm, the best. I love them but turn her down; when any parent is in the area I can't eat fattening things. It's a reflex action.

"I need to watch my weight." Now there's a euphemism to beat all euphemisms, but true, absolutely true. I do watch my weight, I watch it go up and down, down and up; I have no control over it, mind you, but I keep my eye on it constantly. It doesn't do a thing behind my back.

"So does Marsha," Mrs. Green says. Do Jewish mothers see their daughters as fat whether or not they are? Believe me, Marsha is THIN.

"What's this?" Marsha reaches down and pulls out a huge box marked Dietetic Candy. "Yuch, this stuff?"

"Sugarfree," Mrs. Green says to me. "Won't you try one? Only three calories apiece."

I lean over and pick out a cellophane-wrapped hard object resembling candy; the resemblance ceases when I put it into my mouth. It's awful, three calories of terribleness. "My, isn't it surprising what they can do with saccharine?" There, not a total lie.

"Ma, take it home."

"When your roommate enjoys it so much?"

Marsha looks at me like she knows better. "Ma, there isn't enough room for it."

"They cost eighteen cents apiece," her mother says.

I try to cherish the taste eighteen cents worth. It's hard to do, even for me who can swallow an incredible amount of shit.

Marsha puts it on the bottom ledge of the bookshelf. Then she unpacks her clothes, hangs everything carefully, and neatly folds blouses and sweaters. I love watching people do things slowly as though they enjoy the doing, fold, pat in place, it looks sensuous and fun; needless to say I'm too impatient ever to do it myself.

Mrs. Green hands us the identical bedspreads, walks over to Marsha and kisses her good-bye, and then kisses me also. "Come see us soon," she says, so I know I've been adopted. "It's very cramped here." She shakes her head at the door and looks all around the room. How different she is from my father who thinks this is the Taj Mahal. "When you feel like stretching, you'll come to our place, it's a lot bigger." That, as I soon find out, is the literal damned truth.

Chapter Three

❧

"So what shall we do first, get sheets or take a look around?" Marsha wants to know.

Me, I'd been thinking I'd just sit on my bed and worry for a few hours.

"Hey, what's this?" She sees my guitar propped against the side of the bed. "Do you play?"

"A little."

"Terrific. Play something, won't you?"

I pick up the guitar and sing "If I Had a Hammer," heart pounding as though I'm making my Carnegie Hall debut. Marsha gets up and does a little impromptu dance; she loves to dance, she whispers; and suddenly I'm not afraid; it's impossible to worry around Marsha, who doesn't realize how many things there are to be scared to death of. She looks kind of funny moving around in two square feet of free space, swaying back and forth, but she's not self-conscious at all. Me, I *always* feel like I'm on *Candid Camera* making an ass of myself.

"It's clear to me," she says when I finish, "that you're going to be the most popular girl in the dorm." At this moment, verifying, it seems, Marsha's gift of prophecy, there's a knock at the door.

"Come in!" she yells.

Our house president walks in with two girls she introduces as Frannie and Biff. It takes us only a short time to get to know all of them.

Celia turns out to be that rarity of rarities, a happy Harter girl, junior, president of Bailey, and in love with a minister's son back home who was, shocking to relate, one year younger than herself; this was the startling secret of Celia's life. She's a nice and polite brown-haired Gentile girl whose strongest characteristic is her extremely soft voice; that's her really outstanding feature—you have to bend your ears to catch what she's saying. This, we soon discover, is the world's biggest bother at house meetings. Fifty-eight girls in Bailey sit practically on top of each other in the dorm living room, sprawled over sofas and floor, and there's Celia, conducting a meeting by whispers. Fifty-eight girls, nearly all of them with rollers in their hair, Harter never accepted a girl who didn't set her hair; that along with high English Boards was an absolute prerequisite for attending; fifty-eight girls, seven thousand rollers, and one hundred and sixteen ears bending forward trying to find out if Harter had voted in chocolate doughnuts for Wednesday breakfast or voted out Spam salad, or set the date for rush week, or whatever other major issues were being hotly debated in Student Council. And in Bailey Hall no one ever knew, except for the three girls nearest to Celia, and as they varied from week to week, no one ever knew much or for very long.

Celia had shoulder-length silky brown hair, dark-brown eyes, and an incredible mustache that no one had ever told her she had to pluck or bleach or do something to. *She always weighed the same;* when I tell you this, if you were a girl in college, you know I'm talking about a giant in the willpower department. This girl never lost or gained any weight, and she always kept a boxlet of Kellogg's Special K in her room in case she got hungry: 1. because of the vitamins and minerals, and 2. because you could easily filch it from the cafeteria. And when she got hungry in between meals she would open her little box and eat a dry handful of Kellogg's Special K and Nothing Else, or occasionally, if she was starving to death and had ten exams the next day and no date for the weekend, she would heat some bouillon and mix the Kellogg's Special K with the bouillon and that would be her big binge. Celia also sewed her own clothes. There are very few achievements that I admire, but sensible eating is one of them and making your clothes the other. I of course can do neither.

"That guitar sounded very nice," Celia whispers. "However, I must warn you" (Biff and Frannie look at each other as though they disapprove entirely of warnings and think an execution is more in order) "that after seven P.M. when school's in session it's against house rules to make any distracting noises."

Biff adds, "I'm hall proctor here, and I enforce that rule with absolute strictness." Biff, it turns out, occupies a single room across the hall from us and down a little bit from Celia and Frannie, who are roommates. There are maybe ten single rooms in all of Harter and how Biff secured one of them no one ever found out, but she didn't think it was such a miracle; as a matter of fact she might have preferred living with a friend, only her last year's best friend, Pookie—don't ask me what that was short for, I never wanted to know (Biff, we find out, is short for Elizabeth, which her tiny toddler brother could never pronounce, could only say Elizabiff)—flunked out and got married, I believe in that order.

Everyone thought that was real neat of Pookie, too, to have flunked out at the end of her junior year, ten thousand dollars down the drain, but not by their reasoning, for Pookie had married a Harter man, for which privilege ten thousand bucks was hardly a drop. No one but Pookie could have stood living with Biff, I'm sure, because Biff had the year before completed a successful Metrecal diet, had lost sixty pounds and a good deal of hair. Why the hair had gone along with the weight no one knew, but there was Biff with an unusually good figure and three wisps of hair on her head. So her main conversational gambits were: 1. everyone should go on Metrecal, and 2. where could she buy a good wig? After about half an hour she bored you further to tears than Celia did.

"You're lucky to get advance warning," Frannie trills. The whole phrase sounds like a scale going up; it's meant to be a playful tone, I'm sure, but there's something singularly inappropriate in the coupling of those words with that tune. "Don't forget—dinner's at five fifteen, the earlier you get there the shorter the line is." She has a big grin on her face.

Celia was fond of repeating that Frannie would be a perfectly happy girl if Warren Bahnsen would only marry her. Unfortunately Warren only took her out on alternate Fridays and seemed as close to marrying her as he did of changing his sex (which, if he DID marry her, he certainly would've had to do. Frannie was a man in girl's clothing). Which proved to me that Warren was only half an idiot, whichever half of him had decided to date her in the first place.

"Bailey shares a cafeteria with three other dorms, it's quite crowded. Keep your name card on; we'll give out meal tickets at tonight's compulsory meeting," Frannie finishes.

"Mrs. Hibbard will give you sheets," Celia whispers. "My, what nice curtains. Aren't you two well prepared!"

We smile wanly.

"What are meal tickets?" I ask.

"You'll find out," Frannie trills again, huge grin, so we know it can't be any good, and all three dart out the door.

"Next time they come, remind me to offer them some of Mom's candies. That ought to wipe the grin off their faces. I hate people who smile a lot, they always want something from my life." Marsha gets up from the bed.

"Remind me to frown and snarl a lot." I follow her out the door and down the hall.

"I'd prefer it; I'm telling you, evil lurks in the hearts of polite people."

Mrs. Hibbard keeps sheets in a double-locked linen closet near her room; she has a clipboard with our names marked down the sides of a multiruled sheet of paper, dates along the top row, lines and boxes, she looks like she's taking notes for the C.I.A. After she opens the two locks, keys jangling, fumbling, finally finding the right one (how can she keep track of all of them?) she hands Marsha two folded sheets, one pillow case, two towels, one washcloth, and checks her name off, then hands me (counting carefully) the same.

"Do girls steal linens?" Marsha asks. "I can't imagine what anyone would do with an extra sheet or pillow case."

"You'd be surprised," Mrs. Hibbard says.

No doubt she's right. As we walk away she double locks the linen closet once more. Jesus, I think, there are sixty girls in this dorm; she's going to repeat this process sixty times every week all year! And I can't even fold my blouses nicely.

"Oh, girls!" she shouts as we're halfway down the hall, "I inspect roo-oo-ooms once a week." Smile now showing fifty-eight crooked, faded teeth. "Surprise check-up! Beds must always be made."

We smile rather less enthusiastically back, walk into the room, and silently make our beds.

"I'm going to wash up," Marsha says. "How about you?"

The disgusting truth is I wouldn't ever have thought of this on my own; in this small private area I've made my rebellion: 1. never wash hands before meals, and if mother insists, go into bathroom, run water, sprinkle water on soap, rumple towel, leave having wet only two fingers; 2. never wash hands after going to bathroom, even if this means instant death (repeat fake process if parent in area); 3. never brush teeth except in morning or before dates; 4. after shitting, wipe in Wrong Direction. I follow Marsha into the communal bathroom and lather up my hands and face, realizing with a shock that this is actually a pleasant little custom. Who could have guessed?

When we get back to the room, I take my socks off and walk barefoot on the little rug near my bed. Then I step barefoot onto the floor, which to the naked eye is wood, but to the naked foot is unmasked as linoleum. Wood-paneled linoleum, cool and clammy. I point it out to Marsha.

"You have to look closely at this place," she says. "They're gonna try to slip lots of things by us."

"Maybe it'll be easier to keep clean." I try to make the best of what's forced upon me.

I start to put one bare foot into a loafer (this is the absolute best way to ruin shoes, Mom insists). I don't know whether I believe her and am anxious to take the most excellent route to shoe-destruction or whether I'm testing her the way I used to test God to see if He was There. "All right," I'd say to Him, "here's what we'll do. If You're there, make that cloud over the sun start moving." Sitting in a field near our house, staring up at the sky, I used to make these reasonable and scientific tests of the whole matter. If He's such a stickler for bacon, why should clouds be too small for His attention? Once in a while the cloud moves, but I always know it's an accidental wind.

I slip my second bare foot into the shoe, wiggle my toes inside the warm leather, and follow Marsha out the door with this feeling that my life has already changed tremendously.

Down the gray corridor other doors are being opened and shut and locked. I look at the girls and smile, and they smile at me; the ones who are locking up look sheepish: are we afraid of each other already? At college two hours and suspicious of lurking kleptomania. I walk the length of the corridor thinking, which one is the thief? I hope she gets my mezuzah.

Marsha lets the outside screen door bang. I jump a little

nervously at the noise; it sounds too much like an act of aggression. At five ten P.M., right now, the sun is partly hidden by the hill, the tops of the Harter Museum glow, and the red-brick buildings burn with a warm, deep color. The sliver of sun that remains is also red: slice of red sun, I think, and it reminds me of dinner. We follow a herd of girls down the dirt and gravel road into the big glass doors of a new building and down a winding stairway, until we come to a line of girls, no cafeteria in sight, just a winding line of bodies on a stairway, on which we too take our places.

"This is obscene," Marsha says.

I know what she means. I feel like a prisoner of war, something dehumanized, a dog waiting to be fed. Everyone looks embarrassed to be here, or is it only me? Are overweight people supposed to stand in line for dinner? Doesn't that prove what's too clear—that they want to eat?

"Is this the way it is all the time?" Marsha asks.

"Worse," comes a voice from farther down the line. "Wait till the rest of the upper classes get here."

"Maybe we'll get a hot plate," Marsha whispers.

I nod yes. Unfortunately I have no idea what a hot plate is; what comes to my mind is a red-hot dinner plate, sizzling maybe, that, considering my clumsiness, would amputate my fingers. It sounds like something my mother could have invented to keep my hands from ever touching food. See? Eat and you're scorched: the ideal dietary aid.

The line moves slowly forward.

"Too bad they don't hang pictures on these walls," Marsha says.

I shake my head, backside resting on bannister, arms folded, dreaming of burning chinaware. "No nails allowed," I mumble.

"Nails, males," Marsha says, "maybe that's how they make rules around here—according to rhyme."

"Whereas," a voice behind me speaks, "a line is fine."

We turn to look at the red-haired girl behind us. "My

name's Rona Glasser, I'm in Bailey too, we passed you on the way out." She points behind her. "This is my roommate JoEllen Rothstein who didn't get into Wellesley."

JoEllen, dark, tall, overweight, but pretty anyway (another study: why do some fat girls look good? Does the fat not go to their faces, or what?) says, "Go ahead and laugh. I'm so depressed I could die."

"Don't mind her," Rona whispers. "With her, overstatement is a way of life."

"Hey, did you two know each other before you came here?" Marsha moves forward and I follow, jealous. Marsha likes Rona better than me, I think, because I'm not lively, I'm morose like JoEllen. I vow to change.

"We saw each other during the summer," Rona explains. "Jo's from Manhattan and I'm from Brooklyn; we could've stayed home and gone to CCNY, probably more budding doctors there than here anyway, right?"

"Wrong," says JoEllen.

"Jo did a senior project in high school on where Jewish premed students are in the greatest bulk," Rona tells us. "The beauty of progressive education. For biology she did this; everyone else was doing bird migrations. But can you marry a bird?"

"Laugh, laugh." JoEllen is smiling. "I'm here to get married."

"And I'm here not to get married." Marsha explains about Robert.

"I'd like to get married eventually," Rona adds.

"I'm too young to go," I moan.

Marsha moves forward again, off the last step and on to level ground. She peers around the corner; I look over her head; at our left is a fenced-in corridor, big chrome bars to keep us in line, and farther down are stacks of trays, silverware, then the line turns right. I can't believe how much line-standing we're in for. I think of those pictures of Depression breadlines that make me so guilty. How can someone be a fat liberal, an overweight socially conscious person? It's a disgrace. Listen, I know why Gandhi fasted. GUILT. I would too if I could. The only good socialist is a thin socialist, and what about Khrushchev? A fat communist is a contradiction in terms. I know this all too well. Meanwhile I'm hungry.

We round the porcelain bend, dazzling white walls and ceiling, bright chrome bars, lacquered pale green floors, fluorescent lights—this place is a definition of the verb "to gleam."

"What's for dinner?" Marsha asks a woman who's sitting at the end of the long corridor with a clipboard, checking off our names, peering at name cards, peering at her list, looking back and forth suspiciously. "You'll see when you get there, dearie." Big smile.

"Why are you checking names?" Marsha picks up a tray.

"Some girls," the lady looks up at us as though to try to fix us in her memory: troublemakers, "try to sneak through *twice.*"

Marsha whispers, "Can you imagine standing on line two times?"

I barely hear her; believe me, she can stop whispering, we've entered the cafeteria. Trays, plates, eating, talking, clanking, the noise is overwhelming. I stare at the big rectangular white-formica (flecked with bits of glittering silver) tables close together, girls everywhere, then stare ahead at Marsha passing through the chrome-lined passage to a chrome-lined tray-holder and plates of what looks to be chrome-lined food. There are some fifty identical plates behind the counter, identical salads (how did they do this? cut lettuce leaves with scissors?) made of dead lettuce and carrots, big white plates with: a rectangle of meat loaf, lima beans (they must count them to get them this exact), mashed potatoes; another smaller plate with two pieces of white bread, two pats of butter, and for dessert, a plain white cake with orange icing. There's no way to have just meat loaf and lima beans without the potatoes.

Marsha and I take everything and head for a corner table

and put our trays down. Marsha remembers that she forgot milk. "What other protein am I going to get down?" she asks and heads back to the counter just as Rona and JoEllen arrive. She's back faster than she expected. "They don't let you in again." She sits in front of her tray. "I told them I forgot to get milk and they said I had to get whatever I wanted the first time, otherwise it would be pandemonium and unfair to the other girls."

"No seconds?" Rona asks. She's skinny of course.

"There's something you'd like a duplicate of?" JoEllen picks up her fork and cuts into the meat loaf.

"Maybe this'll keep us from gaining weight." I eat a lima bean.

"I don't like to be force-thinned," Marsha says.

"Could we join you?"

We look up at Celia and Frannie and Biff and nod and chew. They are obviously doing their good deed for the day.

I try everything—meat loaf, mashed potatoes, bread, three different enough foods; how is it that here they taste exactly alike? And this is not from someone who's used to gourmet cooking; my mother's best meals are Swanson chicken pot pie and Heinz baked beans; everything else she ruins: 1. because my father cannot have salt or cholesterol with his heart; 2. my uncle has informed her that spices cause Sexual Feelings. Yes ladies and gentlemen, this is true. According to him, oregano and pepper are practically direct causes of pregnancy and God Only Knows What Else. Plus the rabbi's overweight wife believes that anything animal has to be killed personally by her: steak and roast beef she cooks till they can't fight back, she murders them with heat. Chickens she bakes without seasoning until there's no pink under the drumstick and no juice anywhere else. Vegetables without salt and butter, try it you'll hate it. My credentials in this area are impeccable; I haven't been spoiled. But this is the worst I've ever seen. How have they made a meatless meatloaf, leather lima beans, and cardboard potatoes? Later on I get a clue: the oatmeal/glue/

paste that we don't finish for breakfast reappears at lunch as hamburger—it's oatmeal with traces of meat, I recognize it, sort of a theme without much variation.

I eat everything, naturally, because finally there's no one to stop me.

Celia and her friends eat everything because they think it's *good*.

"Is this the way meals always are?" Marsha asks, eating her cake.

Frannie with the bulging eyes and big hands, what an asset to a farm that girl would be, how great behind a tractor, says, "Sunday dinner at noon is sit-down. The scholarship girls serve, and there's a prayer before the meal."

Celia, Biff, and Frannie stare at Marsha's full plate. I hand her my cake. As I'm rolling some of the mashed potatoes around in my mouth—chewing them would be redundant—I notice that Celia is moving her lips, forming words certainly but completely inaudible. I watch her but with no luck; even her lips are unclear, so I say, "What?"

But this is a useless ploy, for nothing can induce Celia to raise her voice. She repeats herself in the same whisper, but this time Marsha is watching too, with better success for she replies, "I can't eat this shit." Her nice clear, loud voice penetrates even to surrounding tables, and I think I hear a regular chorus of gasps join the three at our table.

Celia's mouth starts moving again, this time I squint hard at her. Rona says, "What?" but I have caught on in time to save us from a useless repetition. "She says the food IS a bit starchy." I look at Marsha's untouched potatoes, white bread, and lima beans and smile. What else is there to do?

At the opposite end of the cafeteria girls are still standing on line. The noise in the cafeteria—sipping, chewing, clanging, clicking, crashing, talking—ought to sound lively and gay, but to me, as I look from table to table, it is one long knell.

"Can you wear rollers to the house meeting?" JoEllen asks.

Chapter Four

❧

Rona, JoEllen, Marsha, and I sit on the floor surrounded by whatever Bailey freshmen don't fit on the one couch and seven chairs. There are twenty of us, and we're all nervously here early—seven twenty-five. It's a little cooler now, finally, the promised Boston air, but no one seems much relieved by it.

The window that looks out on the hill is open, and the gauzy white curtains blow back and forth like sails, the middle billows out and the bottom flutters. Oh, Melville, a whaling ship was your Harvard College and Yale, what about me? What kind of voyage can this college-boat take me on? Because if the sea looks scary, think how life looks: uncharted, unplumbed, unknown; only how does a girl go about finding the right metaphor for her terror? I mean, listen, all of *Moby Dick* is one huge metaphor for fear. Those storms and mad

Ahab and the wounded white whale and a dinky boat with leaks—they're so we can feel Melville's fear, but it wasn't whales he was afraid of. It was tomorrow. Like me.

The curtains flutter, and I look around the dim living room, which is decorated in Old Lady Gentile. The couch cover is a brown and white flower pattern. Two lamps on little end tables have brass bases crawling with ornate curlicues, the lampshades have eight or ten beige sides and crisp little skirts, and the most Old Lady Gentile touch of all, the bulbs are forty watt, give off no light to speak of, just an ineffective little glow. There's an olive-green carpet on the floor—thin but extremely clean. The paintings on the wall are: 1. a seascape: little white sailboat on an evenly waved sea, nice neat yellow sand, the forces of nature subdued by a stroke of the brush; 2. a daisy in a burnt-sienna pot; 3. a still life—two pears, an apple and a vase; it looks as though the painter copied wax fruit, a still death.

Jo says, "I wonder how everyone fits into this room. Frannie told me sixty kids are in this dorm. Only half of them are here."

"I bet they use freshmen for floor mats," Marsha says. "Probably we lie down and the juniors and seniors sit on us."

To prove her point, Celia, Biff, and Frannie arrive, clear off the couch and chairs for themselves and the three other upperclasswomen; then Mrs. Hibbard walks in and appropriates the last big chair, evicting a nervous-looking blond girl with bangs, a ponytail, and glasses. So now the freshmen sit on the floor, and our leaders loom above us.

Biff and Frannie then pass out Freshmen Beanies, little yarmulkes, yes, ladies and gentlemen, what else could they be but red yarmulkes trimmed with gold braid and topped by a gold pom-pom.

"Freshman Beanie," I say aloud to myself. Even the word sounds strange, an exotic Protestant-American nineteenth-century expression—does it refer to the pom-pom? Or the whole cap? Does the phrase "I'm going to bean you" come from this?

"Girls, girls," Celia whispers, nearly inaudibly. I can hardly wait for the rest of the crew to get here, then perhaps no sound at all will come from her throat. The living room becomes dead silent with expectation: what can she do for an encore?

"From now on and for the next two weeks," she says, "you must wear your beanies everywhere you go outside the dorm." Celia's grin is splitting her face, and Frannie and Biff are actually giggling.

I look around at my classmates—not a smile cracks any of their faces. JoEllen looks ready to cry, and I know why. For this her hair is up in fifteen steel rollers?

"This is part of the traditional freshman initiation," Celia tells us. "When you are anywhere on campus and an upperclassman blows a whistle, you must stop and hop five big steps backward. . . ."

Like a deranged bunny, I think, and this is what they call orientation? . . .

"With," Celia continues through the chuckles of her friends, "your hand behind your head, and yell 'How!' " She stares into our faces, expecting, no doubt, looks of incredible pleasure. "At the same time you must wear clothes that clash. This has been a tradition at Harter for the past sixty years."

The freshmen are absolutely quiet.

I finally break the silence, shocking everyone including myself by saying, "I think we ought to go out and buy water pistols, and the second anyone blows a whistle, we should soak them." For a split second I flinch, expecting to be hit, then the laughter comes. Even Mrs. Hibbard, give credit where it's due, smiles. The upper-class contingent does not. A couple of my classmates lean over and pat my back, and Marsha says, "Good for you!" I never realized that rebelling could be such fun.

"The other scheduled orientation activities are listed on these mimeographed papers Fran is handing out," Celia whispers.

I look fearfully at the list; maybe a firing squad for big-mouthed freshmen is part of the fun. At the top of a long list that includes library tour, chapel, campus tour, freshman mixer, sorority teas, is a puzzling one: Fraternity Visitations.

Celia explains it. "This is a way for the boys to meet you."

Rona whispers, "At least we'll get something out of it."

"What?" Marsha whispers back.

"What about the guys that don't belong to fraternities?" I ask.

"There are none," Frannie tells me.

"Does everyone join sororities too?" Rona asks.

"Three-fourths of the girls," Celia whispers. "But they're not so important, because girls aren't allowed to have sorority houses; they have to live in dorms. However, sorority bids aren't until second semester. The most important business at hand is explained in the little blue handbook—the college rules and regulations."

Biff and Frannie now pass it out, a thick booklet with a glossy picture of the Harter Museum on the front.

"In order to get your late-night permission you'll have to pass a test at the end of the week on all these rules, so pay attention. Until you pass the test you won't be able to date or anything." Celia smiles.

"And then," Frannie adds, "you'll never be able to use ignorance as an excuse."

"What do you mean, not plead ignorance?" Marsha asks.

"If you break a rule we assume you do it willfully," Frannie tells her. "Because you'll KNOW all the rules."

"Oh," Marsha says.

"Dorm-living rules, page thirteen," Celia says.

We turn dutifully to page thirteen.

"I want to explain them because, except for beer, which is allowed in the dorm until classes begin, all the rules apply from tonight on." Celia looks at each of us as though we're about to jump bail. I find myself as a result looking wildly about for an exit, the way I do in theaters and auditoriums, planning a quick escape before the crowd tramples me to death.

"First of all, no men in rooms, no liquor, no perishables, no hotplates, or any electrical appliances except a lamp."

I stare at Marsha, who looks casual and fascinated by this information, and I relax.

"No hair dryers?" JoEllen asks.

"Correct." Celia looks delighted. Someone has mastered a rule, and so fast!

Meanwhile I know that Jo, whose eyes are staring at a dot on the ceiling, is already planning a hiding place for hers.

"Celia," Frannie says, "I think you should start with dress regulations."

I stare guiltily at my bare legs and loafers. Don't tell me that Peds are required here, that my mother's rule is universal.

"All right," Celia agrees. "Number one—slacks are never allowed on the Hill. You may wear them in the dorm or to meals . . ."

"Except for Sunday dinner, when you must dress up and wear stockings," Frannie interjects.

"Yes," Celia repeats, "no slacks or dungarees or culottes on the Hill."

"No matter what weather," Rona says, a statement, not a question; we already know the answer.

"Correct again," Celia whispers. This group may make up for the way it sits, holding the freshman beanies gingerly as though they smell, by the speed with which it absorbs rules. "You may never come to meals with your hair set or in bare feet, although in the dorm it's okay any time. The hair, that is; bare feet are never allowed. Health reasons."

"Phone duty," Frannie says.

This is so mysterious we snap to attention.

"Oh, yes," Celia nods. "We take turns answering the phone every evening from seven till eleven. A schedule will be posted, and each of you has a different ring, so the person answering the phone can buzz you. If you're not there, she's required to take a message. If you stretch around here," she points to her right, "you'll notice two pay phones."

"Failure to take messages is serious," Frannie warns.

Celia nods again.

"What if we have a lot of work?" I ask.

"We must all share responsibility for the dorm," Celia tells me.

I think, for my parents' three thousand dollars a year they can't hire someone to do this? I'm paying them for the privilege of handling a switchboard?

"Whoever's on phone duty also rings girls when their dates arrive," Frannie adds.

"Thank you," Celia whispers.

"You're welcome," she says.

Oh, they're having a WONDERFUL time.

But what about us? We're reading a list of rules so extensive, they make my father look permissive. The Ten Commandments are a breeze compared to this: "Freshmen have two late-nights a week; they cannot save up from week to week, two must be used every week or are forfeited."

A "late-night" is an extension of the weekday ten P.M. curfew to eleven P.M. or the Friday curfew from eleven to twelve and the Saturday curfew from eleven to one. When you sign out you have to mark "late-night" when you go; you can't decide to take one after the fact, i.e., you can't find yourself late one night and THEN use a "late-night." Oh, no, this can never be.

Why? I soon find out that it's useless to ask; rules are sacred here at Harter by virtue of their existence. They exist, therefore they're right. Probably any other human mortal could see this fact at a distance of ten miles and not have to bang her head against it repeatedly for proof. But me, I'm the type that can't leave anything alone; even if I were Moses being handed the Commandments, I couldn't have kept my mouth shut.

But Moses saw how useless it was to argue with the original Might Makes Right Person, so instead he visited his wrath upon the singers and dancers. When God is a tyrant, you have two choices: be like him or make merry. I bet you think I admire the dancers and idol-worshipers, but I don't; I think they're stupid too, that's the worst part of it; when you have to choose between worshipers and rebels, you're stuck. At least Moses knew when to keep his mouth shut.

Unlike me. I read down the list of regulations: Sophomores have three late nights a week, Juniors four, and Seniors five. If you make Dean's List you automatically get an extra late-night per week. If you break any of the rules, according to how badly, you get late-nights taken away.

And here is the best of all: you have five minutes per semester leeway signing in. That is, you can be late one minute five times, or you can blow all five minutes on a single mad evening. Per semester. This means we must set our clocks to the dorm one, no matter if it's slow or fast. That's the beat we must march to.

Marsha says, "Does this mean that I can't be home Friday, Saturday, and Sunday nights? Not at my own home where my mother is?"

"Right," Celia says.

"This is what college life is all about," Frannie booms out, overcompensating for Celia's whisper. "We're all responsible for each other, our brother's keeper."

"That's the craziest thing I've ever heard," I say. For answer, Frannie merely glowers at me, and Celia pretends not to have heard.

My fellow classmates are so impressed, however, that they elect me hangman, that is, freshman representative to House Council, so I have to participate later on in the little trials held for students who, God Forbid, did not show up at curfew or who were even fifteen seconds late and therefore had to be tried by their peers on the House Council. The Council's punishments were swift and sure and enterprising; late-nights

· 65 ·

were taken away, and the convicted had to sign in and out all day, every time they stepped out the door, even if only to go to breakfast or a class. The House Council met once a week, right before house meetings, which were also compulsory, to try the many cases at hand, only I refused to give in, refused to be a party to the punishments. Instead I instituted the practice of handing out warnings for first, second, and even third offenders, rather than punishments. I yelled how Stalin could have learned from Harter U.; that was always my best tack, I put Stalin and Harsh Punishments on one side, and the old U.S. of A. on the other with leniency, clemency, Eisenhower, and largesse of spirit. So my freshman year I became the patron saint of the few girls who had enough brains to be out getting laid, not getting back by ten P.M. Typical, very typical.

But now, newly elected frosh rep, I don't know anything, I haven't seen anything yet. I haven't seen how the rules are applied, and the catalog, which has described in exceptionally limp prose "A Day at Harter University," doesn't bring the method vividly to life. It says: "The head residents in the Harter College dormitories, with the assistance of student proctors, know that all the girls are in at the expected hour."

At ten P.M., the meeting over, while I'm sitting on the toilet, Frannie comes charging into the bathroom, knocks on my stall, and asks me to open it, just to make sure I'm there. I feel a turd slip out, odor envelop both of us as she marks me present.

"I'm first-floor proctor," she says, and bangs the door shut. I lean forward and lock it, and little tears slip down my cheeks.

Chapter Five

🌷

Monday, Bailey Hall is scheduled to begin its fraternity rounds at one P.M. Each dorm has a different time and that's so the boys can keep straight where the interesting bodies lie. They may be crass around here, their rules are bizarre, but let me tell you, the organization is magnificent.

JoEllen, girdled past all recognition, is the first to be ready. She comes into our room to wait, hair magnificent, ribbon in place, eyeliner straight as a rod.

"Should we go to only the Jewish fraternities?" she asks.

"I think we're supposed to go as a group to all of them," Marsha says.

JoEllen looks uncertain, and Rona walks in.

"Has my roommate been telling you she doesn't want to waste that beautiful hairdo on goyim?" she asks. "Come on, Jo, you're here at college to meet all kinds, don't you remember?"

"I'm not wearing my beanie," she says.

"Me neither!" the three of us chime in.

"You look great," I say enviously to JoEllen. Her clothes are designed to give the maximum impression of thinness on a minimum amount of evidence, unlike my clothes. I've learned all my clothes-buying techniques from my mother, who hates to shop for me because I'm not easy to fit. Besides, she thinks if I look too good, I'll never lose weight. People should never get away with anything: number two of Hannah Fabrikant's maxims. When I was in eighth grade, going to my first real dance, she bought me a gold quilted full skirt and a white starched frilly blouse. Which turned me from plump to obese in the twinkling of an eye. She is my reverse fairy godmother.

JoEllen has one-piece, dark, tailored dresses, empire, A-line, thin material, an interesting collar or bright necklace, so you don't notice that her waist exists not. Her mother is head buyer at Gimbel's, a thin, fretful woman I meet over Thanksgiving vacation, who nags her daughter to diet and buys her fabulous clothes in case she doesn't. This lady, obnoxious ("Why Wellesley DIDN'T accept Jo I'll never know, you should have *seen* how surprised her adviser was!"), crass—the worst kind of Jewish mother, according to my parents—who has produced, God knows, a single-track-mind daughter, at least supplies her with the means to achieve her end. My parents don't even believe in makeup.

I'm wearing a brown tweed suit, full skirt with little tucks on the waist, beige blouse, short-jacket top. I billow out in all directions. Marsha and Rona, on whom my outfit would look fine, are wearing brown and gray skirts respectively with beige sweater (Marsha) and yellow sweater (Rona). Only thin girls can be casual about dress, another law I've observed.

"I'm not looking forward to this," Marsha says as we walk down the corridor.

"So why are you going?" Rona asks.

"For my mother's sake," Marsha answers. "This is for her, and Robert is for me."

"Gee," JoEllen says, "it's funny—this is for my mother AND for me."

"I pass," Rona says.

"I don't know who this is for," I contribute, as we walk into the living room. Come to think of it, I really don't.

In the living room our class is gathered, beanieless except for one sharp-nosed blonde from Muncie, Indiana, whose mother, aunt, and older sister went to Harter. Her name is Nicolette, Nicki for short, and she was overheard (by Rona) saying to her roommate that her biggest fear about college was that she'd be put in the same room with A Negro. Fortunately, in our entire dorm there is not One Negro. As a matter of fact, our entire class (of two hundred) has but one person of color in it. And she, naturally, has a single room. The one Chinese girl, I later discover, is in a single in the basement of Bailey right next to the laundry room. Nicki, believe me, has *nothing* to fear.

The rest of us look nervously at each other, and finally follow Nicki out the door. We have our schedules and maps, and with much noise and cross-consultation follow them to the foot of Fraternity Row, crackling dry leaves underfoot, sniffing the warm autumn air, staring at the fence to our right. The map is hard to follow, the way curves and swerves, and we have to cut through little side streets and byways. Fraternity Row, like every other misnamed thing around here, isn't a row at all; the houses are scattered around the University, here and there, pretty much at random. There's a Professor's Row too—about four teachers live on it; the rest of the three-hundred-member faculty speed in and out of the faculty parking lot in their Fords and Chevrolets from God only knows where.

At the two Jewish fraternities I notice JoEllen asking everyone, "What's your major?" As soon as she hears biochem, her brown eyes glitter, her ribbon bobs forward, and her pretty face glows. Even if the fellow is short, skinny, wears glasses—a creep. I have to give that girl credit. She seems to have mastered way ahead of the rest of us the relative unimportance of good looks in a man. We're staring longingly at the tall, the muscular, the regular-featured handsome—they can talk like idiots, we don't care. Such faces, such bodies. Sorry, women's lib, even to bring up this point, but it isn't only men who are looking for a mannequin-partner, a "living doll."

In every House, for instance, I stare through the green tint of my prescription sunglasses at the most beautiful males. They're the ones I want. Only them. All of them. I have split-second fantasies, that one is looking at me, he'll call me up, I'll bring him home to my parents, he's SO gorgeous they'll never be able to criticize me again. Or else, my version of erotic fantasies: I'm standing in á big auditorium at a dance; across the room I see a Magnificent Specimen, he STARES at me, I look demurely down at my toes, he approaches, asks me to dance, music plays, he puts an arm around my waist and we move together, slowly, rhythmically, perfectly (in real life, of course, I'm a terrible dancer, can't follow *anyone*), no words are spoken, finally he looks down, holds me tight and in front of everyone (including my parents?) he kisses me. Believe me, ladies and gentlemen, this is as erotic as I can get.

And I wouldn't complain about it either, if only reality once in a while would be like my dreams. I guess I'd be satisfied if reality didn't come crashing in upon them all the time, making me hate myself for having them, for being such a fool. How can a fat girl even *imagine* being attractive. It's disgusting.

Naturally I dream anyway, through the afternoon, through dinner (gray meat, unidentifiable noodle casserole, green peas, white bread, vanilla pudding with a maraschino cherry on top, très festive). I sit with Marsha, who's gotten milk this time, Rona, Jo, Nicki (who still has her beanie on) and her roommate Patti (another study: why do so many WASP nicknames for girls end in "i"?), and the three evil genii who seem to be on our trail for good, Celia, Biff, and Frannie. They tell us some unexpected news: tonight's freshman mixer is just for frosh. No upperclassmen are allowed in, on pain of death, I suppose. This is to give freshmen boys a fair chance.

"Well," Marsha says, "that settles that, I'm going to see Bob tonight." Why IS it that we all want Older Men?

"Men are men," sensible Jo philosophizes, straightening the little red bow in her hair.

"And even a lowly freshman may someday become a dermatologist," Rona adds. It's a joke, but of course Jo is right. Why don't we see that, sooner or later, *everybody* grows up?

The four of us laugh, the rest of the table looks puzzled. For a moment I consider trying to explain to them, but how can you condense five thousand years of history into one explanation? I take another bite of the gray meat instead.

That evening Rona walks into our room as I'm about to set my hair. It's hanging down my back, wet and straggly. I set my hair not to give it waves, the curse of Jewish hair, but to keep them out. I start putting it up, sloppily, the way I do everything, impatient to be finished.

"Want me to help you?" Rona asks. Her own short red hair is wound around fourteen tiny little rollers, neat and orderly; when she combs it out it will look just the way it did today, fluffy and lovely. My own hair looks different with each set; one can never predict how it'll turn out; for big occasions I set it as hastily as ever and pray that God will make it work, even though I KNOW this is just the sort of thing that will get Him angry enough to wish on me an ugly new pimple AND a lousy hairdo.

Rona walks over to the bed where I am sitting staring into the big magnifying mirror that emphasizes each pore, pimple, widens the face, distorts it terribly. Ideal for me.

"Would you?" I say.

She sits down behind me on the bed and slowly, carefully, neatly, winds each clump of hair around a roller. I find myself thinking, maybe this is the magic trick, the thing that will turn me from plain to pretty. I'm always praying that something will do it: a new bra (I remember my first, it did one thing—pinched), straight skirt, girdle, dress, new hairdo, perfume, nose job, lipstick, stockings. Each time I tried for the transformation and didn't make it I was sickened looking into the mirror: "Are YOU still there? Where's your replacement, where's the pretty girl I'm supposed to be?"

A new hairdo was the worst, because New Jersey beauticians (and what a word *that* is) treat hair as though it doesn't belong to the rest of you. They set it and spray it and style it—a neat, well-groomed bubble that perches on your head as if to say, "*I'm* attractive enough. What am I doing looming over such a plain face?" A beauty parlor hairdo is a perpetual reproach to the rest of you for not being perfect.

We lock the door, and I take my hair dryer down from its hiding place, put the huge orange cap over my head, plug myself in, and feel the hot air blow up, fill the cap, and swish around, occasionally burning the tips of my ears. The radio is on loud to drown out the whirring sound; Marsha and Rona are sitting on her bed talking, I can see their lips moving, and hear only vaguely the music, the motor blots everything else out. I reach over to the bookcase and start reading *Jane Eyre* from page one.

In half an hour little Jane is telling off Mama Reed—one of my favorite parts—but I can feel my hair about to burst into flame, so I shut the book and turn off the dryer. My ears are bright red from the heat, and the little silver clips holding the rollers burn my fingers as I remove the cap.

"What'a ya gonna weah?" Marsha asks.

After I sneak my dryer back into its hiding place, I take out my one black dress—World War III was fought over it; my mother thought it was Too Old and Too Sexy, but it's the only thing I ever put on that actually improved my appearance. I cried right there in Ohrbach's, so loud that my mother nearly died of embarrassment and bought it. Believe me, I nearly died too, and I'll never go back to Ohrbach's again.

It is a sleeveless black velvet dress, low neck, long waist, definitely slimming.

"Ummm," Marsha and Rona hum appreciatively.

"It even matches my glasses," I say.

"You're not planning to wear your glasses, are you?" Rona asks.

"I can't see without them."

"So what?"

"She looks nice in glasses," Marsha says.

"Take them off," Rona orders.

I do.

"See," she says, "how much better she looks without them?" Meanwhile my hair is still in rollers, my face is entirely without makeup. "Hey, that's not fair. You can't tell till I'm dressed!"

"Your eye makeup won't show with glasses," Rona argues.

"I don't wear any."

"You must be kidding." Rona already has hers on, and it's beautiful. A fine black line over the top lid, lashes curled up and darkened, hint of color on the lid. Rona has huge gorgeous green eyes, her best feature, and she can even *see* out of them.

"She should get contact lenses," Marsha says. "But without glasses she'll squint. I had a lot of nearsighted friends in high school, they used to look terrible when they went around without glasses." She scrunches up her eyes and forehead, doing a good imitation of my sister.

"Let me put liner and mascara on and then you'll decide," Rona pleads.

"Okay," Marsha says. "But she has to wear her glasses to meet Robert, otherwise how'll she be able to know what she thinks of him?"

How is it, I wonder to myself, as Rona rushes off for her tubes of paint and brushes, that other people take over the running of my life so easily?

I'm sitting on my bed, taking off my glasses, holding my lids Absolutely Still, as Rona orders (she's back in ten seconds), and feeling wet things creep around my poor, defenseless nearsighted eyes.

· 73 ·

"Especially when you're all dressed up you shouldn't wear glasses," Rona tells me while curling my lashes with this tiny little clamp. *Squeeze.*

"Agh," I yell. "Be careful."

"I'm careful," she replies. "Your eyes are too sensitive, you need to do this more often to get used to it." Then she takes out a tube of mascara with the roller-applicator, and rolls some paint on. "Your eyebrows are hideous also."

"What do you mean also?" I say.

"You don't take care of them."

"They hurt when I pluck them," I moan, squinting just enough to see her take out a tweezers from the little plastic case.

"It's supposed to hurt. Hold still."

"Owww," I yell. I'm just the way my mother says, a disgrace, unable to tolerate the slightest pain for beauty's sake.

"Look how red the skin's getting," Marsha says, walking over to my bed.

"Give me some alcohol." Rona points to her bag.

Marsha takes out alcohol and cotton, this girl is *prepared,* and I say, "Maybe you should be a surgeon. Then Jo could marry *you.*"

Rona dabs alcohol on the bridge of my nose. "This is all I'll do now, at least your eyebrows don't meet anymore."

"Do you have your malpractice insurance paid up?" I ask. My eyebrows burn, my glasses—where are they? Maybe Rona's confiscated them for good.

"Let's see her with glasses," Marsha suggests. She hands me mine and I happily put them on. It feels like I can breathe again; without eyes my lungs don't work properly. "The makeup looks good under them," Marsha tells me.

I take the mirror and look into the magnified side, but Rona flips it around to the regular one. "That other side's JUST for surgery," she says.

I peer into the mirror; I look pretty much the same, heavy face, set hair, and paint around my eyes.

"Now look without glasses," Rona says.

I try, but I have to hold the mirror near my nose and squint, somehow I don't think that's the effect Rona is looking for, because she grabs the mirror and says, "You must get contact lenses."

Marsha says, "You do look better without glasses, but you look okay in them too."

"With that gorgeous dress," Rona argues, "glasses are the LAST thing she needs."

"With that gorgeous dress, tripping on a foot and breaking both legs I need even less. In the dark I even can't see all the way down to my ankles." Alice in Wonderland, that's me; myopia transforms me and my world till both are unrecognizable. And everything is strange enough to me with corrected vision; I don't need any additional vagueness.

Marsha says, "Come on, both of you, get dressed. Bob'll be heah any minute."

Rona exits, plastic bag in hand.

"It's nice to know someone who makes house calls," I shout after her.

She gives me a silent finger.

"Hey, thanks, really," I say. "It was nice of you to do it."

"Any time," she smiles back. I don't know whether to be pleased at this offer or frightened to tears.

Marsha's dress, red and straight, with a little gold belt, round neckline, looks gorgeous, and I tell her so. How fabulous it is to be thin. Then I take off my pink housecoat and stand in underpants, drooping breasts, and breathe deeply for the last time tonight. I go to the top drawer and take out my one black bra, squeeze myself into it, fasten the four hooks, and sigh. Then I pull on the Bermuda-shorts-length girdle, slowly, slowly, up and up over the mounds of disgusting flab until its waist and my waist meet in one unhappy bulge. Then, a full black slip, and I'm ready for my hypoallergenic liquid makeup, which I spread over my face, aiming the biggest drops at the four or five pimples on my cheek, forehead, chin; another thing

I wonder is, now that I have no bedroom or bathroom of my own, how will I pick and squeeze pimples? Something else I do in defiance of mother, father, uncle, and God.

The makeup swooshes over my face, I ooze it carefully onto my nose and under my eyes so as not to disturb Rona's artwork. The magnifying mirror shows me the completed job; now my pimples and skin have been covered by a layer of beige—is it an improvement? Who knows? I do it for years, feeling naked if I go out on the street without my mask firmly in place. I sit down on the bed, take out the rollers, and brush my hair, flip the ends up, pull the front straight back, spray it in place. It turned out very nice after all, and when I put on the black dress and Marsha zips it up, she says, "You look terrific." I walk into the bathroom where the one full-length mirror is attended by a line; four girls are in front of me. When I finally see myself there, I turn to one side to make sure that the too-chunky profile is still too chunky. Listen, I am no great beauty.

Dash, dot, dot, I hear Marsha's ring and open the bathroom door in time to see her running down the hall. "Hurry!" she yells back. I notice she's carrying a big box of Kleenex with her; the box is blue and white and clashes with her dress. She doesn't have a cold; why is she taking them? I have no time to wonder; I rush and lock the door, take my keys, and charge down the hall after her, wobbling on my two-inch heels that Mom disapproves of, probably because they make my legs look thinner.

By the time I get to the living room, Marsha's happy shouts seem to have subsided and she is merely hugging this tall male who looks even better than his picture. Mrs. Hibbard, Celia, and Frannie look as though they've just swallowed two lemons and an underripe persimmon by mistake.

"This is my roommate, Barbara, she's very smart!"

Robert and I shake hands. I try to look smart.

Mrs. Hibbard approaches and clears her throat. I give Marsha a little nudge with my elbow, and she presents Robert to Madame Medusa. Then Celia and Frannie. He looks around a little nervously, I notice. Maybe he's already planning *his* escape route.

"So, I hear we have to be back by eleven," he says.

"Oh didn't we tell you?" Frannie asks. "House Presidents' Council voted this afternoon to extend curfew to twelve on account of the mixer." She's not smiling as she says this, and I can guess which house president did not vote along with the majority.

"Well, let's go," Marsha says. To me she adds, "Tell Rona we had to leave."

"Remember to sign out," Celia whispers.

"Hope to see you soon," Bob says to me.

Mrs. Hibbard, Celia, and Frannie all nod their heads and smile sourly.

Marsha kisses my cheek and says, "Have a nice time, sweetie. See you at midnight." She's still clutching the box of Kleenexes.

"Nice to meet you," I say to Bob, and watch them go out the door.

"A little rowdy," I hear Mrs. Hibbard boom to Celia and Frannie.

I sign myself out, and Celia walks over and whispers, "This time we'll let you do that, but from now on you can only sign out as you're about to leave the dorm."

"Why?" I ask.

"If the phone rings or someone calls, we'd see your name on the list and say you're gone," Frannie explains.

"But you see I'm here."

"It's against the rules to sign out more than a minute before going out the door," Frannie says. "You better memorize them, the test is Friday, remember?"

"Yes," I lie, just as Rona bursts through the door.

"Where are they?" she asks.

"They were in a hurry to leave." I look straight at Frannie as I say this.

"Yeah," Rona says. "Well, Jo's nearly ready. Shall we go too?"

"Don't forget to sign out," Celia whispers.

Rona nods, and we walk back down the corridor to our rooms. I take out my for-dress-only little black bag with the gold chain and stuff into it a few Kleenexes, compact, lipstick, dorm keys, and one dollar. What the dollar is for I don't know; the dance is a ten-minute walk from our dorm. But that's the way it is with rituals; you repeat them whether or not they're called for.

Jo and Rona are coming down the hall as I lock the door.

"I wonder what would happen if we lost our keys?" Jo asks. "Like if our purses got stolen."

"We'd probably get the electric chair," Rona tells her. "Hey, Barb, why don't you take off your glasses and let me lead you to the dance?"

"Thanks, but I'd like to see what's going on."

It's worth seeing, too. There are guards posted at the auditorium entrance; all males must show their meal-ticket card to prove they're freshmen. (I hear later that some enterprising frosh have sold their cards and beanies for use this evening for five dollars. They must be Jewish, and I don't mean that as an insult.) Also, *everyone* must wear the freshman beanie. Which means we have to return to Bailey for our yarmulkes before we are allowed to enter. Imagine, will you, if glasses look a little odd with a sexy black velvet dress, how little a red and gold beanie adds to the outfit.

Once inside again we're handed those damned name cards, which we're to wear on our chests, but at this most of the girls rebel and put them on the backs of their beanies. We're wearing Good Clothes, and if we can't protect ourselves from the onslaughts of this place, at least we can protect *them*.

I get so crazed when handed my name card that I crumple it, pricking my palm on the pin, naturally, and drop it. I'm going to trample on myself all evening, the Mystery Lady with her name on the floor.

The gym is draped with red and gold streamers, balloons of all colors and sizes, beanies, and freshmen; a record player is manned by the one beanieless person here, the president of the Greek Council; next to him is a microphone.

Four or five uniformed guards patrol the outskirts of the gym floor; covering the rest of this place, wall-to-wall freshmen, AND the famous Harter ratio evident at last. Three males to every female. Another of the prime reasons I came here, figuring the odds would be with me.

What I discover is how many disgustingly unattractive "men" can make up a ratio. I say this with full knowledge that I'm a dog myself and that it's terrible to be judged on looks alone, and yet, and yet, of course I do (and in triplicate) what is done to me.

"Attention all frosh!" booms out over the loudspeakers. "For the first dance, check the back of your name card for a number. I'll call out the numbers, three boys and one girl have the same one, and whoever reaches the girl first gets to dance with her."

A low moan comes from the audience, mostly I think from the girls. Because don't you think many of them have the same fantasy as me? That we'll step forward and: 1. no one else will step up, or 2. three boys will walk slowly backward toward us. Meanwhile "Hit the Road, Jack" now echoes throughout the gym.

The one good thing is that the numbers are being called in rapid-fire fashion; in a minute mass confusion reigns. For a moment I panic, thinking I haven't *got* a number (maybe they kick you out for destroying your name card?), but then I decide not to worry, I'll watch and when no girl claims some number, *I* will. Nobody is noticing anything anyway. Hit the road, Jack, fifty-eight, fifty-nine, out of the corner of my eye I notice Rona and Jo stepping to the center of the gym, what becomes of them in this mob I never see, then number seventy-two is called, nobody responds, so I do. I look at the ceiling as I step forward, wishing I had left my glasses off, and in a while (short while? long while? I don't know) a boy my height taps my shoulder and we dance.

"Hi," he says. "I'm from Akron, Ohio." He looks it, snub-nosed, unattractive, farmerish, with an awful convict crew cut; why does anyone outside prison walls choose to wear it?

"I'm from New Jersey." I look at his name card: William Woodbridge, it says, only the William is crossed out and written underneath it is Billy, of course. What else?

His hands sweat too.

"Hey, where's your name card?" he wants to know.

"I threw it away."

"Then how'd you know seventy-two's your number?"

"I didn't. Just made a lucky guess." I strive for a sarcastic tone.

Old sweaty-palms looks good and distressed, and I want to say to him, to all men really, look, mind your manners—I can't HELP it that I'm not Marilyn Monroe. So you thought you were obliged to dance with me, only to find that you were robbed? that I cheated? It gets me so depressed and angry, that look on his face, that I say, "You're not Jewish, are you?"

"No," he says, real quickly, as though I've just accused him of being a Russian spy.

I slide my right hand through his wet palm and say, "Sorry, then I can't dance with you." And walk away.

The Rabbi's Daughter Strikes Back, I think as I make my way to a corner of the gym. A good title, only for what? I see nondancing males looking at me as I pass by, giving me the same glances men have ever since I was old enough to notice: *eh*. Plain *eh*.

I feel the beanie falling to the back of my head as I walk, push it forward with my right hand, suddenly, FLASH, the image of my father at the pulpit. It so disgusts me that I take the damn thing off and stuff it in my purse, folding it into ten little pieces.

Meanwhile over the loudspeaker comes the next announcement: "The Bunny Hop." The Bunny Hop gets you in the most fascinating position in the world: hanging onto and staring into someone's back. The music begins; you kick left foot left, right foot right, hop forward once, and hop three steps back. Do you know what the quaint little Harter touch is here? Each time before we hop backward, that meshugana at the microphone blows a police whistle into it. Get it? Part of the famous Freshman Beanie Ritual: hopping backward when an upperclassman whistles.

Meanwhile on this mad line my ears are killing me from the piercing whistle. I hate the feeling of someone's hands on my girdled waist; the guy behind me must think I've got armor on, and who can hop backward in heels? Nevertheless I dance till the bitter end; look, college is supposed to be a barrel of fun. Haven't I been reading that for years in *Mademoiselle*, *Glamour*, and *Seventeen*? Staring at pictures of happy college girls on their way to: 1. a date, 2. a football game, 3. a class (only as a last resort, I presume; because as far as fashion mags are concerned, what with matching tartan underwear and school scarves and lipsticks, how important is a book? Flip through one of those College Issues sometime, you'll notice not one of the Scholarly Maidens carrying so much as a small paperback. They occasionally sport lovely, colorful bags that *might* be used to carry books, but how could these fit in with blusher and blender and liner and curler and who knows what else?)

"Jitterbug contest!" shouts the loudspeaker.

This time the moan is deeper and lower, the males are unhappy, and that's because the jitterbug is a dance invented by women for women and can be done properly only by two women. Maybe one percent of the male population could attempt it; ten years ago, sorry to have to say this, fellows, you couldn't dance at all. You were a bunch of stiffs. The Twist saves most of you, but it's not invented until December. I remember it very clearly because in January my uncle writes me his one letter of my entire college career telling me NOT to do the Twist because it will damage my vertebrae. The Twist gets added to my list of things that can kill you with fun, and I keep doing it, naturally. For fun or for death? With me it's impossible to tell.

I walk to the refreshment table and get a paper cup of fruit punch and lean against the cold, gray gym wall, watching the jitterbugging couples. Girl-couples, naturally, and boy-girl couples that look unnatural; they seem to be having A Good Time. I look at my wristwatch, ten-thirty; I'd go back to the dorm right now except that Frannie and Celia and Biff would see me. I have too much pride (or is it shame?) to admit defeat. I wait at the gym wall until eleven fifteen and then walk out, head high. Someday You'll All Be Sorry, down the stairs to the road and up the hill to Bailey Hall.

I like walking alone at night. I become my favorite self, Invisible Me, agony and flesh vanish and I'm a free spirit floating in the night air, unencumbered by the need to look good, to make it, to have a boyfriend, to be, dear God, a woman. I can just stroll along and breathe and stare at the stars and think how strange it is to be alive. I envy Danny—all he needs to worry about are his grades; my parents don't care what else he does. But me, I could get good grades from now till eternity (and I do, of course) and they think it's my way of overcompensating for my fat; if I were thin I could afford to be normally stupid. I'm sure they're right too. All that stands between me and a C-average is thirty pounds.

"Jesus Christ," a voice says as I unlock the dorm door and sign in. "Where were you? We thought you'd never get here." It's Rona sitting in pajamas with Jo in the living room. "We looked all over for you when we left."

"What time did you leave?"

"Nine thirty," Rona says. "Wasn't it awful? How many kids do you think were there?"

"One thousand?"

"Too many, anyway," Jo says. "You can't meet people in a mob like that."

"I had to run away from this jerk who kept trying to dance close with me from the first minute he saw me. Yuch." Rona clears her throat.

"We've been waiting for you so we can have some of Marsha's cookies. You think she'd mind?" Jo wants to know.

"Nope. Come on." And we go to my room and gorge ourselves on Pepperidge Farm chocolate-filleds, all the while Jo moaning, "I better find a boyfriend soon or I'm gonna weigh two hundred pounds."

"Me too," I mumble through a cookie.

Chapter Six

❧

Wednesday morning of Orientation Week I have an appointment with my adviser. It's a damp, cloudy day; finally the knee socks and Shetland sweater are appropriate. The girdle hurts more than usual; I'm sure I've gained some weight. Soon I'll get on a scale to confirm my estimates, cry myself to sleep, and eat twice as much the next day. I have the catalog opened to the map, Harter spreads itself out so that the ten minutes between classes should be used in sprinting from building to building, but today I'm in no rush.

I'm early enough to give myself the campus tour. I start with Marshall Gate, the one across from our dorm that, naturally, is identified by a plaque: this red-brick gate, two huge red-brick columns, white stone on top, iron gate in between "was erected in 1913 to the memory of Gaylord A. Marshall." But wait, there's more, another plaque saying, "From this gate grew the present campus enclosure." I wonder if anyone consulted poor old Gaylord about this, this translating of him into a gate? And how, if you please, did the gate grow? By parthenogenesis?

The path leading up the Hill to the main administration building is smooth and seems a little slippery; I can hardly wait to see it in winter. It's worth waiting for, too; in winter it's impossible to climb—you have to cross to the opposite side of the Hill to the path with steps, and bars you can hold on to to make it to class. There are eight layers of stairs going up this side of the Hill, and on each layer is a round plaque dedicated to those members of Harter University "who, by taking part in the World War, answered a challenge to the ideals of their generation." On EVERY level the same thing is repeated, a clue, believe me, to the principles of education practiced here.

Along the smooth path are millions of trees (this place is crawling with big trees), and at the top the main administration building: Barrington Hall.

Barrington Hall is made of red brick, covered with ivy, and its main entrances on either side are protected by an army of columns, four huge white Ionic columns in front, two on each side of the door; they hold up a little white ceiling from which hangs a tiny little lamp. An ordinary square building preceded on either end by the Parthenon.

I walk to the left toward one of the only two granite buildings on top of the Hill; everything else is red brick except for this other building, which also flanks Barrington Hall but on the right. Fearful symmetry. In front of the granite building is a monument, made of fresh, new-minted stone—it was erected just this year, 1961—a big square block of granite that says: "A monument erected by the Gravity Research Foundation." "It is to remind students of the blessings forthcoming when a semi-insulator is discovered in order to harness gravity as a free power and reduce airplane accidents." I read this one as often as I can to see if I can make sense out of it. No good. First I think it's a monument to gravity, a fabulous invention, without which planes could never fly. But I know that can't be right. Then I think of a free power as opposed to a communist power—thank God THEY didn't discover it first or we might none of us be able to hold on to the planet earth, millions of Americans floating above their native soil just because the Russians had copped all the available gravity.

The monument is fronting the Geology Building; in deference to geology, it's made of big rocks, and two stone lions guard the door; they're also made of granite. Maybe the Anthropology Building will be guarded by live Masai warriors; and the Poli. Sci. Building by J. Edgar Hoover—the possibilities seem unlimited.

I walk back toward Barrington to the other stone building, which turns out to be not entirely granite; the roof is red brick. On top of a chimney high above a stone tower above the red roof is a stone cross. Terrific. Graham Chapel. The stained-glass windows on every side show a man holding a book in one hand and leaning on a walking-stick cross. Moses it definitely ain't. There are little bushes all around this church, and in between the bushes are stone benches inscribed with the fact that they were donated by Tau Omega, the sorority, I later discover, which lets in one Jewess per year. I vow never to set foot in Graham Chapel, only later to find that I'm compelled to present my body here for weekly chapel AND for anthropology. Why anthropology meets here only God and the Dean of Harter know, but four times a week I sit on a pew in a church staring at Christs and crosses and feeling, how can I explain this, morally a wreck. Listen, Judaism is perfectly impossible to buy, but Christianity?

I look up at the cross and shake my head at it; that even their religious symbol should be such a murderous, bloody one bothers me. What can a religion that begins with the killing of one Jew do but lead to the murder of a lot more? My neck hurts from looking up at the cross, where have I gotten such a dislike for it? Was it seeing all those girls in my high school wearing silver and gold ones around their necks, symbolizing what? Nothing to me except that they are the majority, that it's their holidays we celebrate in school, and their country that I'm permitted to live in (and who knows, Jewish paranoia coming on, for how long?). In retaliation I hang one of my Jewish stars around my neck, symbolizing albatross no doubt, proof positive that when you retaliate against idiots you become an idiot yourself.

I trudge to Campbell Hall where my adviser, Mr. Cole, a short, frail-looking young man with wispy blond hair, steel-frame glasses, and pimples, awaits all the freshmen from *D* through *F*. He opens my fifteen-minute session with: "One must achieve a well-balanced program. *All* math and science would not be well-balanced."

Is the entire world filled with rabbis?

"Fine," I say. "I hate math and science."

He looks at me as if a dog had just talked, so I see I'm supposed to keep my mouth shut and Take Advice. The Harter educational model.

"On the other hand, a program devoid of math and science is bound to be overweight in another area," he assures me. I don't like his choice of words. "Have you studied the requirements?"

I nod. Requirements is all they've got around this place; I don't think I'll be due for an elective till my junior year. However, maybe this is what an education is supposed to be—me the vessel, they the water of knowledge. I sit, they pour.

"What are your main interests?" Mr. Cole asks, pen in hand.

Let's see—food, men (in that order, alas), finding the magic fairy dust that will turn me into Debbie Reynolds, happiness, and fun. Oh yes, and being normal. I lick my lips and squint and look up at the ceiling. There must be something I can confide to Mr. Cole.

"I'm interested in politics," I finally say. (I'm in love with John Kennedy, as who isn't, crazy about Edward R. Murrow, fond of Huntley and Brinkley, and don't mind skimming *The*

New York Times.) With those four words I seal my fate—my program is planned out, my future major determined (at Harter you have to decide for good by March of your freshman year, the perfect arrangement for someone like me who just recently figured out which hand was my left).

"Fine!" Mr. Cole beams! "I have a perfect program for you. Composition, required. Gov. One-o-one and One-o-two, I see you have French from high school, so Intermediate French One-forty-seven, One-forty-eight, Geology One and Two for nonscience students, and I suggest Anthropology One and Sociology Two, since you'll be a social-science major and eventually need those courses. Naturally that leaves out history, which you'll take sophomore year. Of course you could take English literature instead, but what use will *that* be to you in your chosen field? Not much, I grant you."

"What do you do besides advise?" I ask as he completes my program card.

"I'm a graduate assistant in chemistry," he tells me. "I just do this during Orientation Week."

The warm, friendly, close personal relationship comes to an end at quarter after the hour, the next *F* is already waiting outside his office.

"Thank you," I say.

"It's nothing," he answers. For the first time, we agree.

A DREARY MORNING. This is something you'll never find in a college catalog or in *Mademoiselle*. A light drizzle begins its careful work of ruining my hair as I set off for the bookstore. I didn't bring any rain gear, of course, so my sweater sticks damply to my skin and my feet get wet and my toes are cold. Trees are starting to get that stripped, starved, fall look. Ivy and moss creep over everything; from a distance some of the buildings look like a dread disease has gotten them, a fungus is eating away at their faces.

The bookstore is on the ground floor of a red-brick

rectangle, again with four white Ionic columns in front of it, form without function, and into the main door are pouring hundreds of students; the upper classes must have already arrived, and I'm swept along with them up the stairs into a room so jam-packed that you can't see the books for all the scholars. I stand in the middle of the crowd and wonder, do I ask for syllabuses or syllabi? And whom do I ask? And how will I find the books? I don't move, feel large and conspicuous, look left and right, finally spot an older woman who looks like she might know something.

"Excuse me," I push over to her, "could you tell me how I'd go about finding the [pause, deep breath] syllabuses for my courses?"

"Over at the desk in alphabetical order!" she shouts and points to the far end of the room.

"Thanks." I'm talking to an empty space; she has already moved away. I move slowly through the crowd to the desk; after about ten minutes of waiting in line I make it to the piles of alphabetical syllabi, and although pushed and shoved, toes and heels stepped on, deafened by the noise, I manage to extract the book lists. It's impossible to read them in here, so I fight the incoming crowd and go out, walk to a big old tree, lean up against it, take out a pen, and go through each list, marking off Required Reading, of which there is not a little. I don't believe I've ever in my life heard or seen the word Required so often. Not even in Real Life, which, our weekly chapel speakers assure us, is what Harter is preparing us for.

Half an hour later, I have five mammoth texts and assorted little paperbacks, such as the *Bhagavad-Gita*, which I have no idea how to pronounce, stuffed into a Harvard bookbag slung over my shoulder, rubbing against my sweater. But as I stroll to the dorm I feel like a College Student for the first time. I look back up the Hill before crossing the road to Bailey; the sky is a gray, wet blanket, the drizzle has stopped but the air feels like a sponge filled with water. I shiver as a breeze cuts through my clothes, listen to the sounds of voices on the Hill, the road, in the dorms, and think, "College." Even after all I've been through, the word "College" has a magic ring, a sound of promise. " 'The air is hummin' and somethin' great is comin'; come on, deliver to *me!* " I accompany myself back to the dorm, down the corridor, and into my room. " 'Could it be? Yes it could, somethin's comin', somethin' good, if I am there.' "

I unlock the door, still humming, and when I shut it behind me (Marsha isn't there) and throw my bookbag onto the bed, I fling my arms out wide and sing out loud, " 'Come on deliver to *me!* " The room has been transformed into a stage and I sing and throw back my head and in the dream—Broadway, Lennie B., crowds of admirers—find a little pleasure. Then I empty the bookbag, lie down on the bed, and feel the heavy weight of books near my legs, fold my arms behind my head, and stare up into the ceiling as if it were the door and I had the key and it was only a matter of time before I could enter.

Chapter Seven

🌷

"Some shmuck just called me for a date for the weekend," Marsha announces on her way to the bathroom; she's gotten her program card and books too, but instead of staring into the ceiling she's been going to the bathroom all night; aggravation gives her the runs, she says. Marsha wants to be an English major, so she has to take Religion, Psychology, Composition, French, and History, and in the middle of every other sentence she's sprinting to the bathroom. "I'd blame the food," she mutters on her way out, "only who's been eating it?"

The answer to that question, of course, is me.

"A creep called me for a date too, his name was Billy," I tell Marsha as she settles back into bed. "Earlier this evening." This, as you can doubtless guess, is a lie. It was my parents, who were calling to remind me that Saturday is Rosh Hashanah, as if I could ever forget. My father asked me in what temple I planned to spend the bulk of the coming weekend. Marsha's, I told him, although Marsha hasn't invited me yet. I only hope the lies stay straight in my mind.

Dad asks, "What kind of temple is it?"

"Reform," I say. For all I know it's Seventh-Day Adventist.

"You'll be certain to tell the rabbi about Your Father," he reminds me.

"Of course." I hope the phone hides sneers better than I do.

"How's your weight?" comes from the upstairs extension.

"Fine," I lie. "Food is terrible here."

"Good," my mother answers. Nothing like terrible food to make her happy. Lisa and Danny get on the phone and say in unison that they miss me. Naturally I cry into the receiver and have to wipe it off with the sleeve of my pajamas just as Mrs. Hibbard walks by. She beams at me, so I figure I must be doing something right, maybe she thinks everybody should polish the phone while using it.

From this conversation I've evolved a date with Billy.

"Are you going?" I ask Marsha.

"Of course not. We're going home for the High Holidays." Marsha looks at me. "Don't tell me a rabbi's daughter accepted a date for Rosh Hashanah?"

"Nope." Rosh Hashanah saved me this weekend, but what am I going to do on all the others, change my religion to one that has a fast of Ramadan or something each Saturday of the school year?

"You are coming home with me, aren't you? Mom's so excited she invited Rabbi Elman over after services." There's less than a look of delight on Marsha's face as she mentions him.

"But you didn't ask me," I tell her.

"You want a written invitation?" She looks hurt.

"No. I just wasn't sure."

"Jesus, for a second I thought being a rabbi's daughter meant you needed things very formal." Marsha thumbs through her Religion text, and I want to say, Look, Tootsie, you'll never find out about religion from a book. Take it from me. "Hey," Marsha looks up, "do you have overnight permission?"

"Of course not! I've got to call my parents, do you think they can wire it?"

"Ask Mrs. Hibbard," Marsha says.

I run out the door and down the hall to Mrs. Hibbard's room to find out if a telegram followed by a letter would be enough permission.

She shakes her curls. "I shouldn't allow it, but since it is for a religious holy day . . ."

"Thanks," I cut her off and run to the phone, make a collect call to my parents.

"Overnight permission?" Dad says. "Absolutely not."

"Good-bye temple, then," I tell him. "How can I go to Marsha's house?"

"Isn't there a temple closer to you?" he wants to know.

"I suppose so, but Dad, I'd rather spend Rosh Hashanah with a family than go alone and come back to ham for dinner; it wouldn't seem like a holiday." I grin into the phone as I say this; finally, *I've got him.* I know it, too; he's doomed. How can the Rabbi turn down this appeal?

"You're absolutely right," he says. "Your mother and I will send a telegram off immediately and write the letter. Is the overnight permission just for this particular weekend?"

"The only way you can get overnight permission is to get it for the whole year," I tell him. "Those are the rules." And do you know what? That's the goddamn truth, that's the beauty part of the rules, sooner or later they're bound to work for you instead of against you—a lot of red tape slows you down, but eventually it slows the taper down too. Hoorah for that little law!

"All right," he says. "You're nineteen years old, we ought to be able to trust you by this time."

Why? I want to say. You're fifty and I don't trust you for beans. However, I manage to keep my mouth shut.

"I got it!" I sing, to the tune of "Maria," slamming the door and flopping on the bed. "I got it, I got it, I got it, tra la la la la la, tra la la la la la, tra LA."

At this moment there's a knock at our door; I get very quiet. It's nine fifteen, am I going to be kicked out of Harter for singing? I open the door.

"Hi, I'm Irene McIntosh," an unknown girl announces. "May I come in?"

"Sure," I point her to a desk chair where she can sit.

"I'm canvassing for Y.A.F.," she says. "We have a very strong chapter at Harter. Would you care to join?"

"I believe it," I say.

"What?" she asks.

"That there's a strong chapter here." I'm already shaking my head to Marsha. *Uh uh,* we do not want to join. Marsha, the least political person I've ever known, wouldn't know Young Americans for Freedom from B'nai B'rith.

"Why?" Irene leans forward in her chair, eager and interested.

"What with beanies and curfews and racist fraternities, it fits right in."

Even Marsha looks shocked. Frankly, I'm surprised myself. Didn't realize how mad I was.

"Hey," Irene says. "I think this place is stupid too. Tell you the truth, three-fourths of 'em don't know what Y.A.F. is. I'm impressed you do."

Marsha relaxes.

"Well, good luck with the recruiting," I tell her. "Still have to sign your name in blood before getting a white sheet? Or do you issue swastikas these days?" I smile pleasantly. Good night, Irene, I am thinking, Irene, good night.

But Irene isn't daunted, far from it. "I'm glad I found you," she laughs. "At least there'll be someone to fight with, instead of all this apathy. I hate apathy even worse than," she pauses as though expecting to be struck by a thunderbolt for admitting it, "liberals."

And I laugh too, because it suddenly occurs to me that the more vehemently you believe something, the more you need an opponent. How boring life would be for a Y.A.F.'er if the entire *world* would join.

"My boyfriend's gonna love you too," she tells me. "He's from South Africa, the only place that tells the truth about Negroes."

"What truth is that?" I ask.

"Let me show you this anthropology book he gave me," she says.

I nod okay and she runs out the door. In two minutes she's back with a book issued in 1918 by a University of South Africa professor of anthropology that proves conclusively, via measuring the circumference of skulls and the use of other enormously scientific devices, that blacks are inferior to whites.

"You don't believe this, do you?" I ask.

"Of course."

Those clear blue eyes, that high white forehead, and neat light-brown short hair, all look entirely sincere. My God, I think, she DOES believe it.

"Even if it were true," I finally say, "which it seems silly to assume, it wouldn't justify anything. After all, Jews are smarter than the Scotch; does that mean we have the right to enslave you?"

"They are NOT!" she huffs.

"Freud, Marx, Einstein!" I yell. Let's see her top that. Who's she got? Robert Burns?

Marsha, who's been sitting quietly on her bed all this time, lifting her books and weighing them in her hand and moaning, leafing through pages of Intro. Psych., laughs so hard and it's so infectious that both Irene and I can't help joining in.

"I like you," Irene announces. "And I know a perfect guy to fix you up with; he's in my boyfriend's fraternity, but he's a liberal."

I accept, naturally. It figures that I would be rescued from a dateless, miserable future by a Nazi.

Chapter Eight

Rabbi Elman hasn't had his heart attack yet, his fingers bulge over his wedding ring and college ring, his cheeks hang down and shake when he speaks; in short, he oozes rabbinical grease. Not that he's disgusting, far from it; even overweight he's nice-looking—tall, dark, graying at the temples. I dare anybody to find an unattractive rabbi in a well-to-do Reform synagogue in the U.S. of A. It's not allowed; they have to be good-looking, have first-class diction like Abba Eban, and say nothing of any importance. The more WASPish they look, the better, so that on Brotherhood Day they'll represent the Jewish community well by being indistinguishable from a Lutheran. See, Jews are ashamed of Jews who look Jewish, and the worst shame of all is having a Jewish rabbi. A rabbi with a British accent is what every wealthy suburban Reform synagogue is looking for. Rabbi Elman, like my father, speaks beautifully, enunciates clearly, gestures moderately, and is working on a cholesterol count that will make my own seem like nothing.

I meet him after Friday night service on the receiving line, and then again in the Greens' mammoth living room. His temple is beautiful and huge, with reserved pews for the rich, like our temple at home, where you have to buy tickets for high holiday services. Marsha's family, aunts, cousins, and grandparents own practically a wing of the place on their own. If I didn't suspect that they were wealthy before, I find out when we arrive at five P.M. Friday courtesy of Jeffrey and a long black Lincoln Continental at the front door of a huge, modern, ranch-type palace.

"Wowie!" I say.

"My father made a killing in the stock market," Marsha tells me.

Later I found out that Mr. Green had worked his fingers to the bone sending his kid brother through college and graduate school in chemistry and that said kid brother had developed a sure-cure for psoriasis and related skin disorders. It sold like wildfire. Then Mr. Green had taken the psoriasis money and invested it in computers, so between psoriasis money and IBM the Greens had a house overlooking the ocean in Lynn, Massachusetts, big enough to house the Eighth Army, with a pool in the backyard so huge it looked like Mr. Green had started a competition with the ocean. There was a cabana (something the ocean definitely did not have) and in the distance, though still on his property, was a greenhouse and a gardener devoted to the care and weeding of every expensive plant that existed, and no cheap ones. Even the weeds were costly, and the plants had unusual problems, maybe even psychosomatic or psychological problems, but they suffered neither drought nor overwatering nor bugs nor lack of sun.

The inside of Marsha's house was distinctly Jewish, and by this I mean the Greens understood creature comforts. Wealthy Gentile families are not concerned that people should be so comfortable they are hardly aware that they're alive. Sleep on a wealthy Gentile person's bed sometimes and you'll see what I mean; they may have skis in the closet, a boat on the front porch, and five private planes, but their beds are either hard or lumpy, and the lighting in their houses is poor (because they don't yet know the Jewish Scientific Facts of Life . . . poor lighting can kill your eyes. Period and No Discussion), and their chairs are not to sink into.

Marsha's is a definitely Jewish house. The rugs on the floor are so deep you sink practically up to your ankles, you don't walk, you foam from room to room, light switches are soundless, closet lights go on when doors open; stereo piped into every room, television sets sprinkled around like ashtrays, beautiful books (who knew if they had ever been opened?), maids and butlers and endless trays of food.

And the food is all dietetic (except when company comes, every other day): fruit, low-cal candies, shrimp and lobster salad, pickled lettuce, and in spite of all these precautions, everyone in the Green family is overweight except Marsha, only nobody notices, not even Marsha. Marsha was not emaciated, and for a long time she'd been listening to her mother moan and weep and wail about the horrors of fatness—Mrs. Green used to grab her own arms and shake them and say, à la Weight Watchers, "See this?" jiggle jiggle, "Fatty tumors"—so between fatty tumors and lobster four times a week, Marsha felt herself to be a fat person.

No wonder when Mrs. Green looked at our room, the size of the closet in her bedroom, she was unimpressed. Mrs. Green had her own bedroom, so did her husband. What depresses me is that one cannot go around asking people fascinating questions like: Why aren't you and your husband sleeping together? Did it pall after the first few years? Or before? Did you ever enjoy sex? Do you know any Jewish woman over forty who did? Do they let you stay a Jew if you like to screw? Is that a poem?

Rabbi Elman, when I meet him, cannot answer any questions because he's stuffing a huge piece of honey cake into his mouth. Mrs. Green has hauled me over to him and introduced Marsha's roommate Barbara, The Rabbi's Daughter, and it takes him a moment of chewing and swallowing before he can get out a "pleased to meet you."

"Where is your father's temple?" he asks.

"New Jersey."

"Large congregation?" The rabbi looks greedy; would he like to swallow it too?

"About a thousand people." I clear my throat and look around for help. "How big is your temple?"

"We have seven hundred families," he tells me, turning around and taking a cracker with wine-cheddar on it. Crunch crunch.

I smile. I've run out of things to say, mad questions fly into my mind: so, how's God? Seen any good bar mitzvahs lately? And how are your kids—also going crazy from you?

Before I have a chance to try any of them, Marsha flies over and says, "Excuse me, Rabbi, I want Barbara to meet my Cousin Stu." She winks at him so he shouldn't be insulted; he'll know that I'm being spirited away to meet the only thing more important than a rabbi—an eligible man. As we walk away, I overhear him say to Mrs. Green that I don't look Jewish. The highest compliment a rabbi can pay anyone, believe me.

Cousin Stu (another study—everybody who's Jewish has an Aunt Rose and a Cousin Stu) is skinny, wears glasses, is a freshman at the University of Pittsburgh, an Excellent School, his mother assures anyone who stands near Stu for more than three seconds. She's Mrs. Green's brother's wife, a very loud lady who spends most of her time surrounding Stuie, stewing, bringing him plates of food, asking him how the flight from Pittsburgh was, what the food in Pittsburgh is like. Even if Stuart and I were interested in each other (we aren't), it would be impossible to establish communication except by carrier pigeon; his mother is a one-woman moat.

Marsha hears the doorbell ring and runs, beating the maid,

to answer it. Robert, of course, is at the door. I walk away from Stu and head toward them.

Robert hugs me hello, and Marsha says, "I'll leave you two alone for a sec while I finish making the rounds. Are you hungry, honey?" she asks him. "There's lots of food around."

"Really?" He has a shocked look on his face, so Marsha gently slaps him before walking away.

"I've gained ten pounds since I met that girl," he tells me. "Just picking her up before dates. They don't let you out of here till you're so stuffed you can't move."

"But everything's dietetic," I say, and we both giggle. Mrs. Green then walks over and greets him and tells him to have something to eat. I have to bite my tongue practically till it bleeds to keep from getting hysterical.

"They're trying to kill me with food, I think," he says as she walks back to the living room. I laugh, but he looks serious. He has such a handsome, slightly round face, neat slicked-down blond hair, Jewish nose, a college grad, a businessman—if I came home with someone like this my parents would cry with delight, maybe my father would even sacrifice a ram to God instead of me.

"They think I want to marry Marsha for her money," he tells me.

"Do you?"

He shrugs his shoulders, which shocks me. I expect him to deny it vehemently.

Marsha and her mother walk over to us, both carrying plates of food. They approach from different corners of the living room, heading for Robert, and don't see each other until they meet in front of him.

"The war of the calories," Robert says, looking at the two piles of food being offered.

Even Mrs. Green laughs. "Barbara, shall I give this one to you?"

"Thanks, no," I say. "I've got to lose some weight." These are the magic words, Mrs. Green's favorite subject.

"My dear," she begins, "I helped Marsha's best friend from high school, Carolyn, lose twenty-five pounds, didn't I?"

"Yep," Marsha doesn't stop kissing Bob on the cheek.

"How about helping me?" he asks, gently trying to remove Marsha from his body.

"Men don't need to worry about such things." Mrs. Green thus accounts for that belly on her husband, a short, bald man who looks like he's in the fifth month of pregnancy. "I took Carolyn aside and told her what a beauty she'd be if she lost weight, and she did, and she is a beauty. AND," ah, the emphasis on that word, "YOU [pause] would be twice as beautiful as she!"

Mrs. Green stops to let that sink in; I know it's supposed to be a compliment so I smile. Practically everyone who's ever known me has told me that (another study—*many* fat women are potentially gorgeous—why are they afraid of their beauty? Forget the study, I may have the answer right here).

"Mom," Marsha says, "Barbara is plenty lovely right now."

"Of course she is. I'm only saying how much BET-TER . . ."

Marsha laughs. "There's no stopping her."

"It's okay," I say. "I'm interested. How did Carolyn lose the weight?"

"Well," Mrs. Green tells me, "she ate only meat and fish and fruit and vegetables, but," lowering her voice to a whisper, "I've got a prescription for a diet pill that's *marvelous*. No hunger pangs at all with it."

"Oh," I murmur, "my uncle won't let me take diet pills, he says they're bad for your kidneys, or something." Kidneys, liver, heart, it's all the same to me; and according to my uncle, practically everything on this earth is bad for some part of your body. To him, reaching adolescence is a miracle, there are so many things that can go wrong. You should see his kids too; you think a rabbi's children have problems, talk to a doctor's sometime. To Susie, my twelve-year-old cousin, a headache isn't something you take aspirins for, it's the sign of a brain tumor, blood clot, leukemia, who knows what else? She's never taken any aspirin either; nothing so primitive is *allowed* in that house. Bayer never darkens their door. Susie takes Darvon and Fiorinal, drinks orange juice to raise her blood sugar level, stays off chocolate to lower her blood sugar level, and thinks that a pat of sweet creamery butter is arsenic, one bite and your heart gives up beating. Cholesterol in that house is the threat God is in ours.

"You don't take the pills forever," Mrs. Green says, "only till you lose the weight."

Which with me might be even longer than forever.

"Maybe I'll try them sometime," I say. I can see my uncle now. "Taking unknown pills is as stupid as jumping off a roof." Waving his arms, a rabbi also, a rabbi of medicine.

"Whenever you want," Mrs. Green offers, "you can have the prescription."

I'm thinking, by the way, that I'd never have the courage to do it, to take her prescription. How little one knows oneself at the age of nineteen (or is it always?). If anyone had ever told me all the things I was going to do this very school year, on Rosh Hashanah night, for instance, I would've laughed in their faces. Not ME, I would have said, thinking that there was only one ME and that I happened to know who she was.

"So what's it like being a rabbi's daughter?" Robert asks after Mrs. Green has walked away.

I think of every other Rosh Hashanah I've known, sitting in temple hour after hour (how would it look if the rabbi's children weren't there?) staring up at my father, bored, with a sore ass, an impulse to giggle every time the list of anniversary dead people is read: Jesse Goldfinkle, Ralph Cornpfeffer, Sadie Spiegelman, Bella Menashawitz, Morris Lipschitz, the most solemn moment in the entire service spoiled because no Jew is named Henry Cabot Lodge. Trying to look pious and good, feeling sinful and evil, knowing (when I was younger) that God was weighing me in His eternal scales and (the only time scales ever register low for me) finding me wanting. Afterward being greeted by every sincerely religious person in the entire congregation—what do they think, we're holy too? Not US, I feel like shouting, only HIM—him with the white yarmulke and the flowing robes, go touch *HIM* and be cured. But we smile politely, HE would murder us if we didn't, and I know my mother is ready to kill me anyway for my fat that makes me not perfect and therefore open to criticism.

"Being a rabbi's daughter is from hunger," I finally answer.

Later on, when Marsha and I are lying near each other in the twin beds in her room she says, "Having a rich man for a father isn't so easy either."

"Why?"

"My parents say that Rob wants me because of my money."

"He told me that," I say.

"It almost makes me want to be poor, do I sound like a bad soap opera?" she asks. "The worst thing in the world is to think to yourself maybe, just maybe, it's all an act, he doesn't love me. That *everything* is a lie. Do you know what I mean?"

"I think so." Listen, I'd like to tell her, on this particular subject I've got the equivalent of a Ph.D. "Still I envy you. What have I got to make men love me—God? I'd rather have money."

Marsha laughs. "You have yourself."

I sigh a real deep sigh. Judging from past experience, that won't be enough. I may yet need God for this job. I think of old fantasies, of being the last woman on earth with some gorgeous, wonderful man who'll *have* to love me, because who else will there be? My way of dealing with the atomic-bomb worries, no great loss without some small gain—so the entire world will be gone, at least I'll have a man. My next fantasy—if I were Negro my fat wouldn't show so much (black is so slimming), and lots of fat black girls are very popular, at least in my high school. And still another . . . if I were extremely rich, I'd have enough money to buy a husband. I'm not proud, I'd never even ask if he loved me, so long as he waltzed me down the aisle and took me to parties, never left me unaccompanied again, I'd be perfectly happy. For me a husband is a piece of Scotch tape over the mouths of the Rabbi and his wife, so I could finally stop all this worrying. And maybe just live?

"This is supposed to be the happiest time of our lives," Marsha says.

"That," I tell her, "is a lie."

Chapter Nine

❦

A typical day at Harter College. Monday. October 2.

My radio alarm went off at seven A.M. I've been sleeping fitfully all night because of the huge metal-threaded rollers my hair is in. The rollers, plus the fact that I'm behind in my work, like everyone else, make me sleep fitfully and have hideous dreams. Last night I dreamt that I was at my high school graduation party and Mom was mad at me as usual for some indefinable reason; my friends were there and Danny and Lisa and their friends; they all had to be fed in shifts, and I was torn between feeding my friends first or my siblings. My alarm clock solved the problem by waking me up. Too bad there isn't some equally effective way to solve bad days; nights we can always wake up from, but what can you do about the days?

My radio alarm goes off in the middle of an advertisement for Ice Blue Secret, something that will keep you dry and cool all day long. America's answer to bad dreams: Ice Blue Secret. I shut off the radio, actually my uncle forbade deodorants on the grounds that they cause cancer; he's a doctor, he's forever reminding us, so he should know, likewise he frowns upon shaving the legs or underarms, I think for the same reason. I shaved my legs and underarms in high school and sneaked Ban on every morning, throwing caution to the winds. Or was it committing slow suicide? With me, it's hard to know.

I shut off my alarm and pull my sore head and flabby body out of bed and stare for one brief moment at Marsha who has not yet gotten up in time for breakfast since her first day of college. She wakes up fifteen minutes before class, makes coffee in her little portable perc and eats a pear; we have a supply of pears in our room you have to see to believe, and pears are all Marsha will touch for breakfast, big greenish-yellow, mottled with brown, soft pears or dark brown Bosc pears with their thick skin and sweet insides. Marsha will even eat little hard green pears if there's nothing else around, but after that she goes hungry. And I don't laugh at her eating habits; you should see mine. You will.

I tiptoe in my red wool housecoat over my flannel, flowery pants pajamas (my mother bought all these things for me and I hated them, but she was right, this is what all the girls are wearing) out the door and into the communal bathroom, six toilet seats in a row, six showers, six basins: there are twenty girls on the hall who share it. Morning in the bathroom is a wonderful time, the smell of discreet farts and shits, only how discreet can they be? Toothpastes, soaps, creams, peeing, shitting, and massive embarrassment. If Harter girls don't like to notice that someone has spinach on their teeth, how do you think they're going to fare in a communal bathroom? Frankly it's hideous even for the liberated; Marsha and I warn each other when we are about to fart and open the window. I'd give anything to know how the rest of the girls do it, but who could ask?

I stagger into the bathroom. Frannie is there with her head

in pink rollers; she looks like a giant bandage in her white, crinkly housedress over white pajamas. I smile at her, but she's brushing her teeth and doesn't notice me; she brushes her teeth as though she's polishing diamonds, another thing I have noticed about Gentile girls, they take all those things their parents and sixth grade health teachers told them seriously. They wash their hands forty-seven times a day, they brush their teeth at every conceivable moment—how do they have time for all this, or strength? At seven fifteen A.M. with three classes and gym in the morning and a geology lab in the afternoon, I manage to pee, wash my hands half-heartedly, brush the green off my teeth, leaving the yellow behind, and walk out of the bathroom with soap still on my neck—I haven't the strength to wash it off—wiping my face dry and sopping up the remaining Noxzema suds that are trickling down to my waist.

Back in our room I tiptoe to the dresser and pull the Iron Maidens off my head; if only I were thin I could wear short hair and never have to set it again. I look at Marsha's short, unset hair, maybe I should stay away from breakfast and have a pear, but no, I can never do that; everybody's got their own eating patterns and much as *I* would like to be thin, my eating pattern doesn't give a damn. I get dressed in a brown plaid skirt over a girdle and a matching brown sweater (everything I own matches).

And do you know the first thing I do after rushing to the cafeteria for a seven thirty breakfast of powdered eggs or toast or cereal and a glass of prune juice (communal bathrooms make me extremely constipated, which I know from my uncle can kill you after two weeks)? I go to gym at eight A.M., I rush down the hill from the cafeteria with my books in the Harvard bookbag, to the gym where I peel off everything I've so recently put on and rush outdoors for field hockey. In my blue gym suit, white sweat socks, gray sweat pants, gray sweatshirt, and no girdle I look like a fuzzy gray balloon topped by a brown head. Luckily only girls are in my gym class. We have fifteen minutes to dress after gym and to rush a quarter of a mile up the Hill, which is a drumlin, extremely steep. Drumlins abound in the Boston area; this is the one real solid fact I learned at College, and when the Harter drumlin had snow on it, it was the biggest pain in the ass you could possibly imagine, except for the classes you were rushing up the Hill to make it to. The only nice thing about a snow-covered drumlin was coming down it on a tray filched from the cafeteria and in forbidden pants. By the time December of my freshman year had rolled around and I'd discovered that I wasn't going to be a teen queen, or a regular person, I wore pants, even dungarees on the Hill and slid down on a tray either by myself or with Marsha. We both had found out the same thing simultaneously: we had not come to college to be told when to wear pants.

After gym, led by a whole fleet battalion of extremely dedicated dykes from the Harter School of Phys. Ed., I flew, panting, up the Hill to my first horror, Intro. Anthro., or Little Details About the Trobriand Islanders You Don't Want to Know So Memorize Them for the Exam. The professor, a bald gentleman of middle age and rotundity that made him look downright friendly, which shows you what a put-on fat can be, was really a skinny Scrooge in disguise, reading from his yellowed notes and giving absurd tests. If this sounds like sour grapes, let me say right here and now that I got an A-minus in the course; bastards like that bring out the killer instinct in me. He used to read out the names of the three highest exams (we had three per semester and a final), and after the first one I made up my mind, son of a bitch, in a class of two hundred I'd make it to the top. I did, too; once after staying up a whole night and recopying four books into my notebook, I walked into the exam, multiple choice, whipped through it, and went back to my room and slept for eighteen hours. And I was only third of the top of three. Can you picture what the other two winners went through?

The class was held in the chapel, an appropriate setting,

with this baldy up front giving us the gospel of the bushmen as told to Carleton Coon. Margaret Mead we never read; she's too interesting, and the primary law of courses at Harter College is that interesting reading is well and good but certainly not an Education. Professor Arthur Hayes Fleming is, whiny voice, fifty minutes without break except for the predictable two or three bad jokes per lecture, and no place to rest your arms while you're taking notes in the pews.

Even worse, however, than the way he waves his pipe or his jokes, is that he's a stutterer. Cured, to be sure, but a stutterer nonetheless. It takes him eighty seconds to say Carleton Coon, long pause on the *C,* breathe, say the hard *C* sound for forty seconds, then finally out with it, Carleton. Repeat process, Coon. I get so nervous listening to him I'm on the edge of my seat each time he pauses for a problem, I feel myself clenching up; even a bastard like this I hate to see suffer, what a Florence Nightingale I am, wishing for him to get it over with. Thank God *tribes* isn't one of his problem words.

Dong. The bell clangs especially loud in chapel. I stuff books into bookbag and rush off across the top of the drumlin to my favorite class, Intro. Poli. Sci., led by the teacher whose sheer pleasantness and lack of hostility, genuine liberalness, and good fair exams lead me, in spite of my entire lack of interest in the subject, to excel in his field. Professor Harris gave out the Civil Liberties Union test for how civilly liberal or liberally civil you were; he didn't grade them of course, for he really was a liberal, but he asked to know how we did, and I proudly showed him my paper after he had had us grade them. One hundred percent. The only one in the class. He beamed through his steel-rimmed glasses and tried to make me feel better when James Baldwin came to speak at Harter and was booed because he mentioned that America was a racist society.

English is at eleven A.M., the lady who teaches it is not a Ph.D. but she's married to a Ph.D. so it's all right; she and her husband have written a textbook one thousand pages long, from which you can learn to read, write, and think. She and her husband look like long-legged birds, thin, long-necked, long-nosed, and soft-spoken. They are such nice people, but why in the world do they think the *Bhagavad-Gita* is good freshman reading? Why do we have to memorize which poem belongs to what poet? Why do we have to memorize grammatical rules? Why do classes have to be so boring, and what is she doing up there writing outlines and comments and notes on the board? You cannot discuss even one little poem in this class without her grabbing her faithful chalk, poised at the blackboard. Jon Swan's "The Opening": she asks us what it's about, the class looks stupidly around, and some genius finally says, "Sex." We look nervously at each other—how will Mrs. Lamb take this?

She walks over to the right-hand side of the room in a rocking gait, like a flamingo really, and writes on the board "I. sex." What else? I look at her and I say to myself, "And *she* is married." There are some people that you can't imagine how they managed to achieve fucking. Mrs. Lamb is a master at prophecy and foretelling and premonitions and all the other little tricks of the writer's trade; she shows us atmosphere and setting, character and plot, allusions and illusions, metonymy and other whatnots I can no longer remember. Harter gives me the feeling that a college education is a conglomeration of things you once knew, and that when you leave you're as stupid as when you arrived, but a good many facts and figures have used your body as a sort of hotel from which they pass almost as soon as they've taken up residence. (Someone else said this, by the way. I don't remember who. Sorry, Mrs. Lamb.)

At lunchtime I have two choices: the cafeteria or fatnesses from the machine in the basement. By October I'm so tired of everything that I go back to the room, take off my girdle, bolt down some cookies, lie guiltily in bed, and try to nap.

Marsha is in bed with her French book; it's occurred to her that being in bed with the French teacher is all that will get her to pass the course, but she takes the book and tries anyway.

"So," Marsha says, *"comment ça va? Est-ce Mrs. Lamb boring tout le monde aujourd'hui?"*

"Marsha," I say, "that's cheating; you have to rush and look up 'boring' in your *dictionnaire.* Otherwise they fine you and throw you out of the French Honor Guard."

"Je suis malade. Shit. *Je suis malaise? J'ai malade?"*

"J'ai mal," I say.

After lunch, geology lab with Professor Wally Pearson, Department Head. I nearly flunk every quiz, and he says, "You always look so intelligent and alert when I lecture, and you don't goof off on field trips; where am I failing?" Naturally he's the best teacher in the entire university; he practically choreographs each lecture, and enthusiastic? He gets more excited over some homely pebble than Professor Fleming over a whole tribe of beautiful Polynesians.

So I say, "Professor Pearson, you're a marvelous teacher, and I'm the world's worst science student; it's not your fault."

Dr. Pearson decides that on field trips I must walk near him, and anything I don't understand I can ask and he'll answer it on the spot and we will therefore solve my problem, only as it turns out the only question I can think of asking is, "What am I doing here?"

Chapter Ten

❦

I have two classes on Saturday, French at ten A.M. and the Geology lecture at eleven.

My French teacher, Mr. Kendall (he's been writing his Ph.D. for ten years, naturally on Camus), is from the Midwest, but he fancies himself—as do all French teachers I've ever known—a native Parisian. He wears a little beret, smokes Gauloises, and hunches over when he walks or talks in a fashion that must be to him either chic or French but that to me looks like he's ruining his spine. He shrugs his shoulders a good deal and sits on the edge of his chair and makes little jokes *en français* that no one in the entire class understands, but luckily that doesn't bother him; it's enough for him that he should be rolling his *r*'s and pursing his lips and raising his eyebrows and dropping his shoulders. It's enough for us too; we read all of Sartre and Camus in translation, not to mention an excerpt from Proust, the homosexual-seduction scene between Charlus and the barber, which, when we first attempt it in French, we think is about the pollination habits of the bee as witnessed by two charming male individuals. Imagine our shock when we find out it's about two fags trying to attract each other. Mr. Kendall is not shocked, of course; nothing shocks him, for he is French.

He insists upon calling us Mademoiselles, and there are so many girls in the class that if he calls on fifteen of us per hour, he wastes at least ten minutes buzzing out all those Mademoiselles, so we restrain our fits of giggling and try to appreciate Gallic ways. Anything to waste some time.

This Saturday afternoon, lunch is over, and classes are through for a blissful day and a half, during which I have to catch up on last week's work, prepare for two quizzes, write a composition for Mrs. Lamb answering the question "Who am I?" and get ready for the blind date Irene has gotten for me." The Rabbi's daughter is actually going out with a Christian, breaking the First Fabrikant Commandment. Two weeks ago I would've sworn that such a thing would never come to pass.

Saturday afternoon I take checkbook in hand, this is my first year with a checkbook, and I mismanage, overdraw, and spend so much money that my parents have a fit; I consider myself, however, like the surviving German Jews in relation to their fatherland; I feel I'm getting reparation monies. Checkbook in hand I go first to the Wetton drugstore where I buy Metrecal (a huge container of the dry powder, which I then mix with water and have between meals) and Ayds (I DO eat them like candy and they add calories the exact same way.)

Then I take the MTA to Cambridge, where I get dietetic chocolate. Then I go to a bookstore and buy: 1. *Learning Swahili*; 2. translations of Sartre, Camus, and Proust; 3. yet another book on counting calories; 4. a present for my father, Sholem Aleichem's short stories. I love buying my father presents with his money, it seems so *right*.

I get back to the dorm after dinner, mix myself a glass of Metrecal, and nervously eat two chunks of dietetic chocolate while sitting under the dryer. Marsha has already gone. Her note says, "Wear your glasses, sweetie, else how are you going to know which boy is yours? Regards, Maaaasha." Ever since I've been in Boston I've taken to leaving out my r's when I write notes to her on the theory that what you don't pronounce you don't deserve. Marsha thinks I speak funny, she asks me to say "water" and "wash" and chuckles like mad. I am the foreigner here; almost everybody at this place is from Massachusetts.

My date, Allan Dobsen, is a junior from Boston; that's all I know about him besides that he's liberal, tall, and blond. When dates come to Bailey Hall, they're received in the living room. Can you think of what it's like when ten blind dates are out there waiting? That means twenty people don't know to whom they belong, and the stares and sighs and looks of disappointment or disbelief are enough to pilot you through years and years of trauma. No wonder I can be easily convinced to take my glasses off; the sighted and the blind are equally at a disadvantage, and I at least don't need to know if my date is miserable that he drew me. Rona makes up my face and tells me, "You look only three thousand percent better without glasses, so what if you can't see him? He'll see you."

"What if he's living according to the same principle?" I ask.

"That's his problem," she says. "Black looks excellent on you."

"Slimming."

"You know," she says, "you're really good-looking, although too heavy," these Brooklyn Jews give it to you straight from the shoulder, "but what you don't realize is that there are men who like heavy women; that's the truth, not everybody needs to be skinny."

"Only creeps like heavy women," I say. "The only guys who like me are creeps."

Rona shakes her head. "Sometimes you give me the creeps."

"I give them to myself, too," I say. "You're a doll, anyway, to help me with this makeup. Thanks."

"Maybe you'll learn to put it on yourself and use it every day?" She thinks this will solve all my problems.

We smile and part, and I walk down the long corridor, glasses in pocketbook, unsteady on my heels.

At the desk in the living room is Biff, trying to sort out and correctly pair the people hanging around. She says, "Barbara Fabrikant, who is here for Barbara Fabrikant?" I wish I were dead, I look around and see many fuzzy pink heads, fuzzy hair colors, and even fuzzier bodies; I can't tell gender in all cases either. Without my glasses, according to those TV ads that show you how many ways blind people can be blind, I am legally blind the fuzzy way. Whether legal or illegal, I see nothing, so I stare nonchalantly into the heart of the shadowy crowd and try to look intelligent and alert. My constant pose.

A body moves forward to claim me; as he gets very close I see that he's an inch or so taller than me, with blond hair, thin, and wearing, thank God, glasses. I heave a sigh of relief. At least one of us will know where we're going. He takes my hand, a nice gesture and a very practical one, for I can barely see the steps that lead to the sidewalk, nor can I see when the sidewalk melts into the road that leads to his House.

"So how d'ye like it heah?" he says.

"Oh," I say hesitantly, "I don't know yet." That's a slight understatement, for by now I'm ready to leave forever, only where would I go? Home is even worse than here. "How do you like it?"

"It's not Harvard," he says, "but I like it a lot. Especially the kids."

"Oh," I say. "Why?"

"They're fun, like my House, we have the best times. Last night we all took turns jumping off the porch into an old bed."

"No kidding."

"You should've heard the bed squeak," he laughs.

An idiot, right? Plus probably a bigot—Beta Delta has no Jews, no Negroes, maybe not even Catholics. Naturally, I'm beginning to like him. I become very attentive the way they say to be in *Mademoiselle*, and he tells me he wants to be a lawyer and he likes football, beer, sailing, the Upper Clahss, and that his high school sweetheart who went to Wellesley got married recently and maybe he should have married her when she wanted him to. I ask him how old he is. Twenty-one, he says.

"Don't you think that's a little young for marrying?" I myself envision meeting someone, falling in love, then waiting five or six years before the ceremony, until he's thirty and I'm at least twenty-five. I don't understand people who want to get married young, least of all men.

"I don't think I want to get married for a long time," I say. And this, Mrs. Lamb, is extremely prophetic.

Allan and I walk into the fraternity house, music is blaring, people are packed in together, there are huge kegs of beer on the floor and little Cheez-Its, pretzels, potato chips, M & M's, and sour cream and onion dip. 1961. People are jitterbugging and lindying; there are kids all over the house, from basement to third floor; we walk down to the basement, where the dancing is; talking is in the living room; and God only knows what's going on in the bedrooms. Allan leads me downstairs, does he know intuitively that I can't see a foot in front of me? Have I been squinting more than usual? Or does he actually like me? I think that's probably impossible.

In the basement we stand on the outskirts of the crowd, this place is more packed than the Long Island Expressway at five P.M. Are these people dancing? Or fucking upright? Is it a mass orgy? No, it's actually jitterbugging, but you'd have to see this to believe it, this is where the good clean fun is, down here. This is where the house mothers want us to be, not in some empty room with a bed in it, but down here where the company is. And you wonder that middle-class, average Americans are the ones who are swinging nowadays with group sex? Listen, you should've seen them in college; group sex is exactly what they were being prepared for.

Allan says, "Wait right here, I'll bring us beer."

I nod yes, of course I'll wait, where will I go if I care to move? Standing there alone, ringed about with bodies I can't clearly see, I'm frightened. What will I do if he doesn't come back? Do I know anyone here? Are people laughing at me? I feel so alone, I smell the beer, perfume, hair lotion, after-shave, sweat; the music attacks my ear, I think I see balloons on the ceiling, or are they lights covered with paper lanterns? I'll never know; I stand very still and wait.

Finally Allan jiggles my arm and hands me a beer. "Jesus Christ," he says, "this is a madhouse. Want a pretzel?"

"No." I can never eat around men because then they will know my fat isn't glandular.

He finishes his beer, and I give him mine, which he also finishes. Then he wants to dance, so we force our way through the body-wall to the center of the writhing people and join them, in time for the fast dance to be over and a slow one to be beginning.

We dance close, no choice in the matter, for all we have is four inches of floor, impossible to talk; I smell the Old Spice on him, he must smell the Tabu on me. Very pleasant. Then I feel a tap on my shoulder.

"Hi, kiddo," a blur says, "it's me, Rona." (Later on she comes up to me when Allan has left for a moment and shouts, "This guy is crazy for you." "No kidding," I say. It's lucky she told me, otherwise I might never know.)

Allan asks, "Why did she say who she was? Didn't you know?"

"I'll tell you about it later."

But he looks worried. "Tell me now."

"I wear glasses, only I'm not wearing them now, so I can't see anything."

"Not even me?" There's relief in his voice from finding out that during the week I don't use a seeing-eye dog. Then he pulls me closer to him so that our faces are about an inch apart. He has lovely blue eyes behind his glasses, and a nice Aryan face, nice mouth, small nose, like mine.

When I look at Allan, my crotch gets wet and I worry: will it drip or smell? Still, it feels lovely, and when Allan tightens his grip around my waist, I suck in my breath so that the roll of flab that the girdle accentuates will not be so noticeable, and we dance close and I think to myself, with the greatest wonder you can imagine, maybe this fellow likes me.

Actually, all I know for sure is that there's something lovely between us. His cock.

No, that's a joke. I mean to say, there's chemistry here, you know what that is. Dr. Theodore Isaac Rubin, who writes such travesties as *The Thin Book by the Formerly Fat Psychiatrist*, from which I wish him such a craving for peanut butter and jelly that his brain should fall out from trying to fight the urge with boiled chicken, that fountain of helpful erudition says somewhere that you can forget a marriage that doesn't begin with chemistry. Hence the fabulous success of most marriages. Chemistry? I'll tell you what chemistry is responsible for: fantasies and daydreams of a particularly venomous and life-sapping variety, DDT, U.S. Steel, and Zsa Zsa Gabor.

And me. I am a victim of chemistry.

But that Saturday night, pressed close to Allan, feeling that magical, delicious sensation, the sensation that can make you see good where there's evil, happiness where there's disaster, which makes you young and hopeful and, in sum, a living, breathing idiot, I am happy happy happy. You could get addicted to this stuff. Don't most people?

After a while, pressing together rhythmically in this smoke-filled, beery room with the lights dim and the potato chips crackling, Allan says, "Let's go for a ride or somewhere so we can talk."

Talk? I think warily. But out loud I say, "You have a car?" because this is another rarity; to have a car you need special permission and a good reason—a place to neck is not acceptable.

Allan says, "I tutor kids in Cambridge once a week; I do it because it's a good excuse for the car."

He helps me on with my coat and leaves his hands on my shoulder for a moment, and I shudder with pleasure. We hold hands and go out into the cold night, and I say, "Will you hate me if I put on my glasses? I can't see a damn thing when it's dark."

"Of course not," he says. "Only women worry about such things, men don't care."

"Are you serious?" I open my bag, fumble around, feel for the glasses case, find it, and put on the black-frame cat's-eyes glasses (remember them? with the upturned corners that if someone tried to kiss you on the cheek they could get their own eyes poked out?) and *voilà*, there are stars in the formerly black sky, the black mist surrounding us has turned into a road with trees on the side, and I can see the shapes of things, even in the distance. I can see all the way to the top of the Hill, where the large twin towers hover over the campus, where the famous Harter mascot is stored, Jumbo the Elephant. On my first campus tour the girl-guide took me to the stuffed elephant, and showed me how its trunk was full of pennies that students threw in there before exams, wishing for aid from on high. "Don't you get it?" she asked. "An elephant never forgets." The hilarious Harter sense of humor.

"Bailey gave more than the elephant," Allan told me. "Lots of money, so the legend says."

"Somehow it seems like the right thing for this place, don't you think? to have been financed by a three-ring circus?" Then I remember that Allan likes it here, not that that would make a difference. I always mean to be a lady and keep my mouth shut, but I never do.

"Aha," Allan laughs, "your first radical statement of the evening."

"Is it radical to criticize Harter?"

"It's just unusual," he says. "Most people aren't critical of where they are."

"Aren't you?"

"I'm torn between discontent on the one hand and sports cars on the other."

We walk down the road from the fraternity house to the big parking lot at the foot of campus and weave around the cars, mostly old, mostly jalopies, though Allan points out an Alfa Romeo, a Triumph, a Corvette, a Thunderbird; he looks at them lovingly and then sighs as we stop before a 1955 green Rambler.

He opens the door to let me in. "The only good thing about this car is that the front seats go all the way back."

He shows me, and then we don't ever leave the parking lot. Is it my two sips of beer that make me this way, or what? I've never done anything like this. Before Allan I had hardly necked, only been hot, hot and bothered and pent-up and crazed and ignorant, and all he does, lying near me in the car, is to reach down between my legs and touch me through the slip and pants and girdle on my crotch, and I have an orgasm. There was an orgasm bursting to get loose. I realize two things immediately: what I've been missing, and what a terrible mistake this is. Only a rabbi's daughter can hold two such contradictory thoughts in her head at the same time, but during the rest of our stormy relationship it's my firm conviction that my necking and petting so precipitously with Allan has ruined all chances for a decent relationship.

And what was actually going on? At first Allan would kiss and touch me and I would do him the enormous favor of kissing him back. Later on I jerked him off, and don't think I didn't think that was a big deal; I thought I was a princess for letting him take off my bra, and I felt damned loose and wicked too. I used to ask him whether or not he loved me, whether he was just using me for my body. Can you beat that? I was coming to the left and right, and all I can think of is, What a doll I am to him. I used to sing to myself, " 'I'm just a girl who cain't say no.' " Isn't that bright? Allan, Allan, wherever you are, my only excuse is, I didn't know any better.

So I wondered why our relationship had such terrible ups and downs, why you were sometimes so mean to me. To the princess with the big boobs that you, mere mortal, were permitted to play with.

Chapter Eleven

❦

Sunday morning is Doughnut Morning in the dorm, and the members of Council have to take turns going to the cafeteria and picking up four huge boxes of every kind of doughnut imaginable.

Today it's my turn, and I curse everyone, with my gloves clutching the four big boxes and my breath freezing around my nose, breathing in the delectable smell that causes me to bargain with myself: at the beginning of the semester I say, one doughnut, you can have *one*. But this is quite the silliest thing I've attempted, and by today, October eighth, I'm saying, three, you can have three. Three huge, filled-with-jelly doughnuts. Then I get back to the dorm, set up the doughnuts and the money box in the living room, and take four and tiptoe to my room, laden down.

I make coffee and go through the doughnuts one by one, reading *Heart of Darkness*. Soon I'm nauseated, short of breath, and miserable. I work straight through to dinner. It's a dark, cloudy day, I decide that Allan will never call again (he does, this evening), and I have Metrecal instead of going to dinner. Two glasses.

Afterward I go downstairs to the washing machines; until college I never washed my clothes or made a bed; my mother may be difficult to live with but she's an excellent maid. Now I even have to iron. Some things I hang up to dry, others I put in the dryer. Later on I return with my hair in rollers and I hum to myself and iron my blouses. This is the pleasantest moment for me at Harter, except the necking. I'm clean and at peace and doing something constructive. Maybe I should be a domestic. Maybe I will. Other girls' clothes are hanging all around, they have a damp and sweet odor, and the iron smells like some kind of toast, steamy and crisp; it's quiet, I'm alone, and I'm not wearing a girdle. The nausea has passed and all I feel is remorse. I vow to go on a diet.

"How can a rabbi's daughter go out with a Gentile?" Marsha asks when she returns at ten o'clock from her weekend with Robert.

I'm saved from answering by a knock at the door—Rona and JoEllen, clad in matching muu-muus, arms linked, jig in. Their heads are rollered, their feet covered by big furry slippers, and they're singing, " 'Sisters, sisters, there were never SUCH devoted sisters . . .' "

Marsha sings, "Snow," and slightly higher I go, "Snow," and Rona and Jo, entirely out of key, finish up the snows and then flop down on our beds.

"We're going crazy," Jo informs us.

There's a knock on our door.

"Come on in, Frannie!" Marsha yells. "The door's open."

"How did you know it was me?" she asks, stepping one foot in.

"Just a lucky guess," Marsha says, and we start giggling.

"If you're going to make this much noise AFTER seven thirty, you have to go to the living room." Frannie is good and offended. "And YOU," she addresses this to me, "freshman REPresentative should keep your classmates in order."

"Hush up, girls," I say. They giggle. "See?" I tell Frannie. "Incorrigible. Criminal elements."

"If you're not quiet I'll bring up your names for disciplinary action at the next Council meeting," Frannie says and walks out of the room.

"Don't you love it that she can?" Rona asks.

"They're so stupid around here, why couldn't she politely ask us to keep quiet?" Marsha says. "She reminds me of a Jane Austen heroine, always in love with rules instead of men."

"I've never read a word of Jane Austen," Rona says.

"Me neither," I say.

"I read *Pride and Prejudice*," Jo says.

There's silence for a moment, we're drifting off in four different directions, where the others are going I don't know, but me, I'm wondering if Allan *really* likes me or is only *using* me. Am I too *easy?* or what?

"So my roommate is going out with a Gentile a second time," Marsha announces.

"Crazy," Jo says. "You could never marry him."

"Marriage isn't *all* there is." I surprise even myself with these words.

"What else is there?" Jo demands.

There's a moment's pause while the answer dawns on me.

"Sex!" There. I've discovered it, my white whale, ship, ocean, adventure, and metaphor.

"Yeah!" Marsha agrees. "Are you a virgin?"

"Of course," we say in unison.

In 1961 at Harter there was an epidemic of virginity. Very few girls there fucked, and those who did almost immediately got pregnant. God was watching Harter girls. As it turns out, God must have had a special eye on Marsha, He fixed up *some* miracle for her. In our dorm there were three girls who screwed. Two of them were on the third floor, one we knew about because she got pregnant, of course, and the other was always worried if her period was ten minutes late. This girl used a diaphragm faithfully, but worried anyway; she would march around her room with no bra on, hitting her small, high breasts and saying, "They feel sore. I think they feel sore."

She thought that if she hit her breasts often enough, maybe until they were black and blue, it would bring her period on. Even I knew that sore breasts are a symptom of a period, not the cause, and I tried to tell her this, but in the area of sex you know how rational people are. She went on blithely hitting her breasts, and because each time her period did indeed come, there was no talking her out of this method.

She was our sexual sophisticate. She had overnight permission and didn't care if you knew that she stayed in a motel with her boyfriend. She even showed me her diaphragm. What a shock. It looked so big, and I expected something the size of a nickel.

On the second floor was only one girl who screwed. Elaine, the Nut; she took Dexamyls to keep from getting pregnant and was happy to pass on her foolproof method to anyone who asked. She was an unusual girl, even at Harter. Her theory was that Dexamyl so destroyed your system, so crapped up your eating and sleeping, made your heart race, and occasionally caused black spots to appear before your eyes, that it was doubtless confusing the eggs and ovaries too; probably they had lost all sense of what they were supposed to be doing, black spots appearing before their eyes also. "A little Dexamyl can cure anything," she said, only with her "cure" and "kill" sounded synonymous.

In the men's communal bathrooms (Allan tells me) there are bull's-eyes painted on with lipstick on the inside of the toilet doors where you're supposed to aim when you masturbate. In Bailey there are no such provisions; luckily for me I didn't know a girl could masturbate, even though my uncle had told me. He said there was nothing wrong with masturbating except that it made it hard for you to *transfer* the sensations from clitoris to vagina. And he mentioned that I should not masturbate with a candle because I might leave wax in my vagina. I think I never would've considered using one because I couldn't even get a Tampax up me. Frankly, I wasn't so sure I had an opening there.

Otherwise the only provision for sexuality was the front door of Bailey Hall, where you were allowed to kiss goodnight. Every weekend at curfew the steps were littered with couples clinging to each other, glued together; this was considered *comme il faut,* but men in the rooms—*verboten.* Thus the mind of Harter.

"What did your parents tell you about sex?" Marsha asks.

"Nothing," Rona answers. "They gave me a book to read, *The Stork Didn't Bring You.* But I had already stolen some of their Scientific Sex Books—they have quite a collection. By the time they gave me the stork book I knew how I had got here and not only that, how many positions they could've used for maximum penetration."

"Whatever that is," I mutter. Listen, I'd read books too, even *Lady Chatterley's Lover,* which I'd stolen from my parents, and still I knew nothing about sex except what I'd discovered with Allan last night.

"My mother told me I could fuck when I was engaged, not a minute before," Jo says. "So I always keep my girdle on when I pet with someone."

"You're kidding." Marsha's voice has a question mark in it, but I'm thinking how my mother would have approved.

"Nope. What do you do?"

"I use Kleenex," Marsha tells us.

Now it's our turn to look surprised. Into my mind floats a picture of Marsha wadding up her hole with little balled-up tissues, nothing should get through.

She explains her method to us, foolproof she insists. First she places a tissue over her private parts, then she and Robert can rub and be wildly inventive, he can be naked, his penis can be right near her little, unopened hole, and when he comes, she can sop him up with the rest of the Kleenexes. No trace of him, at her house or his. Perfect.

"Jesus," Rona says.

"It keeps me a virgin," Marsha points out.

"My father told me my virginity was my most precious possession, that no good Jew would marry me unless he got it," I tell them. Dad and my uncle separated the sex lectures between them; my father gave the moral side and my uncle took care of the disgusting details. From neither of them did I learn anything.

"Do you suppose that's true?" Marsha asks. "That men really want you to be a virgin?"

"With my luck," I say, "it probably is."

"Anyway, if you use Tampax, how'll he ever know?" Marsha asks.

"That's why you shouldn't use Tampax." This is the one bit of sexual information my mother ever passed on, otherwise she won't talk about sex at all. She disapproves of it entirely.

"Well, I do," Rona, Jo, and Marsha say in unison.

"I can't. I've tried."

"You have to aim it toward the backside," Rona says helpfully.

I nod; what can I do, tell her the problem isn't where to aim it, but where to put it? After I get fucked I'll use Tampax— I'm probably the only girl in the world who works in this order, fucking so I can use Tampax. Is there a better reason?

Chapter Twelve

❧

"I heard what you did with the sororities," is Allan's opening remark on our second date, next Saturday night. He's taking me out to dinner, and his car is parked in front of the dorm, and he doesn't deliver this line until we are safely inside it. He has a tremendous sense of privacy.

What I've done is the following: I have out loud and in public asked the charming sisters if they have any Negro members and why not. This is the most astonishing thing that has ever happened on this campus.

"It got around even to the fraternity houses?" I ask.

"Sure," he says. "The guys said to me, 'At least you got a dame with balls.' Only I'm not sure I want one with them."

"Listen, I have good news for you. I haven't got them. Do you?"

Thus the beginning of a heartfelt fight, in which I assure him that: my ancestors were writing Bibles while his were digging bogs, Mahalia Jackson sings better than his mother, and so forth.

When I've finished, he says, "Are you a liberal fanatic idealist who'll murder me with my boots on?"

I promise to take them off first.

Later on that evening, after dinner, Allan says, "You're cool, you really are." He's driving me to see the Charles River by moonlight, he insists, but I know he's looking for a place to park; sex, sex, sex, is all that's on his mind. How do I know? By the surest and most excellent method: because that's all that's on my mind.

He says, "You've got style, and I don't. You can carry on and scream about sororities and be everybody's favorite person anyway."

"Which shows you how hard I work to be liked, some great trait. Maybe I should go into public relations."

"I would like to be cool and smooth and have people admire me," Allan confesses. "I would like an Alfa Romeo convertible."

"I like the way you are because you're a little rough yet." I turn to look at him and pat the back of his head, his soft hair. "It shows that you're alive."

"Will you come back and see my room?"

"Why?" I ask. I feel safer in the car, isn't that smart? My impression of sex is as yet quite hazy, and I think I need external protection: pants on, in a car, his slacks on; I think, what will happen in a room with closed doors and a bed? Maybe the passion will be too much for us, as they used to tell us in Health Ed. Mrs. Ferne, Chairman of Health, I remember her so well, she taught us hospital corners, how a car engine works, and not to fuck. Bless you, Mrs. Ferne, all I remembered was the last.

"Look," Allan tries, "it's much pleasanter to sit in my room, I have a hi-fi, a comfortable chair, and I also don't have to drive the whole night."

We go back to his room; it's huge and he shares it with

another junior who's mysteriously away for the evening. Allan's half of the room is neat, spotless; his proudest possession, besides his hi-fi, is his file cabinet. In the file—every paper he has written since freshman year of high school, carbons of all the letters he's written and originals of all that have ever been sent to him, a list of every book he's read since high school with a little summary of what each book is about; he has sports cars filed and probably women too, only these he doesn't show me. He keeps lists of: his expenses, the books and records he owns, his assignments, his supplies, his dates. At the end of every month he tallies up where he's been, how much it has cost him, and what he's learned.

I say to him enviously, for I am the sloppiest, least organized person I've ever known, "This is wonderful, being so clear-headed. It must save you lots of time."

"Actually," he explains, and now you'll see why I like him, "the filing takes me so long I only have about an hour a day to study."

"Why don't you stop filing?" I ask, genius that I am. Why don't I stop eating?

He answers, "I couldn't study more than an hour a day even if I had time. You know what happens to me during exams?"

"No."

"According to all charts and records I spend more money on dates and movies at that time than any other. My need for femaleness, would you like to see a chart? peaks around the time of my hardest exam."

"Do you really have a chart?" I ask.

He pulls one out, from last semester, the end of his sophomore year. There are weeks, first to last, of the semester, number of dates, exam times marked in red, and sure enough, each week with an exam the little jagged line jags up furiously, and at final-exam time, it nearly throws itself off the graph in a frenzy.

"Money spent on candy bars, beer, and cheeseburgers also triples during exams," he says very seriously.

This I understand without a chart. "Why do you keep these things?"

"I don't know, sometimes I have the feeling that unless I can account to myself for time and money, it will all go and I won't have any idea where."

"Your memory?" I ask.

He shrugs his shoulders and puts the chart neatly back in the file cabinet, under *T* of course—for Time.

I look around the room, two prints, Van Gogh, yellow and orange and very nice, and a Picasso toreador, books and bookshelves, two big windows overlooking the Harter drumlin, and a roommate who throws his jackets on the bed and the rest of his clothes on the floor. Allan says he's very nice in spite of it.

Allan pours Christian Brothers sherry because I've told him that I like it better than beer, and then, holding the glass in his hand, he entices me to the bed. Entices is not the correct word. I'm dying to neck with him again, it's been nearly a week since the last time, and addictive as my personality is, you know what is the next thing it gets addicted to. I want to come, it makes me feel good and relaxed and healthy, and I don't know yet, as I've said before, that there's a way I can do it even without Allan. So like him or not, I *need* that boy. We lie on the bed, him on top of me, both of us clothed, and after necking for a while, him touching me outside bra, outside blouse even, just rolling around clinging to each other, kissing so hard it feels like sucking or eating, I come. One, two, three. After I come I'm disinterested in: 1. sex, and 2. him. Imagine how he loves me then, and it never occurs to me that I'm not going to win the Miss Congeniality Award in this relationship.

He says, "You know, you ought to be able to come again, a lot more."

"I don't feel like it," I say. I'm ready to get up and go to a movie or for a walk. "Is this all you care about, my body?"

Chapter Thirteen

❧

Without knowing it, Allan gets his revenge; he introduces me to Mr. Appel. He took Mr. Appel's course because the hippest Harter girls were in it, all sixteen of them, the Theater Group girls. They wore long hair, more eye makeup than lipstick, and sandals. And, it was rumored, they fucked. The name of the course, by the way, is Oppressed People: A Study of Minorities in America, but that isn't why Mr. Appel is a campus hero.

He's one of the few teachers who has anything to do with students, for at Harter the whole point of being a professor is to lecture a few times a week and then get out of the neighborhood. To say that most of the teachers were uninterested in the bodies in class is to exaggerate in their favor. Take Professor Fleming—his notes are fifteen years old, he reads them six hours a week, and graduate students grade his multiple-choice exams. Then what with his time? Committee meetings, a few graduate students, and home for his yearly vacation. Thousands of hours of training have gone to produce this.

Mr. Appel even has parties for his students. It is to one of those parties that Allan, the last week of October, takes me.

As he and I drive in to Boston, we discuss what to buy Mr. Appel.

"Flowers?" I suggest. But that seems kind of silly. "Candy?" Allan says, "Let's get him a bottle of bourbon."

"Booze?" I say. "You can't bring booze to a teacher. It's not right."

Allan says, "Boy, are you something! He's just a person, a nice guy, he even once said he likes bourbon."

"This is what you discuss in class?"

"I was walking with him up the Hill one day and we got to talking, and somehow we got around to bars and liquor." Allan is driving around one of the rotaries leading to Boston, skids in front of a car that's trying to cut him off, and makes the necessary right turn. I shut my eyes. "You're so sheltered," Allan continues, "that's what's surprising about you—with all your radicalness, you're the most sheltered person I ever knew."

I open my eyes, lean over and peck him on the cheek. "Luckily I have you to unshelter me," I say. Little do I know that all I need for the job is me.

We stop at a liquor store and buy a bottle of bourbon, and on impulse I offer to pay half. Not for Allan's sake, although he's properly grateful, but for the sake of the unknown bourbon-drinking teacher who gives parties, actually gives parties, for his students. He's worth at least half a bottle of bourbon, isn't he?

I sit in the car and clutch the gift-wrapped bottle nervously. I've never been to a teacher's house before. I'm going to be surrounded by upper-class students, I won't know anybody but Allan, and I'm embarrassed because my black dress (what else?) doesn't conceal the flab around my middle. I'm puffy and ugly, except in the eyes of Rona and Marsha and maybe Allan. Then Allan sets the stage for all that is to pass.

He says, "I've even told Mr. Appel about you, how gutsy you are and how you hate Harter. He said he was real interested in meeting you."

"Allan, you didn't."

"Why not?" he wants to know. "You two will probably get along famously what with your politics and all."

"For God's sakes, you act like I'm some kind of cell leader, when all I have is a big mouth. Besides, he probably likes Harter, otherwise why would he be here?"

"He hates it," Allan tells me. "He hates it so much that even though he has a Ph.D. he won't let you call him Professor or Doctor. He doesn't want to be associated with the rest of the creeps with the degree."

"No kidding?" I say, impressed. For this shows something, doesn't it? The man sounds unique. "So why is he here?"

"He says maybe he can do some good, shake this place up a little. Besides, Dr. Harris loves him, treats him like a son, that's how he got the job in the first place, Harris had him at Hamilton when he taught there."

"How do you know this?" To me, teachers have always been a closed book, unopenable, you didn't know their past, present, or future. They just stood up in front of the class, words flowed out, and you took them down and memorized them and moved on to the next course.

"Mr. Appel told me. I like to talk to him."

We're looking for a parking space, actually Allan does both driving and looking; I'm already preoccupied with this fascinating new experience: a teacher who is also human.

Allan parks, we get out of the car and he asks, "Shall I carry the bourbon?" and then sees that my glasses are off. "You don't mean to tell me you're planning to go that way, do you?"

I shake my head yes.

"This isn't a fraternity party, this is going to be with people discussing and being intelligent and you're going to sit there and not even know when someone is talking to you unless I jiggle your arm? Over my dead body. I don't want to come in there with my girlfriend the idiot; they'll think you're a foreigner or something; it'll look like I'm your U.N. translator."

"Oh, it's not that bad."

"How would you know?" he asks. "You can't see a thing."

"All right, all right," I acquiesce. Not wearing glasses has made me nervous too, and I don't know why I took them off, I had every intention of wearing them. "Will you carry the bourbon?"

He takes it and we walk down this huge street with a park in the middle, until we come to Mr. Appel's building, a five-story house with a big front porch. He rents the whole second floor.

We go up to the door, ring his bell, and he buzzes us in. I walk in front of Allan up the stairs, my heart pounding. I feel scared to death. Allan is clumping behind me, obviously not nervous at all. If you asked me then what I was nervous about, I don't think I would have been able to tell you. I don't know if I can now. All I know is that for me, nervousness and love are inextricably intertwined; fright seems to be at the bottom of all my passion. There are better things to have as a foundation for love, too, believe me.

Mr. Appel opens the door to his apartment. I'm out of breath, and my hand trembles as he takes it and says, "You're Barbara. I've heard so much about you." Luckily I walk in without fainting and murmur unintelligibly that I've also heard a great deal about him. He's greeting Allan, however, and thanking him for the bourbon and he probably doesn't hear me. It's just as well, I figure, because how conventional and trite can you be?

Allan takes my coat, I cling to my pocketbook, and Mr. Appel introduces us. The boys are with their dates, and the girls are moving in and out of the kitchen, giggling and laughing and helping Mr. Appel put out plates of cheese and fruit and cookies. They're relaxed, just plain relaxed, as though he weren't a teacher.

One girl with long dark hair, dark eyes, no lipstick, and a long face full of profound seriousness, asks, "Mr. Appel, can we make hot cider and rum?"

"Sure," he says, "if you can find the ingredients."

The mass of bustling girls flows back to the kitchen, and I hear pots clinking and cups jangling, and soon the smell of hot cider and alcohol steams out from the kitchen. The girls pour cups for everyone, only it seems they've poured out five extra cups, all for Mr. Appel, and there are five of them trying to give him a cup.

Mr. Appel finally takes one, from the lovely dark-haired girl who's wearing a dungaree skirt, can you believe it? in the home of a teacher a dungaree skirt, black tights, boots, and a red ribbed turtleneck sweater. Her hair is straight and long and it looks as though it were trimmed by a lawn mower, that jaggedy. But she has a smashing figure and an unusual face, very strong, mannish, high cheekbones, a long nose, not too long, but the line is etched off her face sharply. It would be easy to draw her profile, it seems to me, as I study her, for study her I do, and carefully, because there's no fuzziness and no fat; she's lean and spare.

Mr. Appel is sitting on the couch, there are two girls on either side of him, it's a very long couch, but they're all crunched in together, the three in the middle looking quite happy, the two on either end trying to give the others more room. On the floor near the couch are the rest of the girls in the class, and seated like proper ladies and gentlemen around the edges of the room, are the boys and their dates.

There's a lot of conversation going on now, about the results of the election. I hear Mr. Appel attacking Kennedy, much to the consternation and shock of those who are of the opinion, better anyone than what's-his-name, the red baiter. Mr. Appel attacks everyone in politics and national life. He hates them all, he hates the Boston *Globe*, *The New York Times*, UPI, AP, high finance, unions; the only two human beings he admires are I. F. Stone and Charlie Chaplin. He hates large universities and small ones, and, as far as I can tell, he believes we should all be Populists, whatever that is.

The one thing that's clear to me is that he would like the world to begin again, preferably under his direction. Just what I'm looking for.

I drink my cider with rum, there's more rum in it than you realize at first, and my head gets steamy and fuzzy. Allan is joining in the conversation, and I'm just looking around. Mr. Appel's apartment is everything I imagine a teacher's should be: one entire wall is lined from floor to ceiling with books, hardbound and paperback. And they all look read! There are original oils on the walls, they look very depressing to me, all browns and dark blues and blacks, but I chalk my dislike of them up to the fact that I'm bourgeois and know nothing about art. There's even a poem on the wall; now this I'm interested in. I put down my cup and walk shakily over to read it; it's a poem by someone I've never heard of, dedicated to Mr. Appel, and it's about the Statue of Liberty. It makes fun of the statue and all her bad promises, why it even calls her a whore. As I'm reading I suddenly notice that Mr. Appel is standing near me, he's very tall, must be over six foot one or two, and he says, "My dear friend Helen Baermann wrote that for me after she read my book on the fantasies immigrants had about America in the early nineteen-hundreds.

"Oh," I say. "What were they?"

"Would you like to read it?" he asks.

"I'd love to."

He goes to the bookshelf and takes out a nine-hundred-page hardcover book; meanwhile the room has gotten quieter, as though he's the hub of conversation even when it's about Nixon. He walks over to me and hands me the book. I clutch it and say, "I may not be able to get to this until after finals; may I keep it for a while?" I'm trembling.

"Sure." He looks delighted. "Are you cold? I know this apartment doesn't get enough heat."

"I'm all right." I'm looking up into those incredibly small brown eyes. What a face on that man, what a long nose, balding head, rotten posture, huge mouth with the teeth not close enough together. (My, I bet he's a great whistler, Marsha says after meeting him.)

"Let me get you a sweater," he offers, and over my protestations he goes into his bedroom and comes back with a gray cashmere sweater, huge, he's a big man, and I slip it on and thank him. Now I'm wearing something of his, holding his book, sitting in his apartment. I may faint. Instead I return to my seat, and Allan takes my hand and says, "What did I tell you? Weren't you stupid to be nervous?"

I shake my head yes, oh yes, I was stupid to be nervous.

I sit quietly listening to the conversation, watching everyone blithely eat and drink, while I'm doing my best to sip the cider without choking to death on it and making a spectacle of myself. Later on two girls come over and sit on the floor near us, their names are Jeannie and Cara and they live in the next dorm over, McDowell Hall. They tell me they've heard about me too, and then they invite me to visit them, maybe we'll go to dinner together. I accept gratefully. Cara tells me she's a sophomore and that this is her last year here, that she's transferring to Bennington.

"No kidding?" I say, and another seed is planted, the notion that there is actually a way out of this place.

I whisper to Allan, "Let's offer them a lift home," and he does, and they accept.

Then there's a little commotion on the couch; one girl is holding her stomach, a look of pain on her face. She says she has cramps. Right out loud, just like that. Then she asks if she can lie down. Mr. Appel says sure and takes her into his bedroom. He comes back and sits down again on the couch.

When we leave, quite late, five girls have already called

Harter and had their friends sneak-sign them out for an overnight.

On the way home Allan says, "He's a nice guy, but what do those girls see in him?"

"He's so sexy," Cara says, and we giggle.

Chapter Fourteen

❦

The next day, Sunday, it's not my turn to pick up doughnuts. I can lie in bed, propped up against my special bed-reading pillow with the arms, which I bought myself as a present the week before. Marsha is lying on her bed fast asleep, wearing the present she got herself, a sleep mask. It's violet-colored and clashes with her hair and the blue pajamas and green blanket, but it works, keeps out the light, and saves our relationship. Because Marsha and I may be well matched according to Harter's criteria—we listen to classical music, are Jewish, and didn't care what race or religion roommate we were given; however, Marsha doesn't study, and I do. She prefers to sleep and come in unprepared. I cannot sleep if I'm unprepared. She can't sleep with lights on; I can't study with lights out. The living room is too noisy for study. I have to be back from the library by ten P.M. Marsha gets a sleep mask.

I'm propped up, facing my Gov. textbook with its explana-

tions of The Age of Reason and Our Founding Fathers, two of
my least favorite topics. I look upon our Constitution the way I
do everything else, as an irrational act that occasionally
manages to work. The Age of Reason? The Enlightenment?
How's a person like me supposed to appreciate any of it? Can
it be that most people are so different from me, that they go
through life neither crazed nor scared to death? I find it hard to
believe. However, I force my yellow magic marker through
the pages, underlining important-looking passages, highlight-
ing key words; I have to train my unruly, uncomprehending
brain to absorb this material. For if I am a poli. sci. major, and
haven't I sworn to Mr. Cole that I will be? I had better be
good at this. Then I might even have Mr. Appel in class. I
stare at the yellow line I'm drawing and think of last night, all
those girls surrounding him, the cider with rum. I can't wait
for Marsha to wake up. I cough. I shuffle my notebook around.
I get up to make some coffee. It's eleven A.M., where is that
girl? doesn't she know the words of Solomon, "Look thou O
sluggard to the ant and be wise"? Finally she starts stretching
and moaning, how she hates to get up.

"Good morning!" I say cheerfully. "Coffee's ready."

"Mmmm." She pulls the sleep mask over her forehead.

"Into the air, junior birdmen." I hand her a cup of black
coffee. I don't know how she drinks the stuff; even when it has
milk and sugar it's only bearable. She breathes in the smell and
sips it.

"Where's MY armchair pillow?" she asks.

"Right next to you," I tell her. "Left side."

She leans down and thrusts it behind her and straightens her
spine.

"I'm too tired to pee," she says.

"Pee in bed. Who'll know?"

"Mrs. Hibbard, next bedcheck," she groans. "It better not
be today; I plan to stay in bed all day." She puts her coffee on
her desk and goes to the bathroom without putting on her
slippers. Naturally she's caught, by Frannie, and has to return

for them. She doesn't say a word, slips her feet into the furries, returns to the bathroom, and is back in two minutes.

"For that I needed covered soles." She picks up the coffee again.

"I wonder what Mr. Appel does for sex, social life, and etcetera?" I muse.

"WHAT?" Marsha's eyes open wide. "First of all, what's the etcetera?"

"Oh you know, fun and things."

"And who, pray tell, is Mr. Appel?" Marsha is finally awake.

That's just what I wanted her to ask, so I tell her all about last night.

"He's a *dream!*" I conclude. "He's like a combination of young and old, sort of youthfully mature."

"Yuch," Marsha says. "What do you mean, he's a forty-year-old man who likes teen-age girls?"

"Oh Marsha," I say. "He hates Harter."

"He's not entirely an idiot," she agrees.

"He's extremely intelligent," I say doubtfully. How can I judge intelligence? "Allan says his course is hard work but that everyone tries to get into it, even the nerds."

"Why did Allan take it?" Marsha asks. "I thought he was a math major."

"Probably to meet the Theater Group girls. They ALL take Mr. Appel."

"Oh," Marsha says. "What happened?"

"I guess he met me instead." That seems impossible; could he have mistaken me for one of them? "They seem a lot older than us," I tell Marsha. "Very sophisticated and relaxed. I'd love to be that way. What do you think makes people sophisticated?"

"Fucking," she suggests. "What else is there?"

There's Mr. Appel, I think; the thought pops into my head, and I don't know what it means. I see him tall and bald and hook-nosed, round-shouldered, in baggy pants, a slob, his house with all the books, miles and miles of books, Venetian blinds that he put up himself, poor divorced man, and the spare bedroom for when his three kids visit him. I see the girls, cigarettes, drinks, and my heart starts pounding again, the way it did last night when we were climbing the stairs. *There's something there for me,* I think.

"Could it be just fucking?" I ask.

"What else is there?" Marsha repeats.

Chapter Fifteen

❦

The only good place to drive is far away from Harter; everything around it has been divided up into two-hundred-foot plots with houses and garages on each. These people in Wetton would probably DIE if they had to live in A City, Boston say, or worse, New York; they've probably scrimped and saved for years to escape such a dreadful fate, like my parents. Run from Brooklyn to The Suburbs. Only, is there a law that decrees: what you most fear you eventually build for yourself? Because these suburbs, what are they but cities made of houses instead of apartment buildings? I can't stand to see the hilly streets with the four trees on each side, the tiny little lawns bisected by driveways, the ticky-tacky homes stacked next to each other, the cars parked end to end on the streets or jutting out of garages. There's nothing here to look at.

"So," Allan tells me on our next date, as we head for some real country, "Mr. Appel is having an affair with Lenore."

I recall her, the thin girl with the uneven hair. "You're kidding. He *wouldn't!*"

"Why not? He's divorced."

"How do you know?"

"Lenore told me," Allan says. "Actually she told everyone."

"No fooling? Some nice kid."

"Eh," Allan says. "Everyone else he ever screwed spread it over the campus in half the time it took Lenore. I remember Melissa from two years ago; she told everyone her family wouldn't let her marry him because he was Jewish. And before that Kathy Fitzgerald—was she a knockout!"

Thus I discover what Mr. Appel does for sex, social life, and etcetera.

"Lenore says," Allan continues, "that he buys her little presents and says he loves her."

"No kidding. I wonder if he'll marry her."

"You don't necessarily marry everyone you fall in love with."

"I wonder why not," I say.

Allan laughs. "Would you marry me?"

God no, I think. "Sure," I say. "Would you marry me?"

"Yep," he says. Even I can guess what he's thinking.

We drive on in silence; we're on a back road somewhere in the hills beyond Wetton; we both love to ride around, it soothes us, makes us feel as though we're actually going somewhere.

It's bitter cold; I'm wearing my suede jacket over a heavy sweater. Only in a car am I warm enough in it, and that's because I've *taken out* the woolen lining of the jacket so I won't look so fat in it.

Even the first week in November at Harter is freezing; Boston may be only four hours from New York, but in those four hours the air goes through a giant transformation. Instead of being breathable but cold, it becomes so bitterly freezing that your nose prefers to stop inhaling, you have to force it to work, nostrils ache, tip of nose burns; fingers, no matter how good the gloves or mittens, are killing you as are toes; the Hill is a giant icicle, like the glass tower built for the beautiful princess by her father to keep her safe from men.

Today there's a tart smell in the air, a little acrid, as though smoke from some factories has fused with the air, and you can smell under that fresh winter-cold wind the year-round odor of work and exhaust.

We've been driving along quietly, no other cars on the road, when suddenly behind us we hear the screech of a horn and see a car with three teen-age boys swerving around to pass us. The boys are screaming, "Get off the road, you faggot," as they honk and pass on the left about two inches away from the side of the car.

"You little fucks," I say, but Allan looks at me, pale, his knuckles turning white, gripping the wheel.

"Shut up," he says to me. The boys pass, Allan says nothing, I shut up.

"Well thank God at least for once you listened to me," Allan says after the car disappears in the distance over the next hill.

"What are you angry at me for?"

"You give me the feeling that if I shout Stop to you, you'd just turn around and ask why instead of stopping. Suppose a truck were coming at you," his voice is getting louder and angrier, "and if you move you'll get hit. You have to be able to follow directions sometimes, you know."

"Listen, Allan, I like to know the reason people ask me to do things."

"You drive me crazy. All I want is a nice, docile woman who looks up to me, and what have I got?" He looks at me with real disgust. "You."

"Take me home," I yell.

Perhaps you think this is one of the many times we break up, but it's not. For our idiosyncrasy is: we never break up with each other except by letter or by phone, because if we're sitting next to each other long enough, no matter what the fight, we're going to end up petting. It's something neither of us can help. So we yell a lot and finally park on a deserted road.

Afterward, driving back to school, Allan says, "You know,

· 151 ·

it's funny, I keep saying I want docile girls, but my last girlfriend was just like you."

"How awful," I say.

"She was the one who got the stomach cramps at the party."

"You didn't tell me you had any former girlfriends at that party."

"I knew it would upset you," he said.

"So why are you telling me now?"

"I just felt like talking about a crappy thing she did to me, when I started dating you and breaking up with her. She had a hysterical pregnancy."

"What?" I ask. Some new horror I've never heard of?

"Her belly blew up and her period was late, and she had about as much chance of being pregnant as I do, that's how careful I was. The stupid bitch."

"Good grief," I say. "The poor girl was probably at her wit's end."

"Christ," he says, "any tack to hold on."

"What did you do?" I feel sorry for the girl. Listen, couldn't it be *me?*

"I told her to go home, that she wasn't pregnant and that she damn well knew it."

"Well, she doesn't sound like me at all. If I were her I'd be there with a gun. Or my father. She sounds unpleasantly docile."

Allan says, "There's no such thing as a docile woman; she was quieter than you, but with a grip of iron."

I'm thinking: this is what you do with girls who love you? So I discovered that the best way to deal with him was to love someone else. Then he was fabulous. I believe this is what *Cosmopolitan* magazine calls playing it cool. Which is the same advice my other favorite Reuben, Dr. David, the Jacqueline Susann of psychiatry, gives to women who want to get married. From this I deduce that they are all as crazy as Allan.

"Anyway," Allan says, "she wasn't pregnant. After I told her to go home and not bother me, her period came. She called to say so."

Chapter Sixteen

Compulsory chapel has occurred on the first Tuesday of every week since the beginning of school; on that day at one P.M. all freshmen except those in the infirmary or with a doctor's excuse are required to present their bodies to the church. There we sit in alphabetical order. The very first chapel we had to line up outside the door, all Harter freshmen, with alphabetical lists in our hands and total disbelief in our eyes. We had to line up in order, with people saying, "I'm Deller, are you Danielson?" and so forth. It took nearly the whole hour, so it was better than the chapels where we actually have to sit still and listen to someone; that day we got to stand in the nice fresh autumn air, brisk but not yet too cold, with leaves falling and piles burning in the distance. Then we marched inside and were assigned, each row, our own pew, and there we were to be one Tuesday a week, or God only knows what would happen. Probably you got a late-night taken away; that was the standard punishment for everything but murder on the Harter campus.

After the first Tuesday we're subjected to lectures on the meaning of life, the meaning of college, the meaning of college life, and so forth. To say that the speakers were dull is to admit that they were alive, and I was never sure. The only good thing about chapel is that you can sleep through it. As a matter of fact, chapel is in many ways good practice for class; after you've mastered the art of sleeping in one, you're sure to go on and experiment with the other.

This particular Tuesday, the second in November, I weave in to my pew and snuggle down for a little snooze, when I'm awakened by a youngish voice, a familiar one. It's Mr. Appel. Up there in front of five hundred people, and he's talking about the new politics, the involvement of the young in social issues, the need for new idealistic blood to be pumped into our old corrupt institutions. It sounds wonderful, I think, except he should only have to live in a dorm with the young blood. It makes me feel I'd take my chances with the doddering and corrupt. But he is exciting to listen to, this man—what power there is in that voice, what magnetism in the flow of words, the surge of feeling. Talk about rhetoric, he is a marvel at it.

His final words, and the whole speech has taken only half an hour, are: "I believe that there should be no compulsory chapel in the program of a liberal education." I don't know exactly how this fits in with the new politics, but believe me, it doesn't matter. He gets a standing ovation. That man is a genius at winning people over.

Chapter Seventeen

❧

"Here we are, practicing to be normal," Marsha snarls, the next Saturday afternoon, when the four of us march out of the dorms, with nearly everyone else, and head toward the football field. It's Homecoming Week and the crowd today should only be immediately photographed by *Mademoiselle* as it rushes toward the football field; everyone is decorated in the most highly recommended fashion: knee socks (colored), dark plaid skirts (mid-knee), extremely bright scarves (knitted during a fun dorm meeting), bulky jackets, white teeth, shiny set hair, bouffant and teased, loafers on the feet, and underneath the jackets, Shetland sweaters. Hopefully we'll be mistaken for cheerleaders.

V-i-c-t-o-r-y.

Of the four of us, only Marsha's hair is not teased, there isn't enough of it to tease. Even so, we fit right in, and if Marsha would quit snarling how she wishes she were with Robert, our experiment might have a fighting chance of success. We want to find out what we've been missing.

At the gate to the field are vendors from the fraternity houses, with little elephants (stuffed), pennants, popcorn, streamers, confetti, balloons.

Marsha says, "This far I can't go."

Rona, Jo, and I debate for a moment what's required of us, and decide, nothing. The tickets cost $4.50 apiece, with our student card yet. We walk inside the gate, hearing Marsha mutter, "I'd like to buy fifty of those pennants and stick them up . . ." but then she fades off and we can't hear her, the roar of the crowd drowns out her anger. People are scrambling up the wooden bleachers, the sun beats down, but the wind is cold, all sorts of strange-looking older men are sitting on the fifty-yard line, taking deep sips from little pocket flasks; as a matter of fact, all sorts of younger men seem to have the same flasks—are we here to see a football game or is this a meeting for A.A. dropouts?

"You know how goyim drink," Jo sighs. She has come reluctantly too. Are premed students likely to be here?

We climb to the middle of the stands. Rona leads—her twenty-twenty vision has spotted five big, attractive men who are wearing bulky sweaters and slacks, no jackets, but to compensate are passing back and forth the familiar-looking silver flask we've seen glinting on both sides of the field. We sit in front of them.

"Want a drink?" one asks Marsha, who's in the middle of us.

She shakes her head, no, makes no smartass observations, for I've dug an elbow into her side, signifying that these boys are part of our experiment too, they're reeking of normalcy and enjoyment. AND there are five of them and only four of us; one of them will HAVE to take me. Besides, I have on my prescription sunglasses; with my face half hidden I always feel infinitely more attractive. I look around as far along the rows as possible; maybe some faculty members are here. Maybe even

. . . but no, I wipe that thought from my mind, not him. He wouldn't come to something this foolish.

"Who're ya lookin' for?" the white sweater behind me asks.

At this moment, the kick-off, everyone rises on both sides of the field, there's a roar as someone (their team? our team? who knows?) catches it and begins running. Six female and one male cheerleader are up screaming "Let's go, HARTUH! Let's go, HARTUH!" The boys behind us are roaring, Rona's yelling, Jo is saying it, and Marsha is absolutely quiet. And me, I'm thinking, where are they going? We sit down again, so I see, they're going north, until the tackle, loud moan from our side of the field, and then relative calm and quiet.

I look back at the boy in the white sweater just as he's lifting the flask to his lips. I receive another one of my moments of spiritual illumination; there's no way that an overweight owl like me can go out with him, a regular Harter man. I can't experiment with being normal until I'm thin. And at that moment, staring at him, hearing the cheerleaders start up again, the noise begin, I vow to call Mrs. Green, get the prescription, and go on a diet.

"Who were you looking for?" the boy repeats.

There's a moment of silence on the field and in the stands.

"My lover," I say, facing his direction long enough to see his mouth drop open.

"Hooray," Marsha says. "NOW can we get out of here?"

I nod my head. Rona and Jo signify that they'll stay for a while; Marsha and I link arms and annoy at least fifty people during a Very Important Play on our way out.

We walk away from the field up the road to the Hill to our dorm, and I wonder, will I be like Marsha when I'm thin? I mean now I'm me, bored at football games because I'm fat; will I be the same way thin? On the road with the nearly bare trees on each side a car passes us, a black Volkswagen, and in it I think I see Mr. Appel. My heart goes bump (thank God I'm not my uncle's child, I'd probably check into a hospital with a coronary), the car whizzes by; I try to think about the blond boy in the white sweater, but I can't. The face staring at me through the trees in my mind is Mr. Appel's.

We walk silently up the Hill, interrupted only once by our names being called; we turn around and see Rona flying after us.

"I couldn't stand it either," she confesses.

"Where's Jo?" Marsha and I ask in unison.

"Sitting next to a boy from ZBT."

Rona comes into our room and sits on my bed while Marsha puts a record on the hi-fi. No one is in the dorm, so we turn it up loud, an all-Chopin record beginning with the piece that sounds like "I'm Always Chasing Rainbows" with the wrong ending tacked on.

"Robert says he's still waiting for me," Marsha tells us when that piece is over and another one beginning.

"What waiting?" I ask. "You see him nearly every weekend."

"To marry me. Do you think he's after my money?" She bangs the bed with her foot. "My God, I hate to be in school, and how will I know that some other jerk isn't after my money, answer me that? If I can't tell with Robert, how am I going to tell with anyone else?"

"You won't," Rona says reasonably. "Just marry who you please and hope for the best."

Marsha gets out of bed and walks to the desk, where her books are piled. "There must be a reason for this, but I don't know what it is. How is being an English major going to help me?"

"Maybe that's our mistake," I say, "that we want to be helped. Maybe if we didn't expect anything from college, we'd enjoy it more."

"I want college to make me happy!" Marsha shouts. "Which I used to be. Or to tell me how to know whether I should marry Robert. I already know ALL I want to know about Julius Caesar, and there's not a tiny chance that he'll propose." Her short blond hair glints in the sunlight that comes through the one window, even her hair looks fierily angry, and she bites her bottom lip—around here, what else can you do with your anger except bite yourself?

"Take Physics," Rona says, "at least there are lots of men in the course; that's the best thing about math and science. I'd like to meet a nice Jewish guy and have a good time." She looks at me. "What about you?"

"I want to be thin and beautiful, and then I want more than some nice guy. I want Love."

"Ah, love," Marsha bites into a Pepperidge Farm plain. "I wonder if there is such a thing."

"You love Bob, don't you?" I ask.

"I don't know," she says. "First I was twittery, if that's what you mean, because he's good-looking and a terrific make-out. Now I'm so comfortable with him it's hard to date anyone else. Is that love?"

I think, no. Not for me. Love is an ocean wave knocking you down and an undertow dragging you where you normally wouldn't go. It's when your whole soul belongs to someone else. When all you do, day and night, is to look for that person.

"Anyway, good luck," Marsha says.

"I'm going to call your mother for the diet-pill prescription," I tell her. Maybe that'll be all the luck I need.

Chapter Eighteen

🌷

The prescription comes special delivery Monday morning. All day Sunday I diet and on Biff's scale I weigh one hundred and sixty pounds. I need to lose thirty-five pounds. I take the prescription down to the drugstore in Wetton and get it filled, one hundred huge black capsules, bigger than any pills I've ever seen. They look powerful. As a matter of fact, they look deadly. They cost me $18.95. With tax. From Monday to Wednesday I eat *nothing*. As a result when I go home Wednesday late afternoon for Thanksgiving vacation I've taken off five pounds, my face has narrowed, and with my body girdled up my mother has nothing to complain about. My midyear grades are excellent, I also have a boyfriend who calls me on Thanksgiving eve; I tell them his name is Allan Rabinowitz.

Best of all, as we sit down to Thanksgiving dinner, after Dad has boruched us to tears, I, thanks to the lovely black pill, pick at the turkey and have no stuffing. My mother is delighted.

"Tell us about college," Dad says.

I look at Danny and Lisa, how much I hate Harter they already know from letters. I cast about wildly in my mind for something I can say that's pleasant and not entirely a lie. "Allan took me to a party at a teacher's house. He was so nice. Really liberal and interesting, you should've seen all the books he has."

"Allan, dear?" Mom asks.

"No, no. This teacher. Mr. Appel." Suddenly I'm overcome with the feeling that I want to talk about Mr. Appel, say how he makes me feel, describe him, share him. Just talk talk talk about him.

"How old is he?" Mom asks.

"I don't know. Late thirties maybe." Actually I looked up when he got his Ph.D., and figuring that he was in SP all the way from first grade on *and* did his Ph.D. in three years, I can whittle his age down to thirty-nine.

"Married?"

"Divorced." I try to sound nonchalant; this mother of mine is a regular homing pigeon for trouble.

Mom gives me a long, severe look, her specialty.

"Oh, MA," I say, "he's a teacher."

"Hannah," Dad tells her, "don't be foolish." Being a rabbi for so long, so out of touch with any part of reality, thank God, he misses everything of importance.

"You know, he's the only Jewish teacher I've seen at Harter."

My father nods his head approvingly and looks at my mother with one of his don't-make-me-crazy-with-your-silly-female-fears gazes, and says, "Perhaps we should have the A.D.L. look into this."

"Good idea!" I say.

Danny chokes on a piece of turkey, then quickly swallows it and smiles.

We beam at one another, and I think, perhaps now is the right moment.

"Dad," I begin, "I've been thinking about this for a long time." (Six days, at the outside. Lisa leans forward, I've already told her and she is Very Interested; this idea applies to her too.) "Could I get contact lenses?"

There's a moment's pause, I see he could go either way, ranting and raving about how I can never leave well enough alone, or indecision.

"Look!" I whip off my glasses. "I'd be so gorgeous without them, Harter'd elect me Homecoming Queen!" I flash him a big smile; listen, if I thought it'd work I'd sing *Hatikvah* and dance at the same time.

My father, who responds better to flirting than anything else, says, "We'll talk to your uncle about it."

"Moses," Mom says. "The expense." How that woman wants me to be pretty; it's touching, really. Listen, how do you think I got fat in the first place? Whose food was I eating at age seven, if you please?

"I didn't say yes, Hannah. I said we'll see."

I rush over to my father and hug him.

"Now remember," he says, "I didn't say yes *yet*."

I smile and push food around on my plate, and tell stories about geology field trips, all the while with an eye on the clock. At eight thirty Uncle Charles, wife Dowdy, and brood of hypochondriacs arrive for dessert—sherbet and fruit, naturally, so none of them should die right there and then on my mother's nice gray wall-to-wall carpet.

I spend the first half hour of their visit sitting on Dad's knee, he loves that, then help Mom serve dessert; in short, I play the part of A Darling Girl. After coffee and the dispersal of the brood to the TV set, bad for their eyes, they can only watch it half an hour a day, except Sundays and holidays, Dad says, "So Charlie, what do you think of contact lenses?"

I have a momentary impulse to run and perch on my uncle's knee, but I don't think it would work with him. The Scientific

Mind, more detached than the Religious One. I look at them sitting next to each other on the couch, the Brothers Healing, Body and Soul, and think, "My life is in their hands?" I put a fingernail into my mouth and bite it. The Fabrikant brothers look like two editions of the same person; the Rabbi, older, heavier, grayer, with a tendency to cast his eyes heavenward and translate from the Hebrew, how that man can preface things with Hebrew phrases; and the Doctor, trim to the point of boniness, taut, he's so on edge he makes my father look relaxed, and when he speaks, he fixes his eye on you as though he's an x-ray machine, and prefaces everything with a long Latin diagnosis. With my family, it's amazing I'm not a language major. In fact, for a while my ambition was to be a translator at the U.N., only my training in Hebrew and Latin, where would it get me: a mission from Ben-Gurion to the Pope?

"Uncle Charlie," I say, "I've gone on a good diet."

"Oh?" he says. "What are you eating?"

"Just cutting down," I say modestly. For I already know from him that there isn't a doctor who breathes who thinks there's any plausible diet except the sane and rational Cutting Down. "Now that I'm getting thin, I want contact lenses."

My uncle, who has a lurking respect for me and my good grades anyway, says, "Excellent. I have patients twice your age who can't go on a diet."

Listen, Charlie, I want to say, give 'em Dexedrine sometime, maybe they'll have more luck.

"As a matter of fact, I've been reading up on contact lenses," he manages to tear himself away from his favorite subject, his rotten patients, "and I think if they're fitted by a good ophthalmologist and you keep them clean, there's nothing to worry about."

"Hooray," I yell. Lisa, who's been sitting quietly on the sofa next to Dad watching my maneuvers, and taking mental notes I hope, also cheers.

Meanwhile Uncle Charlie is going on to his Latin descriptions of the cornea and God knows what else, no doubt any and every eye disease that he remembers from med school. I run over and hug him, maybe THAT will shut him up, then I hug my father. Soon they're talking about the medical history of the Jews, the only subject both are experts in at once, and I'm safe.

On my way to bed that evening Danny corners me and says, "No wonder I can never get my way. I can't go around hugging and kissing everything in sight."

"You'll just have to slug him, I guess."

"Slug him and run," Danny says mournfully. "Only who can hide from the eye of God, don't I remember that from one of His Holiness's sermons?" He stands at the top of the stairs, towering over me in his striped pajamas, just like Dad's, his hair unruly, a lock keeps falling over his eye. "I'm doing lousy in history again, I hate school so much, all I want to do is play basketball." He sighs. "You know of any med schools that give basketball scholarships?"

I shake my head.

"Listen," he says, "if you find a way out of this mess," he gestures toward the living room where Mom and Dad are sitting, having an early nightcap, good for Dad's heart, "take me with you. Please?"

"Oh Danny, poor Danny," I whisper. "I'll try." What can I tell him? The way out for me looks like the homely face of a forty-year-old professor of political science; he's the first exit I've ever caught a glimpse of. I'm going to be a beautiful and thin woman: absolute guarantees that I'll be saved.

"Promise?" Danny asks.

"Promise," I say.

Chapter Nineteen

❧

I'm allowed to get a pair of contact lenses only after my uncle
has done extensive research, and has located the world's most
careful and squeamish ophthalmologist, Dr. Qualer, practicing
right here in Boston, one hour and fifteen minutes by MTA
from Harter, fifteen minutes away by car.

Dr. Qualer's opening remarks are, "Contact lenses are
uncomfortable, difficult to wear, and if not kept perfectly clean
can lead to painful infections of the cornea."

Sure, sure, sure, Dr. Qualer, I say, gimme de lenses, gimme
de lenses.

"You'll have to practice wearing them, and for the first
week only *I* will place them in your eyes."

Yes, sir, Dr. Qualer. I'd let him walk right into my eyes if
that would help, I'd just grit my teeth and clench my hands,
but contact lenses I'm going to have.

"These little things," Dr. Qualer is holding two tiny pieces of round glass on his finger, "are a scientific miracle." By this I know he means that his practice has trebled since they've been on the market.

He places them into my eyes, and they are murder; then I get more used to them and they're only crippling, not killing. I see I'll never be able to read or think in them, but since I do little of either, who cares? My eyeballs feel like they're popping out, the lids are obviously being sawed through by sharp bits of glass. I don't care.

I walk over to a mirror; this is the first time since third grade I've seen myself without glasses. And there, ladies and gentlemen, there in the mirror is, really, the scientific miracle. I see a potential beauty staring back at me.

I'm not kidding, and I've never looked like anything to myself, but now I see, my God, what big blue eyes! (heightened by the fact that the lenses are tinted light blue, Dr. Qualer strongly recommends tinting). My eyes are beautiful, my eyebrows, I've never seen them before, are lovely, but do need plucking. Why didn't my mother teach me? No, my uncle had not told them that tweezing causes cancer, although why not I don't know; the fact is my mother tweezed her eyebrows once or twice when she was quite young, and the hair never grew back again. She didn't need glasses till she was forty either, and she still only needs them to read.

So you see, I was doomed from the very start.

However, to get back to my salvation, two tiny little pieces of glass that when stuck on the eyeball cause tears, pain, thickening of the upper lid, total torment if dust gets in the eye—when not causing pain they enable you to see better than with glasses, clearer, brighter; but even more important (because I'm not a big one for seeing) they cause you to look ninety percent better than you ever did before.

When I was in third grade I used to pray for: 1. world peace, and 2. an operation to cure my eyes. Miracles. You can imagine how I felt when the second came to pass. I knew that for me this was the start of a new life.

Chapter Twenty

❧

Considering who I am, it would make sense not to worry about a "new life" but rather be grateful that the old one didn't end in suicide. Unfortunately, people like me are never suicidal. I say that with real regret, for even suicide is more mature than eating. It's also a lot more interesting to be *really* self-destructive—an alcoholic or a drug addict—than to need a shot of chocolate nut fudge brownie to get through the day. Where's the glamour in dying of an overdose of peanut butter and jelly? I plan to remedy that situation someday. Meanwhile, I'm on a diet.

The first morning back at school I take a pill and I wake up with a zing—and my appetite? Nonexistent. I have half an apple for breakfast and a cup of tea with lemon and saccharine. I'm full. Lunchtime I go to the student union and have half a container of prune-whip yogurt. Dinner is a piece of lean, gray meat, it could be beef or veal or lamb or horsemeat, we never know, plus a few vegetables, weak tea and lemon. I'm stuffed. The next day all I have from dawn till dusk are two apples and diet soda.

Then I make the discovery of a lifetime: I find out that with these pills I only need to chew, I don't care about swallowing. The third day I buy two packs of Double Bubble gum and two packs of Juicy Fruit. That's all I have for food. I feel great. At the end of the first week I weigh one hundred and fifty pounds and I look wonderful. Every so often I have a meal, just to stay alive, but most of the time I'm strictly a Double Bubble addict. I make Rona, Jo, and Marsha buy packs of bubble gum wherever they go when the Wetton drugstore runs out of it (which is in two weeks, the way I eat it), while I rush to Newberry, the other nearby town, to stock up. Occasionally I trek all the way in to Cambridge for the sake of the gum, because without it I take food into my mouth.

Can you imagine the looks I'm getting as I scour the Boston area for big supplies of Double Bubble? Do you know what drugstore ladies look like when you're placing on the counter twenty-five long tubes of bubble gum? I go through those weeks with a permanent blush on my face.

Even Marsha is starting to give me strange looks as I lie in bed studying, chewing five wads of gum at once. She says it's the most disgusting thing she's ever seen and she wishes I'd go back to food. But then I leap out of bed and stand in front of her in pants and bra, profile view, and smack my stomach and say, see? Thin!

Marsha says, "Your body may be getting thin, but your mouth is getting strangely fat. Look how it puffs out—even the jaws are increasing in size."

"You're just jealous."

"Do you know what it's like to study in here with you bubbling and blowing and cracking that damn gum?" she asks.

"Put on some music," I answer, and she does, but then she complains that it sounds like Beethoven's Sixth suddenly has percussion accompaniment.

So I switch for a while to Life Savers, but I eat too many of them, and chewing is what I need to do, sucking does not have that *je ne sais quoi* I need to survive. Besides, Life Savers are too fattening; they're too close to food, which is the one thing I don't need on a diet. Food is what did me in in the first place, and I'm getting even with it.

Marsha in her own way gets even with me too. She writes a fan letter to the Double Bubble company and asks them if it's possible to order their gum directly from them. Then she signs MY name. For the entire year I'm in touch with some branch manager of Double Bubble interested in finding out if I wish to order by the truckload, and if so, how often to make deliveries. Double Bubble may think a new trend is starting here in Wetton, Mass., for their sales have doubtless quadrupled in the last few weeks.

Don't think I wouldn't have ordered it direct either, and maybe even by the truckload, except where would I store it? That's the insoluble problem. Our room is not big enough. Meanwhile I practically need a job to afford my new habit. I can go through fifteen packs a day without blinking an eye. Sometimes twenty. By bedtime my jaws ache, and I have to take an aspirin to ease the pain. So here, ladies and gentlemen with a weight problem, the miracle diet that actually works. Throw away your Irwin Stillman, forget about Dr. Rubin's boiled chicken, and don't bother with Weight Watchers. Just have gum, coffee, tea, diet soda, Life Savers, occasionally an egg and salad, drinks on all dates, and every evening one or two aspirins before bed. I'm sorry I still don't know the name of that wonderful big black, powerful pill; I finally threw it away when I stopped being able to sleep altogether. Lack of sleep is another good dietary aid, by the way, only not for forever.

Chapter Twenty-one

❧

As a surprise, I don't let Allan see me the whole first week of December; I spend all my spare time with Dr. Qualer. When Dr. Qualer puts in the lenses he presses up close to me with his extremely fat body. Does he need to lean against my breasts this way? Just to put in a contact lens?

I think he's testing me for breast cancer as a sideline, and I wonder if he charges extra for this service. His belly against my boobs makes me want to scream; luckily my mouth is too busy with gum, the vocal cords are buried under a mound of Double Bubble. I chew gum on the bus and subway into Boston and on the way back every afternoon (except Monday) for a week, and by Saturday night, another five pounds off, I'm ready. Rona is so excited she paints my eyes extra well. Then I put the lenses in, blink, tear, open, ah, bearable. Cover pimples, comb out hair, put on skirt and warm bulky sweater, eighteen degrees out there, walk to bathroom, look at myself in long mirror. Ah. Bearable.

When my buzzer rings, I practically dance out to meet Allan, boots, jacket, and all.

"Hi!" I force my eyes wide open.

He squints through his glasses as I throw my arms around him and kiss him on the cheek. Which I know he hates. He hates holding hands too—is it for the reason he says, that his Old New England parents brought him up to detest "public displays of affection"? Or is it that he's ashamed of liking me? Naturally I lean toward the second explanation.

He unwraps my arms and leads me out the door to the car.

"So? So?" I ask when he's gotten in and shut the door. "You like? Baby blue contacts!"

"Who're you doing this for?" he wants to know. "Certainly not for me!" Another homing pigeon, like my mother.

"Why not for you?"

"I don't believe in character change in such a short time," he tells me, the creep. "You never do *anything* for me."

"What am I supposed to do?" My lenses are killing me. Even if they're not for him, can't he at least enjoy them? God knows *I'm* not.

"Sleep with me." I've heard this now three thousand nine hundred and ninety-nine times.

"Allan, you know I can't." I'm saving it for my True Love. No false loves allowed; no Tampax, no ersatz cocks. I want the real true thing.

"You've lost weight," he accuses me.

"Yeah."

"Why?" he demands again.

"Why not?" I say.

He starts the car and drives through Wetton toward Boston. "You look better in glasses," he says after a while.

"Goy," I mutter under my breath.

"I'm going out with Doris again," he says. He must not have heard me.

"That's nice." I feel calm; why should I care? I don't love him.

"At least she fucks," he points out.

"What can you expect from a shiksa?" This time, believe me, loud enough.

"Don't be a reverse racist, you big-mouth, overweight Jewess!" he yells. Just what my parents told me, your first fight, and his Nazi tendencies will leap to the surface.

Meanwhile I notice he's turning around, driving back toward Harter. Taking me home? I don't care and don't say anything, just watch the snow-covered streets and little boxy houses roll by. In a way I feel sorry for him, I feel like saying to him: "You don't hate me nearly as much as you'd like to." Even *I* can see this, even with the lousy, painful contact lenses.

"You make me crazy!" he screams. Then he drives back to his dorm, opens the car door on my side, polite—well-bred to the end. I follow him upstairs to his room, allow him to take off all my clothes except underpants, and we neck and pet, and I come, twice. Look, he's not the only crazy one here.

On the way back to Bailey I make up my mind, orgasms or no, it's enough. The End.

"Good-bye, Allan," I say in the car. He always refuses to walk me up the seven steps to Bailey through the couple-maze. Usually his refusal makes us part fighting, but tonight I lean over and kiss his cheek. After all, it's farewell forever. "Tell Doris I hope her belly stays flat this time."

Allan laughs. Sure, a man who finally appreciates my most excellent points: my glasses, my fat, my hostility.

"It could be you," he says.

"Not with the diet I'm on. I *definitely* want a flat belly." Yes and my pearl intact too, waiting for the diver-prince to take it from me in a ceremony so magnificent that it'll dissolve and I'll dissolve in perfect bliss.

"My God," he looks at me, "I wonder if you can do it. Go from fat to thin. And who's it for? Some football star? Some Harry Handsome?"

"I'll give you a clue." I open the door, get out, bend over and scream, top voice, into the open window: "HE'S JEW-ISH!"

The entire crew of glued-together couples unglue to watch me run up the stairs in the dorm.

That night I have a terrible nightmare, so bad that I wake Marsha with my crying. At four A.M. she turns on the light and shakes me awake. She asks what's wrong, so I tell her the dream: I'm in a strange house, where it is I don't know. I'm upstairs and I kill someone by accident. A man. I don't know how. Then I steal some candy from his room and run away, terribly afraid. Then suddenly I'm in our room in the dorm and Allan appears in the hall. He's still my boyfriend but he's sleeping with Rona, and they're both laughing at me. I yell for Allan, but he won't come because I'm not sleeping with him. I need a Kleenex (guess where this comes from), so I go upstairs to look for some, and I run into Rona and Allan. They're holding hands, laughing, and looking for a record with "Climb Ev'ry Mountain" on it.

At the end of this recital, Marsha says, "Relax, kiddo, Allan's not sleeping with Rona."

"Yeah," I say, "but he's sleeping with Doris. He told me he is, that he can't hold out forever."

"Do you want to sleep with him?" she asks.

"I can't, so I broke up with him."

She nods her head. Dream, shmeam, this she understands. "You can't do what you can't do," she philosophizes. "Try not to feel so bad." She pats my rollers and says, "No wonder you have nightmares with these things on your head," turns out the light, and wishes me a better night.

Chapter Twenty-two

❦

Right before Christmas vacation we are allowed to request course changes. *Request* and *required*, the two most popular words on this campus. I make an appointment with Professor Harris. Naturally, that day we're in the middle of a blizzard. I have to start out half an hour early to ford the Hill. Marsha makes me drape a scarf across my nose and mouth and wear her big furry hat; I'm afraid she's going to drop hot bricks into my pocket.

"If I'm not back in two hours send a Saint Bernard." I spit four wads of gum into the trash can near my desk.

"Why can't you phone him?" Marsha asks.

"I've got to make the appeal in person," I mutter through the lousy-tasting scarf. "*Au revoir.* Good luck with your studying."

"*Merci et la même à vous,*" Marsha answers.

"You're supposed to *tutoyer* me," I point out.

"Yeah, but I never know when to use *tu* or *toi*, I'm better off with *vous*."

"That sounds like the beginning of a popular song, 'I'm better off with *vous, mon choux . . . ,*'" I improvise on my way out.

"Hey, what's *choux?*" Marsha shouts as I shut the door.

"'Cabbage,'" I yell back.

Frannie passes, looking glum. No doubt Warren hasn't called again. "Shut UP!" she says.

"*Ah, oui, mon choux,*" Marsha yells through the door.

Luckily the scarf muffles my laugh.

I walk through the foyer, open the door, and a blast of wind nearly shuts it in my face. I heave it open, bend down to give the wind less surface to play over, hold onto the railing, and slide down the seven steps. Head first into the wind I go, along the sidewalk down Professors' Row, across the big intersection over to the Hill side, till I hit the stairs. The eight Harter World War I plaques are covered by a layer of hard-packed, slippery snow. Soon they may have to erect another monument: to those students who, on their way to classes and conferences, fell and broke their necks in pursuit of their ideals. All the way up, pulling hand over hand, I invent small plaques: A memorial railing in honor of Barbara Fabrikant, who lost her grip and plunged the length of the Hill. An Honorary Barbara Fabrikant Chair Lift for those students who came to Harter standing on two feet and left as paraplegics.

Finally I get to the top, to where two buildings are joined by a bridge; it shelters me from the driving snow, and I stand and catch my breath.

Then I set off across the quadrangle, grab trees for support, and by the time my lungs are frozen from breathing the icy air through the scarf, I've made it to Parsons Hall. Inside the warm building my toes and fingers tingle, my face smarts, my hair is wet under the hat. It's too late to do anything about it; I run to the second floor.

Dr. Harris opens his door. "Barbara," he says, "why didn't you cancel the appointment? My other students did."

"I wanted to talk to you." The words are half articulate through stiff, cold lips.

"Come on, sit down. I'll make you coffee." He pulls an electric coffeepot from his desk. "Illegal," he says and plugs it in. From the same drawer emerges a bag of chocolate chip cookies, which for him SHOULD be illegal with those flabby arms, huge ass, that belly.

My hands are so numb they can hardly hold the spoon; I warm the right one over the steaming cup, then sip the coffee—which for the first time tastes good. I think: maybe I'm finally growing up.

"Dr. Harris," I say when my lips thaw, "why do I have to take the second semester of Intro. Gov. with Jamieson? He's awful—can't I skip to a more advanced course?"

"Professor Jamieson is a good solid teacher," he tells me.

I interrupt him before he goes any further (where is this chutzpa coming from? another study?), "ALL my teachers are solid and ALL my courses next semester are introductions. Intro. Lit., Intro. Soc., Intro. Geology, Intro. Gov., except French, which I detest anyway."

"Is it all that bad?"

"You're the only one who's relaxed enough to run a class," I tell him. "The rest of them, why don't they TAPE their damned lectures, why do they even pretend to *need* us there? Is this what college is about? I have to put on a skirt and stockings to sit and take notes, memorize EVERYthing, splurt it back on exams, is this IT?"

A guilty look crosses his face; a nice guy like him, how can he help knowing I've got a point?

After a long pause he says, "You're one of my best students. I'll talk to the Dean and see if we can't waive second-semester Gov. Now if it's possible, what would you like in its place?"

I take a deep breath. "Mr. Appel's course on minorities. Oh, Dr. Harris, you're terrific."

"Wait, wait," he says, but with a smile. "You've chosen the hardest one to get into, it's an upper-class seminar, don't you know how many *seniors* didn't make it?"

I shake my head.

Dr. Harris drums his finger on the desk and gazes at me. I hope I look smart and sweet or forlorn and Jewish; whatever he's looking for I hope is there.

"All right," he says. "I'll do my best. Henry is an excellent teacher, and his courses are usually lively. Now, I want you to wait here till the storm dies down. You have the text with you? No? Okay, I'll lend you mine."

I take it and open the book to the chapter "Trial by Jury: What We Inherit from England," but all that appears on the page, stare though I do, is the word "Henry." Henry, Henry, Henry.

Chapter Twenty-three

❦

" 'Love is a many-splendored thing,' " I sing while packing to go home for Christmas "vacation." Harter celebrates ITS holiday by piling on work, God forbid any of us should be like the lilies of the field—one of the two and one-half good things Jesus said, and who listens to it?

Marsha complains, "That song makes no sense at all. No love songs make any sense."

"They're not supposed to," I tell her. Ever since I got into Mr. Appel's course we've been arguing.

"Don't be in love with him," she pleads. "How can you be in love with someone you can't call by his first name?"

"Love isn't like a faucet, you can't turn it off so easily." I'm becoming positively prophetic.

"You're not even trying!"

"How am I supposed to try?" This isn't a sincere question. Nothing could induce me to give this up, it's too wonderful, a cloud of happiness, a turtle shell of pleasure—it makes me thin, unafraid of home, unafraid of Harter. The world is transformed, believe me, from a place of misery to one of ecstasy.

"First of all, you might ask yourself what kind of man fucks girls half his age? Who are his students yet?"

"A lonely man who hasn't found the right girl," I answer.

"Not from lack of *trying*, I have to hand him THAT!" Marsha says.

"Not EVERYbody sticks like a burr to their first love!" I yell.

"I don't mean to insult him," she tries again in a softer tone, "but think what it means to marry someone twenty years older than you. When you're thirty, he'll be fifty."

"So?"

"It's unnatural! When you're forty, he'll be sixty! He probably won't want to fuck more than once a month."

"So?" Listen, I could tell her, I myself *never* want to fuck. Once a *year* will be plenty for me. Petting is so much fun, why does *anyone* go on to fucking? Even the thought of it scares me half to death, a knife at my crotch tearing through. For him I'll grit my teeth and bear it, so great a love have I. I hum again as I pack my books—I'm taking home more books than clothes. If I've been a good student before, think of the incentive now; I plan to *gleam* with brains for Mr. Appel.

"Can you picture bringing him home to your parents?" Marsha demands. "Isn't he your father's age?"

"Dad's fifty."

"Forgive me, old enough to be Mr. Appel's . . ."

"Don't say it!" I yell. "Look, I don't plan to tell them anything." No, as I see it, one day I and Mr. Appel (hopefully I'll call him Henry by that time) will saunter in married, and by then I won't give a damn what they say. I'll have HIM!

"I thought you decided you didn't want to get married," Marsha says.

"That was before Mr. Appel. His apartment needs cleaning, he needs someone to work for him." I throw into the suitcase my pamphlet on the Trobriand Islanders. "I want to be his mate."

"Jesus Christ," Marsha moans, "you can barely make your own bed. And you HATE to vacuum; if you're so hot to be a little homemaker, why don't you practice HERE, right HERE in this sty!"

"You don't understand," I say. "I can't do it except for him." The truth is—I look at myself in the mirror, girdleless, ladies and gentlemen, twenty pounds lighter, nothing is bulging, and I'm finally comfortable in these damned wired bras—the truth is, I can't do any of this except for him. This thin body—listen, have I ever been able to diet before? "Look, aren't I even flying? Disobeying my parents? Do you think it's for ME? No, I don't want to be a fear-ridden nut for HIM!" I finish yelling.

Marsha comes over and sits down on my bed and puts an arm around my shoulder. "You poor kid," she says, and I burst into tears.

"Am I afraid of that plane," I cry.

"Rona and Jo are going with you," she says.

"Do they keep the plane afloat?"

Marsha pats my shoulder. "You know what you need? A drink. What time are you leaving for the airport?" She looks at her watch.

"Four thirty. We're making a six o'clock plane."

She gets up and walks to the closet. "It's only one thirty, plenty of time for me to buy a bottle of Scotch."

"How many calories are in a glass?" I want to know. "Oh, anyway, you won't be able to buy it, you're not twenty-one."

"I have an old face," Marsha says, bundling up. "I only hope I don't drop the bottle in the living room on Mrs. Hibbard's toes."

She waves good-bye and walks out the door, leaving me to my half-filled suitcase and fears. I told my parents I'd take the train in to Grand Central and then a bus from the Port Authority. But Jo's parents, on the million to one chance that the plane makes it, are meeting us at the airport and driving me to Port Authority. I've already called the *Herald-Traveler* (with a name like that they must know something) to see if they have a list of the last ten years' worth of plane crashes. I want the company with the best track record. Rona tells me to save myself the trouble (and the man I talk to at the paper, their publicity department, clearly thinks I have lost my mind), we're booked on Eastern. I can't believe this is happening to me; Mr. Appel had better appreciate all I'm willing to do. My God, I'm willing to DIE for that man.

I walk to the closet and stare at the rack of skirts, dresses, cardigans, coats, and try to figure out how many Friday night services fall over Christmas vacation. Two? Three? I take three good dresses, a pair of dungarees, and the Yankee T-shirt. Pajamas and bathrobes my mother keeps for me, ironed of course; thank God she can't see what happened to her handiwork, the flannel p.j.'s crushed together in a bottom drawer, the mashed sweaters. I've decided to take everything to a cleaner's before summer vacation, even my bras, so they'll be pressed once again. Me, I only iron what shows to the outer world. For Marsha or myself, underneath, I'm rumpled. Maybe when I'm seeing (is that the right expression?) Mr. Appel this will change. I throw seven pairs of white cotton underpants and four unrinsed stockings into the suitcase.

Into my mind pops an image of Mr. Appel standing in the middle of his living room, clasping my hands, holding me away from him to admire me. I see us frozen there, him with a look of overwhelming love in his eyes, and me beautiful and silent and shy.

I finish packing in a trance, makeup, Ban, hair spray, rollers; Temple B'nai Jeshuran, you're gonna plotz when you see me. That may even make Dad's sermons bearable (though I'll hear them at dinner twice before he delivers them in the pulpit), knowing how aggravated the sisterhood will be when they see my pretty (yes!), thin (yes!) face, and nearly okay (fifteen more pounds and it'll be magnificent) body.

I look at myself in the mirror above the dresser and smile, and then, right in the middle of gazing at my white teeth, I think: if the plane crashes, no one will know how thin I got. (Would they believe a sworn statement from Marsha?) Why am I doing this to myself just when life is getting to be worthwhile? Am I crazy? Why should I commit suicide now?

I take my pocketbook from the top of the mess on my desk, get out a dime, and head for the phone to call the Back Bay Station. Maybe a train leaves soon. I open the door and run into Rona and Jo.

"You must be telepathic," Rona says. "We just got here."

"I'm calling the train station."

"Sit down and play us a song on the guitar." Rona pushes me into the room. She's little, but wiry. Also she's eaten recently. I'm weak from lack of food; a baby could push me around.

"We're counting on you," Rona tells me, "to keep the plane up. It's probably better than having a nun aboard, to have a rabbi's daughter."

"Just the opposite." I fall on the bed and take the guitar out of its case. "I'm a liability, not an asset. I'm dangerous cargo. Maybe another Jonah. God is probably hunting up a whale to toss me into!"

"Shut up and sing," Rona says.

I oblige her with several verses of "Deep Blue Sea," hoping to make her nervous, but she and Jo join in cheerfully: " 'Bury him with a starry crown, bury him with a STARRY crown, bury him with a starry crown, it was Willy that got drownded in the DEEP blue sea.' " I give up. Seeing them relaxed, remembering how I'm Making Myself Over for Mr. Appel, I try to calm down too, but the songs I think of continue to have an unmistakable note of gloom. "In Tarrytown" (" 'Wide and deep,' boom boom, 'my grave will be,' boom, boom, 'with the wild goose grasses growing over me' "); "Barbara Allan" (" 'O father, father, dig my grave, O dig it deep and narrow, sweet William died for me today, I'll die for him tomorrow' "); "Blue-Tail Fly" (" 'Beneath this stone I'm forced to lie—Victim of a blue-tail fly' ").

Rona and Jo sing, I harmonize to keep my mind off my troubles until Marsha walks in with a brown paper bag, ice cubes (did she chop them from the sidewalk in front of Bailey?), and paper cups. They have a thimbleful of Scotch apiece and I have half a cup, swallow it like medicine, one horrible gulp at a time. A burning sensation spreads from my throat to my esophagus to stomach; I can't tell whether I feel better or worse till I start giggling. Then it occurs to me that I must be feeling better.

"I want a butterscotch sundae," I announce.

"Why?" Marsha looks shocked.

"If I'm going to die, why should I worry about my weight?" I giggle, and they laugh. Meanwhile I want a butterscotch sundae; for death I dieted?

I can see it now, God welcoming me to heaven. (Outstretched arms, benediction.) "Welcome BARBARA FABRIKANT, daughter of the well-known rabbi, Moses FABRIKANT."

"Dr. Moses Rabbi Fabrikant," I'll correct him, looking wildly for an exit. Can you imagine me trapped for eternity with Him?

Marsha refills my cup, and I swallow the liquid fire. "How do you feel?" she asks.

"Hot," I say. "Very hot." That makes me think of hell, thank God Jews don't believe in that, for us death is enough, we're satisfied; crazy Gentiles have to go on making bad into worse. Listen, God, I bargain, only let me live this once and I promise I'll, what? Be good? Nice? Cheerful? Thin? I don't know what God wants from my life. To do justly, love mercy, and walk humbly before Him? But what does that mean? I want to be left alone, in peace, by my parents; I'll certainly return the favor to them, but I'm not Felix Frankfurter, I'm not *anybody*, there's *nobody* I can do justly TO! Don't you see, God, old boy? *Everything is so far being done to me.* Only let me live, and when I get my chance I'll try never to be mean to anything that's weak and helpless. You think the Rabbi could say the same, and you let HIM live through a massive coronary? Or his wife, Madame Rye Bread and Butter? How come they live and I CAN'T?

I start crying.

"Somehow," Marsha says, "I don't think this was my most brilliant idea."

"Why not?" I weep. Then I fall back on the bed.

Marsha laughs.

"What was the idea?" I screw up my forehead and try to remember. Then I fall asleep.

Two hours later Marsha is pulling me out of bed. She leads me to the bathroom; it takes a few minutes to pry my eyes open—I've fallen asleep wearing contact lenses, which according to Dr. Qualer means that blindness is imminent! I hope I can make it to New Jersey before it hits. I splash water in my face and wonder, will my mother still be pleased at my thinness if I'm blind? Knowing her, she might not notice my groping with a cane, feeling for the chair before I sit down, as long as my face is pimple-free and my fat is gone.

My eyes are killing me, and my stomach doesn't feel good. I go with Rona and Jo to the cab, we get to the airport and onto the plane, and then I puke all the way from Boston to New York. The stewardess keeps saying she's never seen anything like it, never seen anyone VOMit on a shuttle. When I have nothing left to vomit I just retch, I bet she's never seen anything like this either, the dry heaves on SUCH a SHORT flight.

In between retches, somewhere hovering over Long Island, the pilot announces that there's too much air traffic to land, we'll have to circle for a while. I realize this is God's way of letting me know the jig is up. A little later the pilot walks to the back of the plane; as he passes my seat I look up at him and say, "Who's watching for flocks of geese? Who's keeping the eye out for Piper Cubs?" Then I retch again.

He pats my head and says we'll be landing in five or ten minutes.

"He was gorgeous," Jo whispers to Rona.

I'm dying, the pilot is probably bailing out through the rear door, and they're admiring his body.

Ten minutes later everyone is strapping themselves in and we're going down. I murmur, *"Shema Yisroel, Adonoi elohenu Adonoi echod."* When we land, I feel like Amelia Earhart coming back from the dead. The Scotch seems to have worn off, and I think to myself, I've done it!

"Hey," I catch Rona's hand first, then Jo's, "thanks."

"Jesus Christ," Rona says, "remind me never to do *anything* like this again."

"Was I that bad?"

"If God had meant YOU to fly He would've given you wings," she says. "In His Infinite Wisdom He didn't; you woulda made SOME bird."

As I walk down the aisle and out the door, past the stewardess who's hoping we had a pleasant trip (how CAN she say that with a straight face?), I think, it may not have been a great trip, but at least I got where I was going. I flew!

Headline:

Barbara Fabrikant Flies:
Rabbi's Daughter Disobeys Parent
AND
God Does NOT Smite Her Down!

I follow Rona's neat red hair and Jo's ribbon down the ramp. Once on solid concrete I look back at the plane. All right, God, I'll put in a good word for You. I'll say: Occasionally You are an improvement over the Rabbi. I think that's the best I can do. Is it thanks enough for letting me live?

Chapter Twenty-four

❦

This is the first Christmas that goes by without my noticing it. Usually I'm conscious that the entire world is bent on my learning the words to every Christmas carol known to man. I usually feel like yelling, MERCY already! I know most of them by heart, me, a rabbi's daughter, and I don't mean only the first verse. The world is bombarding us with carols, "Sing all ye citizens!" from department stores, radio, TV, street carolers, the Salvation Army (and what a name that is), church belfries.

This year I'm locked in my room, first at home, then at school, for a month. Long papers, short papers, quizzes, exams, finals. Christmas sails by; the old year is rung out, bing! and the new one rung in, bong! while I'm incarcerated. Harter stands between me and the forces of conversion.

With all this work I make Dean's List and get an extra late night per week, also a letter from Dean Pringle (whom I've never met) saying how proud she is of me and how she hopes I will keep up the good work, and continue to uphold the high Harter standards of education.

I now weigh one hundred and twenty-five pounds. Over intersession my mother has: 1. taken in my clothes, and 2. yelled at me for chewing too much gum. She's never satisfied, unlike me. I'm happy because I love the beginnings of things—new sharp pencils, fresh clean notebooks, desk in order, unopened bottle of ink, everything neat and expectant. Mr. Appel's class is on the Tuesday, Thursday, Saturday shift at ten A.M. Perfect scheduling—no gym before it, time to get up extra early to wash and set my hair.

The first Tuesday of the semester I wake at six A.M., lie in bed fidgeting till six thirty, intolerable, then put on slippers and housecoat and walk to the living room. Dead quiet. The silence is so heavy, my breathing sounds loud, and I think I hear my heart beating. Tiptoe to window, pull curtains aside; they shriek as they're moved. The light is gray, the old snow around the road and sidewalk is dirty, a signal for it to melt already, but the temperature refuses to rise above freezing. The Hill is a ball of ice; I can see the hard crust of snow from here. It's impossible even to tray-sleigh down it—you'd crash into the fence; ice skates are what's required, or shoes with spikes. The steps on the other side are layered over every morning with kosher salt, I love that, which erodes boots thoroughly. My good suede ones are permanently ruined; a line of white covers the whole front.

Some trees have hard snow packed between branches. Once when it sleeted, during finals naturally, the trees became coated with ice, they glistened, and icicles hung down from them. They look absolutely dead, frozen to death: when winter comes, who can possibly believe in spring?

Icicles dangle from most of the buildings, in a row sometimes, so thick and hard they're difficult to break off. It looks like it's going to be another bitter-cold day.

Alarms start going off. I rush back to our room, grab

shampoo and towel, and head for the shower. Two hours later I'm out of the dryer, making coffee, yelling at Marsha to wake up. Finally, nine fifteen, put on the radio.

"Pity," she whispers, "have some pity."

"You want to be late for your first day of class?"

"Cleyass, cleyass," now she's imitating me. "Clahss sounds so much better." She sits up. Progress! "So does lahfter and ahnt; admit it for once, won't you?"

"I admit it. I just can't say it. You want to see my outfit?" I put on the lights, stand in front of her in red turtleneck (tucked IN, the accomplishment of a lifetime), black wool skirt, earrings, stockings, boots, eyes made up.

"Everything looks gorgeous." She throws herself out of bed and rushes to the bathroom. One thing I've got to hand her—she may be slow getting up, but she's fast getting ready. Even before my hair is combed, she's fully clothed, booted, books together, sipping the last of her coffee and finishing a pear. For breakfast I've had a black pill, coffee, AND a muffin. Food is permissible on my diet, but only in teeny portions. Let me tell you, fat people of the world, a little secret about maintaining weight: when you're thin, it takes a diet to keep you thin. Fat people can eat more and not gain weight, merely keep their same fat cells in nice working order, whereas thin people, at the drop of a chocolate chip cookie, have put on a pound. Thus proving once again that if there is a God He's a sadist. A thin sadist.

"Do you think I should wear my star?" Remembering Lenore's last name, Fitzgerald, decides me.

I go to class untagged except for my beauty, which, dear God, is more than I ever dreamed it could be. I'm prettier than Lenore, sexier, bigger eyes, bigger boobs; surely this will lead somewhere. Don't pretty women get whatever they want? Isn't that the rule?

Marsha and I part at the top of the Hill. We've linked arms all the way up, rescuing each other every minute; first she slips, then my boots slide. I'm sorry to see her go off in a different direction; I could use a prop, especially today. The wind is murdering my eyes and nose, my fingers I pull back into the center of the gloves, ball both hands into fists and walk toward Parsons. When I'm about six yards away, I notice Mr. Appel approaching from the other side. I slow down, in this weather yet, and we make it to the steps at the same moment. My heart is trying to hurl itself out of my body and onto the sidewalk at his feet: take me I'm yours! Instead, and this is NOT planned, halfway up the stairs I start sliding, and Mr. Appel grabs me, putting an arm around me until we get to the door. "Miserable weather," he mutters. Miserable, I'd like to say, oh NO, it's wonderful!

"Thanks," I say once we're inside. "How are you, Mr. Appel?"

"Fine." He's trying to place me, I can see from his eyes. I see something else there too, a gleam I haven't gotten from many men. I'm sure it's the beginning of love. "And you?"

"I'm so looking forward to your course."

Now he really gleams. Glows, beams. "That's nice to hear. You'd be surprised how few people ever compliment one. As a matter of fact, I wrote to Joseph Heller, telling him how great *Catch-22* was and how I use it in class, and he wrote back to thank ME for writing. He mentioned how infrequently he gets letters like mine."

Mr. Appel opens the classroom door and walks to the front of the room. I look for a seat near the front, in the middle; none are vacant till the third row. I take my coat off, standing (fat people always sit to remove coats, no one should see them, and I've now joined the ranks of people who show off their bodies). Still standing; is he looking at me?

I pat my coat into place, see Doris and Allan sitting together in the back row (Allan's eyes are popping out, fuck YOU, baby), turn toward front, Mr. Appel is, yes! looking at me. I sit down, burning. When I gaze at him a few minutes later he's looking elsewhere, is it at Lenore, or someone else (Jesus, how MANY attractive girls ARE there in this damned course?) I nearly have to shut my eyes, so wild are the waves sloshing over me.

BONG.

"As most of you know from last semester," Mr. Appel begins, "I think an education means posing problems, not answering questions. In this second part of Minorities we're dealing with the relationship of minority groups to the mass media: what the media have said about which groups, and how each has been affected by the media."

I write furiously, every word, even though some of them are familiar to me from his book.

"What we should be interested in figuring out is: What *really* governs the way people live? Where do we get our models from? And the key question of social science: What is change? Where does it come from? Where and how is it likely to happen? What are the necessary conditions for change? What are the factors making for change? What are the consequences of change? AND, most importantly, what kinds of change do YOU want?"

Me, I think, me? It's quiet; I raise my head, our eyes meet again, my God, he can see right through me. I nearly lower them but for this incredible transfusion of chutzpa (a never-ending well; where has it come from? can it be packaged?) and instead I stare at him. I love you, I think, and I don't give a damn if it shows.

He smiles AGAIN at me. It's incredible.

"Our society is based on a theory that men are rational. Yet it's perfectly clear that many times we're not. Sometimes I feel it might be easier to change big things, like our environment, rather than change ourselves. In any case, to understand social change is of the utmost importance, since only this way can we plan and control it. . . ."

My arm is getting tired, so I rest it and miss some pearls of wisdom. I hope they're not on the exam. I look around and notice that the note-taking in this class is sporadic, nearly indifferent. Lots of students are smoking, against the rules, of course, but Mr. Appel is not much for enforcing rules.

I pick up my pen again, and start drawing hearts, flowers, boxes, and hearts, half-listening, half-dreaming for a long time till I hear . . . "You must separate yourself enough from your culture to look upon it dispassionately, to reach any conclusion about it. And it's a culture from which you *should* be separated, a society of followers and obeyers instead of questioners. This is a period when you're going to have to say NO! to most of your culture in order to say Yes to life."

My God, I think, *yes, yes, yes.*

The bell rings.

"Will all of you please see me after class or come to my office to make appointments for your first conference? Start thinking about papers you'd like to do."

"New students," he says, "are there any?"

I raise my hand.

He nods. "Please submit a sample of your writing to me. We do many papers in this class, and I like to solve writing difficulties at the beginning."

I stand up and start putting on my coat, along with the rest of the class.

"My office hours are the same as last semester: Tuesday and Thursday from one to five."

What about Saturday night? I think to myself.

Chapter Twenty-five

❧

Last semester all freshmen had to write an answer to the query "Who am I?" not only as a course requirement but as part of the traditional freshman essay contest, which, in the inimitable Harter manner, was a contest every freshman was *required* to enter.

I won second prize with my answer, which was that I hadn't the faintest idea: did anybody? I'd have loved to have seen the first-prize winner; he must have *known*. Naturally I give my prize essay to Mr. Appel. At the Saturday class he hands it back with the notation: "This is awful. See me."

Even though my conference isn't for a week, I come that afternoon, and he says, "This is the most self-indulgent, immature drivel I've ever read; you'd better be able to do something about it if this is the way you always write. What do you mean, you don't know who you are?"

I'm shocked; I nearly stammer. "I feel like a stranger to myself. I have no idea what I'm going to do next."

"Well, what have you done already?" he asks. He sounds harsh, but his eyes are smiling, even his mouth with the lousy teeth has upturned corners. And I feel as though there's a double entendre here, if only I can figure out what it is or how to handle it.

"Not much." How is it with the rest of the world I'm such a good liar, and here all that falls out of my mouth is the truth?

"Why don't you do more?" he asks, this time actually smiling.

"I'm trying," I tell him. Believe me, Mr. Appel, I'm TRYING.

At this he laughs, is it at me or with me? I don't care, as long as he marries me. "Why did Harry put you in my course? You're only a freshman, aren't you?"

"He did it because I'm going to be a poli. sci. major and he said it would make me feel better about Harter."

"How do you like Harris?" Mr. Appel asks.

"He's a lovely man and a good teacher."

"He obviously thinks highly of you, although with him emotions sometimes get in the way of reason." Mr. Appel stretches one leg over the corner of the desk; I get a chance to look at his crotch. I don't take the chance; I can barely raise my eyes to look at his face. I stare at my booted feet, his desk (littered worse than mine), the window, the bookcase overflowing with Congressional Records, anywhere but at him. What I can manage in a classroom I can't bring off here, alone. I feel as though I've had the skin peeled off my body, exposing my nerves. I want him to fold me in his arms, pulling down the shades first, of course, and locking the office door, then take me into his arms and press me close, and then, then, then, love.

"I'll try to do you the favor of being reasonable," he says. "In this business you have to be a professional, not a person."

I'm sitting in a wobbly wooden chair, wearing a dark brown skirt (short) and a matching beige sweater that emphasizes (can I help it?) the fact that I have breasts. Look, I want to say to him, look! boobs! But I see clearly, too clearly, that the way to this man's heart is not through my boobs (although they'll help, I'm sure) but through my brains. A big joke on my mother AND her daughter.

"I won second prize in the essay contest with this."

"You're kidding," he says. He looks impressed in spite of himself.

"Of course, considering the idiots here, it's not a big deal."

He looks at me with some new appreciation, I've taken the right tone, finally: critical. A questioner, not an obeyer.

"That reminds me of a funny story about my little girl."

I nearly swoon, His Little Girl, he's getting personal; I try to look motherly and affectionate.

"I was walking around Cambridge the other day with her, she's only seven years old, and I met several students and a colleague in the space of two blocks. They all stopped to chat, and afterward my daughter said to me, 'Daddy, are you famous?' "

I laugh as charmingly as I can. "That's lovely."

There's a knock on the door.

Mr. Appel shakes his head. "We didn't get around to your first paper, would you like to make another appointment?"

"I have one for next week."

"Good," he says. Then he stares at me very hard. "You look different from last semester."

"I lost weight."

"You look [pause] wonderful." He clears his throat. "About this paper, tell me, why did Mrs. Lamb like it?"

I have to drag the answer to that question back through mists in my head, for his saying "You look wonderful" has created a fog through which I can barely see his desk. "She said she thought it was very honest."

"Funny. I would've said the opposite. However, she's a good woman, I respect her." He smiles and stands up, and suddenly I'm jealous of Mrs. Lamb. Old Mrs. Lamb, who looks like a flamingo, my God, the world is full of women. I'd like to murder every one of them.

I put on my coat and walk to the door, depressed.

"I'm looking forward to our next conference," he says.

I'm no longer depressed, but exhilarated. I open the door and nearly run into Lenore, who looks like she was about to barge in. I'm depressed again.

Chapter Twenty-six

❦

Tuesday afternoon neither Marsha nor I had classes, and it was Marsha's custom to rush back after lunch and take a nap. She would say, "I have to study to the sound of snap crackle and pop, at least let me snooze in peace."

So every Tuesday I'm on my own, banished to the far reaches of the Harter campus and parted from my dear Double Bubble, which I never chew in public for fear people will think there's something wrong with me. A mistaken impression, clearly, for now that I'm thin and beautiful I am, in my mother's words, perfect.

This particular Tuesday is a bright, not-too-cold January day. I decide to go to the bookstore; maybe, just maybe, I'll run into *him*. While Marsha strips, I get dressed, take the last chunk of gum out of my mouth, pack my Intro. Soc. textbook and a notebook and two pens in the Harvard bookbag, and walk to the door.

"Good-bye, Mouth," Marsha whispers.

"May you dream of nothing but disaster," I say.

I shut the door and head outside, across the road and up the Hill to the bookstore to see what records are on sale; I've developed something new, a new psychological twist to my makeup. I can't read any poli. sci. or sociology or geology without a symphony in the background, preferably Beethoven.

Sometimes when I have two long assignments from Mr. Appel and my sociology teacher, I go to the record library and borrow all nine Beethoven symphonies (although you can only take out three at a time, so I have to forge Marsha's and Rona's names), come home and put them on the record player, three by three, in any order. As a result I can always identify a Beethoven symphony, as opposed to any other composer's, but I can never tell which is which. I think of them as one grand work.

Rona told me that Rachmaninoff's Piano Concertos Two and Three are as good as a symphony, so it's those I have in mind. I like to buy records that have been highly recommended; I know nothing about music and hate to spend five dollars and get stuck with something that neither I nor anyone else likes. That likes and dislikes are a matter of taste has never occurred to me.

I walk into the bookstore and pass through the aisles of Harter mascots, banners, car stickers, shawls, sweatshirts, sweaters, bookjackets (they must be out of their minds thinking that I'll advertise for them).

I pass by the stacks of books, through the supplies of India and other inks, notebooks, typewriter ribbons, looseleaf dividers, and the other trappings of an American education, and finally I get to one little table holding the on-sale records. I leaf through them, wondering how other people tell which record to buy from mere names and jacket covers, and while I'm leafing, trying to look as if I knew something, a young, tall, dark, nice-looking male asks, "Aren't you in my sociology course?"

"I'm in Cranston's course. Is that the one you're in?" The reason I have to ask is there are two hundred other people in this course, and there are probably ninety sociology courses on campus—this place is hip-deep in learning.

"Yes," this fellow says, "that's the course. How do you like old Cran?"

"He's hideous," I answer, and Steve Something from Swampscott, Mass., nods happily, for I've responded correctly. Soon we're chatting about: his major, my major, his courses, my courses, how much work we have, how hard it is, and then he asks me to dinner tonight!

I'm not the least bit interested in this guy Steve or in any of the others I date, faithless I'm not to the shrine in my heart, but I figure I need the practice. And I do, and I never get it, in spite of all the dates, and the reason I don't is as follows:

Steve picks me up this evening at the dorm in one of the yellow taxis that service the area for a mere arm and leg. Even the cabbie perks up when I slither in, my coat opening to reveal a red dress. Red. Can you beat that? No more black. Steve gets in next to me, is sitting practically on top of me, puts an arm around me, and says, "Shall we go to a restaurant or to my home?"

It turns out that Steve's parents are away on a trip somewhere and he has the house and a maid and a cook to himself. Is this something I want to miss? Of course not. We go to his home, huge and lovely, although Steve isn't Jewish, so the carpets aren't wall to wall, only Persian, beautiful but thin. We walk in the door, and the lights are low, soft music is playing, the table is beautifully set, and a Negro maid, in a little outfit yet, takes our coats and hangs them up.

As Steve fixes me a whiskey sour, he asks, "Where were you last semester? How could I have missed you?"

"Well," I say, "it's a long story. I was here, but in disguise." He laughs and so do I, but the truth is I am here now in disguise.

I take my drink, and Steve shows me the house, big, old,

dignified place with high ceilings, high straight-backed chairs, everything seems to be ascending. Tall mirrors, long windows, tables with thin, long legs, chandeliers that point upward. The very opposite of Marsha's house where everything seems to want to go squash or squish, where you sink downward.

We sit down to have dinner, the maid serves; she holds the dish near your side, you can't grip it and slush peas onto your plate, you have to balance a heavy silver serving spoon with the peas in it and transfer them to your plate. I feel like I'm on a tightrope, and I vow to myself, when I'm rich I'm going to eat the same way I do now, food on the table, everybody serves himself, a free-for-all, the way God intended us to eat. The maid and I do our little dance around baked potatoes, steak, and salad. As I thank her for the fifth time and refuse another bit of salad, I think how I wish she could see me with the five wads of Double Bubble when I'm in my other identity, Barbara Fabrikant, Girl Mouth. Lying on the bed, chewing and blowing and spitting out and taking fresh pieces. I wouldn't mind if Steve could see me like that either, because if I had to live this way year round I'd go out of my mind. I hate having someone in a uniform serve me; alas, I hate cooking and cleaning too, so in real life there's only one solution: find invisible gremlins who enjoy housework. Like all the other brilliant life-possibilities I have. Is there anything, really, that can ever make me happy?

Steve and I eat to the accompaniment of Mantovani, Previn, and an old Benny Goodman record; the candles on the table flicker as we talk. After dinner we have a little brandy, which I don't realize is strong until after the first gulp burns a hole in my vocal cords and my contact lenses nearly wash away with tears. The maid clears off the table, then vanishes forever, except in my imagination, which has her peeking through every available keyhole and crack. Which is what I'd do if I were anybody's maid. Steve and I dance in the middle of the old furniture and on the wine-red Persian rug, and then he guides me to the couch, where the necking has been scheduled.

As we sit down I say, "I get the feeling that this has been choreographed before my arrival."

"What?" Steve asks, for I've been docile enough all evening.

"It makes me feel like a cardboard figure you're moving from place to place that hasn't a will of its own."

"You don't look like a cardboard figure," Steve says.

We neck on the couch, and once, while he's lying on top of me, both of us fully clothed, in the middle of one particularly hot and heavy bout, I say, "I must be crazy to be doing this." Then I come.

And I *must* be crazy. I can't practice on this guy, because I don't love him, and he likes me. Two impossible conditions, and I want to get home and think about Mr. Appel and what I'll wear to his three classes next week. Besides, I don't want practice, and I don't want dates. I want love.

Chapter Twenty-seven

❦

To read the articles Mr. Appel assigns you have to go to the library, a chore I'm able to avoid in my other courses. The library is huge, gloomy, brown, with bad lighting and long tables and miserably uncomfortable chairs. The time it takes the librarian to get a book is breathtaking; you need to bring other work to the library, otherwise you sit around chewing your nails, watching the clock, letting those precious moments of your youth slip by you.

The day after my date with Steve, Marsha and I pack our books, sign out, and head toward the Hill in time to see the Tunafish Heroes Man sail up to the dorm.

"I bet you don't eat that stuff, do you?" Marsha yells to him.

"Three times a day," he says with a smile. Then he walks into the dorm with his wares. Men into bedrooms they don't allow at Harter; men bearing food are always welcome. It figures.

As we walk up the Hill, a stiff wind whips our faces, but the last snow has melted and no new one has yet arrived to plague us. Tall, round lamplights dot the campus, illuminating patches of grass, trees, parts of buildings. In the half-darkness, with only suggestions of buildings visible, Harter looks like a dream college.

"My English teacher prefers the critics to any book of literature ever written," Marsha says. "I must be too stupid to understand their subtle methods of education. Once I thought I was smart, but look at me. Look at my grades. Can this be living?"

I stare at the library windows—from this distance they're yellow squares of light that look to me like rows of blind eyes.

I say, "I wish he'd ask me out."

Marsha moans.

We walk into the library and up to the desk, where we fill out our order forms for books and articles. You can't go into the stacks yourself without special permission; God only knows what would happen if students could pour through the library, taking books here and there, loitering around the stacks, reading. No, no, this can never be. For this is Harter, a university ordered around itself, which exists strictly for the benefit of itself, and has students only because it would look mighty foolish without them.

Marsha and I sit opposite each other at a long, empty table, waiting for the librarian to surface from whatever subterranean depths he has to sink to find our books. I have my contact lenses in, which makes reading torture, but what if I should meet Mr. Appel? Marsha's name is called first, and she goes to claim her little treasures.

While waiting for my article, written by the master himself, entitled "Space Madness: People Starve and Rockets Eat" (doesn't he have a real feel for language?), I'm reading an excerpt from one of the Congressional Records Mr. Appel deals out at every class.

"Hello, Elizabeth Taylor," a voice whispers in my ear as I'm reading a playful exchange between two esteemed senators. I nearly leap out of my seat, for I always expect Mr. Appel to appear and do something like this. Unfortunately, this is only Allan, who's putting his books down next to mine and sitting in the next chair.

"Go blow," I say in a whisper.

Allan says, "I did like you better with glasses, though."

"Who asked you?"

"In the midst of having someone explain why the stepfather in *David Copperfield* is actually not a stepfather but a real father, this too I have to listen to?" Marsha is not whispering.

The librarian calls my name and I go to get my article. When I come back, Allan has disappeared, leaving behind a little piece of paper folded in ten neat sections, which I open. It says, "I love you." Of course. He signs his name, Allan C. Dobsen, so there shouldn't be any mistake as to the author. I fold it and use it for a bookmark in my Congressional Record.

Then I turn to the words of my own true love. I read the article and admire his indignation, but I picture him as he is in class: awkward and gawky, like a big bald tramp, shuffling around, nervous, losing notes, occasionally making some sense, and I say to myself, how sweet he is, how cute, how much he needs my help. He's good and great and lacks confidence.

I dream on through the article and return it to the librarian in time to rush back before curfew. Marsha and I dash out the front door along with thousands of other students and fly down the Hill. As we run, books bouncing, hair blowing, Marsha says, "Nobody can tell me this is anything but crazy."

I'm too out of breath to do anything but nod my head.

Chapter Twenty-eight

❧

Thursday morning starts out like any other normal morning: I stand in front of the mirror, profile view, staring at that amazing body with the genuine waist. Sometimes I'm so happy that when no one's in the room, I dance in front of the mirror, for I've fallen in love with me only slightly less than with Mr. Appel. I imagine, dancing there, that if I can win myself over, surely he should not be difficult.

Today I decide to wear a red sweater, my best color, and a short wool skirt, but only after boring Rona so much she runs off to breakfast, and Marsha, munching a pear, says, "If I hear your voice one more time this morning I'll scream."

I quietly get dressed, put in the painful lenses, comb out the set, and stare at myself for five minutes. Then I hear the chimes sound, and I charge out the door, throwing my wad into the filled basket near my bed.

Marsha says, "This room stinks of gum; can't you throw the garbage out?"

"Later, later. I have to get to class early so I can sit up front." There's a triweekly contest in Mr. Appel's class: who can wear the shortest skirts and sit up front and cross and uncross her legs the most times.

I run out the door and up the Hill. For him I manage to move my legs fast; it's fantastic what he can inspire me to do. I won't bother with details of the amount of work I've done; anyone who can take off thirty pounds in two months can do anything. I'm his star pupil, the youngest one in the class, the baby, except when I open my mouth. Then pours out a stream of information and opinion, sometimes it feels as though my brain has been taken over by a foreign genius who understands the ins and outs of oppressed minorities—I feel like the eighth wonder of the world.

I run into Parsons, up the stairs to Room 203, and take the one vacant seat in the first row, along with six other well-dressed girls. Then I walk to his desk and put my borrowed Congressional Record on the blotter, alongside several other issues of the same. As I put it down, he walks into the room, shuffles is perhaps the word I'm looking for, his head bent over and slouching. We say "Good morning" to him; he's carrying a cup of coffee. Some mornings several girls bring him coffee—I never stoop to such tactics—and once one mad beauty brought him a doughnut (what else?) from the cafeteria. (He threw it out, too, after thanking her politely; said he never ate breakfast. It's a good thing for him that he doesn't, else this class might stay up half the night baking.)

He has no coat to take off because he wears one only when the weather is absolutely freezing (today is a tropical twenty-nine degrees), and he never wears a hat. He picks up the Congressional Records to put them into his briefcase, and out of one slips a folded paper. I look but register nothing until he starts opening it; the neatness of the folding makes me catch my breath. I blush and my heart pounds. Shit, I think, oh shit, oh shit, please don't read it, shit, now he'll think I love Allan and not him.

He reads the paper and smiles a big toothy smile and looks straight at me and says, "Unless young men are starting to write me love notes, I assume this belongs to someone else. Would the owner like to claim it?"

I shake my head.

"Well?"

"You could throw it away," I say quietly, with the class now looking at me.

"Ah, ah," he says, crumpling it in one hand, "unrequited love. So sad, the cruelty of women."

Bong.

Class moves slowly, I don't open my mouth. When the bell rings, he says, "Compare the drive for education among Italians, Irish, and Negroes for the next class. Barbara, would you please stay for a moment?"

"Did I embarrass you today?" he asks. "I'm sorry if I did."

"That's okay. It wasn't so bad."

"You certainly do blush well," he says.

"It's because my skin is thin," I say. "Someone once told me that if your skin is thin, your veins show and your blushes are very visible."

"Is that really true? Let me see your veins."

I turn my hands over, palms up, and he takes them, let me repeat this, he takes my hands; and while I faint in an upright position, he says, "Why, it's true, your veins are very clear."

The better to slit my wrists with, Grandma.

"I'll see you this afternoon," he says.

That last sentence echoes in these spacious caverns of mine that pass for a brain all throughout French, *Le Mythe de Sisyphe*, which I don't understand a word of even in English, and on throughout the afternoon. I no longer hear the sentence itself, just the tone, the intensity underneath the words, the real words underneath the said words, or is it only the echo from my head that I'm hearing? I think not, the way he looks at me, that feeling he gives me, aren't I giving it to him too? Isn't that the way it always is?

"I'll see you this afternoon," fades in and out, like a record being played soft and loud, loud and soft, until it becomes, "I wooed her in the winter time and part of the summer, too. And the only, only thing that I did that was wrong was to keep her from the foggy, foggy dew."

At four fifteen I pack my notebook and a couple of books, spray my hair to a magnificent lacquer finish (you should see the wind out there, what it does to unsprayed hair), and I leave Marsha, who says, "Remember, your virginity is your most priceless possession."

"I can't see myself losing it on top of a desk," I say. Although, who knows, if the passion becomes too great for us . . .

"Make sure you're on top," Marsha says. "That way maybe he'll get deflowered too, by a sharp pencil."

"Yuch," I say. "Suppose I marry him, you gonna go on being hostile like this?"

"As a wedding present I'll give you a round-trip ticket to Reno."

"Ho ho. If I'm not back in forty-five minutes . . ."

Marsha interrupts me. "I'll call Dean Pringle."

"Right." We both laugh. The thought of Dean Pringle walking into Mr. Appel's office as he's fucking me is a wonderful vision. "I wonder if they'd fire him or kick me out of school?"

"Around here, only God knows," Marsha says. She's right. Maybe there's no rule against teachers fucking students as long as they get them back to their dorm before curfew.

I think about that on the way to Mr. Appel's office. Doris has the appointment before mine; she walks out as I'm about to knock. I look at her belly. Still flat. Should I congratulate her? Mr. Appel sees me at the door and says, "Come in!" He looks tired, poor man, I want to run my hand across his brow, pat his bald head. Instead I take off my coat and sit down. My body feels tense. Is my voice going to shake?

"I was thinking about the project," I take out my notebook and pen, "and it occurred to me how hard it was to figure out anything about a culture. I mean, what do you look for? The birth rate? Education? Jobs? Family break-ups? What things do you look for to understand people in the first place, much less what kinds of changes have occurred in the past twenty years?"

Mr. Appel smiles. "Harry didn't make such a mistake after all."

I stare at him and think, does that mean he wants to marry me? Is that what he's saying?

"It seems to me," he goes on, "that to understand a culture or a people, one must know their points of vulnerability."

That sounds interesting; I wonder what it means. I'm afraid to ask, and there's a silence, which, it's clear, it is my job to fill. "I was thinking that I'd like to examine Jews for my conference project."

"No good. Jews no longer have any interesting social problems except what they make up in their heads. There's no such thing as anti-Semitism in this country. Jews can get anything they want." He pauses. "You're a very sheltered girl, aren't you?"

"I guess I am." More sheltered than a rabbi's daughter they don't come.

"Did you read that book on the effect of the mass media on the British lower class?" he asks.

"Yes. It was terrific." Actually the Beethoven was terrific, the book was only so-so, I've got the notes here to prove it, pages and pages of them, dragged reluctantly from my pen.

"What I'm interested in is the disintegration of a primitive, maybe problem-ridden, maybe not, culture when it comes in contact with the mass media."

"So you want to know the kind of change that goes on when a rural culture becomes urban."

He nods his head. "The reason I asked if you were sheltered is, if you thought Jews have problems, you haven't seen urban slums."

"You're right," I tell him. "Where I live there are hardly any."

"You need to see more life," he says.

Again I hear the words underneath: you need to be fucked by me.

"Yes," I agree. Please please please.

He pauses for a moment and drums his fingers on the table, still looking at me. I'm supposed to be quiet, I can tell. Then suddenly in the silence I remember this girl in my high school class, a lovely shiksa, beautiful, I mean, whose name also began with *F,* Fraser, Carol Fraser, who was my book-report partner in English (in my high school everything was done alphabetically). We had to choose books together to read, discuss, and present jointly. I persuaded her to do *Exodus.* She loved it; she never knew how Jews had suffered—no history class of ours ever got past Archduke Ferdinand, and she wasn't up on World War II, not having a rabbi-father who liked to dwell on hideous details. She presented *Exodus* to the class and cried right in the middle of her report. For her I devise a new category: Gentiles When They Are Good Are Great. I remember her now, bawling in front of thirty students, and it strikes me, my God, Mr. Appel thinks I'm that shiksa. I feel I ought to confess, say to him, by the way, Jews interest me because . . . but I don't. What if he likes the idea of me being a Gentile?

He sits there looking at me still; I smile and turn my head slightly to give him my best profile (right) and find myself staring out the window at a gray sky blotted out by square red buildings that are in turn partly concealed by brown, lifeless trees.

"I have some time this afternoon," he says. "How would you like to see a slum?"

I nod my head so eagerly you'd think he'd offered me a tour

of the Taj Mahal. Maybe that's what we'll do AFTER the slums, he'll build me a Taj Mahal or I'll build him one! Which would be more appropriate?

"I'll get you back in time for dinner," he says. "Or will that be too late?"

"That'll be fine." I'm disappointed, but only a little; the Taj Mahal was not built in a day.

"Shall we go right now?" He stands up without waiting for me to answer. I think of what Marsha's fantasies will be when I don't come back to our dorm. Will she call Dean Pringle? I wonder, putting on my coat and gloves. He holds the door for me, then locks it; we walk down the hall together, people say hello to him, look at me, I know what they're thinking (I hope). Yes, it's ME, only I'm not going to be his next, I'll be his LAST. Out the door of the building, down the steps, across the quad to the faculty parking lot, the wind whipping my hair around, dear God, let me still be pretty when we get to the car.

We reach his little black Volkswagen; he opens the door; I try to get in gracefully, utterly impossible. Another thing, fat girls of the world, thinness does not mean gracefulness. I back awkwardly into the seat of the car, he shuts the door. I lean over and unlock his side while trying to smooth my hair down.

He gets in and puts his key in the ignition, then turns toward me, takes off a glove, touches my hair and says, "It looks lovely all blown about," and I vow never to comb or set it again.

He talks as we round Powderhouse Park about poverty and democracy and I stare at him, glow when he glances at me, lean against the door, see myself sitting on his lap, arms around his neck, kissing his ear, cheek, mouth; he's so big I'd look almost petite on his lap, delicate and sweet. What a mirage that would be—a human mirage.

"We have enough money to go to the moon, but not enough to clean up Roxbury," he says, then our eyes meet and hold; I feel knotted to him. This car is a movable, bubble-top bed, and I'm floating to paradise. "Roxbury is potentially beautiful," he says. "If money were invested in it, people could live well there." I study his profile, nothing to get excited over. Terrible nose, weak chin, unfortunate wide mouth. Feature by feature this man is a mess. Together he's magnificent, virile, gruff, rough, sexy. What sort of miracle have we here?

He talks about how capitalism is actually socialism for the very rich; I wish this car were a balloon and, like David Niven and his Indian girlfriend, we were going around the world, eighty days, eight hundred, who would care? I try to pay attention to sights he points out, gaze diligently out the window any way he directs, but all I can see is him, him and me, together, forever, together. Finally he parks on a terrible-looking block, a small, littered side street, noisy, kids playing in the road, peeling wooden frame houses with boarded-up windows and old dirty-gray apartment buildings that look as though they are about to collapse. Some of the houses have yards, but there's no grass in them, just dirt and beer cans and a few bent-over trees.

He gets out, and I sit still, as my mother taught me. When he opens my door, I take a deep breath and try to get out without hitting every part of my body on something. He takes my hand to help, holds it tight and keeps holding it even when I'm standing next to him, looks straight down into my eyes and says, "Now for your education," smiles, lets go, shuts the door. "So there are no slums in your home town?"

My father has been standing in front of us pronouncing us man and wife. I'm dressed in a long white gown and thousands of Harter girls are staring jealously from the temple pews. I nod my head. Yes, there are no slums in Morrisville.

"I like social-science students to know the reality of human misery," he says, "so that when they analyze institutions, words like 'poverty' are more than just words."

I'm wondering what it would be like to hold his hand, feel it grip mine. It's hard to concentrate on human misery when you're experiencing such great happiness, but I'm trying, Mr.

Appel. I watch his arm swing, point, watch him gesture with his big gloved hand, and although I merely look and nod, sometimes say, "How awful," all I want is to grab it, him, hang on forever.

He stops and points to some little kids sitting on a stoop outside a four-story ramshackle building, sitting and shivering and not wearing gloves, only coats with not enough buttons and little white cotton socks and flimsy shoes on their feet.

"Oh," I say, then something gets into my eye, killing me (only contact-lens wearers will understand this), and tears start rolling down. I blink like mad, and Mr. Appel puts an arm around me, and I nearly faint from joy.

"I'm glad you're going to major in political science," he says. "The field needs people like you who are fresh enough to feel things. It's being taken over by apologizers for the status quo, napping behind a mask of scientific objectivity. People who have no hearts."

I try to look full of heart. He takes his arm away, and we start walking again, past the children on the stoops, the decrepit buildings, down blocks and blocks of cold, gray dreariness, until we come to a grim little restaurant. He pulls me inside this place, which has a dirty counter, formica tables, and shaky chairs with red plastic seats. We sit at the counter in between several black people who look at us with undisguised hatred. I stare nervously at a pile of Drake's Cakes wrapped in plastic in front of me and then at a blob of ketchup directly in front of Mr. Appel that looks like blood when it first spurts out. He orders two cups of coffee and a grilled cheese sandwich; I tell him coffee is all I want, more in fact than I want. I wish I could call my uncle, ask him if hot coffee burns off germs.

Mr. Appel leans over and whispers, "Look around," just as our coffee and his sandwich are delivered. I can't believe he's serious; I feel the strained atmosphere—it's clear we don't belong here, and shouldn't be staring like tourists in Paris. Naturally I look around, because, folks (only this I don't fully realize then), I'm more afraid of him than I am of hostile black men.

Hoping not to see anything, I turn casually in my seat, past the signs advertising Coca-Cola and Seven-Up, past the profiles of the quietly eating men, and around to the corner, where I see a woman slumped over a table, either asleep or dead, I can't tell which. I assume dead, but instead of gasping (my first impulse) or running (my second) I merely turn back and take a big swallow of burning black coffee. I hate it, but who knows what's crawling around the cream and sugar? I don't want to find out.

When we leave, Mr. Appel says, "Everyone in there is an addict. I wanted you to see what happens to people when they've nothing left to live for."

"Was the woman dead?"

He shrugs his shoulder. "THESE are the victims of our society, our government, and all the social scientists with the big words who can't feel anything!" Then he takes my arm and puts it through his. "Now you've lost your innocence, you're ready to take my course."

I smile up at him, tongue-tied; how can I tell him how much more I have to lose?

On the drive back I think maybe I'll never have to say anything, but with wordless passion (I see this scene clearly) he'll take me, love me madly; the intensity will wipe away our need for words. Oh love me love me love me, I pray; only inside the words ring: save me save me save me, and I feel like a poor black addict waiting to be rescued.

Then we hit traffic. Ordinarily the sight of cars backed up end to end depresses me (I hate being stuck, not moving), but today it affects me differently—I'm trapped in a car with my Own True Love! I look at him tapping his fingers on the steering wheel, glancing at his watch, and my throat tightens. Can it be that he's not thrilled also?

After a few minutes of moving two miles an hour, shifting from first to neutral and neutral to first, he says, "We'll never get you back in time for dinner—what is it tonight anyway?"

"Gray meat," I tell him. "Gray meat and four different starches."

"You sound hungry," he laughs. "How would you like some Italian food—I hate to see any good, promising social-science majors starve to death."

"I'd love it, but I have to call my roommate to sign me out."

"I'll pull off the highway, and we'll find a phone. Are you sure I'm not making you late for a date?"

"I haven't got one," I say, PROUDLY. For that is the best thing about being thin and beautiful—you don't need to date to prove that you are. My mother thinks only fat girls stay home on weekends, but she's got it backward. Only when I'm thin can I finally (and gladly) sit in my room and read a good book on a Saturday night.

"I find that hard to believe," he says as he pulls over to a street-corner phone booth.

"I hate dating," I blurt out. There's so much anger in my voice that I'm a little afraid; what is this with me—perpetual intensity on tap?

"I know what you mean," he responds in a gentler tone that surprises me because I realize I haven't heard it in his voice before. "There are too many things around that make people feel lonely."

I get out and dial Bailey Hall, ask for Marsha, listen for the three rings, dash dot dot, then her voice.

"Hi, it's me," I announce.

"Where in hell have you been? I was starting to get worried."

"I'm with *him*." I stare out the booth to his car. "He's taking me to dinner."

"Don't let him screw you," she says. "Shall I sign you out?"

"Please."

"Baaabra, you're not planning to do anything foolish, aah you?"

"We went to see some parts of Roxbury, and now we're

· *219* ·

stuck in traffic, so he decided to get me dinner. How foolish does it sound?"

"I have to admit not very," she says, "although why Roxbury?"

"It's a slum."

"No kidding!" she says. "Look, forget I asked. When will you be back?"

"Before curfew."

"Okay," she says. "Don't let him rush things."

"Yeah. Have a good time tonight."

"Thanks. I'm not sure if I should wish you the same."

"Oh Maasha," I groan. She laughs and so do I as we hang up.

I get back into the car, and Mr. Appel drives off. Now that we're no longer in traffic he takes out his highway frustration on these narrow streets near the Italian section. He passes cars, screeches around turns. I find my right foot braking an imaginary pedal, my body lurching from side to side. Why is it that every car I'm in has only two possible patterns: motionless or hazardous?

Before I have time to figure this out (it takes only ten years) we arrive at Margherita's, a tiny basement place with dim lighting, red carpets, red-and-white checked tablecloths on little square tables, and everywhere Chianti bottles with candles in them. At the time I'm enormously impressed.

The one middle-aged waiter with shoe-polish black hair greets us ("Professor Appel," he booms), and my heart swells with pride as I notice him nodding his head to me also, as though he approves. Mr. Appel takes my coat (and how awkward I am at this business I can't begin to describe), and we walk to a table, where the waiter tries to pull the chair out from under me but doesn't succeed.

"What would you like to drink?" Mr. Appel asks.

I see trouble ahead but decide on a whiskey sour. He orders that and a martini, the waiter seems perturbed, but Mr. Appel says, "Bring both to me."

I have the funniest feeling he's been through this before. The waiter comes back, sets the drinks in front of him, and walks away. He hands me mine, raises his, says "Cheers" (what, not "To us"?), and takes a big swallow as I sip my sweet concoction and try to fight off the cherry and orange that insist on slipping down near my nose.

"So you like Harry," he glances at me over his menu.

I nod my head vigorously. "Don't you?"

"I worry about his rhetoric; he seems increasingly to be an enormous collection of words." He picks up his martini, finishes it, signals for another. "They sound fine, but I worry when words are so fluent."

I nod without knowing what he's talking about. "He's such a nice person."

"Of course." Mr. Appel taps his finger on his glass; it has a cheap, tinny ring. "I suppose I hold it against him, even though it's been five years, that he argued with me about my divorce. I can't tolerate being *judged*."

"Was it difficult, getting divorced?" I hide my intense curiosity behind the menu and try to figure out the lowest-calorie, least-expensive thing there.

"My wife and I had very little in common when I came back after the war. The problem was the three kids she insisted on having. I was in the first battalion that opened up Buchenwald; the whole thing, going through the war, made me a different person. We had less and less in common. Well," he pauses, "what're you having?"

Torn between shrimp scampi (too expensive) and eggplant parmigiana (too fattening), I finally decide on eggplant; with my superpill still working I'll only eat three bites, and I don't want to be a financial burden on him *already*.

"I was too young when I got married, let that be a lesson to you, although you at least will never have to pay alimony." He rubs his left hand over his forehead as though he's trying to smooth out the creases; I'd like to lean over and help him, make him twenty years younger and smooth away wife and children.

It's hard for me to imagine that he lives in such a different world from the one I see him in: the Professor dispensing wisdom is also a harried divorced man with money problems. I flush that last image out of my mind and picture instead what a wonderful stepmother (kind and competent) I'd be to his kids, and how he'd admire the way I'd care for them. He's looking at me adoringly as I bounce his little girl on my lap, then she runs off (to some unspecified place) and he takes me into his arms, and then and then and then . . . My fantasies always end right here.

The waiter comes, and he orders. I listen to the soft background music as it oozes through the air.

"Have you ever been abroad?" Mr. Appel asks.

I shake my head.

"I'm going to England this summer with some friends." He swallows more of his drink. "Maybe I'll finally get some work done there. I haven't done anything with the notes for my second book. Ah," he shakes his head, "sometimes I think I was more cut out for public relations work than for scholarship."

"Oh, no, no," I say, again not knowing what he's talking about.

"Don't ever have an unhappy love affair," he tells me. "It wreaks havoc with your life. I've been in a tailspin for three years getting over one."

"How terrible." My voice is throbbing with concern, but my mind can't figure out Lenore's place in his tailspin. I feel like I'm being given pieces of his life, none of which fit together.

Then our food arrives. I pick at the delicious, gooey eggplant, thinking that when I was fat I couldn't eat around men and now that I'm thin I still can't eat; is this any way to live? Then I look across at him, the man I'm giving up eggplant parmigiana for, and my heart pounds wildly; I half-close my eyes from the joy of being near him. When he loves me, it'll all be worth it.

On the drive back to Harter pleasure swells inside me, filling me up. I'm near him, I can touch him. For this I'll give up anything.

"This was so nice of you to do," I say as we near Bailey.

"It's nothing. I'll enjoy reading your papers. Only, please, be SURE who everybody else is, even if you don't know about yourself." He laughs.

"I'll do my best." Here we are, right in front of the dorm. Is this it?

"How's Allan?" he asks. Big grin.

"I don't know." And how's Lenore? I'd like to ask. I don't. Love is the best control of all. "I'm not seeing him any more." There. Is that what you want to hear I hope? I'm listening to the underneath of your words, Mr. Appel, that hum and buzz of implication; it *is* there, isn't it?

"You must've broken his heart." He stops the car.

"He has a very tough heart," I tell him.

"And you?"

I shrug my shoulders, and he reaches over, squeezes my hand, and gives me another long, burning stare. "See you in class," he says.

"Thank you," I say.

Chapter Twenty-nine

❧

For the next Saturday class I buy a small bottle of Chanel
Number Five; I'm running out of things I can do, thin and
beautiful, complexion clear, contact lenses, nose job, Dean's
List, what's left? Why hasn't he called yet for a date?

"You smell like a rose," Marsha says. "You look like one
too."

"If only he'd PLUCK me already." I bundle my stem and
leaves into heavy winter gear. All the way up the Hill I think,
pluck me pluck me pluck me—it has a nice ring to it, much
better than "fuck me." Maybe at the moment he's about to
take me that's what I'll say. Mr. Appel, pluck me.

I'm the first one to class, so I nail a seat in the front row.
Allan walks in and starts to sit next to me.

"Bug off," I say.

"Just wanted to ask if you'd gotten your Harry Handsome
yet," he says, picking up his books.

"I hope *your* belly blows up next time," I snap.

He laughs and walks to the back of the room. "Any time you want me I'm yours," he says, just as Mr. Appel comes into the room.

"No chance," I answer, good and loud, then turn toward the front of the room and blush again.

Mr. Appel appears not to notice anything. He says, "I'm going to announce this in class today; a lot of you are doing projects in Boston; if you feel like dropping by, just call and come over." He writes his address and phone number on the board. "I like my students to feel they can visit, with their friends, if they want to." He's looking at me as though he's afraid I'll get the wrong idea, that he's interested in my body. Jesus, Mr. Appel, that's the idea I WANT you to have. With my luck he'll have had a Change of Heart; he'll vow to take up only with thirty-year-olds just in time for me.

I cross my legs, look, see? a crotch. I don't know if it's in full working order, but at least it's there.

He smiles and plays with his notes, penciled jottings on dozens of pieces of paper, no yellowed lecture notes for him; unfortunately, not too much organization either. If he had me to straighten out his life and care for him, he could stop running after lousy girls who tell everyone about their affair (I'll only tell Marsha and Rona and swear them to secrecy) and relax and devote himself to his brilliant work. Whatever that is.

Bong.

Lenore comes in late, carrying a snowball. I turn around, catch a glimpse of her out of the corner of my eye threatening to throw it, my God she wouldn't, at him.

"Don't do it," he says in a tone that makes me shudder.

I uncross my legs and recross them, let the skirt slide above my knees. Lenore walks out.

"Before looking at minority cultures I'd like us to spend some time on the majority culture. We think of it, in broadest terms, as the Western way." He looks out at the class. "What do we mean by this?"

"Frozen foods and flush toilets," a girl says; the class laughs, Mr. Appel smiles wanly; he prefers jokes to be his own. I love ALL his idiosyncrasies, I barely smile; let that man have ANYthing he wants, he's so wonderful and insecure.

"It seems to me that the Western tradition," he says, "is a group of assumptions about human nature. But is there such a thing as human nature?"

Oh Mr. Appel, I think, you're trying to trap us; of course there's such a thing: everybody loves, hates, fears, wishes . . .

"I think not," he says.

Aha, I say to myself, maybe not.

"And one of the prime assumptions about human nature in our tradition concerns human reason. It's clear, for example, that our Founding Fathers believed that in an environment that supported reason, it would flourish, that one could go so far as to build a government upon it." He pauses. "Is man a reasonable animal?"

"No," I say. On this subject I have no doubts.

"Why not?"

"Because people behave irrationally most of the time," I point out.

"Of course," he says, "the irrational is not necessarily negative. Loyalty, love, all the ties that bind people are irrational. Sometimes the richest parts of personal life may be irrational." He's directing this to me. Yes, Mr. Appel, I'm listening. Am I hearing you right? Are you telling me to be unafraid to love you? I will. I do. But why haven't you called me for a date?

Chapter Thirty

❧

Starvation is all that drives us to Sunday dinner. We're out of food; like squirrels in a too-long winter, our supply of nuts has run out. I'm so low on gum, I'm reduced to Spearmint from the candy machine in the basement of Bailey. Marsha is entirely out of pears, and her Pepperidge Farm collection is reduced to two or three plains, no more chocolate-filleds. In this weather, who can make it to town?

At eleven forty-five Marsha and I get into slip, stockings, dress; Rona will be along in five minutes without Jo, who sleeps till two on Sundays.

"Where'd she go last night?" Marsha asks.

"Another mixer. Harter Med, I think."

Marsha throws a heavy wool dress over her head. "Mixers can be divided into two categories, the merely hideous and the crushing."

Finally I can agree; thinness frees me to be honest, and

believe me, fat girls, take heart, mixers are lousy for every-body—even the girls who're dancing. They were invented by people who like to promote hatred between the sexes. Harter, for instance, has a million mixers a year.

Knock at the door. Rona walks in. "You're not going to believe this. Jo found herself a boyfriend. A med student. Freshman. They have a date tonight, next week, and forever. They fell in love last night."

"Did Jo take off her girdle this time?" Marsha wants to know.

"Don't laugh," Rona says. "She got her doctor. See how persistence pays off?"

"And she never lost a pound," I add, full of wonder.

We walk out the door down the corridor, past Mrs. Hibbard in the living room, out into another cold, gray day. We slide down the half-ice, half-kosher-salt steps, and, arms linked, skid down the road to the cafeteria. We're quiet. I'm thinking: see? Reticence gets you nowhere.

"Listen," Marsha points out, "we don't even know if he's nice. Does she?"

"He's alive, that's all she knows," Rona answers. "What else is there?"

"Phooey." I nearly lose my balance as we navigate the iced-over entrance to the cafeteria. Is that God punishing me for my evil thoughts? Is it a warning? I decide to throw caution to the winds: did He punish Jo? "I'm sick of waiting around. Mr. Appel said we should call and visit; that's what I'm going to do."

"Oh NO!" Marsha shouts.

We're inside now, stamping our feet, taking off gloves and rubbing hands together. Today there's no line, so we walk straight into the dining hall. Only Sunday dinner can make you wish for a line. We sit down, await a prayer and to be served our meal by the scholarship girls. It's disgusting. We find a corner table, throw our coats on the chairs, and sit facing the aluminum knives, forks, spoons, and look around to see which house president is going to be giving us our word from On High today. Celia is everybody's favorite: no one can tell what she's reading, and then for some mad reason (is softness of voice a contagious disease?) when she's finished, the entire room *whispers* the Lord's Prayer. A nice, soft, unintelligible hmmmmmm.

At twelve fifteen the cafeteria doors are shut. No worship, no food: the principle of Sunday dinner. Today a house president with a nice loud voice booms out, "Give not that which is holy unto the dogs, neither cast ye your pearls before swine, lest they trample them under their feet, and turn again and rend you. Ask, and it shall be given you; seek, and ye shall find; knock, and it shall be opened unto you: For everyone that asketh, receiveth; and he that seeketh, findeth; and to him that knocketh, it shall be opened."

I'm torn between two conflicting thoughts: 1. is there a message for me in that? and 2. why are they reading from the New Testament again? They're supposed to stick to the Old. When I was a child in public school and it happened that anyone so much as touched the New Testament, I complained to the teacher. Yes, ladies and gentlemen, even in fourth grade, I was my father's daughter, his spiritual emissary. Because in this particular area he is adamant: no Christmas trees in Jewish homes (don't give him the pagan-tradition routine either) and no Jesus Christing his kids in school. In this I admire him. My first-grade teacher chose me to be one of the Three Kings of Orientar (a little place slightly west of China) because I was one of three tallest kids in class; my father was in school the next day, pushing aside crèches and booming out a sermon on the role of the public school in a pluralistic society. He can't do anything about radio and TV, but I give him credit for this: I never have to follow any big gold-paper stars to Bethlehem, and Chanukah gets equal time in assembly programs.

Today I don't have the strength to complain; we bow our heads: "Our Father Who art in Heaven" (what kills me is that even this is from the New Testament, your basic, Gentile, compromise school prayer. What was wrong with the Twenty-third Psalm? Wouldn't it do the job as well?). . . . "And lead us not into temptation . . ." (this line also kills me. If it is God who leads us into temptation, why in hell are we praying to Him? Why don't we come right out and blame Him? My entire elementary-school education has been spent puzzling over this phrase. Because, if you give God this much *credit,* you're also making Him *guilty.* With this Power doesn't come Glory; Him you can't praise without you also blame. How can people repeat this prayer year after year and not notice?)

I sit down at the table facing my daily bread and temptation, which today is wrapped up into a plate of: slice of dead turkey lying over stuffing, brown gravy, mashed potatoes, green peas, side dish of apple brown betty. Thanks to the big black pill, O Black Pill, which art in bottle, thy will be done, I eat turkey and peas and drink coffee. Led out of temptation and delivered from fatness. For this I'll definitely give thanks.

"It's not *right* for women to call men," Marsha says, "and then run up to their apartments. He won't respect you."

"I don't want him to respect me. I want him to love me."

Marsha takes my dish of apple brown betty.

Rona says to her, "Why aggravate? It's a little crush, she'll get over it soon."

"You don't know her, she's not the light type; I worry if she'll EVER get over this."

I agree with Marsha but not her tone; nothing could be clearer than that I'm on to something big; it's as though all the little breezes that have been blowing me around have suddenly concentrated themselves into one great wind. I feel as if in my old life I was stumbling, now I'm flying. I start singing, " 'Think of the happiest things, that's the way you get your wings, think of rhythm, think of jazz, think of the things that a birdie has, it's easier than PIE. I can fly, I can fly, I can FLY!' "

"She's lost her mind," Marsha says.

I start to laugh. "I know why I thought of that song. It's

because Mr. Appel is young. Marsha, you're so rigid. I'm telling you, he's my Peter Pan. He's not old; he's found the secret of eternal youth!"

"Yeah," Marsha agrees. "He's never grown up."

Rona laughs.

"You've never met him! How can you say that?"

"I don't need to meet him," Marsha argues. "His reputation preceded him."

"I bet you're afraid. I bet you're afraid you might like him."

"Oh, my God," Marsha says. She takes a last bite of dessert. "I have some bad news for you. I heard that Mr. Appel is still fucking Lenore."

"Really?" I say, enormously relieved, why for a second I was afraid she'd tell me he was dead. "I wonder how it began with them." If I could I'd call Lenore to find out. I'm not proud. Maybe I could pick up a pointer or two. Or ten or twenty. The way I am, three hundred pointers might not hurt.

"Doesn't it bother you about Lenore?"

"You don't know about love," I say smugly, and indeed she doesn't; that girl must've been born under an unlucky star. "I'm going to call and tell him I've been wandering around Roxbury."

"In this weather?" Marsha asks.

"He thinks I'm very dedicated. And then I'll ask if he wants some company. Hey, I thought of something else: would he invite the whole class over if he were still fucking Lenore?"

"If he's crazy enough to fuck her, who knows what else he'd do?" Marsha says. "Listen, we're not letting you do this. We're coming with you."

"What do you mean 'we'?" Rona says.

"You're her friend also," Marsha tells her.

"I have enough math problems to do that if I had extra Sundays they'd be filled."

"I'd love you to come," I say, which shocks Marsha. "Then you'll finally see how kind and sweet and gentle and wonderful he is."

"It's very nice of the two of you to make plans for me, but I can't do it," Rona puts in.

"Don't worry," Marsha says, "just say you'll go. She'll call, and he'll say he's busy, and we'll study with clear consciences. I'm giving you a once-in-a-lifetime opportunity to help save a human person."

"All right, all right," Rona agrees.

"God damn it," I yell. "He's gonna say YES! I'll bet *anything.*"

"What can we bet?" Marsha asks.

"How about the cab ride back and forth?" I ask.

"Fine," she says.

"Hurry up and finish so I can call."

"If he says yes," Rona adds, "I'll beat both of you to death with a slide rule."

We finish dinner in silence. On the way back to Bailey I say, "I'll tell him that you two were interested in Roxbury also."

"I've never seen it," Rona says.

"It's a slum," Marsha tells her.

"Oh," she asks, "why would I be interested in a slum?"

"Why would anybody be interested in a slum? Ask Baabra, she's the expert."

"You're interested in comparing Brooklyn slums with Boston ones," I ad lib.

"No wonder she's in political science," Marsha says. "I've never seen anyone think bullshit so fast."

We wipe our boots free of salt on the welcome mat inside the door. Marsha and Rona walk to our room while I go to the pay phone. I don't need to look up his number, I have it memorized, and with very cold hands I dial.

In two minutes I'm in our room. "Come on, you two unbelievers. He says he and a friend are just sitting around and they'd love to have company."

Rona says to Marsha, "You I could murder."

"Don't," I say, "I already called a cab, and she has to pay for it."

Luckily my hair is set, all I have to do is put on eye makeup and contacts and throw myself into a sexier dress. I use the remaining time to fuss at Marsha and Rona. Why are they taking so long to get ready? Why are they putting on so much makeup? Suddenly I wonder how I got myself into this mess, and I make both of them swear hands off Mr. Appel, that they'll leave him to me.

Rona brings her calculus book right into the cab and does problems all the way in to Commonwealth Avenue. She pays us no attention, just bites on the end of a pencil and works away, with the inside light of the cab on. The driver says it doesn't bother him. So there we are, illuminated, three of us sandwiched in the back seat, Rona working, Marsha nagging, and me lost in my favorite dream.

"The thing that kills me," Marsha says in a low voice, "is how you can be in love with someone who's never called you for a date."

I sigh and nod my head. "I think he's shy."

Rona snorts.

"Besides," I say, "think of Rochester and Jane; he never tells her he loves her until the very last second."

"Are you speaking of Jack Benny's chauffeur?" Marsha asks.

I give her my steely stare. "In the book Rochester is trying to test Jane's love, or strengthen it, or something, I forget exactly what."

"If I'm to understand this right," Marsha says, "Mr. Appel is screwing Lenore and not asking you out in order to win *you*."

"Look," I say, "I know this doesn't make sense, but I don't care about *him*, who he's screwing. When you're in love, nothing matters, not even the person you're in love with. Do you understand?"

"No," she answers. "I absolutely do not."

· 235 ·

"This is Commonwealth Avenue, ladies, now which number is it?" the cabbie asks.

"Two thirteen," I say.

"This street looks like Ocean Parkway," Rona says. "How I wish I were there, back in Brooklyn."

"You and me," Marsha tells her.

"You've never even SEEN Ocean Parkway," I say as the cab pulls over to the curb and stops.

Marsha sighs and pays. "Brooklyn has never seemed so desirable as it does now."

We walk up the steps to the door. Before I ring I turn to both of them. "Now, promise. Hands off. And be polite."

"Jesus Christ," Marsha mutters, "make up your mind whether we're gonna insult him or steal him from you."

I ring the bell. "Promise?"

"I'd like to stick my slide rule up . . ."

The buzzer interrupts Rona. "And don't be vulgar," I whisper as I open the door.

"Do you mind if we breathe?" Rona whispers back.

"Don't ask," Marsha tells her. "Don't ask."

"Hi," that beautiful voice with the New York accent yells. "Barbara?"

All the *r*'s where they should be.

"Yes. Hi," I yell back, voice shaking. Hand shaking. Calm down, I talk to myself, calm down. You're pretty, he likes you, relax.

We walk down the hall to where he's standing. "I'm glad you dropped by. You must be freezing."

"We are." My teeth are chattering, not from cold, but what a good excuse to have. We walk in and I introduce Rona and Marsha, and he introduces us to his friend Arthur Wales, whom I call Mr. Wales, but only once; he's one of those people who insist, absolutely insist, on being called by his first name, Art. It's practically a religion with him, and the reason for this is: then no one will feel inferior around him. This principle seems to be the mainstay of his career; white

Anglo-Saxon Protestant helper of the poor, he wants to be mistaken for a black person on heroin. He wears loud shirts, tight black pants, and desert boots, and is going bald at an incredibly rapid rate. In spite of everything he does, he still looks like a social worker. He's young too, he was one of Mr. Appel's students, he tells us, five years ago. It's clear that he's been worshiping Mr. Appel ever since.

Mr. Appel holds my hands between his to warm them while Marsha and Rona are helping Art hang the coats. Can a person die from excess of love? If so, call an ambulance; I'm half dead.

We walk into the living room, and I sit down on the couch. Marsha sits next to me, my own jiminy cricket, and Rona sits in a chair.

"What would you like to drink?" Mr. Appel asks. "Coffee, tea, soup, wine, whiskey?"

I say, "Sherry, please." Marsha and Rona ask for the same. Art sits down on the couch next to Marsha, and Mr. Appel comes back from the kitchen with glasses and sherry, and sits in the chair next to Rona. Off to a wonderful start.

"Art and I were trying to figure out a warmer place to live," he says, handing us huge amounts of sherry. "It has to have excellent beaches and be wonderfully democratic."

Marsha laughs and says, "Before I heard the second half of the sentence I was going to suggest Spain."

No wonder she looks cheerful; if he'd tell her he's about to leave the country it would make her day.

"We've been thinking about it for the last half hour and we've decided that only cold climates have democracies; the better the beach, the worse the government." Mr. Appel takes a huge swig of his drink.

I notice Marsha's eyes narrowing as she watches him; I can read her mind: sure, she'll say, on top of everything else he's an alcoholic. I watch him take a second swallow. I wonder if he is. It bothers me for half a second until I decide that I could cure him of that too. If he had me, would he need whiskey?

"Of course, considering that we live in *this* country, I don't know why we should be so picky about the others," he says.

Art gives us this: isn't he a genius? look. I smile back at him and then turn toward Mr. Appel. He's wearing the big gray pullover he lent me the first night I met him; does he remember that? Maybe someday I'll remind him of it, our first anniversary perhaps, or when our child is born. Nondescript brown baggy pants, loafers, and he slouches in his chair, sprawls, really; I've never known anyone so constitutionally unable to sit or stand straight. My mother would plotz if she could see him. Next to weight and pimples, posture is her greatest concern. I hear myself arguing with her: look, I'll say, so YOU won't marry him; I love him even *with* the stoop shoulders.

"It's not *that* bad here," Marsha says.

"I'm not happy with what's going on in this country," he responds. "I think the way people are unable to discipline themselves is a reflection of a sick culture. The fact that all anyone wants is money and that the biggest business in this society is public relations indicates to me that something is wrong."

"I don't think it's terrible to want money," Marsha argues.

"There are more things to human relationships than a cash nexus." He takes another drink. "Materialistic wants are a small part of what human beings desire. They want love and tenderness along with material goods."

I'm looking at him as he says this; it's clear what he needs, the affection he lacks; and me, I'm overflowing with it, for God's sake; it's practically killing me there's so much of it; it swells up inside me and I have no place to put it. Mr. Appel, take me or call an ambulance. I'm about to explode with unexpressed love.

"Of course, that's true," Rona puts in. Thank heavens for her. "And when you see slums, money seems obscene; the lack of it is so terrible."

Mr. Appel *beams* at her. I'll kill her; when we get back to the dorm, I'll murder her; she's trying to STEAL him!

"The thing is," I get up the courage to say, "it's hard to know what to do about all the problems."

He turns and smiles at me, oh those beautiful crooked teeth, how I love them, the mouth and eyes and glasses and weak chin. "It seems to me that it's possible to know, the harder problem is what to DO. The tragedy of America . . ." he laughs and says, "Wait, now why should I try this without my text?" He gets up and takes his Immigrants book down from the shelf, opens it, and reads: "The tragedy of America is that its problems come from too-weak people, not from too-strong, like dictators. The deep sickness of this country is that it has never been governed."

"Lovely," Art says.

Mr. Appel beams some more.

Art asks Rona and Marsha what year they're in, what their majors are, where they're from, and Mr. Appel and I just look at each other.

Then he says, in the middle of their conversation, "Barbara, would you help me put out some food, please?"

"Sure." I practically leap to my feet; perhaps he'd like me to cook and clean also? Listen, anything, Mr. Appel, I'll do anything, only please, please, ASK.

I follow him out of the living room down the corridor to the small kitchen. I'm shaking again; the two-inch heels on my boots feel like stilts. Am I going to lose my balance and fall? I make it into the kitchen and grip the table, which has bread and cheese and cake on it.

"Will you cut the bread?" He hands me a serrated knife.

"Sure." I bend over and start slicing hard French bread, concentrate on what I'm doing, the happy homemaker, competent and capable. I'm cutting as though my life depended on it, totally unconscious of where he is or what he's doing, till I feel him at my right, putting an arm around my waist and pulling me to him. I'm so startled and frightened that I keep holding the knife at my side until, when he has me nearly pressed against him, it gets him first, right in the ribs.

"Ouch!" He winces and lets go. "Did you do that on purpose?"

"No." My eyes well up; can I slit my wrists with a serrated knife, I wonder? I put it down. "I'm sorry."

He turns me around and holds me and kisses me long and hard; his teeth hurt my lips, his tongue is the longest one I've ever felt in my short career as a sexual being, and I feel like vomiting. At the same time I realize this is the happiest moment of my life and try to cherish it. I put my arms around his neck, and when he takes his mouth away I keep holding on and bury my head in his shoulder.

"You're wonderful as long as you're weaponless," he laughs. "Hey, what's the matter?" He removes my arms from his neck and looks at the tears running down my face. "What's the matter?" he repeats.

"I like you so much," I blurt out. Then the tears pour.

"I know," he says, after a moment. "And I could hurt you so much."

I feel like cold water has been thrown in my face; the tears stop immediately. I don't understand him.

"You're very pretty," he tells me. "You're going to be a beautiful woman. Very aristocratic; you look like a European princess."

Mr. Appel, I want to say, please, write those words down and send them to my parents, so they'll die happy.

"Smile, Barbara," he says. "They'll think *I* tried to stick a knife in *your* ribs."

Remembering makes me smile and then laugh. Besides, it's starting to be real to me, the kiss, for the first time. HE LOVES ME.

"What are you doing next weekend?" he asks.

I hold on to the table; my heels are growing again, the room is spinning; listen, Mr. Appel, next weekend I don't know, but this weekend I'm fainting. "Nothing but work. I have a ton of it."

He shakes his head. "I was thinking, I don't feel like skiing,

I was going to ask you to go with me, but I'm getting too old for it. Just the idea tires me."

I let go of the table and hug him and say, "You're not old," only my arms, resting on his waist, feel a roll of flab around his middle, different from a young man's, looser, sadder, older. "You're not old," I repeat. "Besides that's not my idea of a terrific way to spend a weekend."

"What is," he asks, "besides going to church on Sunday?" He smiles this indulgent smile, looks at me like I'm what? a sweet shiksa princess, who needs a tour of slums to give her a social conscience? "Whatever it is, let's do it next weekend."

"Look," I say. "You stay here, I'm going to take the food in; before I go I have something awful to confess, the worst deep, dark secret of my life. Then when I come back you tell me if it's still on, okay?"

"If you have syphilis, it's off." He's trying to look calm, believe me.

"Worse than that." I pick up the cheese and bread and head for the door. "I'm Jewish."

I hear him laugh as I go out the door to the living room, so I figure I must've handled it right. Art takes the bread and cheese from me and puts it on the table. "What's Henry laughing about?" he asks.

"I told him I'm Jewish," I say.

"What in God's name is funny about THAT?" Marsha wants to know. And that isn't all she wants to know, either; I can tell by the way she's looking at my hair which is, ladies and gentlemen, finally out of place.

"You'll have to ask him." I turn around and walk back to the kitchen.

Mr. Appel is leaning on the refrigerator when I return.

"So am I," he laughs.

Big news. I look at him and nod. Listen, Mr. Appel, with me people might make a mistake, but you, only Helen Keller would have doubts and not if you let her hands play over your face and rest on that nose with the bump in the middle.

"Yes, I know."

"What do you mean, you *know?*" he asks.

"What do you mean, what do I mean?"

"Do I carry a sign?" He looks hurt, insulted.

"Oh, come on," I try to jolly him out of it. "We're both Brooklyn Jews, only I had a nose job."

"I was born in Manhattan." He sounds angry.

Where? I want to ask. The Lower East Side?

"So you're *not* Jewish," I say.

He laughs a little, mollified, I guess, by that. "The trouble with Jewish women is that they're too damned shrewd."

I walk over to him again, press my body against his (feel THAT, you meshugana; in bed we're all alike; shut your ears and you'll never know my religious affiliation), and say, "For you I'll be an idiot."

"How about for me not being so Jewish?"

"I'll try."

He kisses me again. Ladies and gentlemen, my dreams are coming true. Did someone say Jews have no heaven. But I'm in it right now, even with his teeth bruising my mouth; he kisses *hard*.

"What do you want to do next weekend?" he mumbles into my hair.

I sigh, thinking, *I've passed.* "I don't care, I just want to be with you."

"Whoa," he says. "Take it easy, honey. You're pushing me."

I'm absolutely quiet. Have I got a lot to learn! I thought I was saying the nicest thing one person could possibly say to another, the only words I want to hear. I try to understand his point of view: is loving someone an act of aggression?

"Was that a stupid thing to say?" I ask.

"Too pushy," he answers. "Too Jewish."

I pick up the rest of the food. "Where can one take shiksa lessons?"

"Right here." He pats my head and follows me into the

living room. "Right here." He laughs a big deep laugh, so I do too. Shiksa lesson number one: laugh when you ought to cry.

"Tell us, what's funny about being Jewish?" Art asks him as we both sit down, me on the couch, him back on the chair. He's trying to look as though he doesn't know me, only, sorry about this, Mr. Appel, my lipstick is on your mouth. Next time don't kiss so hard, it leaves fewer marks.

"God only knows," he says. Now THAT is funny.

It's a very short time before Marsha starts fidgeting and Rona begins talking about her calculus assignment.

"I think I'd better call a cab," Marsha finally says.

"Don't. I'll drive you home," Mr. Appel offers.

It takes a tremendous effort to restrain myself from leaping up and hugging him. I look at Marsha: see how sweet and kind and considerate he is? She looks back at me with unreadable eyes.

We put on our coats; Mr. Appel helps Rona and Marsha with theirs, Art helps me, then leaves us on the street in front of the little black Volkswagen. Marsha and Rona get into the back, and I sit in front, flying. By the time we get to Bailey, Mr. Appel and I have been married for years, our two children are in the back seat, and I'm basking in the glow of his love. There's so much warmth inside me I feel like I've swallowed the sun. I don't notice how dark it's getting, clouds gathering, snow beginning to fall, until we get home. When he stops the car, I finally notice that there's no light any more in the sky.

"Stay a moment," he says.

"Okay." I let Marsha and Rona out.

I get back in the car; he parks across the street from the dorm, illegal, but at least the front-door light won't touch us here. He reaches for me, and I lean over, straining, so he can kiss me. What a rotten place to neck is the front seat of a VW; should I tell him about Allan's Rambler? My head is about to fall off. He releases me, finally; I sit back and try to straighten the vertebrae. Out the front door of Bailey come Frannie, Celia, and Biff.

"If there were more Jews here," I say, watching them walk, "sororities and rules wouldn't be such a big thing, I could bring you into the dorm, into my room. If there were more Jewish teachers, you wouldn't have to flip out about the lack of political activity and faculty apathy." I look at him. "How come you stay at this lousy place? Being a token Jew?"

"I like it that way," he says, "better than being surrounded by them."

"Your People?"

"Oh, honestly, Barbara," he says. "You have the most parochial mind I've ever seen."

I vow to do something about it immediately.

He lunges at me, kisses me, opens my coat and pushes my breasts around. Ugh, I want to yell, be *gentle*. But maybe he'd think THAT was parochial too, so I just kiss him back, put my hands around his neck, and play with the few remaining hairs on his head.

When he drives away, I watch his car, half covered by snowflakes, white on black, go slowly down the road, illuminated every few yards by a light so that in the darkness it disappears, appears, disappears, until it's finally gone. The light in front of Bailey shines through the falling snow; in its beam you can watch snowflakes drifting down, buoyant and lazy. The light cuts sharply through the darkness where it's nearest the lamp and then, as it gets farther from it, it spreads out, hazes, dims, and fades away. I lift my face up and let the snow fall on it, then walk slowly around the block. If I stood still any longer I'd turn into a snowmaiden: here lies Barbara Fabrikant, love-frozen.

My lungs draw in the cold air, nostrils tingle; I try to blow smoke rings with my breath. In front of the cafeteria all the floodlights are on. I look at them and see, my God, the world is so bright it hurts your eyes. The snow doesn't reflect light, it generates it, and the snow-laden branches of trees aren't fuzzily there, they're piercing the sky, pointing into it; the streets stab me with their sharp lines. I notice how cars look going fast, that you have to keep your eye on one point and let the rest fuzz, that your eye doesn't focus on the whole moving thing, the eye wants to hold it still. I feel myself walking, stand up straight, and no longer think, how beautiful, but how miraculous. I feel, I feel, I feel my muscles, I feel my arms and legs press, I feel the wool against my skin, I feel, I feel, I feel again. It's happened. I'm alive.

I drift back and forth in front of the cafeteria: I'm too happy to know what to do with myself: have dinner, skip it, roll in the snow; nothing makes any difference. I want to hold this feeling, taste it, hang on to it forever. Life is beautiful, I think; maybe there is a God after all.

Someone taps me on the shoulder, Marsha naturally. She pulls me into the cafeteria.

"It's impossible," I say, "to describe what I'm feeling without being corny. Why is that? Where are some new words?"

"For such an old feeling?" she says. "Don't worry about being corny. Do you want to talk?"

I start to cry. Again the same slow, silent, unaccompanied tears. "I love him." I wipe the wet off my face as we stand at the end of the line.

"Yes," she says, "and he?"

"He said I was beautiful and wonderful. He wants to see me next weekend. He *kissed* me. He *likes* me. Why are you looking at me that way?"

The line is moving fast tonight. Marsha picks up a tray and silverware; I imitate her, so unconscious that I even take a glass of milk when she does and forget my tea. We find an empty table and spread our coats on the other chairs. Stay away, please, Harter girls.

"I'm torn," she says. "For your sake I'd like to believe that he cares for you, and maybe I'm jealous: where's MY big romance? But he drinks too much, and I don't trust him."

"You don't need to," I say. "You're not involved with him."

"And you are."

"And I are," I say.

"Baabra, are you sure *he is* with you?"

I think: he hugged me, he kissed me, he said I was pretty, we laughed together, and we have a date for next weekend. I love him. I'm going to marry him. "What more does he have to do to prove it?" I ask.

"Oh, Baabra," she says. "Oh, Baabra."

Chapter Thirty-one

Shiksa rule number two: no one must know about him and me. This he doesn't need to tell me, this I've figured out on my own. Tuesday morning I get up at eight thirty and dress in a Monday/Wednesday/Friday outfit, and walk into class too late to get a front-row box seat.

Here I am, Mr. Appel, your own true love. The image of our getting married before admiring crowds of thousands of Harter women, all hideously envious, has never been entirely erased from my mind. Nor has the other dream disappeared, the one where he brings me back to Bailey after a date and we cling and caress right there on the front steps in full view of Frannie, Celia, and Mrs. Hibbard. However, I'm not up to making love in class, even in fantasy, although I *suppose* I wouldn't mind if he blushed and stammered and dismissed the class half an hour early (because the sight of me was driving him wild with desire) and then bolted the door and drew the shades and pulled me onto the desk on top of him and stroked me hungrily, kissing me and murmuring how he couldn't live without me.

I glue my eyes to him, and the one time he returns my look, it goes right through me. He continues chatting with the girls nearer him.

I open my notebook, business as usual, unscrew the fountain pen. Unfortunately, as soon as he begins to talk, all I hear him say is: "You're going to be a beautiful woman," and since I KNOW that won't be on the test, I content myself with drawing little houses, cubes with nice pointy tops, long rectangular houses, tall thin ones. An entire page full of living quarters.

The class is discussing something, I can hear them buzzing around me; wait, there's an argument, something unusual here. What's more, it's Lenore talking. I snap to attention.

"Mr. Appel," she says, "you think people are much better than they are. You think they want to improve their society, but they don't. All anybody wants is to have a good time."

"No," he answers, "I reject that. That's another sign of a sick society—not to believe in disinterestedness or honesty or altruism. We think everyone has an angle; we're outraged, but we're never surprised when someone turns out to be dishonest. Well, we should be! Not everybody is a crook."

"Or a saint," she says.

"Yes," he agrees. "Saints are people who try to go it alone. *We* need to join together. But I know what you mean, when you say that people aren't good. Even *my* reason occasionally says that to me; however, my glands are hopelessly optimistic. This society was built by people who risked and cared, and I think they're still kicking around."

"Or just kicking," Lenore says as the bell rings.

The class chatters its way out; I stay seated as they go, and then get up and slowly put on my coat; the classroom is empty except for him and me. He's putting his papers into his briefcase.

"Hi." I walk up to the lectern. Now will he fly to shut the door and pull down the shades? Press me to him and say how he can't live without me?

"Barbara, please, don't moon at me during class. Would you like to see me fired?"

"I'm sorry, I didn't realize that teachers could be fired so easily."

"A college community is like a small town," he continues, making me feel like a badly trained dog, "and I want to retain my privacy."

"You want me to drop the course?"

"Don't be melodramatic." Then he looks at me and laughs and so do I. We've thought of it at the same moment, but I say it first. "Too Jewish."

"Where are you going now?" he asks.

"To McElroy. French class."

"I'll walk you there, if you promise to look normal," he says. That's a tall order, Mr. Appel, even on my good days.

"It's hard for me not to be happy around you," I whisper.

"You're pushing." Underneath the playful tone he's serious. We walk out together down the hall and out across the snow-covered campus. He's not wearing a coat, naturally, it's a warm thirty degrees, practically spring. Shiksa lesson number three: if someone wants to catch their death of cold, don't tell them to wear boots. Mr. Appel, if my mother saw you now, bareheaded, coatless, in this weather, she'd have my father say *Kaddish* for you in advance.

He looks as though he'd walk three feet away from me if he could still whisper. Poor him, he can't have both. So he puts up with walking next to me, and I wrap my arms around my bookbag to keep from inadvertently slipping one through his arm. Shit, my dream come true, and nobody knows. They see him walking near me and think, big deal, nothing, a teacher and a student. No, no, no. He's my LOVE.

"About this weekend," he whispers, "I find myself swamped with work. Would you mind just spending it at home with me? You have overnight permission, don't you?"

"Yes." Does he think that means I'm not a virgin? I swallow hard; who knew I had such a number of terrible things to reveal about myself: a Jewish virgin, a double criminal.

"Yes, you have overnight permission, or yes, you'll come?"

"Yes both," I say.

"I have an unlisted number. Use it when you sign out: seven-six-five, three-one-nine-eight."

I write it down; should I thank God he's well prepared, or be sick about it?

"I'll give you money for a cab. Come whenever you want Saturday evening." He looks at me. "You can't expect me to pick you up at your dorm, can you?"

I shake my head. Between wishes and expects there is, I'm beginning to see, an awfully wide gulf.

"I have money."

"That's nice. I don't." He laughs. I laugh. We come to the entrance to McElroy. I stand and look at him, my teacher, my love.

"If you don't hurry, you'll be late," he says.

I walk up the stairs. Oh, Mr. Appel, I'm already late. Born Too God-damned LATE!

I rush into class, bong! just in time. Mr. Kendall is already rolling his *r*'s, launching himself with his usual gusto into a discussion of *La Peste,* another book I could live without. Today's discussion seems to be on the symbolism of disease. I sit in the back of the room and try to sleep. It's difficult in this class because conversation tends to be so jarring. Mr. Kendall speaks only French, which means that we get a vague idea of the general direction we're supposed to converse in; the class contributions are in pidgin French (or is it pidgin English?), which means most of us don't understand each other. Could Alice fall asleep at the Mad Hatter's tea party? It's plenty hard here too.

What is the meaning of disease?

It means that someone has the bad.

They're *sick,* that's what it means. What an inappropriate topic for me, the world's happiest human person. In love, and supposed to worry about a plague? I refuse to worry. I sleep with my eyes open, smiling every so often at Mr. Kendall and trying to look as though I know what's going on and am fascinated and am not contributing today because my throat is sore. I clear it every so often and blow my nose.

Class finally ends. Maybe Mr. Appel is waiting for me outside. Throw my coat on, rush out. He's not there. I walk to geology class. Take out notebook and pen. Bong!

Today we're considering fossils, how they're found, dated, used to date rocks, what they tell us about former surfaces of the earth. From bubonic plagues to millions of years of death; how is one to keep cheerful? Just the word "fossil" makes me shiver—you mean I could be dead that long? longer? forever? Okay, God, here I am trying to believe in you. But for Jews what good are you? What do you promise us anyway? If I were to believe, I'd have to convert, because Jews die (and become fossils), and Gentiles live forever.

"The principle is perfectly simple," Professor Pearson says. "If you find fish fossils in the middle of what's now dry land, you can assume that the land was once a body of water." To me, it's equally possible that some dinosaur caught a fish and dragged it off a couple of miles to enjoy a meal in peace and quiet away from the ocean. Professor Pearson tries to talk us into believing that Harter College was once a glacier; he says you can tell because of the drumlin the retreating glacier left behind. Meanwhile, Professor, try walking down the stepless path, you'll think you're *still* atop a glacier. Talk to Mrs. Hibbard for a few minutes, you'll wish for the entire return of the Ice Age.

I find myself writing: "Should I see a gynecologist? Geology. Gynecology. Genealogy." I see I'm lost to learning today. No wonder Marsha has trouble concentrating; how can you worry about the Pleistocene when you've got a crotch to take care of?

Bong! Good-bye, dead rocks.

I rush back to the dorm. Marsha is already there, lying in her bed, eating a vanilla yogurt. On my desk is a coffee yogurt.

"You made it to town?" I ask.

"Couldn't stand it any more, so I started walking down at eleven."

She has a kind of guilty look on her face; ordinarily I'd never notice it, but today my nerves are strung so tight I think they'd vibrate to radio waves.

"What do you mean 'started'?"

"I was halfway down the hill when Mr. Appel saw me and offered to give me a lift to the market and back."

"You *accepted* a ride from a man you don't trust?"

"I trust him as a driver," Marsha says. "Barbara, don't you trust me?"

"I don't know. He's so wonderful, I can't imagine anyone *not* being in love with him."

"He was very nice. Apparently he's met my father's brother somewhere, I forget where. He didn't make the connection Sunday." She sighs.

"Why are you looking sad? Unrequited love?" I sit down on the bed and start crying. "Or requited!"

"Are you melodramatic!" She walks over to my bed. "I don't like him, remember? I *really* don't. If you're gonna hate me, at least hate me for the right reason."

"I much prefer hating you for that," I sniffle.

She laughs. "Feel free."

I open the yogurt. "Thanks for shopping." Take a spoonful. "Are you SURE you don't love him?"

"I'd like to see him fired, tootsie, for moral turpentine."

"He's not raping anybody," I point out.

She walks back to her vanilla yogurt.

"How would I go about finding a gynecologist?" I ask.

She chokes.

"I'm going to stay with him this weekend."

"That's his idea for a first date?" she asks. "You must be

going crazy. When Allan asked you to sleep with him after two MONTHS you were insulted.

"This is different."

"How?"

"First of all I love him," I tell her. "Secondly you can't talk to a forty-year-old man the way you do to a twenty-year-old."

"My point exactly," Marsha interrupts.

"But I love HIM. I can't help it that he's not my age."

"So you've said."

"You can't *choose* with whom you fall in love, it just *happens*."

Marsha sighs again. "What will he think of you if you sail up to his apartment the first date and fuck?"

"What will he think of me if I say I'm waiting till I get married? Bad enough I'm a virgin, what do you think he'll do if I give him my father's sermon?"

"There must be a happy middle," she says.

"What? I'll let him only halfway in?"

"Barbara, how about *waiting* a while, a *week* or two maybe, see how it develops."

"What develops? Where can it go? I love him." I pause. "This is good coffee yogurt—fresh."

"Can't you wait to see if he loves you?"

"How is he going to love a Jewish virgin who won't fuck, answer me that!" Oh yes, I've worked this out in my head. Being me, just like being fat, I haven't got a *chance*.

"Lots of men manage," she argues.

"He won't." In my head I see the line of beautiful, young, experienced shiksas waiting to snag him, ready to fuck, do God knows what else (is there anything else? does someone have a book on it?). He's not going to wait around for *me*.

Dash dot dash. My ring. I jump up. "It's HIM." Rush out door, fly down corridor, open door, run to phone. Can't speak. Take deep breath.

"Hello?"

"Hi, it's me, Allan."

"Oh."

"Forgive me for living," he says. "I wanted to ask you out for dinner Saturday night."

"Doris's belly giving you trouble again?" I ask.

"No," he says. "I figured out that I love you, although it DOES make me mad that you couldn't get thin for me."

"Oh, Allan." For the first time I feel sorry for him. "I'm involved with someone else."

There's silence.

"Allan?"

"That's certainly depressing news," he says. "Seriously?"

"Yes." How much more serious could it be? "Allan? Would it be wrong if I offered to fix you up?"

He groans. "Of course it would. With whom?"

"Rona. My friend with the red hair. She's very cute. And thin."

"Okay. When shall I call her?"

"Tomorrow," I say. "Hey, listen, I, uh, think you're really fine, uh, a fine person." Again the stupid tears are in my eyes.

"I wish you loved me," he says.

"In a way I wish I did too," I tell him. "It'd be a lot easier."

"Would it?" He sounds immensely cheered.

"Yeah," I say. "Listen, Rona's last name is Glasser."

"Is she my favorite religious group?" he asks.

"What else?"

"You've spoiled me for Christian girls," he says.

"Have I?"

"Thank God, at least I was circumcised."

"Were you?"

"Couldn't you tell?" he asks.

"Yours was the only one I'd ever seen. Except my brother's when he was a baby, and who looked then?"

He laughs. "Hey, if this thing doesn't work out, you know my number."

"Yeah. Thanks."

"I wish you the worst luck in the world," he says.

"The same to you," I tell him.

I tiptoe down the corridor past our room and knock softly at Rona's and Jo's and gently twist the knob and walk in.

"Glad to see you," Rona says. "If Jo tells me once more about the kind of diamond she wants from Cartier's I'll kill her. You came in time to save her life. Jo, be eternally grateful."

"Listen," I say, "you have a chance to make me eternally grateful."

Jo interrupts. "Lenny's taking me to meet his parents over spring vacation."

"Wonderful." I wonder if Mr. Appel has parents, or if they're dead. And anyway, does a man his age take his intended to meet his parents or his children?

"It was love at first sight," Rona croons. "He's a budding doctor, and she's the only child of wealthy parents."

"We were enormously attracted to each other," Jo argues.

"Of course you were." Rona's voice is surprisingly mild. "I'm teasing you; do I still get to be a bridesmaid?"

"Yeah, and wear a pink outfit that'll clash with your hair," Jo answers.

"If you two wouldn't mind postponing the wedding plans," I say, "I have a mission of mercy for Rona."

"Good-bye." Rona starts up from the bed.

"Wait. It's not bad. Allan just called. He's very depressed. Won't you go out with him? As a favor to me?"

Silence.

"Please?"

"Okay," she says. "As a favor to you. But I can't this weekend, I'm busy."

"He'll call you tomorrow," I tell her.

"You already told him yes?" The red is spreading from her hair down.

"I knew you'd do it, you're such a sweet, kind person."

"Between you and Jo," she says, "I could be driven to violence."

"He's a fabulous make-out," I remind her.

"Then it won't be a total loss." She grins. "Hey, who're you gonna fix Marsha up with?"

I give her a puzzled look.

"To keep HER away from Mr. Appel." Rona laughs good and hard.

I blush redder than her hair. "There's a whole list of girls I have to fix up, practically the entire world!"

"Don't worry," she says, "about me. As far as I'm concerned he's yours."

"Thanks. And thanks about Allan."

She laughs some more as I leave and go back to our room. Marsha looks expectantly at me.

"Not Him. Allan. He was very depressed so I fixed him up with Rona."

"You WHAT?" She shakes her head. "You're going out of your mind."

"It wasn't much of a mind to be in anyway," I tell her. "I'm happier out of it."

"Has Rona agreed to this?"

I nod my head.

"I can hardly wait for the four of you to double."

I try to visualize it, Rona and Allan in the back seat of the VW, Mr. Appel and I in the front, off to go dancing. I wonder if Mr. Appel dances. Fox-trots? *I* call Mr. Appel Henry, and *they* have to call him Mister. Allan and he fight over me. If only I could have his love and Allan's kisses: how is it that a twenty-year-old boy necks so much better than a man twice his age? Or is there something wrong with my response? Allan gets me excited the way he goes slowly, touches me, holds back, kisses softly over and over, brushes lips lightly until I open my mouth. I'm the one who can't stand it light any more; he makes me want more of him than he's giving. Is it weird what excites me? Am I not like other women? Just thinking about Allan makes me hot. I had expected, since I don't even like him and he can do such wild things to me, that when Mr. Appel kissed me my head would blow off. Why didn't it?

"Maybe it'll get better," I say out loud.

"What 'it'?"

"Oh, everything. Maybe everything'll work out fine and shock you to pieces." I lie down and pick up my Introductory Literature text and try to concentrate on "Corinna's Gone A-Maying."

"Maybe the Pope'll convert," Marsha says, "and marry Princess Margaret."

"Why Princess Margaret?" I ask.

"Why not?" she answers.

Chapter Thirty-two

❦

Thursday afternoon is my scheduled conference with Mr. Appel. Should I keep it or not? Marsha is in the library, out of consultation range. Will he be angry if I go? If I don't? While I'm ruminating, I'm putting in my lenses, making up, getting dressed. I'm hungry to see him; if I could stare at him twenty hours a day, drink in that face, those big knobby, rough hands, that body, maybe I'd be able to stay away from a conference. But right now I'm insatiable, I'll never have enough of him, never be tired of him, never want to be anywhere but with him. Why have I such an appetite? I feel like a cannibal, a love-cannibal.

I put on earrings, admire myself in the mirror and head up the Hill. He's alone when I get there; his door is open but I knock anyway and walk in.

"Hello," he says.

"Hi. I wasn't sure whether I ought to come."

"Why in the world not?"

Good question, Mr. Appel. Well, see, I thought since I was planning to spend the *weekend* with you. . . .

He pulls out my last paper, comparing the rate of unwed motherhood in various minority groups. "This is fine work, excellent writing; however, I gave you a B-plus."

"Why?"

"I've given you so many A's your record is starting to look odd."

"What in the world does THAT mean?" For my grades I'll speak up.

"I give practically no A's."

"I worked plenty hard for mine." British understatement; first I lose thirty pounds and second I spend half my waking hours being brilliant for YOU, you ingrate.

"I know. You'll probably get an A-minus in the course." He opens my paper to the second page. "And here's another one of your Barbara-isms: 'Jewish women are rarely unwed mothers, why is that?' " He shakes his head. "Why are you always trying to establish the superiority of the race?"

"I thought it was an interesting point," I say. "And I deserve a straight A in your course. Why should it look so odd? You think you'll be the only A I get? Go ahead and laugh—Jewish women get A's instead of babies."

"You're crazy. Jews are goddamned aborigines, no class, loud, obnoxious. What makes you think they're terrific? What have they painted? Where are their great composers? Or writers, I mean real writers, that compare with Shakespeare or Melville."

"Chagall, Mendelssohn . . ."

"Converted," he says.

"Bellow, Malamud, Singer, Calisher, Philip Roth, Henry Roth. Yeah, and Bernstein, Bloch, Stern, Menuhin, Oistrakh, Rubinstein."

"They're just performers," he says. "Not a Beethoven among them. Or a Dickens."

"You forget da Vinci and Rembrandt," I say.

"Jews have contributed comparatively little to world civilization," he tells me.

I sit in stunned silence. Could he be right? All these years have I been misinformed? miscalculating?

"You look as though you lost your mother," he says. Smiles.

"I'll have to think about what you've said." Near tears, of course.

He gets up and walks to his door, locks it, pulls down the shade. Grabs my wrists. "Come here, my little Jewess, don't be sad."

Pressed against him, feeling him hold my body, thin for him, oh, appreciate it please (he seems to), his hands are all over me, that feels *good,* then we kiss and it's awful, so I concentrate on my body against his. Does he have an erection? I can't tell. Anyway, I'm not sad any more.

"I . . ." (love you, love you). "I'm very fond of you," I whisper in his ear, "even though you're Jewish." Hold my breath.

He laughs. Got him. "Same to you," he says. "Actually, you should be highly complimented; I don't usually like Jewish women at all."

"Was your mother that bad?"

"What *are* you talking about?" He shakes his head again, takes his arms away, looks like he'd like to shake me. "Please don't do cheap-jack psychoanalysis on me."

"Well, Mr. Appel," I reply, "you should be highly complimented too. I usually don't like *men.*" Smile.

He looks a little nervous, but manages to laugh.

"I'm a terrible Puritan." He takes me in his arms again as he says this.

"Me too," I manage to get out before he opens my mouth with his and thrusts his tongue in. When he takes his mouth away, I whisper, "I'm afraid."

"So am I," he says. I'm sure he must be joking. What has HE got to be afraid of?

"What am I going to call you?" I ask as he nuzzles my neck.

Just then there's a knock on the door, and he jumps away from me. Straightens his shirt and tie. I wore very little lipstick today, using my head for once, and there's only a smidgin on his lips. I take out a Kleenex and wipe it off.

"You can always call me Doctor," he laughs. "One minute!" he calls in the direction of the door. "Or Rabbi." He laughs even harder. "How about that, would that make you happy?"

The look on my face, if he didn't enjoy his joke so much and was able to see it, must be a study. But he never notices.

Chapter Thirty-three

🌷

I expect Saturday to dawn differently. Maybe the sun will shoot into the heavens instead of drifting up slowly from beneath the Hill. Or the birds will sing a song that I understand. The frost will be jewels, and everything will glitter, not frozen but from this miracle.

I plan to be up at five thirty A.M. but I sleep through my alarm and am finally awakened at eight forty by Marsha's clock radio. Rush out of bed, to bathroom, into clothes, up the Hill. The day continues badly, a lousy combination of hectic (rush to class, rush to next class, rush rush rush) and then draggy, all afternoon, will it never become two, three? I pace around the room. Marsha leaves for a weekend of skiing with Robert. Instead of saying good-bye, she tells me, "Take care of *yourself.*" She must know: all I can dream of is caring for him.

Four o'clock, five o'clock. Pack a few books and clothes and one sexy nightgown (bought at Filene's just for tonight) into one suitcase. Wash hair, set it, dry it, call a cab. Dress. Finally, seven fifteen. Sign out for the weekend.

The cab hits traffic practically the minute we round Powderhouse Park and leave Wetton. Drag, drag. Finally the exit to Back Bay. Almost there. Heart pounding. Take out lipstick from purse. It's cold. Hands shaking, apply the icy pink to nervous lips. Commonwealth Avenue: the park in the middle of the road, beautiful old houses, much prettier than Ocean Avenue. Cab stops. Pay. Walk up stairs. Ring. Bzzzzz.

Suitcase feels so heavy, it's pulling me downstairs while I walk up.

He opens the door. Takes my valise and puts it on the floor, helps me with my coat. Then he holds my hands, just like in the fantasy, and says, "What a beautiful dress." The black velvet, taken in, my neck and arms and part of chest (bye-bye, Mama F.) show. No jewelry except gold earrings.

He leads me to the couch, sits down behind the coffee table stacked high with books and a huge glass half-filled with ice and bourbon; the bottle is there too.

"I haven't eaten yet," he says as I sit down beside him. "Have you?"

"Sort of," I say. "Let me cook for you."

"Absolutely not!" he yells. "Don't start chicken-souping ME; I'll call out."

"Why don't you let me see what you've got in the refrigerator?"

"NO! If YOU want something let me get it for you. Don't start making yourself at home. It drives me crazy. I have a lot of work to do. How about you?"

"Me too."

"Harry said your anthro teacher last semester thought you were talented in the field."

"Fleming should have his notes burnt."

"I want you to stay in political science," he tells me.

"I'll stay." Poli. sci., your arms; they're the same, aren't they?

"My internist told me to stop drinking." He swallows the last of what's in the glass.

"Why?"

"My stomach's been bothering me." Pours more bourbon.

"Don't drink it then," I plead.

"My God," he yells, "you're here two minutes and already ordering me around?"

Shiksa lesson number five: don't walk into a set-up play with your mouth wide open.

He offers me a drink. I say I'll have some sherry later, it's hard for me to work if I drink.

"You're trying to make me feel guilty," he says.

I shut my mouth, walk to the valise, take out my Lit. book, notebook, and paper, return to the couch. Sit down, opening the book. I have to write a paper on "La Belle Dame sans Merci." Thanks to my years of training *en français,* I can translate the title, after that I'm doomed. What can I make of this poor knight standing around some gloomy pond? Why doesn't he get up and move?

I take off my shoes, put my feet up, and stare at the poem. So, we have this haggard knight and a beautiful lady (or is she a dream?). Then a nightmare of other men trapped by the beautiful lady, and finally, a lifetime of loitering. I bite my pencil. Would Mr. Appel understand the poem? Would he mind if I asked? I look up and find him staring at me. Smile, look down again. Shiksa lesson number six: don't spoil a good thing.

Now it's even harder for me to figure out the damn poem. All I can think of, looking at it, are his eyes, my body, the incredible, wonderful fact: I'm *here.* I never want to be anywhere else.

I stare at the poem some more. Hear him get up, walk, dial. "Chicken Delight," of course. He goes into the kitchen, brings out sherry and cheese, sets it on the little table in front of the couch.

"Forgive me my evil moods. My wife isn't doing what I

want her to do with the children, the alimony is killing me."
He pours sherry. "What else? I can't work on my next
project, I need to get a second job, I wish I lived in England."

That last one hurts so much I could cry out. Hey, don't *I*
make you a little happy. He makes me ecstatic and I don't do a
THING for him? That isn't the way love is supposed to be.

He sits next to me on the couch. I take a sip of sherry and
then hold his right hand, run my nails up and down his arm,
wrist, palm; this used to drive Allan wild.

"Why England?" Rubbing his hand may not do anything
for him, but it's hypnotizing me. Smooth skin, coarse hair, big
hand near my smaller one. Smooth and rough, smooth and
rough, touch, touch, rub: am I massaging him or me?

"Because even though the English are class-conscious among
themselves, they're not with foreigners. Or else they don't
know how to place Americans, can't tell by the accent, I guess.
For me it's like being in a classless society."

"Among aristocrats, I suppose."

"That's the best kind of classless," he says.

"If I were Princess Margaret . . ."

"I'd marry you," he finishes.

That stops me cold.

"What were you going to say?" he asks.

"I'd run away from home, I'd chuck my crown and get the
hell out, maybe take a few jewels along, marry my Captain
and leave off curtsying for life."

"You're funny." He grins. "I thought all little girls wanted
to grow up and be fine ladies and marry a prince."

"I don't want to be a lady." The fierceness in my voice
surprises me.

He howls with laughter. "What DO you want to be?"

Yours. Just yours.

"Sophia Loren," I answer. "Rich and earthy."

"What's stopping you?"

I take another swallow of sherry. Listen, fella, you're not
helping me along, that's for sure.

"I'm a virgin."

He picks up his drink and takes a huge gulp. "Wonderful. Is that what you came for? To lose your cherry?"

I wonder if Sophia Loren had to cope with anything like this. SHUT UP, I want to say, don't make something beautiful so *vulgar.*

"I think I came because being with you is nice." The words nearly stick in my throat. For a second I have to think: what the hell AM I doing here, but then I remember. Yes. I love him.

"You're awfully young."

"I'm aging fast." And all on account of you.

"You're playing a game with me."

I shake my head. No.

"I'm afraid of you." He looks down at his knees, flashing to me the bald top of his head. "What does a young girl like you want with an old man like me?"

"You're not old, you're young and sexy and wonderful!" Then I, the new Jewish Sophia Loren, blush fiery red and develop a beautiful nervous blotch on my bare chest and throat. Oh, Mr. Appel, take it from me, all you have to fear is fear itself.

He seems to get the message; he leans over and pulls me onto him and starts to kiss me. Then his doorbell rings. He jumps off the couch, straightens himself out, rings back. I pull myself to an upright position.

"Chicken DeLIGHT!" a young male voice yells up the stairs.

I laugh, he laughs. It serves him right. In a way I'm sorry we weren't in the middle of fucking, it would've proven that God punishes men who won't let women cook for them.

He pays at the door, brings in a big greasy bucket, and sets it down on the coffee table near my books. I snatch them away, put them on the floor.

"Chicken fat on my poetry I don't need. That looks disgusting."

"It's edible," he says. "It sustains life. I'm not one of those people who live to eat. I eat to live."

Shiksa lesson number seven: I eat to live. I eat to live. I repeat that phrase several times in my head while watching him pick out greasy breasts (how can chicken be dry and greasy at the same time? call Chicken Delight and find out). I eat to live. Sorry, Mr. Appel, I could repeat that one eight million times, it'll never get through. Fat or thin, eating or dieting, I LIVE TO EAT. How am I going to hide this fact from him for a lifetime?

"Do you know Irene McIntosh?" Here I am, trying to change the subject of my ruminations.

"Uh, yes, I think so." His tone of voice is different, what's wrong?

I look at him swallowing the last of a chicken boob. Trying to look normal and not succeeding. You can't strive for normalcy, it comes naturally or not at all; listen, I'm an expert in this area.

"Did she take a class of YOURS?"

"Yes."

"Irene the rock-ribbed, Irene to the right of Goldwater McIntosh?" Yes, folks, Irene's favorite politician, Barry G, strikes her as being too much of a liberal. Her favorite author: Ayn Rand. Her favorite color: probably brown shirts. "It must've been some lively class."

"She's an annoying girl." He wipes his hands on the little paper towels that look more edible than the chicken. "Okay now," wipes his mouth, "where was I?"

Molesting me, how could you forget?

"Oh, yes, the Heilbroner." He carries the chicken bucket into the kitchen, comes back, picks up a book.

The Heilbroner? The Heilbroner?

I go back to my poem and vow to ask Irene what happened when she was in his class.

"La Belle dame sans merci thee hath in thrall." I gaze around the apartment in a kind of stupor. There's the wall of books, the overhead bowl-light, the utilitarian floor lamp with wrought-iron stem and plain white shade, the same kind of useful-ugly table lamp with a thick brass base and white shade; no rugs on the floor, faded brown couch, Venetian blinds, no curtains on the windows, cream-colored walls, drab pictures, wooden chairs. What this apartment needs is color and a woman's touch. It's screaming for feminine love, flowers and plants, a Klee print, a bright sofa and an easy chair. It's screaming for me.

He sits on the opposite end of the couch, underlining in his book and taking notes. I sneak a look at him from beneath lowered lids; my heart is pumping out love, filling the air, surrounding him with it, sending a jetty of warm love to massage his head and eyes and body, to comfort and support and feed him. Mr. Appel, love is even better than Chicken Delight. In my mind I see his flaws: insecurity, pomposity, unprepared classes, needing to be worshiped by ten girls sitting at his feet, having to be a good guy jousting with a bad world. Mr. Appel, what are you trying to reform if not yourself? Let me help you, let me save you from this awful life.

"What in *hell* are you staring at?"

I snap to attention; actually I've been staring at nothing, not at the room or him, though my head must be permanently fixed in his direction. I've been looking at a blank.

I return to the poem. His anger doesn't frighten me, because behind it, underneath it, he loves me. I know it. I'm as certain as if he told me. And anyway, has he said he *doesn't?*

The poem is killing me; what does it mean? I get up from the couch and walk into his bedroom. Maybe reading it aloud, as Mrs. Lamb advises, will help. I look at his bed. Should I sit down on it? If he walks in on me, will that make him mad? I pace back and forth and whisper the lines aloud, walking between his bed and the dresser, cluttered with a mirror, comb and brush (what does he need a brush for? his eyebrows?), electric razor, and a box that looks like a lady's jewelry box but couldn't be, must hold his cufflinks. "La belle dame sans merci thee hath in thrall." In thrall in thrall in thrall, enthralled, enthralled, I've got it. I'm so delighted, the Columbus of nineteenth-century poetry, finally seeing land, I flop down at the edge of the bed and start writing.

Solving the poem must be a message from God, a good omen, maybe I'll do my most brilliant work pacing in his bedroom. The thought makes me giddy.

I read the poem aloud once more, get halfway through as he opens the door.

"I came in here so I wouldn't disturb you," I explain nervously.

"That's the most unusual reason for going into a man's bedroom I've ever heard."

"I'm an unusual girl," I say.

He sits down next to me and grabs my shoulders and presses his mouth onto mine. I try to act as though his kisses get me excited, drive me wild, I hold my hands on his neck, press him to me too, as though I can't get enough of him. What would happen if I told the truth now? Yelled, "AGH, too much, more than enough, pull your tongue back, lighten your hands." He's forty years old and must know what he's doing, this must drive all the other girls mad with desire. I moan a little in my throat.

"Fuck me," I whisper. "Please fuck me."

He pulls away abruptly. I'm lying half on the bed, my feet on the floor, staring up into his angry face. What could I have said that was terrible?

"Don't start making demands on ME!" he yells. "Jewish cunt."

The tears pour down my face. That's the worst thing anybody ever said to me, the worst. I roll over on my stomach and hide my head in the bedspread. Then I feel his arms around me, his chest against my back; and, folks, such is the power of love, my tears immediately stop, and I feel fine. He turns me around and kisses my eyes and nose and mouth, gently, finally, my neck and throat and shoulders, earlobes, ear,

I don't need to feign excitement, here it is, the real thing. He keeps coming back to my cheeks, kissing the wet off them. This time I make a sincere little noise in my throat, ohhhh, my love my love. He reaches back and unzips the dress, I help him pull it over my head (why is this never the way it should be? always awkward?), he tosses it on the chair near his dresser. He reaches down and strokes my legs, up to my thighs, until midway up he hits the loose long-line girdle.

"I hate girdles," he says.

I pull mine off, rip it off, stockings, slip, pants and all. Suddenly I start feeling scared, he strokes my legs again, thighs, touches my crotch, and then I realize, Holy God, my body is still in the girdle, in the dress; touch them and I'll come, touch me, and there's no one home. I can't believe it. He's stroking my crotch, my bare absolute uncovered crotch and it's gone dead on me. Maybe, besides not having a hole, I've lost the entire area. Listen, Mr. Appel, are my legs joined together like a Barbie Doll's, just two legs and a belly? He turns away and starts undressing himself. I take off my bra (thank God, at least my breasts are still here) and I pull myself toward the pillows, lie with my head on one, and feel my heart pound not with love, not with passion, but with pure terror.

I shut my eyes as he lies next to me and rubs my breasts, my belly, kisses me hard. I stroke his chest and back, then he lies on top of me and I move my legs, feign incredible excitement, thinking at least I'll give him the most fantastic experience of his life.

"*Hold still!*" Again angry. "Just lie quietly."

Lie quietly? I stop stroking him, stop moving entirely. I stretch my legs straight out and let him touch me and kiss me and feel me, unmoving. I pretend I'm a gingerbread woman being molded; that's it, Mr. Appel, help the orthodontia, push my front teeth back a little; knead my breasts so they stand up like little hills, force them up, don't let them sag; and that belly, it could be flatter, press a little harder, maybe it'll entirely disappear.

After a while he says, "DAMN IT."

"What's wrong?"

"I can't fuck you, you've got to help me."

"Sure," I say nervously.

He gets up and goes to the dresser and brings back a little necklace. I'm already scared out of my wits. What does he want from me that he's bringing me a gift in advance? He sits down on the bed and hands me a little golden cross on a chain.

"Put this around your neck," he orders.

I take the cross in my hand and stare at it, two pieces of metal soldered together, no ornaments, no curlicues, two lines at right angles, one longer than the other, brightly polished, shining. Here I was worried that I might have to take his penis in my mouth; and if Chicken Delight disgusts me, what in the world would that do? But I was prepared to try. For him I thought I'd try anything.

I stare some more at the cross; how easy it would be to put it around my bare neck, how much simpler than sex. Then it begins, the fantasy: I'll put it on and he'll choke me to death with it, strangle me with a cross, and then my parents will arrive to identify my naked body and my mother will say, "At least she was thin"; but my father, my poor old rabbi father, when he sees the cross around my neck (he won't even notice my body, I'm sure) he'll put his hand on his heart as it breaks, and he'll die. Tears come to my eyes.

"I can't wear this." I give it back to him. "Listen, Mr. Appel, I don't care about fucking, if you don't feel like it, we don't have to do it." We're PERFECT for each other, I should say. I hate getting undressed, for God's sake. I'm happier necking with my clothes on.

"Bullshit. Castrating bitch. And don't give me that virgin story either. Why *can't* you put the necklace on?" He holds the tiny cross, which looks *really* ridiculous with his big hands and big nose, and stares at me, the criminal.

"Because I'm a rabbi's daughter," I finally say. Let this be a lesson, I think to myself: the truth always comes out.

He gets off the bed and walks out, still holding the cross, and I throw my naked body across the bed and weep.

When the sobbing subsides (my lenses are getting *some* bath from this), I wonder whether I ought to have put on the damn cross and not made any fuss. I think about my nose job and weight loss, the contact lenses, the shiksa lessons, how much I love him. I see my stupid father standing at the pulpit mouthing absurdities and inanities. "The Lord shall guard thy going out and thy coming in from this time forth and even forevermore." Some Guard. If the Lord got paid for His Guarding, He wouldn't be able to afford a mouthful of manna every hundred years. Some Guard. Some God. For this I'm standing on principle?

Mr. Appel walks into the room. "I hope you're satisfied." He lies down on the bed, as far away from me as he can get. I stare up at the ceiling light.

"I love you, but I couldn't do that."

"Don't give me that love crap," he mutters half into the pillow.

"I'M GLAD I'M A JEW!" I yell.

He gets up and turns out the light. I get up and turn it on.

"I'm going home."

"You'll never make it. It's too late. The dorms will be locked."

I walk naked into the living room, open my suitcase, take out the baby blue lenses, and become blind. Carry suitcase into bedroom, squint hard, turn off light, bump into dresser, bang knee on foot of bed, grope along side, feel pillow, lie down.

"Mr. Appel," I say after what feels like ten hours of silence, "I honestly don't care about fucking. I don't *want* to fuck. I'm scared to death of it."

After a few minutes more of this black quiet I hear him snore. Ladies and gentlemen, I know I ought to hate him. It's clear even to me. So why don't I?

I roll over on my side facing him, reach out gingerly and

touch his shoulder, his back is toward me naturally. Then I edge a little closer so my arm can rest along his back.

· I fall asleep touching him. Sometime toward morning I have this dream: Mr. Appel is in a room doing some kind of important Work. I apparently am with other people in an office nearby. Someone had tried taking a note or message to him and was frightened off, so I took whatever it was in to him. And while other people watched, he put an arm around me, then held me in his arms, and I explained, "You see? He just wants to hold onto someone. Just for a while. He doesn't really mean anything by it."

When I wake up, hearing him get out of bed, that dream lingers.

"Do you want coffee?" he shouts from another room.

"Yes." I get out of bed, wash up, put on makeup and lenses, perfume, and little sexy nightgown. Go into kitchen. He's dressed in a workshirt and dungarees, my hero, leader of the masses.

"You look good enough to eat." He hands me a cup of coffee.

Eat me then, I want to say. I can barely carry the cup to the kitchen table, I feel like my grandmother. The coffee is in the saucer by the time I sit down. I pour it back into the cup. Eat me. Eat me.

"What else would you like?" He's standing near me, towering sixteen feet over me.

I don't say anything.

"I'm not hungry either," he says.

I sip my coffee.

"Barbara." He swallows practically half a cup of steaming coffee; superman, a throat of steel. "You know how fond I am of you, but this is impossible now. I have too many things on my mind. I can't be bothering with women until I've straightened out my life."

Bothering with women? Bothering? Women? What a way he has with words. I keep sipping the coffee.

"I don't want you to start dating Allan again."

"Why not?"

"He's not good enough for you. Don't go running off and getting married. Give me time." He finishes off his coffee in one huge gulp.

I smile. "I'm not in any rush. All I want is to BE with you."

He shakes his head. "I can't handle that. I can't be involved with anyone. First I've got to straighten out my affairs."

That makes even my stupid eyes narrow.

"I'm going to call a cab and send you home," he concludes.

I'm numb, dumb. He gets up and goes to the phone. I spill a few tears into the coffee, then throw it out and leave the cup in the sink. Go into bedroom, pack, dress, carry suitcase into living room. What am I going to do? What am I going to do? I feel like dying. What am I going to do? The words keep echoing through my head, a ticker tape: what am I going to do? I hear the cab honk. He helps me with my coat.

"Can you manage the suitcase?"

I nod. He presses me to him and kisses me. I walk out the door, get halfway downstairs when I hear him shout, cheerfully, ladies and gentlemen, as if nothing had happened, "See you in class!"

Chapter Thirty-four

❧

I open the cab door, get in, say, "Harter College, Wetton," and begin to cry. No shame. Lie down on seat and bawl.

Cabbie says, "Lady, *please*. You want to stop and have some coffee? You want to tell me what's wrong?"

I sit up and shake my head and wait for the sobs to subside. Mr. Pignatelli (his name is tacked to the glove compartment), what's wrong would take more than a fifteen-minute ride to tell; it'd take a book, a huge volume, for the job.

"Is it cold for you back there?" He rolls up his window. "This is some lousy winter, the worst I can remember."

I dry my eyes and look out at the gray sky, gray snow, bundled people, slow-moving cars. This is some lousy winter. I direct him up the Hill to Bailey Hall. He insists on carrying my suitcase to the front door.

"You have friends here?" He puts my suitcase on the welcome mat on the top step.

I pay him and say yes and thank him. Then I tiptoe into the dorm, hoping to sneak to my room before anyone sees me. I walk past the sign-in sheet, past the living room, when, "Don't forget to check yourself in!" booms out from the far corner of the living room. Frannie, of course, back from church, dressed in her Sunday best, ready to do God's Will on the planet earth.

I plop the suitcase down and sign myself in. Then it begins to dawn on me, the first idea I've had all year, the first time my brain is clickety-clacking! *I've got to get out of here.* I unlock the door, throw my suitcase on the bed, grab a notebook and pen, and rush out into the gray day, across the road, up the Hill to the library. There, for two hours, I go through one college catalog after another, only this time I know what I'm looking for. A school without a list of do's and don't's, without Required Courses, without idiots, sororities, house mothers, and Soc. 104 to be taken only after Socs. 1 through 103 have been completed. I go through the catalogs one by one, marking down places that seem promising. Not many. Harter is right smack in the mainstream of American education. As I list the third possible school, I have this fantasy of Mr. Appel on bended knee, pleading with me to stay and marry him. Of course I'll marry you, I say, but I'm going to school somewhere else. He weeps with relief. We get married, and Radcliffe finally admits me. How can they turn down a girl who's smart enough to be Henry Appel's wife?

I shake myself awake, put the catalogs back, and slide down the Hill to Bailey. Once inside my room I lock the door and take out my B'nai B'rith guide; the next school I attend is going to be *crawling* with Jews. I sit at my typewriter and write two letters asking for applications for admission. Type envelopes, stamp them, put on coat, walk four blocks to mailbox. Come back to room, get undressed, take out lenses, rub hands together to get them warm, flop down on bed and bawl.

There's a knock at the door. I dry my eyes and open it. Irene. Bundled up like a little fascist Eskimo.

"I noticed you were back, so I thought you might want to go to dinner." She stands in the doorway.

"Is it that late?" I look at my clock. Five fifteen. Does misery make time fly?

"It's still early," she says. "Hey, Barb, do you mind my asking—aren't you going out with Al any more?" Another study about shiksas—why do they give nicknames to *everybody?*

"I broke up with him a while ago," I tell her. "Listen, I have a question for you. Did you take Mr. Appel's course?"

She nods. Is her face red?

"Why?" I begin to say, and then the answer dawns on me, formerly the world's biggest idiot, but now, clickety-clack, hear that brain go. Does misery improve the intellect too? "Irene, are you, uh, a recent convert to Y.A.F.?"

She nods her head.

"So when you took Mr. Appel's course . . ."

"I don't want to talk about it. He's a loon. You coming to dinner?"

"Maybe later," I say.

"Okay. See you." She shuts the door. I hear her boots clump clumping the length of the hall. Oh, Mr. Appel, how fantastic is your effect upon students, they come to you liberals and they leave, Nazis. I wonder what's going to happen to me? Then I start crying again. Nothing. Nothing. I'll always love you.

An hour later Marsha walks into the room, laden down with groceries. She takes one look at me and asks, "What's wrong?"

"He doesn't love me. All I want is to marry him, and he doesn't want to see me."

"That's some all," she says. "Are you still a virgin?"

"Yes," I sob. "Oh, God, yes."

"Then I don't hate him so much." She hangs up her coat and hat, puts away her boots, while I bang the pillow with my fist and sob. If I keep this up I'm going to be in a hospital with dehydration. Headline: Rabbi's Daughter Cries Herself to Death.

"Sometimes not being fucked is worse than anything," I cry.

"I know what you mean," she says, "but it's nice that he has a little sense, that he cares what happens to you. At least he wasn't just using you."

I cry even louder. "Oh, Marsha, it wasn't that way. He TRIED, but he couldn't."

"He what but he WHAT?" Marsha sits down hard.

"He couldn't because I'm Jewish. What am I going to do?" Marsha sits quietly for a few minutes. "Look," she finally says, "when you loved him it was because you thought he'd love you. If you're sure he won't or can't, then you shouldn't love him any more."

"You," my sobs are slowing down, "don't know anything about love. It doesn't work that way."

"You've got to *try* to get over him."

"How?" I straighten up and look at her, sitting on her bed, surrounded by cookies and pears and muffins.

"That's a good question," she admits.

"You're telling me," I say.

She unpacks the food.

"I haven't had anything to eat all day," I tell her.

"So have something." She gestures in the direction of a box of Pepperidge Farms. I walk over, open them, and take out five chocolate-filleds. When the Tunafish Heroes Man comes, I have two. Later on I go to the candy machine in the basement of the dorm and buy four candy bars. I think: I never understood why I ate, but I do now; I'm trying to mend a broken heart with peanut butter.

Marsha watching me eat and suffer, says, "For God's sake, get a grip on yourself. He's not the only man in the world."

For answer I swallow another Reese's Peanut Butter Cup, put it in my mouth after peeling off the paper, and suck on it slowly, feeling the delicious taste coat my tongue. Good-bye, waist. Good-bye, ribs. If he doesn't care, then neither do I.

Marsha says, "Barbara, stop, if you want older men, we'll find older men for you."

"I love him, not older men."

"My parents met this guy in Italy on a business trip, he's forty and he's here for a few months. I'll fix you up with him. He's *really* good-looking."

"Eh." I'm lying flat on my back, my belly is distended, I'm nauseated; who can think of dating?

Then Rona tiptoes into the room. She has a big smile on her face when she sees we're awake. She comes over to me and hugs me and says, "I had such a lovely time with Allan. Thanks."

I draw a deep breath and say to Marsha, "I'll go out with this guy, what's his name?"

"Bruno Something, he's Jewish and he was in a concentration camp, only he didn't liberate himself with his bare hands. I think you'll like him anyway."

"Yeah," I say. "Yeah." Then I turn over on my stomach and moan.

Chapter Thirty-five

❧

Bruno may be a great businessman, able to convince Italians who have poison ivy that they have psoriasis and should buy the Greens' magic brew, but as a person he's crazy.

He picks me up at Bailey that next Tuesday, the first time I skip Mr. Appel's class. He's a tall, distinguished man with a Roman nose, graying at the temples, but too slick with the pointy shoes, shiny suit, oily hair.

His opening lines are, "What a marvelous wife you'd make for me."

"You can tell this from looking?" I ask.

"Always trust, ah, the first impression. That is said correctly?"

Oh, yes, I say, that certainly is. We walk to his car, which is parked illegally in front of McDowell Hall. He holds the door for me, how can I explain it? with a flourish. It makes me feel like he's saluting and clicking his heels.

Once in the car, he says, "Of course you cannot really be Jewish."

"I am so." Nyaah nyaah nyaah. "And don't tell me I don't look it, you don't look it either."

"An Italian would know right away. But you would fool anyone."

Perfect. Perfect.

Bruno drives us into Boston. He tells me he prefers a hotel to staying with the Greens, that he needs his privacy, short *i*. It immediately makes me think something is wrong with him.

He asks, "Do you want to see my concentration camp number?"

"Yes," I say.

He extends his right arm to me, and I pull up his sleeve and see it there, a long number tattooed onto his skin, fuzzy but legible. If it weren't that my heart belongs to Henry Appel, I would have fallen in love with this man, just for the sake of that number. Don't ask me why. I'd rather not know.

Bruno takes me to an Italian restaurant. It turns out that he's homesick; he never touches pasta in Italy, but the second his plane arrives at Logan Airport, all he wants is spaghetti.

At the restaurant he stuffs me with food, I've never met a man like this before, he practically hand-feeds me. Now I'm not fat yet, but even at my thinnest I don't look like someone who's starving. But Bruno force-feeds me; when I turn down lasagne, he takes some on a fork and puts it in my mouth. In this fancy Boston restaurant what a sight: a gray-haired man feeding a young woman as though she were still in a high chair. I keep saying to him, "Bruno, enough already, I'm getting fatter by the minute," and he shakes his head and feeds me.

"You need to put on a few pounds," he says.

Bruno, stick around a few months, you're talking to the champion in this area. But there's no point in arguing. I swallow everything, even dessert, and I drink wine, and I feel like I'm going to die. When he tells me that he's taking me up to his hotel room, I haven't got the strength to say no. I'm in a pasta trance. The worst kind.

His hotel is the Boston Hilton, and he's on the top floor, a gorgeous suite with no one around; the entire floor seems deserted. I'm nervous; the walls here are three feet thick—I could yell for a year and no one would hear. He marches me straight into his bedroom, unfastens my pearl choker, unzips my black dress, and I say, "Bruno, what are you doing?"

"I'm undressing you, what a gorgeous body you have, only you should put a little weight here," he touches my breasts, "and here," he rests a hand on my hips.

"Wait a second," I tell him. "I'm a virgin."

"Don't be afraid, there are many things you can enjoy."

"Really?" I decide to play dumb.

I stand there with pants and girdle and bra and slip and stockings on, master of my fate as always, looking out through my contact lenses and thinking, "He's going to kill me." Yes, ladies and gentlemen, that's what's going through my head. There's this man undressing me and I'm sure it's a prelude to sudden and horrible death.

He takes off my bra, but I insist, I am the captain of my ship, on retaining the pants and slip. He takes off the slip, pulls it over my head, but the pants stay on. Even if he's going to kill me, *they stay.*

He undresses neatly and carefully, hangs everything up, my clothes and his. Then he leads me to the bed, because right now I'm staring out the window, twenty stories high, with the underpants on, thinking what a splat I'll make if I jump out, filled with so much blood-red spaghetti sauce. He places me on the bed (I feel like an overweight Barbie Doll), lies down next to me, kisses me a few times, touches my breasts and then masturbates me, something that Allan has never done. Bruno reaches down inside the pants, I'm not even slightly excited, and rubs my clitoris a short while, and I come, thinking, "So this is how you do it!" I need to be taught everything from start to finish; there's nothing I can figure out on my own.

Bruno says, "See? Didn't you enjoy that?" Then he shows me how to suck him, but I can't do it. I was right, it *does* taste worse than Chicken Delight. Every time his penis goes any distance into my throat, I gag; nothing like gagging and starting to vomit to turn a man off; so I manually masturbate him, and he comes, and I think, maybe I've been reprieved, maybe I'm going to live.

"Let's take a nap together," he says.

"I'm not sleepy. Let's take a walk first and then come back and nap."

He says, "Fine," and helps me on with my clothes, but when he gets to the pearl choker, he holds his hands at the back of my neck, pulling the pearls tight, and says, "It would be so easy to strangle you."

No kidding, this is exactly what he says; when I have fantasies and fears, there's Someone up there beyond the clouds chuckling and cackling, "Let's give this bird a real scare." Okay already, God. Enough. I believe. I believe.

He takes his hands away and gets dressed, and we walk out down the hall, down the elevator, past the desk, into the street, then I spot a cab and break away from him, he's been holding my hand, and I dash for the cab, open the door, jump in, Bruno seems to be staring at me from a great distance, he probably doesn't know that I'm escaping with my life and just barely, and I say to the cabbie, "Wetton, Mass."

"Where do you think I might go," the cabbie says, "New Jersey?"

Marsha isn't the least bit sympathetic when I describe how I nearly got strangled. "Haven't you ever heard of joking?" she asks.

The answer is no. I mean, I take everything seriously. Everything.

Chapter Thirty-six

❧

Tuesday, Thursday, Saturday I rise at nine A.M., eat a peanut butter and jelly sandwich (chunky peanut butter, blackberry jelly), look in the mirror at my face ballooning out, cry, get dolled up in case I should meet Mr. Appel on my way to French class, but don't budge from the dorm till his class is over. I've decided never to go to his class again. Marsha doesn't say anything to me except, "How will you transfer out with an F in his course?"

I figure I'll kill myself if worse comes to worst: transfer out of *everything*.

A week goes by. I'm working hard in my other classes, eating, and turning down all dates. No substitutes. I'm accepting no goddamn substitutes.

Marsha says I'm crazy, that there's something wrong with me. Rona tells me to stop eating and find someone My Own Age. Jo is worried about how she'll order my bridesmaid dress with my unstable weight. What if she orders a fat dress and I'm thin? Or, more likely, the reverse?"

Marsha keeps repeating, "He's a no-goodnik. Admit it. Find someone else. How can you love a no-goodnik?"

I don't know how, but I'm managing.

"Listen," I try to explain, "he's nasty, self-centered, adolescent, and worse. I see it. See? I'm admitting it. It doesn't help. I want him to marry me."

The middle of the second week, the beginning of March, Marsha says, "Now this is it. We're going skiing. We'll cut our Saturday classes and Mom'll drive us to Vermont. You need a change of activity."

"Okay." Maybe Mr. Appel will call and save me from my friends.

He doesn't. Friday afternoon after class Mrs. Green picks us up and drives us to Wilmington, where their winter palace lies within easy driving distance of Mount Snow.

Mrs. Green brings frozen fish, chicken, soup, wine, fruit, and other low-calorie delicacies; the second we get in the door of the house she's broiling and boiling and stewing. Marsha feels sick after the two-and-a-half-hour ride, so I help her mother unpack.

"Let's get to the bottom of this," Mrs. Green says. "How can such a beautiful, bright girl be making herself unhappy?"

"I fell in love, and the man I fell in love with hates me."

"There'll be plenty of others." She stands at the stove stirring a pot of soup, happy in her big kitchen with Marsha and me to take care of. This for her is "roughing it"; she fusses with the food, makes weak tea for her daughter; how can a woman like this understand me? "You have to get a grip on yourself, you're young yet, you could go through this ten more times before the right one comes along," she says.

"I'll never love anyone but him," I moan.

That night after dinner I sit in the living room listening to Marsha and her mother debate Robert for the umpteenth time—poor Mrs. Green, helpless against the forces of nature that combine to defeat her—and I drink this delicious sherry, Harvey's Bristol Cream, which makes me woozy. I sit in front of the fire and look out the big bay window at the miles of snowy hills, pure, clean Vermont snow, the perfect setting for happiness.

I go to bed in a stupor and awake in one. Marsha again feels sick, so we have tea and lemon with our soft-boiled eggs and one slice of toast with dietetic jam, then Mrs. Green gives us the keys to the car, tells us to be back for dinner and to bring anyone along that we meet. Marsha takes her skis; I'm going to rent my equipment and take lessons while she scouts the underbrush for wonderful men that we can both fall in love with and marry this very weekend if possible.

We get to beautiful Mount Snow, and the first thing I say is, "It's steep here."

"You'll go on the beginner's slope," Marsha tells me, "don't worry."

"Worry?" Fear-crazed is perhaps the expression she's looking for; why, I'm going to break a leg if I'm *lucky*.

It's noon by the time we get the equipment, put it on, and locate a ski class. Then Marsha takes off for the distant slopes.

The ski instructor is a good-looking man named Hal, and he has great confidence that I and my four classmates are going to be aces on the snow. I nod and mumble but pay strict attention to his every word. I never realized what a boon fear was to concentration.

We hold our poles and bend forward and imitate his knees, we lean left and right, wonderful, easy. We're standing still, not moving an inch, clearly the most preferable way to ski, then he takes us to the beginner's slope, where the incline is about fifteen degrees, and he teaches us to snowplow—the most important thing we have to learn: *How to Stop.* God, yes, I think, and I watch him through the goggles and contact lenses. When he leans forward, I lean forward, and if he presses his knees together, so do I. Learn to stop! I hope to be a master at it by the end of the afternoon. We practice on this little bunny slope, and I'm a whiz, the best kid in class, I can stop on a dime. Then Hal comes over and invites me to a party. I nearly accept, only what would Mrs. Green say to a ski instructor as a substitute for one's political-science teacher? For this she didn't schlep me to Mount Snow.

And anyway, my fondness for Hal wanes the second I get on the other slope, the one, I mean, that really goes downhill. The first time I try it, it feels icy, I'm going sixty miles an hour, and maniacs whiz around me, the cold wind stings my face and eyes, and I decide, about halfway down the mountain, it's time to snowplow to a stop before I hit eighty. I press my knees together and grunt, perfect snowplow position as I've understood it, and nothing happens except I fly down the hill with my toes together and my skis pointed out, the world's first pigeon-toed skier. When I tell you my speed isn't cut down, not even reduced slightly, I fly to the bottom of the hill and am stopped at the side by a very unpleasant pile of snow, you can see why Hal is finished in my book.

I repeat this scene all afternoon, and the only thing that improves is my ability to dive off the side; I'm getting adept at picking the less icy drifts at which to aim my hurtling body. The ski lift itself, designed by some sadist, doesn't hit my head as I get off more than five or six times, but it gives me a lot to look forward to on the ride up, adjusting my skis and getting ready to throw myself off the chair and down the little incline. Praying all the while for something less than brain damage.

My toes, fingers, and legs ache, but I continue the same way, down, flop, up, smack in the head, down, and so forth. On my last ride up I see Marsha at the top of the hill looking flushed and pretty with no snow over her red ski outfit; she waves, and I trudge over, one ski gets on top of the other, I maneuver my foot around to free it, the poles crunch in the crust of snow; am I ever ready to get home.

However, as if you couldn't guess, I come back here Sunday. There isn't any sun out, just gray clouds and freezing wind, and I ski until late afternoon, till it's time to go back to school. Finally I understand the meaning of the phrase "a glutton for punishment."

On the drive back Mrs. Green says, "You two girls look wonderful, so healthy and rosy."

Marsha says, "Just think, if we weren't in college, we could look this way year round."

"Maybe it'll be better next semester."

"That's what you said last semester," Marsha reminds her. "That's probably what you'll say next year too."

"If only you had gone to Vassar," Mrs. Green says.

Marsha and I laugh so hard that she has to join us; she's a good mother and tries her best, but everything is against her. Marsha wasn't accepted at Vassar, even with her millions.

Chapter Thirty-seven

❧

By next Saturday, the third week in March, a miracle has occurred. The snow has melted, and the ground is visible again. Kosher salt has been replaced by mud as an agent of boot-destruction, and the wind has finally lost some of its sting. It's lucky too, because I've gained fifteen pounds and have had to remove the lining from my suede jacket again.

The sun glares into my face at one P.M. as I walk out of Geology; it hurts the lenses so much that I shut my eyes and feel my way down the stairs, holding onto the railing, and bump smack into Mr. Appel.

I look up at him, don't move.

"Come with me," he orders. "I can't talk to you here."

We trudge side by side across the muck to his office. My heart is pounding and my hands are trembling; it's fantastic what being near him does to me, as though my very reflexes, involuntary muscles, everything, don't belong to me, are being controlled by him. I don't care what he feels for me any more; I only want him to pretend, be nice to me for a while, let me love him without this much pain. Believe me, it *hurts* to love a louse.

We get to his office, walk inside, he locks the door and pulls down the shades.

"All right," he pauses before seating himself, looms above me, "what's going on? Why haven't you come to class?"

"I've decided to drop your course," I ad lib.

"You can't. It's too late to do it. You'll flunk."

"So I'll flunk." Mr. Appel, a dead person doesn't worry about grades.

"You can't." He pushes his fingers through the stray hairs on his scalp. "What will people say? Have you told Harry this?"

"No. I haven't told anybody. Nobody'll say anything."

"Don't be an idiot. This isn't the right thing to do. This is very unprofessional of you."

"I don't know what you're talking about," I tell him.

"It means that personal matters aren't supposed to get in the way of your professional commitments to scholarship." He gives me a stern, scholarly eye. "It happens that you're an excellent student of political science. You have a lively mind, you're not afraid of hard work. You're one of my best students. You owe it to yourself to continue what you've begun."

"I don't think I even want to stay in the field," I say. "And I'm not much of a professional at anything."

"You're being too harsh on yourself," he says.

"I've got to drop your course." Mr. Appel, this isn't a question of I.Q. here, remember? This is my HEART, you goddamn prick.

"Don't drop it," he says. "I'll give you your A, and you don't have to do one more thing in the course. Don't be hasty. Maybe after a while you'll feel differently."

"I feel differently already. I want to take a course in modern poetry, I'm bored with poli. sci." I see him wince. Finally. Got him the only place (apparently) that he hurts.

"Then take a poetic journey. But you should return to the social sciences. They need people like you."

"They'll have to survive without me."

"Try me for the rest of the semester, that's all I ask. Maybe you'll change your mind."

"I can't do it." I look at him, and big tears start forming in my eyes.

"Don't start waterworks with me," he says. "YOU pushed this thing too far, not me. Surely you didn't think I was seriously involved with you?"

I cry even harder. Mr. Appel, I didn't know there was any other way to be. I get up and head for the door, which is blurred with my tears. As I grope for the handle and open it, he yells, "I hope at least I was good for your ego!"

When I come back to the dorm, a distressed-looking Marsha meets me at the door. She says she's just been on the phone with Mr. Appel, who invited her to go with him to a showing of *Monsieur Verdoux*.

"What'd you say?" I can't believe this is happening.

"I couldn't think of anything, so I hung up on him."

"You did?" I cry.

"I'm sorry, I didn't know what else to do," she says.

"You're wonderful," I tell her. "May God reward you for your wonderfulness."

God, as usual, isn't listening.

Chapter Thirty-eight

❦

I wake up before dawn Sunday, and as I grope my way from bed to the dresser, where my glasses are, I see a vague outline of myself in the mirror, and it frightens me, the way it used to when I was a child, as though there were someone else in the mirror, not me. When I was little, I'd shut my eyes when I went to the bathroom in the middle of the night, feeling my way along the hall outside my bedroom like a blind person, to avoid seeing that apparition. Now I put on my glasses, grab my housecoat, and tiptoe down the empty, quiet corridor to the living room.

I sit on the lumpy couch near the window that looks out on the Hill, and I watch light; you can't see the sun from here—the drumlin must hide it—but the light comes fast. I wrap the housecoat around me, they don't give heat until seven A.M., and I tuck my feet underneath me, and stare at the small, brown yard and the road and the Hill; that Hill nearly fills up the view, except for the bits of sky that show through. I look at the sky and the light and I try to feel poetic, but I don't, you know. I feel hopeless.

Today I'm supposed to see Allan. He called me yesterday and arranged to meet me in the parking lot. After breakfast I dress up and put on my lenses, just in case. Then I walk to the lot.

Allan's opening line as he spots me leaning against his car is: "Hello, dear. I still miss you."

"Two-timing bastard," I say. "Aren't you ever content with one girl at a time?"

"Only if it's you."

"A likely story. Does Rona know you're here?"

"No," he answers. "Why should she? Am I engaged to her?"

"Don't ask me. You'd probably do it to spite me."

Allan laughs and puts an arm around me, it feels good, even though I know it shouldn't. I cry.

"What in the world has been going on with you?" he asks.

"Jesus Christ," I say, "what do you mean?"

"You've gained a lot of weight."

"No fooling. Is this what you wanted to tell me?"

"Mr. Appel is very upset with you; what is this fixation you have with him? Why aren't you coming to class?"

"This fixation is called love. Oh, Allan," I start sobbing, "what am I going to do? I can't get over him."

Standing near his car in the lot, sniffling and sobbing, I'm attracting more attention than a circus; he opens the door and pushes me inside, starts the motor, and drives off.

"You can't possibly be in love with a man his age," he says.

"Show me where that rule is and I'll fall out of love immediately." What an annoying smartass I am. I'm not lovable even when I cry. I thought girls melted hearts the second they resorted to tears. What about me? The volume of saltwater I've shed is enough to make soluble every male heart in The Boston Area. Except that for me it doesn't apply; my tears must be made of the wrong ingredient.

"Get a grip on yourself," Allan says. "Why didn't you call me before this? Don't you think I would have helped?"

I sob.

"This is crazy, this love you say you've got."

"No it's not."

"All right," he says, "let's start on a different tack. What has he got that I haven't? Besides an extra twenty years?"

"Did he tell you to say that?"

"He told me to tell you you're a wonderful girl, but you take things too seriously. And that you shouldn't do anything in haste, like leave."

"I hope he falls into the China Sea and gets eaten by communist sharks," I say. "Slowly too, not in haste."

That makes me feel much better, and I laugh.

Allan says, "Your problem is that you're a virgin. Only virgins could be this wound up over one man."

"Do you really think so?" This appeals to me enormously, the idea that one screw and I'll be cured. So simple, so quick.

Allan senses his advantage and presses the matter with great forcefulness. He's found the line of the century, maybe he's the originator of it: the panacea for the ills of the world, America's interpretation of Sigmund Freud—one good fuck.

"But you're going out with Rona, I can't let you fuck me."

"I'll stop seeing her. I've really missed you, can't you tell?"

"Where could we go?"

"You mean you'll do it?" he asks. "We'll go to a motel."

Then I remember I have my period.

"So what?" he says. "Now I won't have to use anything and it'll be safe."

"What a mess!" I shudder, seeing blood over the bed, over him, drip drip drip. How unromantic.

"Don't worry about a thing." He drives like mad into Cambridge to the Holiday Inn, where everybody's parents stay when they come visiting, and heads into the motel parking area. He leaves me in the car and comes back triumphantly with a key and leads me to my doom, ah, I mean, my room.

"I said it was for Mr. and Mrs. Dobsen, and they didn't ask any questions." The accomplishment of the century.

Allan is twirling the key around on his finger as we step up to Room Eleven; he bends over, fits the key into the lock, and opens the door. The room is big, has a double bed and a television, two night tables, glasses covered with paper, a green rug on the floor, and white bedspreads. We're going to have to get those bedspreads far off the bed. And what about the sheets? What if I bleed all the way through to the box spring?

Allan says not to worry, that we'll put a towel underneath me, only I don't think that'll be enough. He says, "For God's sake, what do you think you have down there, Niagara Falls?"

"I'm scared."

"Don't be. There's nothing to be afraid of." He walks over to the bed and sits down on it, bounces up and down a few times. "This is a perfect bed for fucking."

"Why is it perfect?"

"Because it's there," he says. "Shall I get a bottle of booze for you?"

"No." I'm stoic to the end. "I want to be conscious."

Allan puts his arms around me and kisses me and presses me to him, and I automatically push my hips forward against his, usually the most exciting thing in the world. Only now I feel nothing. I'm not the slightest bit turned on.

I try, I throw myself into kissing him, I rub his neck and suck his lips, nibble at him, fight with his tongue, and it's as though I'm somewhere else, my body is cold. All I can think of is: I've never found my hole—maybe I don't have one.

I keep trying. Allan and I sit on the bed and we take off each other's clothes.

"I'm afraid I'm too small," the fear makes me confess.

Allan places a towel on the sheet. I get on top of it.

"You don't look too small," he says.

"Ho, ho," I say, "sadistic bastard. Put a finger up there first, okay? Or do you mind the blood?"

"Not at all." Gallant to the end. He sticks his middle finger up me, and it hurts. I'm not kidding, it hurts. But I control myself, thinking it's probably just his nail that's hurting me, and even I know that his penis doesn't have a nail, it's much softer and gentler. A bit bigger, yes, then I look at his erect penis, and, my God, it's not a *bit* bigger, it's monstrous; why, nothing that big is ever going to go up little me.

"No," I say as he lowers himself upon me.

"Yes," he says. The ayes have it, too.

He begins by inserting his penis just a little way into what he assumes is my vagina and what I know for a fact to be a solid wall of impenetrable flesh. And I yell. Now this is something D. H. Lawrence never wrote about, so how could I be expected to know what it was? The pain I'm experiencing is excruciating. In the midst of my anguish I realize this must be because although there's not a decent muscle anywhere else on my body, down there in the little nether regions they're fantastic. And they're holding tight; they've received word from that part of my brain that is forever out of touch with me not to let anything through.

I scream. Allan pushes, the muscles spasm, and I have the distinct impression that I'm being crucified, and this isn't a literary image either, I mean, this is the real thing. I'm bleeding, I can feel it drip down, I've never had this much pain in my life, and I can't stop yelling. Allan says, "Shut up," and I nearly bite his hand, which he's placing not very gently over my mouth.

The more Allan drives, the more I hurt. I try biting my own hand to keep quiet; tears rush down my cheeks. Then I make the discovery of the century. My God—I think to myself, with real wonder—there is something wrong with me. And then I scream good and loud, for this, really, hurts.

Allan is more than halfway in; the further he goes the worse it is, contrary to what he's assuring me; the more he pushes and bangs the more I shriek. He keeps going anyway; he must think I'm kidding or playacting or something, who knows, who knows what's going on in his mind.

Suddenly outside the motel, as if in chorus with my yelling, is the sound of a police siren screaming nearby and then driving into the motel parking lot, directly outside our window. It's at this point that Allan comes, pulls out, and I finally shut up.

A few seconds later there's a knock at the door; we cling to each other, I'm lying in a pool of blood, he has red smeared from his thighs to the tip of his penis, even his balls are daubed with color. We must look like a scene from a horror movie.

Allan yells, "Who's there?"

"Police! Is someone hurt in there? Open up!"

"Officer," I shout back, "nothing is wrong, there must be some mistake, no one is hurt here." Allan looks like he could throttle me, so I figure if they don't go away I'm done for. We'll both be kicked out of school, and then one night I'll be found dead, a poisoned mushroom having been slipped onto some nice piece of steak. There'll be a note pinned to my chest that will say, "This girl died of a big mouth."

"Are you sure everything's okay?"

"Yes," I yell back. "Absolutely positive. Thanks anyway."

"All right," they say, and we hear them open their car door and drive away.

Allan collapses back onto the bed in relief, and I get up and go to the bathroom, turn on the shower, and let the water wash over my soiled body, and I think, only I could get fucked for the first time to the sound of a police siren coming to rescue me. *Only me.*

Chapter Thirty-nine

❦

Allan takes me back to the dorm that night, furious at me for spoiling his fun, and I cry myself to sleep. Monday morning Marsha announces that she's going to see a gynecologist; her period is two months late.

Rona, who's just walked in, says, "You're not worried about being pregnant, are you?"

"I haven't fucked, if that's what you mean. But I'm sick every morning, my period has never been this late. I know it sounds crazy, but I have the symptoms."

"Don't worry," I say, already worried. "Do me a favor, will you? Ask the doctor if you can get pregnant if you fuck during your period."

"Sure," Marsha says, "why do you want to know?"

"No reason," I answer, turning green.

A few hours later Marsha walks in the door, flops down on

the bed. Rona and I are staring at her. "He thinks I'm pregnant. He says he's practically certain."

"Oh, no," Rona and I chorus in unison. "How can that be?"

"That's what I wanted to know, too, and he gave me some long explanation the gist of which seems to be he's seen this before and expects to see it again."

I feel as though the sky has fallen in on our room. This is worse than everybody's nightmare; this is worse than Mrs. Ferne warned us.

Marsha continues, "He says you can get pregnant any old time, even during your period."

"Aagh," I say and clutch my throat. I should have known my act wouldn't go unpunished, and my God, if it hurts for a penis to go up me, how is it going to feel when a baby comes down?

"What in the world is wrong?" Rona asks.

"Allan fucked me, and I had my period, so he didn't use anything; he said it was safe." Even as the tears rush down I see she's gotten pale.

"How could you do it?" she asks.

Marsha is looking on in disbelief. How can one room at Harter College contain so much soap opera?

"Oh, Rona, I'm sorry. I wasn't going to tell you." I clutch at my knees and bury my head in my lap. "I was miserable about Mr. Appel."

"Being miserable," she says, "isn't a good enough excuse. For anything."

"You're right," I sob, and she is. However, it's the only excuse I've got. It's very hard, believe me, nearly impossible, to be miserable and considerate at the same time.

She walks out of the room.

"Marsha, what will you do?" I ask.

"Get married. I called Bob and he's delighted; all he's wanted to do for the last two years is marry me." She shrugs her shoulders and then starts to cry. "The thing that kills me," she says between blowing her nose and wiping her eyes, "is that I feel like my life has always been in somebody else's hands. Do you know what I mean?"

I'm crying too and nodding my head yes. Yes yes yes. I know what she means.

"There I was, being such a good girl, not fucking. The least I should have done was to screw." Then she lifts up her head and gives a little hoarse laugh. "When I think of all that wasted Kleenex," she moans.

Chapter Forty

❦

How do most people survive a terrible situation? Do they just stick it out? Grit their teeth? Firm their upper lips? Believe me, they have my sincere admiration.

On May fifth, a gorgeous spring Thursday, I walk out of geology class and stare at the light-green trees, buds, new leaves, new grass, even a robin on the quad pulling a long spaghetti-worm out of the ground. Spring has finally come to Harter, but instead of being a transition period, a leisurely link between cold and hot, it's warm, too warm in fact for the trench coat I wear to hide my fat.

I look over toward Mr. Appel's office: see this, shmuck, the way I sweat under a coat, thirty-five extra pounds, and all on account of you? I shift my Harvard bookbag over my shoulder: books, fat, worries—it's surprising I'm not bent over double. I feel like a beast of burden, loaded down and miserable, walking round and round, never seeing anything new, only contemplating my misery from all possible angles.

I trudge down the Hill, if Mr. Appel came along right now and loved me I'd still marry him, do *anything* for him. Realizing this convinces me that I AM a dumb animal, trapped in a hideous human body. All I can do is walk blindly around, down the Hill, across the street, unable to think or act; someone's dropped this pack on my shoulders, ordered me to march, and this is it. For life? I don't see anything ahead but endless, aimless drudging. Can't drop out of school, can't diet, can't fall out of love. Trapped.

I figure that falling out of love must be as difficult as coming out of a coma. And there's another reason for the similarity; most people would rather be in a coma. I mean, if they're anything like me, what has life got to offer compared to the beauty of a cocoon-wrapped sleep?

I walk into Bailey, over to the mail table; on it is a letter addressed to me from Bennington College. I put the bookbag down and open the letter. It begins: ''We are pleased to inform you,'' and I shut it, hide it in my pocketbook. I did it. I did it. I'm getting out of here. I'm NOT going to be stuck in this mess, this limbo, this lunatic asylum forever. I'M GETTING OUT! Do you hear me, God? I'M GETTING OUT!

''Absolutely NO pants and bras allowed on the roof any more,'' Frannie is yelling. I turn around.

''Barbara,'' one of my classmates appeals to me, ''can't you *do* something about this?''

''I'll try,'' I say.

Even springtime at Harter is crazy. The main activity is to go to the roof of the dorm in pants and a bra or a bathing suit, with the ubiquitous rollers and a bottle of baby lotion mixed with iodine, which is supposedly the magic ingredient for getting a tan, and sunbathe. You can look over the roof of the dorm to the fraternity houses, where the boys have installed telescopes, much to the consternation of Celia and Frannie.

who immediately decided to ban bras and underwear from the roof. That is just like them, spoiling the fun of perfectly innocent girls lying around packed next to each other in various states of undress, broiling and buttered, happy as the Sunday residents of Manhattan Beach. When I myself go up to the roof, I wear a light-pink housecoat that my mother sent me; all I care about tanning is my face, to get rid of some of the pimples, which I usually do. Then as soon as the sun goes in or it rains for two days, the pimples come back with a vengeance, as if they've just been awaiting their chance. My body I've stopped bothering with: it's too fat for *anything*.

Celia and Frannie have banned underwear because of the telescopes. I once argued, "Why don't you ban boys? Or maybe ban telescopes?" But it was a whole lot easier to ban bras.

"Okay," I now say to Frannie. "Where's Celia?"

Frannie accompanies me to their room, and I announce to both of them, in front of this freshman girl who's looking on with admiration: "On behalf of my constituents, I refuse to direct Spring Sing if the girls can't walk around half-naked on their own damn roof!"

The freshman applauds, and Celia, I see, is near tears.

Spring Sing is not compulsory, but there's no way to avoid it. Every dorm in the university has to sing in front of the assembled student body, and the best group wins a prize. I've been elected to lead Bailey's Spring Sing (an unusual honor for a freshman) because I play the guitar. From this accomplishment it is assumed that I'm a musical genius; and at Harter, I was. I have a nice strong alto voice, untrained but unafraid; the rest of the girls used to peep, if you know what I mean. Bailey Hall voted to sing a two-part, jazzed-up version of "Comin' Thro' the Rye." I lead all rehearsals, and does that dorm rehearse! Every spare moment, first sopranos, then altos, then together, over and over. Celia and Frannie make a costume for me: a black skirt, white blouse, and a tartan band across my middle, which makes me look like Miss Overweight

Scotland, and a little matching plaid bonnet. The bonnet had
been in its former life a shower cap, but they covered it with
plaid and put a pom-pom on it, very sweet, very inventive.
The rest of the chorus wears matching plaid skirts, kilts, all
made by Celia and Frannie. Don't ask me when they had time
to study, or if they did study. For them Spring Sing supersedes
everything.

I have Celia and Frannie over the proverbial barrel, so they
agree to let it be a matter of choice, to post a sign saying
"Warning: Phi Hi and Tri Bly and Chi Shmi are Watching
You." By the time May has rolled around, almost everyone but
those two are past caring.

In this manner Spring Sing is rescued, which in a way is too
bad; it means I have to be out on the lawn again in half an
hour, conducting (if that's what you can call it) these girls.
Picture someone who has never done anything more than play
fifteen chords on a guitar leading an entire dorm-chorus. I
wave my arms as intelligently as I can; they ache after ten
minutes; and after two hours I can barely use them to turn
pages. Who needs this? But my classmate pats me on the back
and hustles her thin body up the stairs for a half hour of
ultraviolet rays before the dorm bell is rung and everybody is
summoned to Bailey's lawn for the rehearsal.

I go to my room, a single now, thanks to God's little miracle
on behalf of Marsha. She was too upset to memorize one word
in her religion text; she went home. The room used to be
crowded, and now it's empty. I lie down on her bed for a little
variety and look at my empty bed. Then I take out the letter
from Bennington and read it all the way through. I read and
reread it, my passport, my visa, my ticket out of hell, for the
entire half hour. When the bell rings, I stuff the letter back in
my bag, press it to my body, walk out the door. *I'm getting out
of here.*

Outside, the girls assemble on the lawn, Frannie yelling and
Celia whispering for everyone to hurry up. They get in place,
I blow the first note on my pitch pipe and stand on the top of

the stairs so everyone can see me clearly and follow my brilliant directing.

I wave my arms, wave my arms: " 'Every lassie has a laddie, nane they sae ha' I. But all the lads they smile on me, when comin' thro' the rye.' " It sounds nice, even with the chirpy voices. I stare at the green Hill half-lit by a dying sun, watch other girls stop and listen and admire us, listen myself, wave my arms, wave my arms.

The girls sing, and I think, If I ever write a story I want the title to be "But All the Lads They Smile." That's one of my favorite hobbies, making up titles to stories I'll never write. I get the idea for "But All the Lads They Smile" while trying to cue in the stupid altos; they're looking at me like little birds needing to be fed, anxious eyes, anxious mouths. Finally I tilt a finger at them, and they gobble down the first notes and then enter full-voiced into the song. I watch them and listen. Behind me is Bailey, in front of me on the Hill are the red buildings nestled on green grass and surrounded by trees. The sun and blue sky make everything look like a picture postcard: College Life. I ache; one more year of my life is over, gone, finished, kaput, and I'm still a mess. Harter looks pretty, the song sounds lovely, and I think: sometime I have to write down how close to tears you can get from leaving a place that you utterly despise. Sometime. Sometime.